Praise for *Land*
That Moves, Land That Stands Still
by Kent Nelson

**Winner of the Mountains and Plains Booksellers
Association Award for Best Novel**

"I would like to take every serious reader of fiction by the elbow and say 'If you are looking for a fine novel that tells you important things about the world of love and family and work, all set against a pastel-driven, Western American setting, then you must read this book.' . . . Nelson . . . opens up the lives [of his characters] with sharp psychological skill and the deft hand of a man who knows how to leaven his story with just the right amount of emotion without ever veering towards the sentimental."　　—*Chicago Tribune*

"Nelson has an endless capacity for invention; the twists and arc of plot in *Land That Moves, Land That Stands Still* carry forward pell-mell and surprise you at every turn. It's the vivid story of an unusual kind of family, formed out of hard necessity and peculiar circumstances, and written with courage and clear-eyed affection."　　　　　—Kent Haruf

"An impressively sweeping novel. . . . Nelson writes with a powerful sense of place . . . that gracefully melds the landscapes of the contemporary American West with the arcing landscapes of the human heart."
　　　　—*Rocky Mountain News*

"The novel is a reminder that families, not individuals, are the heroes who built and continue to build the West. . . . Nelson captures a rugged and harsh land with a direct, occasionally poetic language.".
　　　　—*The Salt Lake Tribune*

"Never less than engaging . . . an accomplished and moving novel that is sometimes charming and sometimes witty. . . . [T]he issues facing [the characters] are . . . the same as those we all face as human beings . . . how to get along in the world."　　　　—*The Denver Post*

"A story of how the bonds of family can sustain humanity, and how the land can heal, if it's protected in return. Kent Nelson traces the cycles of farming with a nearly rapturous marvel that parallels the characters' emotional journeys."
　　　　—*Midwest Living*

"[*Land That Moves, Land That Stands Still*] draws you in and keeps you there as much through its deft and engaging storytelling as through its trio of dissimilar yet intricately connected female characters . . . each woman faces her own complex questions of trust, self-identity, and reconciling present and past."
　　　　—*The Santa Fe New Mexican*

W9-CTS-392

"Rare is the novel that contains both a sense of place so evocative the reader feels he has been there himself, and characters so vividly drawn that they tenaciously lure the reader into their inner lives . . . [the characters learn] how to help each other come to terms with what is missing from their lives, empowered by the loyalty to the new family they have created."

—*BookPage*

"The landscape of South Dakota comes alive in this affecting tale of three women at life's crossroads. . . . Nelson's skill in delineating three different, complex female protagonists is remarkable, and many of his precise, dialogue-driven scenes are little gems. Yet this is not frothy women's fiction, but an authoritatively controlled tale with mounting suspense and violence that builds like a thunderstorm in the Black Hills."   —*Publishers Weekly*

"Nelson makes every element urgently interesting, from a stone to a tractor, a field of alfalfa, a South Dakota sunset, the sting of a clever retort, the touch of a loving hand. And he tells a western tale unlike any other thanks to a remarkable cast of on-the-run, battered, grief-stricken, resourceful, smart and sharp-tongued skeptics."   —*ALA Booklist*

"I know Mattie Remmel and her neighbors, which is not surprising since I am a South Dakota rural woman. I'm not sure how Kent Nelson, a Colorado writer certifiably male, grew to know them so well. His portrayal of the land and the people of southwestern South Dakota is flawless, sympathetic, and so real readers may be driving around my neighborhood looking for them."

—Linda Hasselstrom

"With nothing more in common than their ability to survive, four people find their place on the land and with each other. *Land That Moves, Land That Stands Still* is a story about family in its most honest terms, about moving beyond survival and back into life. Nelson's prose is as clean and sparse as the landscape it evokes, as tough as its characters. This is a great, lusty, read."

—Claire Davis

"A beautifully realized piece of writing, a poignant story full of memorable, meticulously drawn characters. No reader will forget Mattie, Elton, Dawn, or Shelley, and no reader will fail to be spellbound by the extraordinary bravery, tenacity, and love of these seemingly ordinary human beings. Here again is proof that no human life is ordinary."   —Tim O'Brien, author of *The Things They Carried*

"I loved this big-hearted, moving, expansive novel of the West, its land and its people. Deeply satisfying, full of darkness and the incandescent light of enduring hope."   —Brad Watson, author of *The Heaven of Mercury*

PENGUIN BOOKS

LAND THAT MOVES, LAND THAT STANDS STILL ·

Kent Nelson's books include the novel *Language in the Blood* and the story collections *Toward the Sun* and *The Middle of Nowhere*. He has worked as a tennis pro, city judge, ranch hand, and university professor. An avid birder and mountain runner, he has searched out more than seven hundred North American species and has run the Pikes Peak Marathon twice. He lives in Salida, Colorado.

Land That Moves, Land That Stands Still

Kent Nelson

PENGUIN BOOKS

PENGUIN BOOKS

Published by the Penguin Group
Penguin Group (USA) Inc., 375 Hudson Street, New York, New York 10014, U.S.A.
Penguin Books Ltd, 80 Strand, London WC2R 0RL, England
Penguin Books Australia Ltd, 250 Camberwell Road, Camberwell, Victoria 3124, Australia
Penguin Books Canada Ltd, 10 Alcorn Avenue, Toronto, Ontario, Canada M4V 3B2
Penguin Books India (P) Ltd, 11 Community Centre, Panchsheel Park, New Delhi – 110 017, India
Penguin Group (NZ), cnr Airborne and Rosedale Roads, Albany, Auckland 1310, New Zealand
Penguin Books (South Africa) (Pty) Ltd, 24 Sturdee Avenue,
    Rosebank, Johannesburg 2196, South Africa

Penguin Books Ltd, Registered Offices:
80 Strand, London WC2R 0RL, England

First published in the United States of America by Viking 2003
Published in Penguin Books 2004

10 9 8 7 6 5 4 3 2 1

Copyright © Kent Nelson, 2003
All rights reserved

Grateful acknowledgment is made for permission to reprint excerpts from the following copyrighted
works: "Long-Legged Fly" from *The Collected Works of W. B. Yeats, Volume 1: The Poems, Revised*,
edited by Richard J. Finneran. Copyright © 1940 by Georgie Yeats. Copyright renewed © 1968 by
Bertha Georgie Yeats, Michael Butler Yeats, and Anne Yeats. Reprinted with permission of Scribner,
an imprint of Simon & Schuster Adult Publishing Group. "Hymn to St. Cecilia" by W. H. Auden.
Copyright © 1941 by W. H. Auden, renewed. Reprinted by permission of Curtis Brown, Ltd.

PUBLISHER'S NOTE
This is a work of fiction. Names, characters, places, and incidents either are the product of the author's
imagination or are used fictitiously, and any resemblance to actual persons, living or dead, business es-
tablishments, events, or locales is entirely coincidental.

THE LIBRARY OF CONGRESS HAS CATALOGED THE HARDCOVER EDITION AS FOLLOWS:
Nelson, Kent, 1943–
    Land that moves, land that stands still / Kent Nelson.
    p. cm.
    ISBN 0-670-03226-3
    ISBN 0 14 20.0460 X
    1. Women—South Dakota—Fiction.   2. Women Farmers—Fiction.   3. South Dakota—Fiction.
    4. Farm life—Fiction.   I. Title.
    PS3564.E467 L34 2003
    813'.54—dc21   2002193378

Printed in the United States of America
Designed by Nancy Resnick

Except in the United States of America, this book is sold subject to the condition that it shall not, by way
of trade or otherwise, be lent, resold, hired out, or otherwise circulated without the publisher's prior consent in any form of binding or cover other than that in which it is published and without a similar condition including this condition being imposed on the subsequent purchaser.

The scanning, uploading and distribution of this book via the Internet or via any other means without
the permission of the publisher is illegal and punishable by law. Please purchase only authorized electronic editions, and do not participate in or encourage electronic piracy of copyrighted materials. Your
support of the author's rights is appreciated.

For Lulu

Silence is the destroyer.
Silence is the teacher.
Silence is the joy of life.

Acknowledgments

The author acknowledges and thanks James Barr Ames, a kind patron from the very early days, and those friends who believed enough to contribute financially to the writing of this book. Special thanks to Dick Hazen for the use of his house on Lopez Island and to John TePaske, whose place this is.

Part I

Like a long-legged fly upon the stream
His mind moves upon silence.

—W. B. Yeats

Chapter 1

From the edge of the mesa, Mattie Remmel heard meadowlarks and the riffle of the river below and the wind sighing in the grass. The sweep of sky was more than seemed right—too blue overhead and paling toward the Lakota reservation in the east, where the cirrus brushed the distant plains. To the west, the first storm clouds of spring spilled upward over the Black Hills.

The river curved directly beneath them along the base of the mesa, pooled in gray and blue reflection before the plank bridge, and then ran swiftly over rocks and downstream into the cottonwoods. In April the trees were leafless still, gray trunks and upper branches ragged from wind and age. Across the river was the 135 acres Haney had plowed in a circle. An unattached pivot sprinkler lay across its radius like a huge silver mantis with two dozen pairs of symmetrical legs. Around the plowed ground was what the land had been before: sage and rabbitbrush and prickly pear, switchgrass, prairie dog mounds, and rocks. To the north, hills and gullies and more mesas were layered in shades of blue and gray.

In the scrub cedar was a line of wooden fence posts canted at odd angles in the clay bank. The barbed wire was loose, disappearing into the eroded gully or caught in tangled coils around itself. The fence stopped where Haney had cut the road to the bridge, then continued to a corner cedar post braced with braided wire. From the corner the fence turned east and petered out into the floodplain.

"That old fence," Mattie said, "dividing what from what, do you think?"

"Nothing from nothing," Haney said. He was standing shirtless in the ditch and lifted one end of a thirty-foot section of aluminum pipe. "Help me here, will you?"

Mattie came around the Toyota pickup and stepped down into the ditch at the other end of the pipe, and together they hoisted the pipe onto the mound of earth parallel to the ditch.

"Maybe they ran sheep," she said. "That explains Sheep Table and the erosion of the hills."

Haney didn't answer. He heeled his shovel into the ground and lifted earth. His shoulders and neck were muscled from work, and his sinewy wrists and forearms shimmered with sweat. His graying ponytail was wet on his back.

They'd been married twenty-two years, and she loved him still, but felt sorry for him, too, less for his age—forty-eight—than for his intractability and silence. He hadn't expected to be farming. He'd inherited the ranch fifteen years ago with his brother, Earl—four thousand acres, mostly dry mesas and hills. Eight hundred was irrigable, two-thirds in alfalfa, one-third in corn and Sudex. Haney had been sculpting in Maine when his parents died, and he'd agreed to take the place on, at least for a few years. At first he'd worked with a fury, building fences, buying equipment, learning about crops. But in the last several years his stamina had waned, and she sensed he wished for a life he didn't have.

Haney would have denied his unhappiness. He'd have said he chose his life and had no regrets. But she understood his unease in other ways—from the ponytail he'd let grow, from what he said to Shelley on the telephone, from the projects conjured up to absorb his time, the pivot sprinkler among them, the latest and biggest.

Last fall he'd pulled the biggest rocks out with the tractor, scraped away the sage and rabbitbrush, and plowed the ground. In winter he'd moved the pivot piece by piece, dangling the sections from the bucket of the front-end loader and hauling them across the river ice. In March, in terrible wind, while the ice broke up, he assembled the pivot, and now he was trying to get water to it.

The sun went under a cloud, and the shadow was cool. Storms normally drove to the north, but in spring the air was volatile, and already a dark curtain of rain obscured the hills. "Why don't we stop for the day?" she asked. "Let's ride up and see where the museum people want to dig."

"I know where they want to dig," he said. He leaned on his shovel, breathing hard, and looked west. "We could use half an inch of rain on the pivot. I seeded it last Sunday."

"I thought there were rocks to pick up."

"The hired man can pick up rocks, if we get one from the ad."

Lightning flashed, and Mattie counted six seconds to the thunder. Haney reached up and rolled the aluminum pipe back into the trench.

The idea was to take water from the main ditch, run it through the pipe he was laying now, and let gravity take it from the mesa to the river. Somehow the water had to go over the river, or under it, and uphill again to the pivot intake. Haney had explained the physics. "It'll work," he'd said, "because gravity is more powerful than your imagination."

Lightning flickered down again into the Black Hills, and the thunder was closer. The pipe still wasn't right, and Mattie climbed down and they lifted it out again. "I'm going down to the house," she said. "I'll leave you the truck."

"You could ride the ditch on the West Main," Haney said. "See if we're getting water from the district."

"All right." She tugged her shovel from the pile of earth and slid it under the rubber straps on the front of the Honda four-wheeler.

"Take the rake," he said. "If the water's coming down, there'll be weeds."

She leaned into the truck bed, jostled a rake from among the tangle of barbed wire, boards, and tools, and strapped it beside the shovel. Then she swung her leg up and over the seat and started the engine. Thunder boomed again, and without either of them touching it, the pipe rolled off the mound of earth into the ditch.

"Fuck Jesus Christ," Haney said.

She downshifted and waved, but he was struggling with the pipe and didn't look up.

She steered off the mesa and down the rutted road along the edge of a dry ravine. During the winter the road had washed, but it was passable, and with spring rain still to come, there was no point yet in filling the ruts. Cedar and chokecherry grew in clumps along the hillside, and at the curve, a doe jumped from cover and white-flagged away.

At the bottom of the ravine, the land opened out a little where Haney had built a runoff pond. A shallow quarter moon of water lay in the bottom of it, and two avocets, black and white with pinkish heads, stirred the water with their bills. As she drew closer, they flew, trailing their blue legs and chattering, though above the noise of the four-wheeler she barely heard them.

The pond was another of Haney's projects she thought unnecessary. Haney's contention was that rain was free, so why should he pay the district for water? But building the pond wasn't free. He'd bought pipe, put in a gate and an overflow valve, and spent two weeks shoving and carrying earth in the loader. They could have bought water for thirty years for the cost of the pond.

She supposed the real reason for the pond was the Pollards, though Haney had never said that. The Pollards were mean and unpleasant. The father, Lute, shot hawks and coyotes and about anything else that moved, and from years of riding the school bus, Shelley knew the son, Jimmy, and stayed clear of him. Haney's rights were prior on the ditch, but it ran through the Pollards' property, so they took water whenever they wanted. Haney had had several run-ins about the stealing and even sued them once, but he couldn't prove damages. How could you show what your crop might have been?

A few raindrops blinked in the pond, and she curved past it and dropped down the next steep pitch to the West Main. The alfalfa was only a few inches high, but was brilliant green against the drab gray cottonwoods and the paler hills beyond the river. She rode through the dry weeds along the ditch and saw water, but there wasn't enough flow to flush the ditch. She pulled a few tumbleweeds out by hand, then felt a few more drops of rain. To the west all she saw was gray.

She crossed the four-wheeler bridge at the West Main and came out onto the lane adjacent to the horse pasture. Tom Mix and Dale Evans grazed the far end of the pasture fence and, when they saw her, galloped partway across the field. But she didn't stop. She rode along the fence, descended into the swale and over the creek culvert, and accelerated up the hill toward the greenish halo of a single cottonwood.

At the crest of the hill the house appeared—her place in the world. The house wasn't fancy. The kitchen sagged off to one side and had a leaky roof, and the living room was sterile for her taste, but overall the place was large enough. Upstairs were two gables, one for each of the children's rooms, though neither was occupied now. Shelley was a junior at college, and Loren had died seven years ago, when he was nine. At odd moments like now she still grieved for him.

Besides the house, there were several outbuildings—a wooden barn not in good repair, several smaller storage sheds, and a huge, garish, white aluminum Morton shed where Haney fixed machinery. It had been expensive, too. The sin of money was indulgence, though Haney called it investment.

She coasted up under the cottonwood tree beside Haney's Lincoln and turned off the four-wheeler. Wind whined under the eaves and rattled the dry cornstalks in the garden. Singular heavy raindrops dinged on the car and thudded on the ground.

She liked weather, especially the dark brilliance of storms. She liked not controlling what was going to happen next. A gust of wind lifted the blue tarp from a pile of lumber near the barn, and she walked through blown-up dust to her garden. It was bordered by a six-foot chicken wire fence that kept out the deer and loose cattle, but now it was fallow. Three rows of dried cornstalks and the rotted leaves of cantaloupe and squash and tomatoes were all that remained after the winter.

Her gaze shifted to a movement by the Morton, a shape passing behind the International tractor and moving toward the jellyroll bales in the hay pen, a shadow with substance. Dark. But she wasn't sure she'd seen anything.

The rain suddenly came harder, and in seconds she was soaked. Drops stung her face, dripped down the back of her neck; her blouse clung to her skin. As she walked toward the house, she took apart her braid and spread the wet hair with her fingers. Then on impulse she unbuttoned her blouse and held it open so each raindrop was a needle on her skin, a pain lasting until she felt no pain, but only reveled in the rain's washing over her.

A bolt of lightning snapped her from her reverie, and she covered herself, half expecting to see Haney splashing along the lane in the truck. But the lane was empty. Gray rain rushed across the fields, and she went inside, trailing water through the kitchen.

She dried her face and hair with a dishtowel, then sat and unlaced her work boots, pried the left one off with the heel of the right, and wrenched the right off with two hands. Wet socks dangled from her toes.

The telephone rang.

"Hey, Mom, it's me," Shelley said.

"Hello, sweetheart."

"You sound out of breath."

"I just came inside. It's pouring rain."

"I guess you can use it."

"Your father wanted half an inch on the pivot, but we've already got more than that."

"He told me he seeded the field already," Shelley said.

"He didn't tell me till today. How's school? How's Warren?"

"I have a midterm in journalism tomorrow. Warren's okay. He wants to go to Kenya this summer."

"Alone, or with you?"

"I don't think he knows. But I'd rather stay in Boulder."

"To do what?" Mattie braced the receiver against her neck, peeled off her wet jeans, and carried them to the laundry room.

"Maybe get a waitressing job. The ranch isn't exactly a place to come to."

"Your father doesn't make you do chores."

"You know what I mean, Mom. It's the middle of nowhere. And I don't have any friends."

Mattie took off her blouse and underwear and put everything into the washing machine. Out the laundry room window a lake had formed in the yard, and the fields beyond seethed in rain. "Listen, Shel, I have to put on some dry clothes. Let me call you back after supper."

"Whatever," Shelley said.

They hung up, and Mattie walked through the living room and climbed the stairs. Shelley wasn't much help on the ranch. She irrigated some and weeded the garden, but Haney had never taught her to run machines. Still, Mattie didn't like the idea of Shelley's wasting her summer in Boulder. Maybe Boulder was more fun than Hot Springs, but why wouldn't she want to go to Kenya?

The upstairs hall was dark. She passed Shelley's room and Loren's closed door. Theirs, opposite Loren's, was ajar, and she pushed it open and went in. The bedroom had space enough for two bureaus, a soft chair no one ever sat in, and a Nordic-Trac. There were paintings on the walls; Haney's artist friends shared their work. Mattie liked Arlo Smith's gouache of a woman sitting with her eyes closed, asleep or not, as the viewer chose.

The bed dominated the room. In the angle of light from the window, Mattie noticed the two pale indentations in the beige quilt, one on either side of the middle—shallow, shadowed depressions made by their separate bodies.

The rain slacked on the roof, and she went to the window. A wedge of turquoise was emerging from behind the clouds, and the storm was moving east. From the mist and rain, the gullies and mesas re-formed themselves.

She turned away to the mirror across the room and measured her naked reflection. Physical work so dominated her days she never thought of being incapable of anything. Still, her body's aging disheartened her. Her skin, lightly freckled, was beginning to soften, but at least she was blessed with tight cheekbones so that as she'd grown older, her face had held its shape and texture. And her hair was beautiful, dark chestnut brown, which in a certain light shone red. When it was wet, as it was now, it looked almost black, and when she pulled it back, her face had an uncommon, angular look.

Instead of getting dressed and starting dinner, she pulled back the covers and lay down on her side of the bed. She didn't think she'd sleep, but she closed her eyes and was aware of her body's radiating heat. What would Haney think if he found her in bed?

It was dark when she woke. She listened for Haney downstairs, as if perhaps his footsteps had wakened her, but the house was quiet. That wasn't unusual. After his field work, Haney often went to the Morton until she called him. She rose and looked out, but the truck wasn't there.

She put on a flowered housedress and descended the stairs with some disquiet, as if her sleeping required apology. Being late with dinner was her only acknowledgeable sin, and the person who would eat it wasn't there, so there was no one from whom to ask forgiveness. Haney wasn't at his desk, and the truck wasn't in the yard, either. Just the Lincoln. Maybe he'd gone to borrow pipe gaskets from Sigurd Olafsson or to talk to Sam Appleton about something.

She turned on a lamp in the living room. The blue sofa faced the fireplace, and on one wall was the glass cupboard with the china her aunt from Phoenix had given her. On one side of the fireplace was the piano that had come with the house, and on the other, Haney's rolltop desk. A piece of paper protruded from a closed drawer. She went through the room and turned on the light in the kitchen.

She took chicken from the refrigerator, spilled five potatoes into the sink, and set the kettle on the gas burner. She peeled a potato, and as the skin fell away in her hands, a preternatural feeling came over her so intense she took a deep breath to calm herself. She set down the half-peeled potato and listened. Water still dripped sporadically from the eaves. Out the window was darkness—nothing to see, no hills, no trees, no light from another house. No headlights.

She called up to the Olafssons', but there was no answer, and then the Deckers. One of the boys answered. "Is Haney up there?" she asked.

"No, ma'am." It was Keith.

"Is your mother home?"

"She's in the shower."

"It's all right," Mattie said. "Don't bother her."

She hung up and went to the vestibule and put on her rubber boots and a down jacket and a red plaid hat with earflaps and stuck a small flashlight into the pocket of her coat. As she went out, she turned on the porch light.

The storm had left cold in its wake, and a wind blew from the north. The jagged black mountains rose against the stars. Mattie revved the four-wheeler and turned on the single headlamp and gave gas, shifting quickly from first to second to third as she splashed out of the yard. She tilted her face sideways to the wind and, heedless of the puddles, ran the straightaway past the horse pasture, crossed the four-wheeler bridge, and gave gas on the hill to the pond. She hoped momentum would be the answer to the slick gumbo, but the four-wheeler lost traction anyway, and she had to angle it into the grass at the side of the road.

She scrambled off and climbed on foot. She could barely see anything, even with the flashlight. The gumbo was slippery, and she walked at the edge of the track on rocks and clumps of grass. When she reached the pond, she shone the light around, but the beam petered out into dark.

"Haney?"

Cold air washed into her lungs. She climbed above the pond, her boots muddy and heavy, her heart drumming, her breath loud in her ears.

"Haney!"

Water roared in the ravine to her left, though she couldn't see it. Halfway to the top of the mesa, she made out the pale outline of the truck on its side in the gully.

The spray of the flashlight didn't reach. She scrambled down the hill at an angle, sliding, catching herself on thorny brush. She fell headlong and got up blindly. The truck was on its passenger door, wheels tilted uphill. She shone the light in through the windshield. Haney wasn't in the cab. She went around the tailgate, and there he was, pinned under the right front wheel, already dead.

Chapter 2

Rain melted the snow in the Black Hills, and the creeks and rivers rose. The Angostura Reservoir, already near capacity, was in full release, and the Cheyenne and Fall rivers flowed high and heavy with silt. On the plains to the east there was nothing to hold the water. Shelley flew to Rapid City and rented a car and arrived late the next morning, but Haney's brother, Earl, and his wife, Greta, coming from Denver, had been turned back at Edgemont because the bridge was washed out. They called from Lusk, Wyoming, and were coming back around by way of Chadron, Nebraska.

At noon the rain tapered off, but didn't stop. Mattie and Shelley walked up to Sheep Table in drizzle. The plank bridge over the river was gone, and careless of where the channel had been, floodwater swept through the cottonwood lowlands. Debris, caught against tree trunks, caught more debris—branches, grass, sections of fence, and a drowned heifer. Upstream, the river pounded against the curve of the mesa, and dump truck loads of soil fell into the water.

"It isn't the first high water we've had," Mattie said. "Sometimes you're rescued by water, and sometimes you're ruined."

"All Daddy's work gone," Shelley said.

"Alfalfa can take a lot of water."

"So what'd you do when you found him?"

"I sat with him. I took off his glove and held his hand. I wanted to be close."

"You think he tried to push the truck back from the lip of the ravine?"

"That's my theory. Somehow it slid more and tipped over on him."

"Maybe he didn't die right away," Shelley said. "It's terrible." She started crying.

"After a while the cold came right through him into my hand. You know what I remember most? Water. It was dark, and I couldn't see anything, but there was water everywhere."

"Then you came back and called me?"

"And the sheriff. I didn't want him out there any longer than he had to be."

"Well, Jesus," Shelley said. "Now what do we do?"

"Now we bury him."

Rain was still falling that afternoon when Mattie and Shelley drove the pickup into the circular driveway to the Southern Hills Mortuary. The building was beige, one-story, with junipers in front. A man with an umbrella came out to greet them. "I spoke to you on the phone, Mrs. Remmel. We've done our best on short notice."

"So have we," Mattie said.

He opened the door, and they walked into a foyer that smelled of flowers. Mattie was familiar with the surroundings. A month ago she'd been to services for Dot Wilkins, who'd had a heart attack getting a cow and calf back to pasture. Mattie took Shelley's arm, and they followed the man down a carpeted hallway.

"Do you do the burial, too," Mattie asked, "or does the church do that?"

"Usually we work with the church," the man said, "but in this case we've been instructed to send the body back east."

"What do you mean, back east?"

"Maine," the man said. "Mr. Hanratty told us Mr. Remmel will be buried in Maine." The man rested his hand on the handle of a closed door. "Would you prefer to go in together?"

Mattie and Shelley stood in silence for a moment, and then Mattie said, "You go in first. I'm going to call Barton."

The man opened the door, and Shelley went in. "The telephone is in the alcove down the hall."

The alcove was deep red—drapes, chairs, a curved sofa. Mattie dialed. "Let me speak to Barton, please. It's Martha Remmel."

A moment later, Barton Hanratty came on the line. "I tried to call you," he said. "I'm sorry."

"What's this about Maine?" she asked. "Haney and I agreed we'd be buried with Loren."

"He revised his will last February," Barton said.

"He never said anything to me."

"You're generously provided for, Mattie. Don't worry about that."

"I don't care about being provided for," Mattie said. "I care he's being buried in Maine."

"The arrangements have already been made. We have to respect his wishes."

Shelley came from the viewing room weeping. Mattie embraced her and spoke what words of solace she knew and then went in and closed the door.

Haney's face was blue as glacier ice. His eyes were closed. Mattie lifted the sheet back and revealed his hands folded across his chest as if he were in prayer, a pose she'd never seen Haney in, even asleep. He worked with gloves on, and his hands were pale. She imagined them on the steering wheel of the Case tractor, on the handle of the shovel, on the pipe he'd lifted the day before. His forearms were darkly tanned and nicked with cuts, and inside his right elbow was an inch-long scar she'd never noticed before. She felt its smoothness. A scar told so little, not where or how or when, and now such questions were unanswerable. She moved her hand up over his arm to his shoulder, to his stubbled chin, to his lips and his closed eyes. His hair was not in a ponytail, but was folded under his neck and shoulder.

She had no doubt he'd loved her. He boasted to others how hard she worked, how he couldn't get along without her. He said it in buying her a new television and VCR, in ordering her the parka and boots from L. L. Bean, the dress she had no occasion to wear until now. A week ago he'd held her hand crossing the street to a restaurant in Hot Springs. Why was it so much harder to say "I love you" than to order boots from a catalog?

Who had closed his eyes? When she found him under the wheel of the truck, his eyes were open. Had his last vision been gray sky and rain? Or stars, after the storm had passed? Had he thought of Shelley and her? Or Loren?

This was their last moment alone together, without Shelley, or Earl, or the friends and neighbors who would gather. "Why couldn't you tell me you changed your mind?" she asked. "There must have been a reason. What was it you couldn't say?"

He worked such long hours exhausting himself and slept so fitfully at night; she'd listened for years to his breathing, imagining beautiful words to make of the moving air. What had he meant by his silence? Now there was no answer and no time. Now his silence was incomprehensible. The last words he'd spoken on the mesa in her presence were "Fuck Jesus Christ." He hadn't even looked up when she waved goodbye to him.

Chapter 3

Earl's beige Mercedes pulled through the gate at four o'clock with its headlights on, and Mattie went out on the porch. Earl was older than Haney by two years, bulkier and taller—six-two and two-forty—with short gray hair and a mustache. Distinguished-looking, Mattie thought, though appearances were deceiving. Earl was a jerk. He was an orthopedic surgeon and had to have everything in precise order, including his automobile, his wife, and his opinions on the world.

Greta was Earl's third wife, a tiny woman in her early thirties, slender. She wore jeans and a white shirt, and when she got out of the car, she took a puff on her thin cigar and threw it into the wet grass. Haney had liked Greta because, as he said, anyone who put up with Earl deserved some credit.

Earl lectured, scolded, and ranted, and usually Mattie steamed silently, because what was the point of exacerbating family conflict? Once, though, at Haney's parents' in Boston, Earl expounded on the Southwest—"a godforsaken wasteland," he called it, "inhabited by retired people and the buzzards that prey on them."

"I'm from Tucson," Mattie said. "I'm neither a buzzard nor retired."

"I meant Southern California," Earl said, "and the illegal immigrants really frost me. I earned my money. I don't want to support gangs and welfare cheats."

"What's your objection to spreading the wealth?" Haney asked.

"People should be productive. That's what gripes me about Haney. He doesn't work."

"Doesn't work?" Mattie said. "What are you talking about?"

"He makes useless objects."

"What about Sarah?" Mattie said. "She sits around at home. How do you tolerate that?"

Earl's wife then—Sarah with an *h*—shot her a furious glance. She divorced Earl a year later.

As far as Mattie knew, Earl had approved of her marriage to Haney, though she doubted Earl's approval of anything ran very deep. Earl thought Mattie might steer Haney from sculpting to a more practical career, though she never tried. Even when she agreed to come west, it was, from her side, so Haney could get a new perspective on his art, though he got so busy with the ranch he'd quit his real work.

Earl and Haney had been raised in Lexington, Massachusetts. Haney had gone to Haverford, then started architecture school at M.I.T., but he quit when the Vietnam War was over. It was the seventies, and everybody was a little crazy then, except Earl. While Haney traveled in Europe, Earl finished at Princeton, went to Johns Hopkins Medical School, and started a practice in orthopedic surgery in Denver, where he'd done his residency. He thought Haney's traveling in Europe pointless.

Haney called it a fact-finding mission, though what facts he uncovered were unclear. Mostly he sketched and painted. Then in Florence he had a revelation in front of Michelangelo's slaves that sculpture was his calling. He returned to the States and enrolled in a night class at the Museum School in Boston.

Boston was where Mattie had met him, one June when Haney came into her friend Jill's kitchen holding a bunch of daffodils. His shirt was rumpled, and an edge of his collar was turned up, and as Jill took the flowers, he'd glanced at Mattie, and she blushed. Her first thought was: *This man is a force.*

Someone, a woman with long dark hair who tried to sound like Joni Mitchell, had brought a guitar to the party. The guitar was passed to Haney, but he was too embarrassed to play. He tinkered with chords and notes, and finally sang a single verse:

> Somewhere in the forest glade
> A maiden meets the stranger
> At such hour as is bade
> In the country of the Danger.
> Here-a-loo, loo, loo.

He had a sweet voice and a sad look in his eyes, and from the start she was lost in him. He called her the following Sunday. "Haney Remmel," he said. "Is this Martha?"

"Yes."

"I sang at the party," he said. "I'm driving up to Maine for a week. Do you want to go?"

"A week?"

"I'm leaving in an hour."

"Well, I . . . maybe. But I have a job."

"Bring rain gear," he said. "I'll pick you up. Where do you live?"

They stayed at Ames McGill's house, a converted stable that was once part of a larger estate. Downstairs were a tiny kitchen and bath, a breezeway living room that opened to the water, and a small bedroom. Upstairs was a loft where Ames wrote. Their friends gathered in the evening on the rocky beach: Arlo Smith, a painter, married to Jen, a ceramicist, and Ames, who had roomed with Arnulf Gorcyk at Yale. Arnulf was an entomologist. Celia Frederick was a painter. Ray Worth and John Kipp Wessel were lobstermen in Sedgwick. They were, among one another, more than friends. They were allies in laughter and talk and drink and a place lush with rain and water and sunlight. Each of them had a life beyond the summers, but the separateness made them closer for the moment.

That first night they'd built a fire and cooked mussels Arlo and Jen had fetched from tide pools and lobsters Ray Worth brought in a crate. They ate too much, drank more wine than was reasonable, and made fun of their own seriousness. It got cold. Jen and Celia had brought blankets, and Ames lent Mattie his sleeping bag. They sang to the sea fading into dusk and to boats passing among the islands.

Finally the fire burned down, and people drifted away. Ames smoked a cigarette and stared at the dark sea. "I'll take the loft," Ames said. "You two can have the bed."

"I'm staying here by the fire," Mattie said.

"There's the sofa in the breezeway," Ames said. "You could sleep there."

"I'll be fine."

Ames and Haney left her, and she curled beside the coals and listened to the sea. She'd made her statement: She might take leave of her job on the spur of the moment, but not of her senses.

The second night it rained. Ames built a fire in the woodstove in the living room, and the three of them ate salad and sardines, drank beer, and talked politics. "Watergate gave America the chance to prove itself a nation of laws," Haney said, "but we showed we're a nation of special interests."

"We knew that before," Ames said. "Carter, now that man—"

"Carter's another example that democracy doesn't work," Mattie said. "Even with a huge mandate, a president can't accomplish anything."

"And meanwhile," Haney said, "we stand by and permit, no, *facilitate*, the killing in Guatemala and El Salvador."

"Whoa," Ames said. "I'm going to bed before the shit really flies."

"You don't believe in justice?" Haney asked.

"I believe in art," Ames said. "And art must be made every day, early in the morning. Finish your argument in there." He pointed to the bedroom.

"Are we arguing?" Mattie asked.

They adjourned to the bedroom, but the conversation died. She was nervous, never having been in the presence of someone so outspoken and respectful, so insistent and kind. Haney agreed not to turn on the light, and Mattie slithered from her clothes and got under the covers. Haney undressed on the other side of the bed. Neither of them said anything.

Rain drummed on the roof. They slept without touching.

That night she dreamed of Rosa Saenz's bakery in Tucson, where she used to work, the place she thought had rescued her. It was a dream of smells—raisins, cinnamon, yeast. Rosa sang a hymn in Spanish. In the morning Mattie woke to sun burning through the mist over the water.

Haney was gone from the bed.

That week they sailed to Bar Harbor and played mixed doubles with Arlo and Jen and camped near Mount Katahdin and climbed it the next day via the Knife Edge. Evenings their friends came to the beach and ate and drank and sang. Each night she and Haney undressed and slept in the same bed, breathed the same air, but never even held hands.

At the end of the week they sailed with Dennis Burke—painter, gay actor, singer—and other friends to Isle au Haut. The sun was out, the wind strong, and when they got back, she went to bed with her clothes on, light still in the air. She woke in darkness and heard the singing from the beach, voices half lost on the sea waves. Haney was in the room silhouetted at the window. He unbuttoned his shirt, unbuckled his trousers, and slid them down. She couldn't help but watch. His arms and shoulders were facets of moonlight. He had a laborer's body—thick arms and shoulders, muscular thighs. For several minutes he stood before her naked, gazing toward the moonlit sea. She'd never had the leisure to study a man's body before and was thrilled as much for the chance as for what she saw.

Then, finally, he turned toward the bed. "I know you're not asleep," he said.

She didn't answer.

He stood for a minute, then knelt on the bed and folded the covers back. He moved slowly toward her through the air, and she felt him there, even before he touched her.

"How's Shelley taking it?" Greta asked.

They were sitting at the kitchen table, Earl with a spiral-ringed notebook at hand, while Mattie, at the counter, spread mayonnaise on homemade bread. Rainwater leaked through at the seam where the kitchen joined the rest of the house, and Mattie had put out pans and towels to catch the drips.

"Pretty hard, I guess. She's not saying much." Mattie put ham on the bread. "Do you want lettuce, Greta?"

Greta nodded. "It's never easy for a girl to lose her father, or a woman, either. I lost mine two years ago."

"It was like Haney to try to lift the truck," Earl said. "Was he thinking he was superman?"

"It's a Toyota, not a Ford," Mattie said. "It wasn't that heavy."

"It still wasn't very smart." Earl pushed the notebook across the table. "These are the ranch ledgers Haney sent me over the years. You can see how you did."

"I know how we did."

"A lot went into Haney's so-called improvements," Earl said. "He bought that grader to build the pond, and this crazy pivot sprinkler idea . . ."

"We've used the grader for other things," Mattie said. "He planned a new road out north."

"So what do you think you'll do?" Earl asked.

"I haven't thought about tomorrow," Mattie said. "Maybe I never will."

She cut the sandwiches diagonally and brought them to the table, along with three plates.

"The last time I saw him, we were looking at that investment property in New Mexico," Earl said. "Dry scree covered with juniper and piñon. How's anyone going to develop property without water?"

"Did you know Haney wanted to be buried in Maine?" Mattie asked.

"No. What the hell for?"

"I thought maybe you'd know. We had friends in Blue Hill, but—"

"Haney didn't talk to me," Earl said. "Have you been through his stuff?"

"Not yet."

"Maine," Earl said. "You mean we have to go back to Maine for the funeral?"

The memorial service was the next day in Hot Springs. Mattie had made the necessary telephone calls to friends in New England, but because the funeral was back east, only Ames McGill flew out for the memorial. The neighbors came: Trini and Allen Decker, the Olafssons, the Parsonses, Hector Lopez, the Appletons, the Westcotts, the Bishops from over in Oelrichs, even Lute and Jimmy Pollard. Gretchen Wright, eighty years old, got her hired man to bring her. Barton Hanratty came, and people from town Mattie barely knew: Grebe Martin at the supply store, the loan officer at the bank, a waitress named Rae Ellen from the Maverick Café, where Haney ate dinner when he went to town for a meeting. Shelley's boyfriend, Warren, drove up from Boulder.

The closed casket was surrounded by flowers; Mattie and Shelley agreed Haney in the coffin did not look like himself. The pastor, Lamont Furze, spoke of a man deeply cared for, who, in the ten years he had been among the community, had made a lasting difference in their lives. Earl spoke, too, more generously than Mattie would have wished, of a loving, brotherly relationship. He cried once, surprising Mattie.

She and Shelley didn't speak, and Mattie knew their silence would be interpreted as grief. Mattie felt grief and anger and absence—all of these. She felt as if she were looking out from her familiar perch on Sheep Table without comprehending what she saw, hills, mountains, sky rendered meaningless. How could everything be changed?

After the service, people departed, talking among themselves in low voices, maybe about Haney or about the weather or the baseball game at the high school. Mattie and Shelley, holding hands, were the last to leave.

Outside, people gathered in clusters. Mattie was aware of the daffodils by the steps of the mortuary and the blooming forsythia. She and Shelley endured the neighbors' respects. Shelley talked to the Westcotts for whom she had baby-sat in high school. Mattie hugged Trini Decker and Allen, and shook hands with Hector Lopez, who farmed shares of corn with Haney. Hector held Mattie's hand in both of his and said nothing, though there were tears in his eyes.

Mattie invited Ames McGill to the ranch to be with the family, and he wrote the directions on the palm of his hand. Of Haney's Maine friends, Mattie liked Ames best. He was tall and gangly, shaved his head bald, and eked out a living without family money or a nine to five job. To support his writing, he sometimes worked in the IGA bagging groceries.

When Mattie was ready to leave, she nudged Shelley toward Earl and Greta, who stood on either side of the Mercedes, talking over the hood. Warren took Shelley's arm and steered her in that direction. Then Mattie saw the Pollards a few cars ahead.

Lute was slouched against the fender of their red quarter-ton Dodge, and Jimmy stood a little distance away, eyeing the crowd. They both had shaved and for once looked almost clean, though not at ease, either one of them. Lute reminded Mattie of a swarthy crooner—Al Martino, maybe—curly hair tinged with gray, a hawkish nose, and a paunch. Jimmy was only two years older than Shelley, and he was already his father in the making.

As Mattie came nearer, Lute poked Jimmy to attention. "We're sorry about the boss," Lute said. "We waited to tell you personally."

"Thank you," Mattie said.

"We got a tractor available," Lute said, "and Jimmy has free time. We could do some helping out for you."

"No one has free time," Mattie said, "but I appreciate the offer."

"We mean it," Jimmy said.

"We're neighbors," Lute said. "I better check on you once in a while." He said this almost as a threat.

"I'll call if I need help," Mattie said.

Earl honked the horn, and Mattie excused herself.

"You give a holler," Lute said.

The Mercedes rode smoothly on the highway, Greta, Shelley, and Warren in back, and Mattie in front with Earl. From Maverick Junction, it was eight miles south to the turnoff onto the county road and then another eight miles east to where the gravel started.

"I thought it went well," Greta said. "Haney had a lot of friends."

"He didn't go out of his way to alienate people," Mattie said. "He thought you had to get along with the neighbors, unless they were named Pollard."

They zigzagged along section lines. Windbreaks of thick spruce grew alongside the cattle pens and backyards of most of the places they passed. The houses were old, though most of the barns and grain silos were aluminum now. Good farmers traded unreliable machines for equipment they could count on, and bad farmers fixed the old and prayed. It was easy to tell as they passed their houses which farmers were which.

They drove by the Parsonses', past fallow fields, and alfalfa turned green. They passed Hector Lopez's mailbox, the road into the Pollards', then the Deckers' house next to the road, a clapboard box with a cement stoop and a screened porch. Trini and Allen and their two boys were just pulling up in their Suburban, and Earl honked as the Mercedes splashed through puddles in the road.

The long view east was of rolling hills and sky. The Lakota Sioux and the Cheyenne had fought each other for this country, and then later the army had driven the Cheyenne north into Montana. The Lakota were forced onto the reservations—Rosebud and Pine Ridge just east of the ranch.

The place had fallen to Haney and Earl after their father died. By then Haney had been sculpting seven years, and he and Mattie had been married five. Before they took over, the ranch had been leased to a family in Omaha who had boarded horses and hunted deer and pheasants. The alfalfa had been worked on shares with Sigurd Olafsson, the remainder sold in the fall.

It had been Earl's idea Haney should run the place, and Mattie sensed Haney was restless in his work. By his own admission, his sculptures were becoming stilted and inward, and he thought a new landscape might open him up. Mattie was ready, too. She was tired of Maine. Autumn and winter were foggy and cold, and spring never came. Besides, Shelley was five and about to start school, and Loren, only a year old, hadn't thrived in the dank climate. Change for all of them might be what was needed. Haney agreed he could sculpt anywhere, so they came and made a living, and now Haney was dead.

It was cool on the lawn under the cottonwood. Barn swallows scissored the air, and meadowlarks sang from fence posts in the Ironweed Patch, where stacks of pipe, worn-out machines, and old cars had sat for as long as Haney and Mattie had been there. They drank margaritas. Mattie sat in the only wooden chair, Earl and Greta at the picnic table, Greta smoking her thin cigars. Shelley sprawled on the grass beside Warren, who pretzeled himself into a lotus position. Ames McGill stood a little apart and turned his face to the sun. "In Maine we don't see the sun until July," he said.

"My father never sat around like this even once," Shelley said. "He never enjoyed this place."

"He liked being busy," Mattie said.

"He was that way around a boat, too," Ames McGill said. "If someone had to scrape barnacles or paint a hull, he called Haney."

"Daddy should have been an engineer," Shelley said.

"He was an engineer," Mattie said.

"I remember once he built a catapult," Earl said. "He tossed rocks into an open field across the road. Even back then he was fiddling with impractical inventions."

Warren opened his eyes. "The one time I was here he asked if I knew how to run machines, and when I told him no, he said, 'Good, I'd be worried if you said you did.'"

Shelley laughed. "He told terrible jokes," she said. "The one I remember is about the cowboy in spring thaw. These ranchers haven't heard from their friend in a few days, so they drive over to his place, and all they find is his cowboy hat lying in the mud. They lift up the hat, and there's Jed with only his head showing. 'You all right, Jed?' they ask. 'Yeah,' Jed says, 'I'm on my horse.'"

Earl and Warren laughed, and Mattie smiled. "I never heard him tell a joke," she said.

"He joked about his work," Ames said.

"Not around me."

"His work was a joke," Earl said. "At least he got responsible in his old age."

"He kept all his sculptures in the barn," Mattie said. "He didn't want them in the house. I thought he'd set up a studio out there, or in the Morton when he had that built, but he always had to mend a fence or fix the baler."

"It's full-time work, or nothing at all," Ames said. "That's how he thought of it."

"I mostly knew Daddy as a rancher, not a sculptor," Shelley said. "That's my image of him."

The sunset bloomed hard and faded fast on the clouds, pinks and oranges sliding into gray. Neighbors had brought casseroles, potato salad, and a ham, and Greta went in with Shelley to set out the dinner, leaving Earl and Warren arguing about the stock market. Mattie and Ames walked to the barn to look at Haney's sculptures, and Mattie was glad to have a few minutes with him.

"Do you know the cemetery where Haney wants to be buried?" she asked.

"It's on the hill above town."

"Do you know why he wanted to be buried there?"

"He loved boats," Ames said. "He loved the sea."

"I know," Mattie said, "but he loved his son, too."

She unlatched the door and swung it open, and dusky light poured in over the dirt floor of the barn. A gray cat stared at them for a moment and then squeezed out between two weathered slats. The stall on the right was filled with dead refrigerators, boxes of fossils Haney had collected, and assorted tack and saddles for the horses. On the left were the sculptures, stacked willy-nilly behind bags of Sudex seed. Mattie went around the sacks and slid aside the door on the east for more light.

The sculptures were of different sizes—Oscar size to the size of a man—and they were oiled and waxed and wrapped in clear plastic.

"Go ahead and open one," Mattie said.

Ames slit the plastic with his pocketknife and held up a misshapen bird, half heron and half man. The bird's head was tiny, the man's neck and body were elongated, the wings too small ever to let such a creature fly.

"It seems as if these are from another life," Mattie said.

"They are from another life," Ames said. "It was Haney's talent to see what was real in other realms. The magic of this is the impossibility of flight."

"Do you think he was happy here?" Mattie asked.

A noise, something falling, made Mattie turn toward the ladder to the loft. She walked over and looked up, but saw only the gray cat looking down at her.

Then she heard Shelley call, and she went to the door.

"Dinner's ready," Shelley said. "And Uncle Earl wants to talk to you. He's going to make plane reservations to Maine."

"We're coming," Mattie said. She turned to Ames. "Please take that bird. Haney would want you to have it."

The burial in Maine took three days. Greta didn't go; she said she made her peace with Haney via satellite. Earl chaperoned Mattie and Shelley, and they flew to Bangor on the afternoon of April 24. Ames and Jen and Arlo Smith picked them up and drove them to the Down East Bed and Breakfast. They had dinner together, and in the morning, as mist moved across the islands, they went to the cemetery.

Haney's friends spoke at the grave: Ames, of course, and Arnulf, who'd traveled with Haney in Europe, and Tom and Maria Schneider from the early Boston days. Arlo and Jen Smith came from New York, and Ray Worth and John Kipp Wessel read several of Haney's gallery reviews. Shelley spoke about her father, the rancher, who worked with the hope of a future that never came to pass. Mattie could not bring herself to speak.

The only two people Mattie knew who were not there were Wilson Ward, drowned three summers before off Nova Scotia, and Dennis Burke, incommunicado in Spain, who presumably hadn't heard the news.

Chapter 4

Early the following day Mattie and Shelley and Earl flew from Boston to Chicago to Rapid City, and Earl dropped Mattie and Shelley by the house. "I can't stay," Earl said. "Greta thinks money is electricity. You flip a switch, and there it is. I'll be bankrupt in a week if I can't cut on somebody's knee."

"I know you own half," Mattie said. "I don't know how it'll work without Haney."

"The house is yours as long as you want to stay here," Earl said. "We'll talk. Let's stay in touch."

Earl drove off, and while Shelley slept, Mattie used what was left of the afternoon to haul out the pickup. She could have asked for help of any number of neighbors, but it was a private matter. She chained the back axle of the pickup and spliced a double length of chain to the winch on the tractor. The sheriff and deputies had lifted the truck to get Haney out, but hadn't got it upright, so she did that and then dragged the truck to the road. For another half hour, in the fading light, she fetched the tools and lumber that had spilled into the ravine.

Shelley was waiting for her on the porch when she got back. "You got the truck, huh?"

"We don't have Earl's Mercedes anymore," Mattie said. "We have to get around."

"We could drive the Lincoln."

"I told your father when he bought that fancy car I'd never ride in it, and I won't start now."

"I know, Mom. You always keep your word."

"I try to."

"I'm hungry."

"You could have heated up one of those casseroles," Mattie said.

"I didn't know what you'd want."

"Why don't you make a salad and set the table, and I'll see if the truck runs."

They ate at nine and left the dishes in the sink. Mattie went to bed, and Shelley watched TV in her room. For a while Mattie was aware of a dim babble of voice through the walls, but then she slept. She woke at midnight, cognizant that Haney was missing. She walked the hallway back and forth, as if looking for him, and when she returned to her room, he still wasn't there. She lay awake awhile, thinking of the work that had to be started. The rain had postponed irrigation, and she couldn't get the tractor onto the eighty acres of corn stubble at the West Tip that Haney wanted to put into Sudex. She could put off the road to the north gate. That was no emergency. While they waited for the fields to dry, she had in mind fencing the north pasture. Haney had already started that, and it had to be done. Getting rocks off the pivot field was necessary, too, before the alfalfa started growing.

She had to visit the neighbors and thank them for the food they'd provided and to gauge their promises to help. Sam Appleton owed Haney for feeding his cows when Sam had surgery the winter before; Avery Bishop had offered a tractor if they needed it, and they did, because their own Case was disassembled in the Morton; Vern Haffner was going to take a vacation, he said, and bring over his Vibra Shank and drag the grass out of the alfalfa in the Upper East. Mattie counted on Trini and Allen Decker for sympathy, but not for farm work, but sympathy was useful. She didn't underestimate it.

As she was thinking these things, she heard the drone of a motor outside. She thought it was an airplane at first, but it might have been a pickup or an ATV coming closer. She got up and went to the window and looked out at the barn and the white Morton illuminated in its own light. She couldn't see the driveway from that side of the house or the track to the west, but she opened the window and listened. The motor was louder; it wasn't a plane.

Sometimes people got lost out in that ranchland; it was easy enough to do because there weren't many road signs. She went across the hall into Loren's room and looked out to the west and south. It was dark beyond the yard. She made out the shapes of trees by the creek, the lilac bush, and the white fence, but nothing much else. Then movement:

A truck without headlights was coming down the driveway slowly—obviously not lost. It came on to the gate; then whoever was driving revved the engine and spun the truck around. It stopped there under the far side of the cottonwood.

Mattie turned and banged into a chair and went out into the hallway. In a moment Shelley came out. "What's going on, Mom? What're you doing?"

"Stay in your room."

"Who is it?"

Mattie scrambled down the stairs in the dark, feeling her way along the wall, and ducked into the living room. She crossed to Haney's rolltop desk and found the .44 pistol he kept in the second drawer.

The light came on in the room.

"Turn off the light."

Shelley switched off the light. "What are you doing with that gun?"

"I'm going to warn someone."

She got to the kitchen door when the truck revved again and took off back down the driveway. The headlights never came on. All Mattie saw was the shape of the truck cab against the stars.

"Was that Hector?" Shelley asked.

"Hector wouldn't do something like that. Maybe it was someone poaching deer. I don't think they left their names."

"Do you think it was the Pollards scaring us?"

"They'd be the first ones I'd think of," Mattie said. "But it wouldn't make much sense. We could follow the tracks right to their place."

"But we're out here alone," Shelley said. "I don't like it."

"Let's not get paranoid right away," Mattie said. "We have time for that."

"Then what'd you get the pistol for?"

Mattie looked at the gun in her hand. "I don't even know if it's loaded. I don't know how to tell."

She opened the door and held the gun outside and pulled the trigger. It went off with a flash and a blast and a kick that shook Mattie's arm to the shoulder joint.

In the morning Mattie was up and calling to Shelley from the bottom of the stairs to get moving. Then she was outside and let the door slam behind her. She walked out to the gate and looked at the tire tracks in the dirt. They didn't tell much, except she hadn't been dreaming. She picked up two Pabst cans from the weeds.

She threw the cans into the back of the pickup, got in, and started it. There was a high-pitched whine when she pressed the accelerator and backed around.

Shelley came out of the house. "Jesus, Mom, can't I even get coffee?"

"You could if you were up early enough."

"You might have left some. Did you find some tracks?"

"Kids," Mattie said. "I found two beer cans. Come on. Get in. Work's waiting for us."

Gumbo was gumbo when it was wet, but cement when it dried. Mattie pried with a crowbar between the back tires and the chassis of the four-wheeler, while Shelley whacked with a shovel at the mud under the front. After a few minutes Shelley stopped and looked out toward the pivot field, just barely visible as a brown circle against the yellow-gray grama grass and yucca. The river had diminished from its flood, but was still roily and brown. Twenty miles away the Black Hills were dark blue silhouettes.

"Did Daddy have insurance?" Shelley asked.

"Car insurance or life insurance?"

"Either."

"He had life insurance, but not much. He didn't believe in it, and he had enough money, at least until he came out here and threw it into the ranch."

Mattie cracked off the last chunk of dry gumbo and threw the crowbar into the truck.

"So what do we need to do out at the pivot?"

"Clear the rocks. That's the first thing. Then we assemble the pipe and find someone who knows how to get the sprinkler running."

"You know, we don't have to finish everything he started."

"We don't have to, but I feel some obligation, especially to the sprinkler. Besides, we can't take the seeds out of the ground."

"Why'd he seed it if he wasn't sure he could get water there?"

"I guess he was sure he could."

"Daddy used to say picking up rocks was the world's oldest profession," Shelley said. "I may go back to school sooner than I thought."

"You do what you have to. Your father put an ad in the *Star* for a hired man, so maybe we'll find someone."

"Warren said he'd come up if we needed him."

"Do you want him to?"

"I might. I'm not sure."

Mattie got on the four-wheeler, and the engine coughed and died. She tried again with the choke, and it caught. Mattie backed it around. "I'll meet you back at the yard," she said. "I want to string up the fence up north so we can rent that pasture."

Shelley headed the truck downhill, and Mattie followed. Then on the flat, she shifted the Honda to fourth, barreled around Shelley, and ran the straightaway full throttle along the pasture fence. She felt the air, the close weeds at the side of the track, the sky rushing past. She liked the jiggle and the blur, the thrill of ripping through shallow water and over sand. She liked the ground zooming under her.

She braked for the creek, then gave gas up the hill and into the yard. Toward the house a bit of color caught her eye: a patch of red in the garden. Her wheels spun on the lip of the embankment, and when she came closer, the color was gone. She coasted around the house.

Someone had dug among the dead debris from last fall, in the carrots and potatoes. There were footprints in the earth. She got off the four-wheeler to look, and Shelley pulled up beside her.

"I can't believe you, Mom. You're going to kill yourself driving that way."

"If I were going to kill myself, I'd have done it awhile ago. Let's get the fencing gear into the back of the truck."

"I don't know how to build a fence," Shelley said.

"You're in college. You can learn how."

Rolls of barbed wire, posthole digger, tamper, and post pounder bounced in the bed of the truck as they drove past the hay pen. The downstream bridge hadn't washed out partly because the embankment was shored up with boulders and cement, but mainly because the river decided to cut several new channels around it. They forded the shallowest places, Mattie keeping up speed through the water. "We'll run the river back where it belongs," she said. "There's no sense letting the river make us build more bridges."

"Mom, why don't you relax?"

"Not today or tomorrow," Mattie said. "When it dries out."

They climbed out of the river bottom to the flats. To the east, high-tension wires were attached to a row of miniature Eiffel towers, all built with bribes and promises, never mind the blight on the land. There was nothing to be done about them unless someone had the courage to use explosives.

They took the old road north, switchbacking up above the gullies. Haney had started the new road—he started everything—but the bull-dozer blade had cracked on a rock and was left in the weeds at the bottom of the mesa.

"Who are you renting the pasture to," Shelley asked, "assuming we can build the fence?"

"Hector said he was interested."

"Mom, Hector killed somebody. That's what people say."

"People say all sorts of things. He didn't kill anybody. We've worked with Hector for years and never had any trouble. Anyway, we need the income."

"I thought we had income."

"We have capital. I want to make the ranch pay for itself."

"Like how much capital do we have?"

"Earl accepted your father's projects because he liked the tax write-offs. I don't know what capital we have."

"I thought Daddy's ideas were pretty sound."

"Theoretically. The pivot will give us more alfalfa and more acreage to borrow on, if we need to borrow. These days that's success."

"It gives us more work," Shelley said.

"That, too."

Mattie raised the two handles of the posthole digger above her head and brought it down full force. She was 131 pounds, and because the ground was soft from rain, the blades bore in a good four inches. She squeezed the handles together and lifted out a portion of earth. Then she did it again. And again. And again.

They were at the far north end of the ranch, not quite to the county road heading to Buffalo Gap. She finished one hole, then pitched the digger into the pile of earth and wiped her forehead on the back of her arm. "You do it awhile."

"I don't know how," Shelley said.

"You just saw me. That's how."

Shelley picked up the posthole digger. "Daddy used the gas-powered one."

"It's heavy and too hard to start. And it's like holding a wild animal."

Shelley lifted the digger above her head and brought it down in the hole.

"That's all there is to it," Mattie said. "Where're your gloves? You'll get blisters."

"If I get blisters, I won't have to work."

"If you get blisters, the work will hurt more."

Shelley put on gloves and picked up the digger again.

"At least your father put in most of the steel posts," Mattie said. "He's got in every other one to the bottom of the ravine."

"Daddy wouldn't let me join 4-H," Shelley said. "Now he's making me build fences."

Mattie wrestled two creosoted posts from the truck bed and tipped one of them into the hole she'd dug. She kicked in dirt and small rocks around it.

"Look over there," Shelley said.

Two does and a buck had come out from a patch of brush and were making their way up the ridge. The buck paused and stared at them.

"What's he know, do you think?" Shelley asked.

"Danger," Mattie said. "That's all most men know."

The buck snorted once, but never moved.

"You tamp the post in," Mattie said. "I'll start the next hole."

When the three wood posts were set, Mattie measured the distance between them and cut two two-by-fours and nailed them together. Then she notched the corner post and fitted the cross brace into the notches. Shelley held the brace, and Mattie toed in four-inch nails.

"How'd you learn all this, Mom?"

"Doing it," Mattie said. "Now comes the hard part."

She yanked a roll of Red Brand barbed wire from the back of the truck and let it fall to the ground. She looped the end of the wire around the corner post and twisted it tight, then kicked at the spool. The spool weighed ninety pounds and was too heavy and prickly to hold and too unruly to bend over and keep on the ground. Mattie kicked it again, and it started downhill. In a few feet it was rolling, but the wire had a mind of its own about where to go, and it veered off-line and got hung up in the sage twenty feet down the hill.

"Not very scientific," Shelley said.

"If you've got a better idea, you're welcome to try it."

Mattie sidestepped through rocks and sage and yucca, freed the spool and righted it, and let it go again. This time the spool bounced like a stone on a skewed path all the way to the bottom of the ravine.

"Now what?" Shelley asked.

"Now we stretch the wire."

"Now we need the hired man," Shelley said.

Chapter 5

Mattie gave Shelley credit for youthful rebellion. Growing up, Shelley had endured minor scrapes and explorations of the edges, and she'd emerged from these, if not unscathed, at least free of nightmares. She'd survived adolescence without losing her life to drugs or insanity and had made it to college. Haney had spoiled her by not making her do more chores, but she was independent of the ranch. As Haney put it, she was not condemned to rural existence.

Mattie hadn't agreed with him about all that, but she thought a unified front was better than one divided. Anyway, it was too late now. Shelley was who she was.

They sat that evening at the kitchen table exhausted from fence building, nibbling at leftover ham. It was eight o'clock and easing to dark. In another month it would be dark at nine, and the thought of more light to work didn't comfort Mattie in the least. Tomorrow, the day after, the day after that: There would always be work to fit into the time.

"It's funny," Mattie said, "I feel his disapproval even when he isn't here."

"Disapproval about what?"

"I want a cigarette."

"You don't smoke."

"Maybe I don't because he didn't approve."

"Greta left some cigars," Shelley said. "They're in the middle drawer of the sideboard."

"Thanks."

Mattie found them and took one from the pack.

"What else did he disapprove of?"

"I could never let on I was tired."

Mattie took a match from the box by the stove, lit the cigar, and went outside. Parallelograms of yellow light fell from the windows, and to the east the arc light at the Olafssons' house shimmered under a moonless sky. She puffed the cigar, while Shelley clattered dishes inside.

The yard was a still life—the tractor, weeds growing, the facade of the barn door, the plane of adjoining shadow. She half expected to see the boy who'd been in the garden that morning, the ghost she'd seen at odd moments for the past several weeks. He was skittish as a barn cat, though apparently not dangerous. She assumed he was watching her now.

She took a last draw, pinched out the cigar, and went inside. The dishes were done, and the blurred sound of the TV came through the ceiling from Shelley's room upstairs. Mattie turned off the kitchen light and went into the living room.

She rarely had the leisure to sit in the living room, even if she'd wanted to. It was Haney's room more than hers. The rolltop desk, given to him by his father, was there, and the photographs of his sailing days were on the walls. Anyway, the ceiling was too low, and only two small windows looked out. She thought maybe she'd bring in several of his sculptures and make it more alive. There was an irony: to liven the space with lifeless objects made by a man now dead.

She remembered seeing the desk for the first time when she visited Haney's studio on Trowbridge Street. The apartment smelled of clay and burned marijuana and something metallic. The drawers spilled out drawings, photographs, letters. On the top shelf was a bouquet of dried flowers in an empty glass. A pair of women's blue panties was draped over a drawer handle.

Haney cleared wine bottles and books from the sofa so she could sit down.

"What are those?" she asked.

He looked up to see what she meant. "You don't know?"

"Perhaps I should have asked, whose are those?"

"Are you asking?"

"No."

"I have wine, cabernet or chardonnay?"

She was conscious of light entering through the high windows along the street. "Cabernet."

After they were married, the desk went with them to Maine, where it was the messy centerpiece of his studio. "Haney's junk heap," Jen Smith called it, "an archaeological treasure."

"It's his soul," Ames said.

"Are you saying a soul can't be cleaned up?" Mattie asked.

"Would you want to cleanse his soul?" Ames asked.

When they migrated to the ranch, the movers carried it into the living room and set it where it was now. Haney had kept the desk neater over the years, the way he himself had become. The living room wasn't a studio, and the people who came to the house weren't painters and sculptors. Haney had never said she couldn't look in the desk for anything or sit there to write a letter, and so far as she knew, he never locked it. But it was his private place, and when she sat down and raised the rolltop on its sliders, she felt as if she were in violation of a trust.

The papers on top were sketches of the pivot, calculations of grade and distance and water pressure from gravity feed. Water could flow uphill if it started higher than where it came out at the end. Sheep Table was 260 feet above the pivot field. Haney had worked out in a notebook how much water it took to run the sprinkler, the requirements of the generator, the different methods of laying the pipe across the river.

He'd considered six alternate routes for the road to the north gate, and apparently he was tinkering with the idea of a new baler that would run faster and make larger bales, though none of the hay haulers could accommodate them. There were designs for a bedroom deck, notes and sketches for cattle guards, a water-pumping system from the river to a storage tank.

She sorted through the unpaid bills and stacked the current ones. She looked at the phone bill. Most of the calls had been to Shelley in Boulder, a few to Rapid City, several to Earl. None to Maine.

There was no personal correspondence, except one recent letter from Ames McGill and an unsigned postcard from Spain, dated February 6. "In Algeciras, looking at Gibraltar. Wine okay. No women. Some song. Tomorrow, onward to Morocco."

The photo on the card was of a painting at the Prado, *Idyll* by Mariano Fortuny y Marsal (1838–1874), a naked boy playing a fife. She assumed the card was from Dennis Burke.

She'd read Ames's letter before. He'd asked Haney to crew on Arnulf's sloop when they took it to Key West in October. If Haney could fly to Maine, they'd have two weeks to get the boat south, and Mattie could meet them in Key West. Her compliance was solicited.

But Haney must have had more letters than just that one. A couple of days before he died, he'd told her Jen and Arlo had seen the new Terrence McNally play in New York and that John Kipp Wessel had broken his arm on his lobster boat. But where were the letters? She saved the ones she got. Wouldn't he?

The idea of Haney's hiding letters disturbed her as much for her thinking of it as for his doing it. There wasn't anything in his life to hide. She knew where he was almost every minute.

Out the window headlights caromed down the driveway, and the night before came into vivid relief. They were vulnerable out so far from town. It wasn't an hour for visitors. She knew that. And Trini would have called. She got up and went outside as far as the gate. It parked at the edge of the arc light at the Morton. Whoever it was, Lute or Jimmy, was smoking a cigarette. It disturbed her either one would be there.

The truck started, and Lute—she saw it was he—pulled on the headlights and kept the brights on all the way to where she stood. Then he stopped and leaned from the driver's window. His face was shadowy and reddish in the refracted light, and she smelled liquor.

"You weren't out here last night, too, were you, Lute?"

"Last night? No, me and Jimmy was worried about you. You haven't called. I told him I'd just right now ride over and see."

"Well, you did that."

"You want a beer?" Lute handed a can out the window.

"No, thanks. We haven't needed any help."

Lute hissed the can open and drank a long swallow. "Well, I should warn you about that boy."

"What boy is that?"

"We had him up to our place for a while, but we run him out. Injun boy. He's a stealer."

"No one's stolen anything from me."

"You need some help getting rid of him, here I am," Lute said. He paused and spit. "You taking any water yet from the district?"

"With the rain, there's been no need to irrigate yet."

"Hay'll be cheap," Lute said. "I knew it was gonna rain a lot. I can dowse water, too. I got a special sense."

"Is that right?"

"Did Haney ever get that Case back together? There's something we could help you with."

"Sigurd Olaffson said he'd look at it. There hasn't been any hurry because of the rain."

"I'll send Jimmy down tomorrow. He's a real mechanic, Jimmy is. Or I could look at it myself right now."

"Maybe sometime next week," Mattie said, "if we haven't got it fixed."

"No problemo," Lute said. "I'll send Jimmy."

There was an awkward silence, and Mattie backed away from the truck. "Well, Luther, I've got some bills to pay. Thanks for checking on us, but we're doing all right."

"You watch out for that little Injun bastard," Lute said.

"I will. And I'll call if I need anything."

Mattie backed farther away toward the house, and finally Lute got the picture and started his truck. She was relieved when he turned around and his one working taillight receded down the drive.

Most of the bills were straightforward: electric coop, AAA Auto Parts, Reimer's Feed. She wrote checks on their joint account, though Haney's accounting system was an enigma. He entered the checks, but didn't subtract, so there wasn't a balance. The previous bank statement showed over $4,000.

There was an invoice from Hector Lopez for $462.17 for trucking jellyrolls to the feedlot last fall, though Mattie couldn't tell whether it was a receipt or a bill to be paid. It was a strange amount, too. And she couldn't remember Hector's moving bales. The Visa charges seemed high: several for gas at the Texaco station in Hermosa, odd only because they had their own farm gas, meals at the Maverick near Hot Springs, and four at the Colonial House in Rapid City. The big charge was for one airline ticket on Continental, $385.

She knew Continental didn't fly to Maine, so it couldn't be to meet Ames to take the boat south. Where was he going? Haney was quiet, but over time he'd become silent. Lately, when they drove to town, he gazed at the road, but she felt certain he was thinking of other terrain. When they worked together, he was more irritable. And at night he said good night in such a perfunctory manner it hurt her feelings. She didn't blame him, or herself—no person made another unhappy—but she wished he'd shared his doubts. Why hadn't he spoken to her? Doubts were honest; so was fear.

She looked for the airline ticket in the niches and drawers, under papers, and in notebooks, but the only unusual thing she found was a fifth of Jack Daniel's behind some files.

She drank a capful of bourbon, then got up and went upstairs to Shelley's room. From the TV there was canned laughter, then a *boing*. Mattie looked at the movie posters on Shelley's wall—*Pretty Woman*, *Cocktail*, and *2001: A Space Odyssey*.

"Can I talk to you?" Mattie asked.

Shelley muted the sound. "I guess you're going to. Who was here a bit ago? I heard voices out there."

"Lute Pollard wanted to check on us."

"In the dark?"

"I told him we were doing all right, but he's going to send Jimmy down tomorrow to look at the Case."

"Jesus, Mom, I don't want Jimmy here."

"Neither do I. But he offered, and we need the Case fixed somehow."

"Did you ask him about last night?"

"He said he was home."

Shelley looked away at the TV. "So what do you want to talk about?"

"An airline ticket. Did you ask your father for one, or did he offer?"

"No, why?"

"I'm trying to figure out why he wanted to be buried in Maine."

"What's an airline ticket have to do with it?"

"Do you think he ever had an affair?"

"What are you talking about, Mom? Daddy wouldn't do that. Would *you*?"

"We're talking about a man, not a woman."

"But he loved you, Mom."

"I didn't say he didn't. I was paying bills, and I found a charge for an airline ticket he never told me about."

"He didn't exactly plan on dying, Mom. Get a grip."

"I'm trying to."

Shelley looked at her mother, then back at the TV.

"He never talked to you about going anywhere? Well, I'm sorry to bother you."

"It's all right."

"Don't stay up too late."

"Have a little faith, Mom."

Mattie nodded. "I guess that's what's required here."

Shelley turned up the volume. "Good night, Mom."

Chapter 6

The next morning was clear, and sun angled into the corner of the bedroom, striking her bureau and the white lace bureau scarf and the painting of the woman asleep. Mattie thought the woman was day-dreaming with her eyes closed. The distant mountains were powder blue and lilac, and darker blue in the canyons, and the nearer hills were yellow-pink with sunlight. The sun struck the tops of the mesas and left the gullies deep in shadow.

Mattie put on her robe and slippers and went downstairs. She started the coffeemaker and stepped into the yard. The air was chilly, and there was dew on the grass, but the light was so clean she could not imagine a purer place. She pulled her robe more firmly around her shoulders.

She saw hawks—specks a mile away—dozens of them above the mesa, spiraling, soaring, dancing in the air. Without her own knowledge she moved across the wet grass. Her slippers absorbed the dew, and she didn't notice the cold. The lane was soft with rain and rutted by the tire marks of the four-wheeler, the pickup, and the tractor. The fields were an expectant gold, as though light were made of sounds, the howls of coyotes from the night before and now the songs of meadowlarks.

An upland plover flew from one fence post to another, rattling its complaint at her intrusion, but she kept her eye on the hawks. They wove a pattern of random circles around one another in the air, coiling and uncoiling with such ease Mattie felt the palpable magnetism of their movement. Their numbers grew. She couldn't count how many there were, and she stopped and let the moment enter her body.

"Mother!"

Shelley's voice drifted from the house behind her.

"Mom, what are you doing?"

The screen door slapped closed. The truck started.

The hawks drifted on the invisible currents above the place where Haney died, not even moving their wings. Buteos—Swainson's hawks—with broad white wings, dark collars, broad tails. She knew her birds.

Behind her the truck engine revved up the hill from the creek, the tires slapping mud under the chassis. The noise grew louder, and then Shelley stopped beside her with the driver's side window open. "Earth to Mom, what are you doing out here?"

"Walking."

"In your robe and slippers?"

"Obviously I am."

"Where're you going?"

Mattie turned toward the mesa. The hawks were dispersing to the north, over the cottonwoods by the river. "I thought I saw something."

"Like what?"

"Well, hawks, if you want to know. Swainson's hawks." Mattie screened her eyes with her hand, not from glare, but from distance.

Shelley followed her gaze. "I don't see any hawks."

Mattie was herself uncertain now. The hawks flew north, singly or in small groups, but disguised by distance and almost invisible.

"Mom, you're in trouble here. And aren't you cold?"

"No. Why am I in trouble? I'm taking a morning constitutional."

"Come on, get in, Mom. You need some coffee."

Mattie climbed in, and Shelley turned the truck around by gunning it and sliding on the gumbo.

The sun was well up when they came out after breakfast. Mattie carried the lunch cooler, and Shelley the jackets. The mountains were stark now, black as their name, and the hills closer in had hardened under the higher light to yellows and browns. They barely needed jackets except maybe later against the windchill higher up on the mesa.

"Get the yellow daisy and fence clips," Mattie said. "I'll put gas in the four-wheeler, and then we'll load the steel posts."

"This isn't going to be fun, is it?"

"Why were you so adamant last night that Jimmy shouldn't be down here?"

"I just am, that's all."

"Is it about that time you broke your arm? You never told the whole story."

"I told enough," Shelley said. "I don't want Jimmy down here to re-mind me." Shelley took the cooler and put it and the jackets into the bed of the pickup. "Why're we taking the four-wheeler?"

"One of us has to go to the store later, and the other will need a way to get home. There's a list in my jacket—milk, eggs, vegetables. And yeast. I want to make bread."

Mattie revved the Honda and kicked down into first. She was halfway across the yard before she remembered the water thermos. She looked back to see if Shelley had thought of it, but Shelley, in the truck, was almost to the Morton.

The gas tanks, two of them set ten feet high on braces, were by the barn. Mattie stopped under the rusty red one, pulled the saddle seat off the four-wheeler, and ran the nozzle into the tank. She turned her head away from the fumes.

Dew steamed from the grass and misted around the barn. A shadow sailed close by over the ground—a turkey vulture, early for the season—and she followed the vulture's tilting flight, its black wings raised above the horizontal, its skin head just visible. It disappeared beyond the barn, and as she lowered her eyes, she saw the boy looking down at her from the loft.

He was hidden by slats, but the light falling between the boards highlighted his red shirt. He was Indian, she could see that, though she couldn't see well enough to tell how old.

She topped the tank, replaced the nozzle on the pump, and screwed on the gas cap. Not looking at the boy, she stretched her arms and walked toward the barn, pretending to look at something low in the cottonwoods along the creek. When she was closer, she gazed up to where he was. "What's your name?" she asked.

The boy didn't answer.

"Where did you come from?" She spoke gently, not wanting to frighten him.

The boy didn't move or let on he was there.

The sound of metal banging metal made Mattie look across the yard. Shelley was throwing fence posts into the back of the pickup, and the sound echoed from the side of the Morton. When Mattie looked back, the boy was gone.

They set double wooden posts at the bottom of the ravine to stretch the barbed wire to and another double post on a rise halfway up the slope to the west. Mattie ratcheted the wire tight with the yellow daisy, while Shelley, back up the hill, clipped the barbed wire to the metal posts.

There were gaps in the line of steel posts, and they took turns with the post pounder. The pounder was a hollow piece of iron three feet long and four inches in diameter with a heavy head. The head fitted over the top of the post and had to be raised high in the air and thrust downward, so the downstroke, with her weight, drove the post into the ground. Haney had done it with some effort, and liked to, but for Mattie and Shelley it was brutal work.

Toward noon they sat on an outcropping and ate ham sandwiches. There was no shade, but the breeze made them put on their jackets. The sun felt good. Shelley passed Mattie a hard-boiled egg. Mattie gave Shelley carrot sticks and olives and water poured into the top of the thermos.

They were about the same altitude as Sheep Table opposite, and below them the hills and gullies and the river were without shadow. A mile away, the Upper East lay fallow, and standing water in one corner reflected the blue sky. Beyond that field were the county road and the Appletons' farm and a wide swale that emptied the higher plateau. To the west, two miles away, the tin roof of the Pollards' house caught the glare of the sun.

"So what did you see out there?" Shelley asked.

"What did I see when?"

"This morning when you went running out of the house."

"I told you. There were hawks over Sheep Table."

"And you were going to join them?"

"I wanted to get closer to them. Was that wrong?"

Shelley peeled her hard-boiled egg. "I wonder about you sometimes, Mom. You have tangents."

"Like what kinds of tangents?"

"Like that time in New Mexico you got lost."

"I wasn't lost. I wanted to sit on that outcropping."

"It was a cliff, and it was four miles from the road."

"I know where it was. Near Clayton. I was curious how far you could see from the top."

"You didn't have to spend the night up there."

"I didn't have to, but when I got up there, I wanted to. You all knew where I was."

"Daddy made us sleep in the car," Shelley said. "He was worried about you." She tossed a stone idly, and it bounced down the hillside, clattering against other stones. "I could never do that."

"Never do what?"

"Spend a night like that. And then, let's see, you climbed Devils Tower."

"Yes, well . . ." Mattie took another bite of her sandwich and drank some water.

"You panned for gold."

"Lots of people pan for gold."

"Not in winter, when there wasn't any."

"I didn't know there wasn't any."

"You knew it was winter. And what about skydiving? Daddy even said you couldn't, but you did anyway."

"He forbade me. That was his word."

"You could have been killed."

"You can be killed driving a truck home from Sheep Table," Mattie said. "You don't think I was a good wife?"

"What's the definition of a good wife?"

"Don't you have one?" Mattie asked. "You might have to be one someday."

"Maybe I won't."

"Is it the woman who's faithful? A woman who makes a man happy? A woman who obeys?"

"I don't obey Warren very much," Shelley said, "but I make him happy."

Mattie stared off toward the Black Hills. "Your father wasn't happy. I couldn't change that. I wish I could have."

"It wasn't your fault."

"Maybe not, but it was difficult, thinking he wanted another life from the one he had."

"What life did he want?" Shelley asked.

"I think a good wife would know," Mattie said. "I thought he wanted to sculpt, but he didn't do it." She got up and picked up the post pounder. "We'd better get back to work."

Mattie did four posts, and her shoulders ached. Her hands ached. She worked around the barbed wire Haney had stretched, holding it away with her leg so the post would go down straight. She set a fifth post, her leg bowing out with the wire. The barbs nicked her skin through her jeans. Just as she raised the pounder, the door of the truck opened, and she looked up at Shelley on the mesa. "Where are you going?" Mattie called.

Shelley ignored her or didn't hear. Either one made Mattie mad, and she brought the pounder down hard. Her leg buckled, and the pounder struck the top wire, and the wire recoiled and drove a barb into her right wrist, just at the edge of her glove above the thumb.

Mattie dropped the pounder and sat down hard on the ground. "Fuck Jesus Christ!"

"Mom?" Shelley scrambled down the scree. "Are you all right?"

"No, I'm not all right." She peeled off her glove.

The wound bled and swelled quickly to a hard blue knot the size of an egg.

"You must have hit a vein," Shelley said. She poured water from the thermos onto a corner of her shirt and dabbed at the wound. "You'd better get some ice on it. Let's get you up to the truck."

"I thought you were leaving without telling me," Mattie asked.

"I was getting a shovel."

Mattie stood up, holding her wrist. "I guess that decides who goes for the groceries. I'll take the four-wheeler down."

"Mom, you can't drive with that."

"I can drive," Mattie said. "You stay here and finish the fence."

"Mom . . ."

Mattie climbed on a zigzag up the hill to the four-wheeler.

She drove slowly with one hand along the rim of the mesa, keeping her right hand in the air. The old road wound in and out of the gullies and down into the breezeless heat. Where it leveled, she passed the broken bulldozer blade and kept on another mile to the river. She was dizzy, but not enough to stop.

In the kitchen she felt better, though the knot above her thumb was hard as glass. She filled a sandwich bag with ice, got a beer, and went back out into the yard. She sat on the picnic table, held the ice to her wrist, and breathed deeply to stanch her nausea. She looked west for the hawks and was surprised to see nothing: not anything. No fields, nothing. No hills or ravines, no mesas, no mountains. Tears welled up in her eyes. She tried to force back the tears, but she couldn't, and she struggled to breathe.

Then she gave in, and the tears came beyond her reckoning. Haney should have been pounding in the posts. He should have been laying the pipe across the river. She heard her sobs, felt the impossible ache. She cried for a long time and woke as if from a dream. The ice hurt her wrist as badly as the wound, but the swelling had gone down. Did the cells shrink? Did the blood rush away? Water dripped from the sandwich bag. She dabbed the cool plastic on her forehead and opened the beer.

The land appeared to her again, the amber hills and mesas. She heard water running—the hose, maybe—and she got up and walked around the corner of the house. The Indian boy was drinking, holding the nozzle of the hose so the arc of water ran into his mouth. The sunlight's striking the water made it look as if he were drinking light.

He straightened up, surprised.

She guessed he was thirteen or fourteen. He had a round face and long hair, and his jeans were ragged. A red plaid shirt was unbuttoned over a dirty white T-shirt. He looked at her wrist.

"I'm all right," she said. "It's good of you to be concerned."

He lifted his eyes to hers.

"Are you Lakota?" she asked. "How did you get here? Did you walk?"

The boy stepped into the shadow and turned off the hose. Then he gazed past her, and Mattie turned to see what he saw. A red and white truck was coming down the drive a half mile away, moving through the green alfalfa and the heat haze. At first she thought it was the Pollards' truck, Jimmy coming to look at the Case, but when it crossed the culvert, she saw it was newer than the Pollards' Dodge. It splashed through a puddle at the last curve before the house.

A woman was driving, and a man sat in the passenger seat. No ranch couple Mattie knew would ride that way. The woman pointed at something to the east, but Mattie didn't know at what or what they saw. When the truck neared, the boy took off running for the barn.

Mattie walked to the gate, and the truck stopped. The woman got out carrying a manila folder. A stranger with a folder was not good news. She was in her mid-thirties, dressed in a skirt and a white blouse. The man was a little older and wore a short-sleeved business shirt, his tie loose, his hair longish under a Rockies' baseball cap. He leaned into the cab and got out three scrolled documents. He walked over tentatively, Mattie thought, as if he knew she were going to be a royal pain in the ass.

"Are you Mrs. Remmel?" the woman asked.

Mattie drank a swallow of beer and held the cold can against her wrist. "What if I am?"

"I'm Jane Arnold," the woman said, "and this is Lee Coulter."

The man smiled halfway, like an embarrassed child. His tie was blue and had buffalo on it. "We're from the museum," he said, looking at Mattie straight on. "I spoke with your husband about a month ago. We're sorry about what happened."

"He was a generous man," the woman said.

"He was when he wanted to be," Mattie said.

"We know this isn't a good time," the man said, "but we hoped to do some site preparation before the ground dries out."

The woman opened the manila folder. "We're talking about in the next week or so," she said. "You probably know how eager your husband was to go forward with this, but he thought you might be concerned about the noise—"

"I am that," Mattie said.

"We have a small crew, and we'll minimize disturbance."

"But I'm just as concerned about moving bones around," Mattie said. "I don't want any crew."

"He gave us written permission," the woman said.

"When did he do that?"

The woman drew a paper from her folder, but the man stepped forward and took her arm. "Look, this isn't a good time," he said. "When should we come back?"

"Never would be all right," Mattie said. "When did he give you permission?"

The man smiled. "I'm going to leave these aerial maps with you. Heat imaging shows the land in different altitudes and compositions. I think you'll find them quite beautiful."

"I already know the country," Mattie said.

The man laid the maps on the picnic table. "Take your time. If you have questions, call me."

"What about the ground?" Jane Arnold said. "The ground will be cement."

The man looked at Mattie. "I'd like the maps back, though, when you're through." He paused. "That's a mean-looking wound you have there. Be sure to keep ice on it."

Chapter 7

Shelley didn't like working alone. The wind was spooky, and the land so empty and colorless it unsettled her, made her feel lost. She felt sometimes as if she were her father, a déjà vu sense of feeling as he did. She was a coward, and so was her father. He'd been so unobtrusive when he was alive that now his absence was scary, as if he'd never existed. But he did still exist in her.

An accident made no sense. One moment her father was healthy and alive, and the next moment he was dead. And there wasn't even a marker in the cemetery where she could visit him. The fence posts were markers. He'd driven one in every fifty-four feet to show the line, so she had to pound two posts eighteen feet apart in between. It took her forever to get one in, and when she'd done ten, her shoulders ached, and gloves or no gloves, her hands were blistered.

God, how could her mother allow Jimmy Pollard to work on the tractor? He was such an asshole, and nasty insane, and there was no way she was staying if he was going to be around. No way! Of course, her mother didn't know what had happened. All she knew about was the broken arm, and that Shelley had fallen out of Jimmy's truck. She should have told the truth, but she'd been scared, and she was still scared every time she thought of it. Lute and Jimmy were lowlifes.

But she couldn't walk out and leave her mother.

She did another post, and then she realized there weren't enough posts to finish, and she sure as hell wasn't going all the way back down for more. Besides, she had to go to the grocery store.

The truck squealed and screeched, but gravel didn't allow for speed anyway. She was on the back road to Hot Springs through Buffalo Gap, named for the cleft between two hills where the Indians had funneled buffalo for easy hunting. Now and then, across a grazed pasture or wheat field, a house appeared in a clump of trees, but mostly the land was barren. That's how she saw it—windblown dryland farms, no water except rain.

She slowed coming into Buffalo Gap, passed the seed store and repair shop, and turned right onto Main. There was no grocery store or gas station, and the bank had closed, but there was a post office and two bars. Work had made her thirsty, and she pulled into the Stockman's beside three other pickups already parked.

On weekends the Stockman's was a dance hall poorly attended, but it was dead now. Her eyes adjusted to the light, to the cement floor, the pool table and three video poker machines, a fireplace that hadn't been used in a while. Posters of the Black Velvet girl were taped to the walls. At the bar, two blue helium-filled balloons wavered above a display of chips, crackers, beef jerky, and a five-gallon jar of boiled eggs in brine. A loner sat at the curve of the bar, and a man and woman about halfway down. Two farmers in overalls were at a table in the middle of the room.

Shelley went to the center of the bar, where a half-empty beer glass was sitting, and ordered a Budweiser.

"Shelley Remmel, is that you?" The woman beside her stood up from her barstool.

"It's me," Shelley said. She didn't know the woman, but she looked vaguely familiar.

"It's Thella."

"My God," Shelley said. "It is you."

"It's all me. I didn't get tits until I got pregnant." Thella laughed and pulled her shirt down tight over her breasts.

"She's sure got 'em now," said the cowboy beside her.

Thella's hair was dyed platinum, and she had put on forty pounds. She patted the open barstool next to her for Shelley to sit down.

"I don't want to crash the party," Shelley said.

"You are the party, sweetheart," the cowboy said. He slid a glance over her, head to toe. "Give her a shot, Tom. Let's get started."

"That's Hank," Thella said. "He doesn't know any better."

"I try not to," Hank said. He took off his cowboy hat and set it on the bar. His hair was short at the sides and long in back, and he wore a red T-shirt that said "I TRIED TO CONTAIN MYSELF, BUT I ESCAPED."

The bartender delivered her Budweiser and then a shot.

"So where've you been all these years?" Thella asked.

"In school down in Boulder."

Thella turned to Hank. "Shelley and I used to run cross-country together."

"Thella still runs," Hank said, "but everybody catches her."

"They did back then, too," Thella said. "I've been married and divorced twice already. Did you run at college?"

"Till I hurt my knee."

"What're you doing home?" Hank asked. "It isn't vacation, is it?"

"My father died, and I came home to help my mother."

"He the one who turned the truck over on himself?" Thella asked. "It was in the *Star*."

A door slammed behind them, and a man barged into an empty chair and came toward them. He stopped a few feet away. It was Dwain Skutch, and he was about as Shelley remembered him—slender, hawk nose, except he'd lost some hair.

"You know Dwain," Thella said.

"Sure as shit she knows me," Dwain said. "We used to go out."

"Is that what you call it?" Shelley said. "I was fifteen."

"She was a cocktease from the git-go," Dwain said.

"You could have been arrested," Shelley said. She drank the shot of whiskey and a gulp of beer and stood up.

"Come on," Thella said. "Dwain doesn't mean anything."

"Of course he does."

"Of course I do," Dwain said. "But no offense." He grinned at her and hoisted his leg like a dog over the empty stool and sat down.

"Give her another shot, Tom," Hank said. "And one for Dwain there."

The bartender poured two more shots.

An hour later Shelley was still there, but the grocery store was farther away. She'd had three shots and was on her third or fourth beer. The bar was noisier. Hired men done for the day had filtered in, along with a couple of codgers let loose from home and several women from the grain elevator. Ruby Randall was singing "Lonesome for You" on the jukebox.

It turned out Dwain was working on the highway crew repairing the washed-out bridge at Edgemont. His supervisor had sent him to Hot Springs for a concrete drill bit, and he ran into Hank at Yogi's Bar, and they'd played pool. Around five-thirty they'd picked up Thella at the Battle Creek Texaco in Hermosa, where her ride from Rapid City ended. On the way back, two hours ago, they'd stopped in at the Stockman's.

Shelley pieced this together from the conversation, and somewhere it came clear Dwain wasn't going to get home to Edgemont, and there was talk of moving the party to Hank's trailer while they could still drive and not get arrested.

Tom put another pitcher on the bar.

"Do people really eat those eggs?" Shelley asked.

"People eat 'em when they're drunk," Tom said. "They bet on whether they can."

"Would you eat one, Hank?" Thella asked. "For me?"

"I'm not that drunk," Hank said.

A woman from the grain elevator, a heavyset blonde, started in wailing loudly with Ruby Randall.

> I'm tired of crying, tired of trying,
> but I'm still so lo-oh-ohn-some for you.

That jolted Shelley to her feet. "I have to shop for groceries," she said. "I promised my mom."

"Let's you and me go talk in the bathroom first," Thella said.

She put her arm inside Shelley's, and they reeled together across the floor. An old geezer at a table whistled at them.

"Keep it hard," Thella said. "We'll be right back."

In the ladies' room Shelley shook out her hair and washed her face, while Thella used the stall.

"So what do you think?" Thella asked from behind the partition.

"I could use a shower," Shelley said.

"I mean about Hank and Dwain."

"What's to think? They're animals."

"Hank's a cute animal, though, and he's real good when he wants to be."

"When is that?" Shelley asked.

The smell of marijuana wafted from the stall. The toilet flushed, and Thella came out. "He's an orderly at the VA," Thella said. "He gets some amazing drugs." She offered the joint to Shelley.

"If I do that, I'll never get out of here," Shelley said. "I told my mother—"

Thella laughed and took another hit. "So look, why don't you come over after? We're in the Sunnyside Trailer Park, number sixteen."

"Sixteen," Shelley said. "Well, maybe."

"Bullshit. You're chicken."

"I might," Shelley said. She took the joint and inhaled.

Chapter 8

S helley wanted to eat. She was giddy, teetery, and *starving*. It was dark now, and she turned south on State 79. She was drunk, but there wasn't much traffic, and when she saw headlights coming, she slowed to forty. It was only three miles to Maverick Junction, if she could wait that long for food.

Dwain Skutch—God, how had he lived so long? The last time they'd gone out was early spring of her sophomore year. She'd just got her driver's license, and her father had wanted her to take a tractor tire to get fixed, and she'd met Dwain at Butler Park. They'd sat in the bucket seats of his father's hardware store van at the far end of the playground, listening to Roseanne Cash. Dwain kept the engine on for heat.

They'd parked before, and she knew sort of, but not exactly, what he was after. They argued it out in aggression and avoidance, he touching and she resisting. Apparently he thought if he tried often enough, he'd get what he wanted. But that night he didn't try. He sat against the window and looked at her with a pained expression on his face.

"So what's wrong?" she asked finally.

"The baseball game was canceled," he said.

"Oh, come on, Dwain, it'll be rescheduled."

"You don't care about me, do you?"

"What are you talking about? Sure, I care about you."

"Not enough, though."

"What does that mean, not enough? I'm here, aren't I?"

"Enough means enough. You won't put me in your mouth."

"What?" She stared at him. He was serious.

"See? You don't want to."

"Well, Jesus, Dwain." She'd heard rumors about girls doing that, and heard that was what boys wanted them to do, but she didn't know anyone who had done it, or admitted it.

"If you will, I won't ever ask for anything else."

"Here?"

Silence. It was cold outside, and the park was deserted. Across the street a row of houses threw sharp lights into the air.

"So ? And?"

"I don't know. I don't know how."

"What's there to know?" he asked. "Here, make some room."

He slid over into the passenger seat, and she got on her knees in the footwell.

"Now what?" she asked.

He unzipped his pants and pulled them down. Of course she knew vaguely what to do. She wasn't that dumb. She'd touched him before through his jeans and once inside his underwear, but she'd never seen his cock. It was standing up and hard, and she ran her hand over the tip of it. It was smooth and warm. She couldn't help thinking it was an odd thing to be doing.

"You'd better hurry," he said.

She moved her fingers gently, and in two seconds he groaned and gushed over her hand.

Rae Ellen Kurtz gave her a menu. "I just loved your daddy," Rae said. "He ate here all the time. When he died, I cried and cried."

"So did I," Shelley said.

She was sitting in a booth at the Maverick Café.

"And he was so funny. Like once he said he was going to show me a picture of naked women, and you know what it was? A herd of cows!" Rae laughed and took a pencil from her hair. "He tipped well, too. I liked that."

"Did you ever see him with another woman?" Shelley asked.

"Heavens, no," Rae said. "No way on God's earth."

"I want a hamburger," Shelley said. "Make it a cheeseburger, no onions. And a Pepsi."

"Gotcha," Rae said.

After dinner Shelley felt better. She wasn't sober, but she wasn't hungry, and she was less likely to drive into a tree. From the Maverick, Hot Springs was five miles, and on the way she passed the Sunnyside Trailer Park stairstepping up the hill off to the right. She had no illusions about what would happen if she went to Hank's. She wasn't fifteen anymore, and Dwain would try to fuck her, at least he would if he were conscious and could get it up, neither of which was likely. She wasn't about to find out. On the other hand, she might not mind fucking Hank. He was a cute animal. Her friends at CU called it sportfucking. They went to fraternities and got drunk and fucked someone. Sex wasn't just a man's sport. Women weren't all sweetness and light. They could fuck, too.

There were only a few cars in the parking lot at the SunMart. She searched her mother's jacket, but there was no list, not in either pocket. She remembered milk and eggs, and they needed coffee and vegetables. What else? She could call, but her mother would ask her where she'd been. And she might still go to Hank's.

Inside, she got a cart with a wobbly wheel and pushed it down the vegetable aisle. It was bright inside, fluorescent. Lettuce, what kind? There was head lettuce, romaine, red-leaf, green-leaf, butter. She didn't want to decide. Beans, peas, carrots, broccoli, cauliflower? Major in journalism? Work in a bank? Go to law school? She wanted to sit down at dinner and be served chicken curry and wild rice and fresh peas with butter.

She put a head of red-leaf lettuce into a plastic bag, chose broccoli crowns and cauliflower that wasn't too brown. No beans. They'd have beans forever later in the summer. Vegetables solved. She wheeled her cart over to the meat display and got a pork roast. And then there was Mr. Adler, her English teacher, behind her in the pasta aisle.

She was sure it was Mr. Adler from his slouch and his red hair, though she'd never seen him in shorts and a T-shirt. In school he'd been her savior, not only in class, but also at one of her disciplinary hearings. God, she'd forgotten she'd dyed her hair pink! She'd done it one noon hour in Thella's basement, and when she went back to school, the principal sent her home.

Boy, her parents, especially her father, were unhappy. She'd never seen him so angry. "What the hell would you do that for?" he'd asked.

"Don't I have the right to wear my hair how I want?"

"Not when you live in this house."

"Since when do you care about appearances?"

"Goddammit, I do care about appearances. People will think you're crazy."

"What people? I don't care what people think."

"Your father means people will think *he's* crazy," her mother said.

The next day the principal suspended her, and she appealed to the school board, but the board was adamant: no pink hair.

"They're one intelligence level above plants," Mr. Adler told her. "This is a Republican town."

"So what do I do?"

"Shave your head, and come back to school. You learned how the real world operates."

"I don't like how the real world operates."

At the dairy case she got milk, butter, and yogurt, but there was something else her mother wanted. She was trying to remember what it was when Mr. Adler pushed his cart down the aisle. He glanced at her and stopped.

"I'm Shelley Remmel," she said. "I was in your English class."

"Of course. Shelley," he said. "My body's here, but my mind's in New Orleans."

"Who's in New Orleans?"

"William Faulkner. I'm going to a symposium. I'm sorry about your father. I saw the notice. You're at Boulder now, right?"

"Well, not anymore. I had to come back to help on the ranch. How's school?"

"Almost over, thank somebody. I think of resigning, and they think of firing me. So far it's a standoff."

"Are you still writing poems?"

"Alas, I am. It's a nasty job, but someone has to do it."

"So you shop at night?"

"At night I avoid irate parents."

"I just ran into Thella. Remember her? She works at the John Deere factory in Rapid City."

"I saw her last winter at a basketball game. She's put on some weight."

An awkwardness drifted between them, and Shelley put a carton of half-and-half into her cart. "There's something else I'm supposed to get, but I can't remember what." She looked in his grocery cart: rice, celery, carrots, spices, flour, and yeast. "Yeast," she said. "That's it, Mr. Adler. Yeast. Isn't that amazing?"

"What's so amazing?" Mr. Adler said. "I have a breadmaker."

"But that is *so weird.*" She was suddenly conscious of being foolish. She was drunk, and he wasn't. She turned her cart around, though she had no idea where yeast was in the store. "Have a good time in New Orleans."

"Thank you."

She glanced back. Mr. Adler hadn't moved. She stopped her cart.

"Can I ask you something, Mr. Adler?"

"Of course."

"Are you, like . . . do you go out with anyone?"

"I went out with Miss Suarez a few times, but we didn't speak the same language." He smiled. "I suppose I'm a recluse, which, however, is not a sexual orientation."

"Would you go out with me, say, like Friday?"

"If you call me Bryce," he said. "I thought you'd never ask."

Chapter 9

The last low sun spread itself into the corner by the rolltop desk. Shelley wasn't home yet; Mattie was sure she'd stopped work early and had gone to town. She stared at the black-and-white photograph Haney liked best of himself: He was at the helm of the *alouette*, canted to the horizon, a sea spray riding from the bottom right of the picture, blurring islands in the background. Ames McGill, shirtless, was balanced beside him, reading a novel, and Arlo Smith in a bathing suit, arm upraised, held a stanchion and pointed at something out of the picture. Haney was in his twenties then, before Mattie knew him, and his long hair was blown sideways by the wind. He wasn't so much happy as *there*, completely absorbed by what he was doing. The picture had been shot from a dinghy trailing behind, and inked in below on the raised white keel was the line "A bad tack wins the race." Who'd taken the picture? Had the owner of those blue panties written those words?

Mattie laid down the scrolled maps the museum man had lent her and peeled off the rubber band. She'd never liked maps. She preferred to think of the world as what was in front of her at the moment—fields, valleys, rivers, and mountains in relation to her own body. Natural landmarks informed her where she was and how far she had to go—the hawk's nest in the dead cottonwood, a rock outcropping shaped like a bear, the oxbow that used to be in the river.

But she had to admit, as far as maps went, the heat-imaging ones were beautiful, deep greens and blues expressing the contours and elevations of the land and orange and brown denoting its composition. The dig site, marked with an arrow, was just below the Upper East.

She didn't doubt there were bones in the sinkhole. For years they'd found fossils along the river and in the gullies after a rain, and Haney had saved the best ones, thinking someday Shelley or Shelley's children might want them. But he'd hoped to find a mammoth tusk or the bones of a wolf. "They're around," Haney used to say, as if the animals still roamed the countryside. And then he'd found the fragment of a mammoth's tooth.

She believed in privacy, and going through Haney's possessions was not her desire. They both had secrets. Most of hers were mundane, of course, wondering whether it would rain, whether Trini Decker still loved Allen, whether Haney would be on time for dinner—secrets only because they weren't worth telling. She'd told him the important things about her parents, about working at Rosa Saenz's bakery, about her college beau, but to reveal every moment was impossible. And what purpose would it have served to tell about the fling she'd once had with an ornithologist before she'd ever met Haney? Besides, other secrets she kept later were more serious—thoughts of Loren, fears of getting old, wanting to be held. She'd never told Haney such things, and he'd never asked.

Would it do her any good to know who'd taken the photograph of the *alouette*? She trusted him. Each of them relied on the other to tell what was necessary, but it was exactly this that set Mattie to doubting; he hadn't told her what she needed to know.

She glanced out the window at dust in the winnowing light. She hadn't seen or heard a car, but something had raised the dust, and a low-slung gray Mercury was parked just beyond the cottonwood tree. Mattie got up from the desk and went outside, letting the screen door bang behind her. The car had Utah plates. Clothes and two pillows and a basketball were jammed into the ledge at the rear window, and a piece of cutout cardboard was duct-taped into the back window on the driver's side. A sparkling dolphin hung from the rearview mirror.

She didn't see anyone, but at least it wasn't one of the Pollards.

She went around the house and saw a woman kneeling in her garden. As Mattie came nearer, the woman stood up. She was slender, and as tall as the deer fence, and dressed in jeans with holes in the knees and a blue work shirt. Her blond hair was tied up carelessly behind her head. She was in her late twenties, Mattie guessed, maybe thirty. She worked something nervously in her hand, Mattie couldn't see what, but she could see the pink fingernails moving.

"You planted too many beans last year," the woman said, "and it wouldn't hurt to put more nitrogen in the soil."

"I like beans," Mattie said.

"So do I, and they freeze well. Did you know it's bad luck not to leave an empty row?"

"Is that so?"

Mattie looked at the woman more closely. She had eyes too blue to be decent, a wide mouth, cheekbones that showed through. Her nose had character, a slightly off-center bump that made each eye take a different angle of light. Even without makeup, or especially without it, she was beautiful.

"I could sure use a beer," the woman said.

"There's the garden hose, but no beer in it."

The woman nodded at the bandage on Mattie's wrist. "You had tetanus?"

"I've had the shot, if that's what you mean."

The woman looked off toward the mailbox and the county road. "You know, I might have been driving around forever out there."

"People who live here know where they are," Mattie said. "And you can ask. Who are you trying to find?"

"I wanted to find the Remmels' place."

"You found it."

"Then I'm batting a thousand so far," the woman said. She pulled a wadded bit of newspaper from her shirt pocket. "What do you mean, 'hours and wages depend on competence'?"

"It means we're looking for a man who can fix machines."

"What kind of machines?"

"I have a field generator that doesn't work, a windrower to grease and lube, and a pivot sprinkler frozen with rust. I guess the first priority is a Case three-eighty-six tractor that needs to be put back together."

The woman looked toward the Morton. "It's a shame they make those buildings so ugly," she said. "Is that where the tractor is?"

"Yes, but I sort of have someone who's going to look at it."

"I sure do hate wind chimes, don't you? Oh, I'm sorry." The woman moved the object she was fiddling with to her left hand and put out her right. "I'm Dawn, your new hired man."

Dawn left her hand midair, and Mattie felt obliged to shake it.

"I better go see the tractor."

Dawn strode off toward the Morton, and Mattie had to run to catch up.

Dawn pulled open the sliding door of the Morton. Along one wall was Haney's workbench with a welter of tools and parts of various two-cycle engines. The shower stall Haney had put in smelled of mildew, though mostly Mattie noticed grease, and she was suddenly conscious of the wind chimes. The Case sat in the middle of the cement floor surrounded by parts laid on a tarp.

"You got a lot of welding gear and air pumps," Dawn said. "That's good. You can't have too much air. And a three-wheeler. Does it run?"

"No."

She looked at the Case. "I see why you advertised for a hired man. I hope you weren't paying much to whoever was working on this."

"I wasn't," Mattie said.

"He sure didn't know much about engines."

"It was my husband."

"Is he going to be mad if I fix it?"

"No, he won't be mad," Mattie said. "He's dead. He was killed in an accident."

"Well, I'm sorry, but he wasn't a mechanic. Here, hold this."

Dawn gave Mattie the piece of quartz in her hand and then lay down on the tarp and looked up under the tractor engine.

"What do you see?" Mattie asked.

"A mess of stuff."

"That doesn't sound too scientific."

Dawn got up again and brushed dirt from her hands and took back her piece of quartz. "I sure could use a beer," she said.

Dawn set her Budweiser can on the kitchen table beside her piece of quartz. "Well, before I got to be Dawn, I was Yvonne, and before that, Sage. I outgrew Sage—that was a joke. I didn't want to be Rosemary or Thyme. I was never real good at Yvonne."

"So why Dawn?"

"I want a new beginning," Dawn said. "Do you think things happen by fate?"

"Either that or by random occurrence."

"I stop in Hot Springs for gas, look in the newspaper by pure chance, and here I am."

"Random occurrence," Mattie said. "Now I told you I can't hire anybody until I talk to my daughter."

"I know you did, but some stones have power."

"Does that one?"

"I'm not sure yet. I got it in Death Valley a few days ago." She picked up the piece of quartz and rubbed her fingers over it.

"Your car license says Utah."

"I know, but that's not important. There aren't boundaries. I'm not really from anywhere."

"You had to grow up somewhere."

"I grew up in Lolo, Montana. I learned to fix machines at a vo-tech school in Kalispell."

"Your fingernails don't look as if you fix machines."

"Of course not. I had them done a few days ago in Las Vegas."

Mattie looked out the window at the Mercury. "Is all that your stuff in the car?"

"It is now." Dawn finished her beer and got another from the fridge. "I don't drink on the job, but you said I'm not hired yet. Are you a religious nutso or a Sunday school teacher? I can't work for someone who believes in that shit."

"I don't consider it shit," Mattie said, "but no, I'm neither of those."

"Dog," Dawn said—she pronounced it Doog. "Dog is God spelled backwards, and doog is good spelled backwards. That's what I believe in. Good." She leaned forward over the table toward Mattie. "All right, here's what we'll do. I work a week as a trial for room and board, and then we'll decide what I'm worth, retroactive to today."

"Who's we?"

"We'll vote. You and your daughter and I."

"There's no vote," Mattie said. "This isn't a democracy."

"Will I have to go to town very much, like for parts and things?"

"There'd be some of that. Do you have an aversion to town?"

"No, but I can tell I'll like it here. Have you thought about getting buffalo calves?"

"I don't want buffalo calves," Mattie said.

"When will your daughter be back? Is it all right if I camp out at the river for a couple of nights?"

Mattie took a breath. "Dawn, listen—"

"Just one night, then, and in the morning I'll fix the Case tractor for free."

"One night," Mattie said.

"Thank you," Dawn said. "And I'm environmental."

"Good."

"See, it's fate," Dawn said. She worked the stone in her fingers. "Can I take a beer with me?"

That evening after supper Mattie studied the maps in more detail, more for Haney's benefit than her own. It was impossible not to think of him, his coat still hung on the rack, the desk littered with sketches, the book on hydrology still on the sofa where he was reading it. He was everywhere in the house.

But he was not there.

Around nine Trini Decker called, wanting to know how she was.

"Busy," Mattie said. "Shelley and I worked on the north fence this afternoon."

"Have people been helping out?"

"Well, Lute Pollard showed up in the dark, and this afternoon I clobbered myself with the post pounder."

"But how are *you*?" Trini asked.

"There are bad days and worse days."

"And Shelley?"

"I don't know. I don't think she knows. There's so much work we don't have much time for anything else."

"You need help."

"I may have a hired man," Mattie said. "I'm not sure yet."

"Homer Twardzik?"

"No, a new person. Not from here."

"But something's wrong."

"No, not really."

"Tell me."

Mattie hesitated. "Sometimes I think I didn't know Haney very well."

"He was quiet. He always was."

"I don't mean that. There are all these things I'm finding out about."

"Like what?"

"Like, he gave permission to the museum to dig the sinkhole. And he bought a plane ticket he didn't tell me about. I found the charge on our Visa."

"A plane ticket to where? Was he leaving you?"

"I don't know to where."

"That was a joke," Trini said.

"It's not a joke," Mattie said.

"I'll be right down," Trini said, and she hung up the phone.

Mattie regretted immediately opening her mouth to Trini. Trini was Haney's opposite; she believed in getting it out. Nothing good ever came from repression. Confession was a blessing for the soul.

"Looks sixty, acts thirty," was how Haney described her. She was Mattie's age and height, but bulkier. She wore shifts and baggy clothes. Her long brown hair was straight to her waist, or up in a twist, or sometimes fastened in a clip at the nape of her neck. Her eyes were brown, the right one slitted narrowly from a BB gun accident as a girl. From the side the wound gave her a heavy-lidded Asian look.

The Deckers weren't ranchers. They were partially reformed hippies who'd come to South Dakota twenty years ago with two other couples. They'd bought sixty acres for fifteen thousand dollars and lived in a tepee while they built a house. As Trini told it, everyone in the county hated them, and some people still did. Allen had a degree in physics, but worked for years as a carpet installer, and Trini had been a history major from UC Berkeley before dropping out. She sewed and proofread business documents and kept a garden three times the size of Mattie's. The other couples gave up the commune, but Trini and Allen stayed on for the children, Keith for Richards, and Dylan after Zimmerman. They home-schooled them through junior high and then, out of frustration, sent them to high school in Hot Springs. To Trini's disappointment, Keith was president of Young Life, and Dylan read science fiction and played computer games.

Mattie knew more about Trini's marriage than she ever wanted to—how often she and Allen made love, what arguments they had, the newest vibrator they bought. Mattie was informed they "screwed their brains out" on their front lawn after a potluck at the Bishops' and that Allen had the hots for a paraplegic woman at a convalescent hospital where he volunteered.

Trini tried to get Mattie to talk about her marriage, too, but Mattie thought what she and Haney did was their business. Trini of course knew a few things by observation—how she and Haney moved together or around each other, how they looked at or didn't look at each other, the way they conversed in public. Once at a tool auction a year ago Trini had said, "What's going on with you two?"

"Which two?"

"You and Haney are barely being civil."

"He's buying more junk," Mattie said.

"That's not it," Trini said, "but I understand what you mean."

"What do you understand?"

"It's easy to see what's there," Trini said, "but not what's absent."

Trini had brought brandy, and they sat in the kitchen and drank tea with brandy in it.

"Really I'm fine," Mattie said. "You didn't have to come all the way down here."

"It's only two miles. Now what's all this about a plane ticket? He didn't tell you about a trip he was taking? Maybe he bought it for you? Where's it to?"

"I can't find it. It's not in his desk."

"Did you call the airline?"

"I don't want to investigate him," Mattie said. "I don't want even to be suspicious."

"So you think it was for someone else?"

"Or for him to meet someone else."

Trini poured more brandy. "Let's see the Visa bill. We need the reference number of the ticket."

Mattie fetched the credit card statement and came back. "Remember when I had dental surgery in Denver two years ago? Haney stayed here because the Morton was going up, but three days later he showed up at Earl's with a sprained knee from skiing at Vail."

"As I recall, the Morton contractor was delayed."

"So he went skiing? He had to go through Denver to get to Vail. Why didn't he stop and see how I was?"

"There's no underestimating the insensitivity of men," Trini said. "Are you holding that against him, too?"

"Yes."

"Give me the bill." Trini picked up the phone.

Trini dialed the number, then pressed a button and waited for someone to answer.

"I mean, he goes to Rapid City all the time," Mattie said. "Maybe he meets her there."

"They put me on hold," Trini said. She drank her tea and brandy. "And in your life, are you blameless?"

"Yes, mostly."

"You've never thought about going to bed with another man?"

"There's a difference between thinking and doing."

"You've never flirted?"

"We're not talking about flirting."

"Who've you wanted to go to bed with?"

"William Hurt."

Trini laughed. "Oh, Jesus, me too. And Jeff Bridges."

"But not Redford," Mattie said. "Too many wrinkles."

"I don't mind wrinkles," Trini said. "What about Robert Duvall?"

"A genius," Mattie said. "*Tender Mercies* and *Lonesome Dove* and *Wrestling Ernest Hemingway*."

Trini hung up the phone. "I had an affair once," Trini said.

"You never told me that."

"Would it be so terrible if Haney had one?"

"Yes," Mattie said. "It would change my world."

"Then maybe your world is screwed up," Trini said. "If he did, what are you going to do about it? You can't yell and scream at him. You can't get revenge. You can't even divorce him."

"I don't know what I'd do, but I can't erase what I know. Could you?"

"No, probably not."

They were quiet for a moment.

"Well, I'm here," Trini said. "And I have plenty of brandy."

Chapter 10

Trini left a little before ten, and Shelley still wasn't home. Mattie cut three slices of her last loaf of bread and put a thigh and a drumstick on a plate. Then she got a sleeping bag from the debris in the hall closet and took the plate and the sleeping bag and a kitchen chair outside to the bottom of the steps. There was no reason the Indian boy had to be hungry and cold in the hayloft.

She stood for a minute in the yard. The land unlit frightened her, but she liked its mystery. To accept darkness was what every creature had to do. She wanted light, but darkness beckoned her, put her between wanting to believe and being unable to, between knowing and not knowing. Deer slept in the day and fed at night; rabbits, voles, kangaroo rats braved the night because it was safer. But safe was relative. Owls hunted at night because their prey was moving, and so did coyotes and mountain lions and snakes. Would the Indian boy be more likely to come to the house if the porch light were on or off?

The arc light at the Morton made a shadow of the house, and Mattie circled the shadow and made her own shadow behind her as she walked toward the light. She entered through the side door and flipped on the light, and the cavernous interior came alive.

Haney's workbench was neat. He had come to order his possessions. There were hundreds of tools, and he had bought more at every farm sale—boxes of loose tools for ten dollars, sets of socket wrenches, miscellaneous screwdrivers. He owned ball peen hammers, finish nail hammers, claw hammers, rock hammers, sledgehammers. He owned socket wrenches, crescent wrenches, pipe wrenches, saws, chisels, pliers, ten pairs of Vise-Grips. He had air-pressure tanks, a drill press, table saw, Skil saw, Sawzall, and all the heavy wrenches for big machines, which he was just learning about when he died.

Mattie searched everywhere for the ticket—in the drawers of the workbench, the toolboxes, the cabinets where he kept screws, bolts, and fence clips. She looked inside old tires, under the tarp, in a roll of plastic irrigation pipe—anywhere he might have hidden things. She even looked in the red toolbox in the cab of the tractor.

The Case set off the memory of when it had broken down, September of last year, when Haney was optimistic there'd be enough dew to bale the Upper East. After supper he towed the baler up the hill, but he hadn't gone ten feet into the field when hydraulic fluid spurted from the cylinders. He had to walk to the Appletons' to call her to bring up the red toolbox.

She was canning apricots and didn't want to stop, but she'd washed her hands, found the red toolbox, and driven up the farm road. It was almost dark, and a rim of blue outlined the Black Hills. In the field, Haney was a silhouette against the cut hay.

She held the flashlight while he tinkered, but the problem was more serious than he could solve right then. He levered out the linchpin and unhooked the hydraulics, and she drove the tractor to the turnaround and idled it down. She was still sitting there when Haney climbed in to get his thermos and some tools he wanted. They gazed at each other. Her hair was pulled up and out of her eyes, her apricot-smelly apron still tied around her waist, her face spattered with juice. Suddenly he kissed her hard on the mouth. One hand grasped her hair, and the other opened her shirt. He set his calloused hand on her breast. She moved her hand tentatively up his leg. Then he lifted her from the seat and sat down and pulled her over him. She slipped her underwear aside and pressed against him. There was no word for what she felt, only a sigh that obliterated every other sense. She lifted her body and eased down again.

Eight months ago—that was the last time they'd made love. She hadn't known it was the last time they ever would.

Chapter 11

Earlier that evening, sunlight dappled the cottonwoods and shone gold on the hills, and the swinging glass dolphin sprayed out its colors on her leg as Dawn coaxed the Mercury downhill toward the river. She didn't see why Mattie was opposed to raising buffalo. Bison, really. They'd lived in South Dakota forever, and telling her relatives in Georgia and her children and her grandchildren how she'd raised buffalo would be a good story.

Mattie would hire her, how could she not? What difference did it make where she'd learned to repair equipment? If she could fix the tractor, she didn't need references or recommendations or a license. Whether she was from Montana or Georgia didn't matter.

The shocks on the Mercury groaned as a tire dipped in a pothole, and the muffler scraped. She turned the corner, and in front of her was a plank bridge. Upstream a pale yellow light diffused from the stream, and she envisioned dolphins leaping over it from the lower pool to the upper one. She stopped on the bridge and got out. A flood had gone through not that long ago—a riprap of brush and barbed wire and grass was caught on a jumble of logs—and someday there'd be another. A flood washed everything to the next river, and on to another after that.

Dawn picked up two pale, hand-sized stones from the ramp—not magic stones—and dropped one of them into the deep pool under the bridge. It sank to the bottom and shone dully against other stones. She dropped the other one closer to the bank into deeper water, and it disappeared.

"Good," she said. "Perfect."

She opened the back passenger door, and a striped tom jumped out. He rubbed up against her, as he always did. "You stay here, Hercules," she said. She lifted a hand dumbbell from the back seat and tossed it into the pool.

She lifted the trunk and, from the jumble of clothes, extricated Styver's set of TaylorMade titanium golf clubs. How many hours had she waited for him at city courses in small towns or at country clubs where he glib-talked people into letting him make a threesome? How many bad jokes had she endured in seedy nineteenth-hole bars and posh lounges? *Golf is a game that needlessly prolongs the lives of some of our most useless citizens.* Too fucking many.

She lugged the golf bag to the edge of the bridge and, one by one, tossed the clubs into the pool, where they sank under the bridge not quite out of sight, but good enough. She got out his black-and-white golf shoes and put a fair-sized stone in each and tossed the shoes. They looked like zebra fish on the bottom.

Then she filled the golf bag half full with stones and dragged it back to the car. In the back footwell, under dirty clothes, she found the duct tape she'd used to tape the cardboard into the window Styver had broken when he threw the barbell at her and missed. Good thing the car was moving. Reason number sixty-three to leave him. Or was it sixty-four?

Hercules rubbed against her again, and she sneezed; the cat had the same sadistic qualities Styver did.

"*What about the rashes and sneezing? What about the watering eyes?*"

"*Fuck you, Yvonne.*"

"*It doesn't matter to you I'm allergic?*"

"*No, it doesn't matter. It's my mother's cat.*"

That was reason sixty-five.

Dawn dug under the dirty clothes and found the urn of Styver's mother's ashes and tossed it into the river. Then she got out a bandanna from the dirty clothes and tied it over her nose. In one quick movement, she picked up the cat and jammed him into the golf bag. She duct-taped a gray star over the opening, lugged the bag to the edge of the bridge, and toppled it into the water. Styver's mother had said she wanted to be buried with her cat.

On the flats above the river, Dawn followed a four-wheeler track west until it descended into a rocky gully. There she parked and walked, carrying two cloth wind dolphins, her tent and bedroll, and the bottle of Stolichnaya, which was the only souvenir of Death Valley she wanted to keep. She walked until she found a campsite she liked, on a finger butte about level with the tops of the cottonwood trees at the river.

There she staked the wind dolphins and rolled the tent out on a flat spot and then sat down with the bottle of vodka. The river beneath her was slow and clear, and she imagined dolphins surfacing languidly in the green pools. Upstream the sheen off the water was silver in the calm stretches and bluish white where it ran over rocks. The water looked oddly unmoving, the drops in every riffle replaced by other drops. Though it was flowing, the whole river looked still.

For the first time in months she was where she wanted to be. She'd jettisoned Styver's possessions—his golf books, his coffee cup, his clothes. The only thing she'd kept was his laptop, which had no emotional significance, but might come in handy. Money, money, money—her life with Styver was over.

She liked the ranch and being in one place. She liked the quiet. Shadows crept down into the gullies toward the river, and a honey light lit up the clouds. She could disappear into this place. It would be this way day after day. Styver wouldn't find her. Or the police. The land would not tell on her. She closed her eyes and fingered the piece of quartz and saw buffalo all over the humpbacked hills. Wind dolphins swam in the breeze. She uncapped the bottle of Stoli and drank once to the new dawn.

Chapter 12

When Shelley came out of the SunMart, the thought of sportfucking Hank Tobuk was totally reprehensible. She must have been really shitfaced to think of it in the first place, and she felt ashamed asking Mr. Adler on a date, not because she didn't want to go, but because of Warren. She'd have to tell Warren, or not tell him.

Or she could not go out with Mr. Adler. *Bryce.* She wasn't betraying Warren, exactly—it wasn't as if she were going to sleep with Bryce—but it wasn't fair. Still, if she found she didn't like Bryce, wouldn't Warren profit? He'd seem all that much more attractive to her.

She drove east to Maverick Junction, turned south, and then east again. Driving that stretch of road always made her feel so vulnerable. Only a few sporadic lights shone from the void. No wonder she was lonely—houses so far apart and the lives within those houses so solitary. Who would know if anyone died? She thought of her brother. Did anyone remember him?

How many nights he'd endured that brutal coughing. She remembered the attendant panic, her parents opening and closing doors, the raised voices, the humidifier, the telephone calls. One night they'd dragged her with them in the car—she was twelve and couldn't stay alone—and they'd driven to Hot Springs and then to Rapid City and Loren had died.

She set the groceries beside the scrolled maps on the kitchen table and took out the sherbet and got a bowl from the cupboard. She heard footsteps on the stairs.

"Is that you?" her mother called.

"It isn't Hector Lopez."

Her mother came into the kitchen. "Now why would you say that?"

"How's the wrist?"

"Better. I'll have some, too. Are there more groceries?"

"I'll get them, Mom. What's that food doing out there on the steps?"

Her mother went outside.

"Mom, I said I'd *get* them."

But she let her mother go and got down another bowl and spooned out sherbet. Then she put the lettuce in the crisper and opened the 1 percent and drank from the carton. Her mother came back with the other bags.

"Did Jimmy Pollard show up?"

"No, but we may have a hired man. I said I'd talk to you."

"Good. Anybody's fine."

"Her name's Dawn. She's camped at the river."

"A woman?"

"She says she's going to fix the Case tomorrow. That'll be a test." Mattie hefted two chickens from one of the bags. "You bought more chicken?"

"Guess who I ran into in the store?"

"William Hurt. No, who did you run into in the store?"

"Remember my old English teacher, Mr. Adler? We're going out Friday night."

"Is that where you were all this time?"

"I went to the Stockman's in Buffalo Gap and ran into Thella."

"I thought you were living with Warren."

"It's not a date, really. We're just going to talk." She put the juice in the cupboard under the sink. "So what's the food outside on the steps for?"

"There's an Indian boy living in the barn. I've seen him a few times, and I think he's hungry."

"And you're feeding him?"

"Would you rather I called the sheriff? I thought if we could draw him in, we could find out where he's from and help him get home." Mattie took up her bowl of sherbet. "Thanks for remembering the yeast."

"There was no list in your pocket, but I have a steel trap mind. I don't know what to do about Warren, Mom. He's sweet, but he's oblivious."

"I thought you loved him."

"Why does it have to be either-or? Can't I go out with Bryce and love Warren, too? Warren's more like a habit."

"That's what commitment is, a habit."

"Is that what you felt about Dad?"

"Maybe instead of going out with Mr. Adler, you should go see Warren and decide what's what. But I gather you are not asking me for advice." Mattie finished her sherbet and rinsed the dish. "How'd you do with the fence?"

"The fence won."

"You didn't finish?"

"I ran out of posts."

"Tomorrow I want to pick up rocks," Mattie said. "I want to see how long it will take."

"Maybe the Indian boy can help."

"That's a good idea. Maybe he will."

"Mom, come *on*. Don't get involved."

"Why shouldn't I?"

"At least talk to the sheriff and find out if he's missing."

"All right. I can do that when I go to Barton's office tomorrow."

"Thank you," Shelley said. "That's what I'd do. And Mom?"

"What?"

"Who's William Hurt?"

Chapter 13

At sunup frost rimed the Lincoln and the leather seat of the four-wheeler. White etched the grass and the north side of the cottonwood tree. Mattie walked directly across to the barn, listening to red-winged blackbirds chirring in the marsh beyond the Iron-weed Patch. She didn't want to frighten the boy, so she sang as she walked:

> The dancing cowboy
> Is hiding his crying
> The dancing cowboy
> Is losing his blues
> > tonight.

She swung open the door, jostled a sculpture aside, and climbed the ladder to the loft. Sunlight fell in streaks through the vertical boards. A barn owl watched her from a rafter, and Mattie knew if the owl was there, the boy wasn't. She climbed back down.

The sculptures: What was she going to do with those thousands of hours of Haney's life? She unwrapped a small one that was part of his Man/Woman series, a man lying on his back with a woman floating above him, *Man and Woman Separated by Air*. She carried it and another one, still wrapped, outside and saw Dawn's Mercury parked at the Morton.

Mattie detoured over to see what Dawn was doing. The wind chimes were gone, and Dawn was up on a stepladder, her hair clipped up, leaning into the engine of the Case. The radio on the workbench was playing classical music.

To Dawn's credit, she seemed to be a self-starter and adaptable. She might believe in fate and in magic stones and change her name every so often, but she was self-sufficient. Mattie liked that quality in a woman. The problem was, How could someone so pretty not be trouble?

Mattie nodded at Dawn, and Dawn waved, and that was that.

When Mattie came into the kitchen, Shelley was dressed in a pink robe and sneakers and was cooking Cream of Wheat on the stove.

"He wasn't in the hayloft," Mattie said.

"Who?"

"The Indian boy."

"Is the sleeping bag gone?"

"Yes."

Mattie set the sculptures on the table and unwrapped *Man and Woman Joined by Earth,* a man and woman clinging to one another, half buried beneath a birch tree.

"What are you going to do with those?" Shelley asked.

"I thought I'd clean them up and put them in the living room. How're you feeling today?"

"Hung over a little."

"Dawn's already working on the tractor."

"Good for her."

"You might go say hello to her and see what you think." Mattie poured herself coffee. "Where would you sleep if it was cold out?"

"In my bed."

"With the sleeping bag, he could sleep anywhere."

"He probably sold the bag and went to a Holiday Inn," Shelley said. She spooned Cream of Wheat into two bowls and carried one to Mattie. "Breakfast is served."

"I know where he is," Mattie said.

"Where?"

"Let's go look."

Mattie set down her bowl and went outside.

"Mom, the cereal will get cold. And I only have my robe on."

Shelley followed out to the porch, where Mattie was pointing at the Lincoln. "Look at the windows."

All the windows were white with frost. They went down the steps, and Mattie motioned Shelley around to the passenger side.

"What are you going to do?"

"I don't want to scare him. If he runs, let him go."

"I don't care if he runs," Shelley said.

They looked at each other, and Mattie opened the back door.

The boy, startled from sleep, sat up quickly and scrambled to Shelley's side, but she held the door closed with her hip.

Mattie leaned down into the car and smiled. "Don't be afraid," she said. "Breakfast is ready when you are."

Mattie followed the seasons by the direction of sunlight into the kitchen, and that morning it shone from an angle just east of the cottonwood tree and made the air alive with particles of dust. The Indian boy sat between them without speaking, eating his Cream of Wheat. His hair was matted with bits of hay, and his eyes were tired. And he smelled of days of sweat and dirt.

"He's another version of Daddy," Shelley said. "Maybe he can't speak."

"He'll say something if he wants to."

"Maybe he's mute."

"More coffee?" Mattie asked the boy.

The boy pushed his cup forward, and Mattie poured it half full, then added some to her own.

"You never let me drink coffee when I was eleven," Shelley said.

The boy looked at Shelley. "I'm not eleven," he said.

"How old are you?" Mattie asked.

"Sixteen."

"Bullshit," Shelley said.

"Where are you from?" Mattie asked.

Outside, a swallow swooped under the eave with a bit of mud in its beak and added the mud to its nest. Inside, the boy reached out and grabbed a fly from the air.

"He must be from Pine Ridge," Shelley said.

"Why don't you let him answer?" Mattie looked at the boy.

The boy didn't say anything.

"Are you lost?" Mattie asked. "How did you get here?"

No answer.

"We're going to pick up rocks today. Do you want to earn some money?"

The boy looked at her. "Are you serious?"

"Yes, I'm serious."

"Jesus," Shelley said, "you want to hire him?"

"Why not? It was your idea."

A truck drove from behind the house; they heard the rumble before they saw it.

"Pollards," Mattie said. She looked out the window. "I bet it's Jimmy coming to look at the Case."

The Indian boy ducked down below the windowsill.

"Get rid of him, Mom," Shelley said.

"I intend to."

Mattie got up and walked out to the Morton and found Jimmy standing in the open bay watching Dawn.

"What's all this about?" Jimmy said. "How come you got a woman doing this?"

"Is that a problem?" Dawn asked.

"Do you even know what you're doing?"

"I'm fixing this tractor."

"This is Jimmy Pollard, Dawn," Mattie said. "He's a neighbor."

"He could learn some manners," Dawn said.

"I guess you were a little late getting here, Jimmy," Mattie said. "But we're about to go pick up rocks. We could use some help doing that."

"If you know how," Dawn said.

Jimmy looked at Dawn a moment longer than he needed to. "I ain't picking up rocks."

He turned and looked back at Dawn again and then went out and got into his truck.

"Not very nice, is he?" Dawn said.

"Not very," Mattie said. "Remember that."

Standing in the middle of the pivot field, Mattie couldn't tell it was a circle. The thin pale green looked as if it extended all the way to the river, and beyond it were the eroded cliff and the mesa they called Sheep Table, from which they had to bring the pipe down.

They stayed apart from one another, gathering rocks of all sizes and shapes into piles. A rock could break the teeth of the cutting bar on the windrower, and the feedlot didn't want rocks in the bales. They tossed rocks into heaps, picked them up again and put them in the cart, then picked them up a third time when they unloaded them at the edge of the field. Some of the rocks took two of them to move, and they rolled them up a plank into the cart.

Midmorning Mattie and Shelley rested on the back of the cart and drank diet Pepsi from the cooler. Mattie's wrist was sore, but not weak, and she rationalized the pain as healing. The boy continued working. He moved over the ground, hurried and unhurried, as if he knew exactly the energy required to pick up each rock. To him, movement was resting and working at the same time.

"Brave-No-Name," Shelley said.

"I guess we shouldn't let him do all the work," Mattie said.

"Why not?" Shelley finished her Pepsi and stood up. "He's a better worker than I am. I know that's not saying much."

"You're learning," Mattie said.

"I thought I might drive down and see Warren," Shelley said. "To see what's what and to get some of my stuff."

"Are you thinking of staying, then?"

"I'm thinking of it."

"It's your house, too," Mattie said. "I'd be glad for you to be here."

At noon Mattie invited Dawn to join them for lunch—tuna sandwiches, coleslaw, chips, and lemonade—but she'd brought her own food.

"How's the tractor coming?"

"It's coming."

"You need any parts?"

"Not yet."

"You sure you don't want to eat with us?"

"I'll finish here," Dawn said, "but I'll need to know whether I have a job."

"Shelley will come over after lunch," Mattie said. "She has a vote, too."

Mattie, Shelley, and the Indian boy ate at the picnic table under the cottonwood tree. No one talked much. The Indian boy ate as if he hadn't seen food in weeks. He stuffed the bread into his mouth, finished the coleslaw right from the bowl, and drank a quart of lemonade.

"He'll calm down," Mattie said.

"I'm not so sure," Shelley said. "I wouldn't offer room and board."

Once in a while the boy gazed into the sky—at a seed floating, clouds, a distant hawk? Mattie couldn't tell. "More?" she asked.

He nodded, and she made him another sandwich.

"I can pay you for this morning," she said, "and give you a ride into town. I have some errands to run."

"There are more rocks," the boy said.

"Shelley's going to finish up fencing. You want to pick up rocks by yourself?"

He nodded.

"It's going to be hot."

"You could get a bus in town," Shelley said. "My mom will point you in the right direction."

"I know the right direction," the boy said.

He got up and walked west across the yard toward the pivot field.

"You should take water," Mattie called after him.

But the boy didn't stop.

Mattie and Shelley looked at each other and then again at the boy moving away.

"Is he going to work if we're not watching him?" Shelley asked.

"Don't you?"

"Not always."

Mattie got up and collected the empty plates. "Take some water out to him later," she said. "You can see how big the piles of rocks are."

The boy disappeared into the creek bottom and came up the other bank and kept walking along the dirt track by the horse pasture.

Chapter 14

The Black Hills were sacred ground to the Indians. They had no boundary lines, no land offices, no court records, and when the whites came into their country, the Indians for the first time encountered the idea of private property: This is mine; that's yours. They didn't much like the idea.

In 1803 the United States bought the Louisiana Territory from France, and a year later Lewis and Clark explored all the way to Oregon. The country opened up. Wagon ruts deepened as homesteaders joined the fur trappers and gold panners. They fenced the land and shot buffalo indiscriminately, and naturally the Indians resisted this encroachment. By 1868 enough skirmishes and battles had been fought that the United States negotiated a treaty at Fort Laramie to establish the Great Sioux Reservation "for the absolute and undisturbed use and occupation of the Indians." The government made reparations for land already taken and promised to keep whites from settling or hunting on all of South Dakota west of the Missouri.

Six years later, in 1874, gold was discovered in the Black Hills.

There was nothing like greed to make a treaty obsolete. Prospectors poured into the Black Hills like ants. Towns sprang up overnight: Lead, Deadwood, Black Hawk, Silver City. Wagon ruts widened to roads; a railroad was planned to Rapid City and westward.

The Indians resisted as best they could, attacking homesteaders and making hit-and-run raids on soldiers, but they were doomed from the start. Smallpox decimated many tribes, and the government sent wave after wave of fresh troops. Though they routed Custer and triumphed at Rosebud, by 1890 the Indians' struggle was over.

Greed proceeded apace. Hot Springs, already a haven for weary miners, became as well a resort for the rich. Hotels and spas drew people from Chicago, St. Louis, and Kansas City. For a few years it was a boomtown. Then disaster: The gold petered out. The mining towns declined, and Rapid City, because it was on the railroad, became the commercial center of the region. Hot Springs, eighty miles south, barely survived. Mount Rushmore and Wind Cave had a trickle-down effect, but the Veterans' Administration hospital became the centerpiece of a year-round economy. The once-glitzy Evans Hotel became a convalescent home.

To Mattie Hot Springs was another desolate, decaying town. The main highway was littered with modern trash—Dairy Queen, Pizza Hut, Subway, and Taco John's. Video outlets and trinket shops eked out their overheads; a business services/fax/copy shop took over the defunct movie theater. The county seat and turn-of-the-last-century office buildings, built of stone quarried from the Hills, were gray and somber, set against plastic gas stations and the neon signs of motels and bars.

She had an appointment to sign papers at Barton Hanratty's, but she stopped first at the Amoco to leave the pickup to get the axle looked at. From there she walked to the *Hot Springs Star* to put in her ad: "FOR SALE CHEAP: 1994 Lincoln, 87,300 miles."

She hated that car. Earl had owned it, and it was a gas guzzler and *maroon,* and a person who drove a Lincoln was almost as pretentious and arrogant as one who drove a Mercedes or a Cadillac. Earl had said he'd give Haney a deal, but it was no deal, and when Haney bought it, she vowed she'd never ride in it, and she never had. The neighbors thought it funny that they drove separate cars to potluck suppers and farm sales, even to town. But it had never been funny to Mattie.

After that, she stopped at the sheriff's office and asked whether anyone was looking for a missing Indian child. "What's he look like?" Sheriff Nolan asked. "Do you have a picture?"

"I thought you'd have the picture," Mattie said. "I don't even have a name."

"Who'd be looking for an Indian kid?" the sheriff asked.

"His parents, maybe? He's been at my place three weeks."

"They probably don't know he's gone," the sheriff said.

"I'll bring in a picture," Mattie said.

Mattie was furious walking down Chicago Street. What kind of attitude was that? What an ass! At a tourist store she bought a disposable camera and muttered to herself all the way to Barton Hanratty's office next to the VFW Post on River Road. She was still steaming when she climbed a flight of red-carpeted stairs.

A secretary showed Mattie into Barton's office, and he stood up and shook her hand. He was a heavy man in his fifties, prematurely gray, and sentenced without parole to what she knew was his unwanted calling. Mattie gave him credit for supporting his family, but mostly she felt sorry for him. His wife had to drive a Volvo, and the two children attended boarding school in Rapid City.

"It's good to see you, Mattie," Barton said.

"Since when?"

Barton sat back down and pushed across a sheaf of papers. "There aren't any surprises here," he said. "Final probate report, transfers of assets, title to the car. You can read the documents if you want to."

"The surprises were before," Mattie said. "Or maybe they're still to come. Did you know Haney signed a permission for the museum to dig on the ranch?"

"No, but I could ask Cal Fiori about it. He does the museum's work."

"Wouldn't they have to consult Earl?" Mattie asked.

"I'd think so."

Mattie drew the documents toward her and sat down, but she didn't sign anything. "Did Haney confide in you, Barton? Did he ever discuss personal matters?"

"I wouldn't say he confided in me. We had a drink together now and then."

"Did he ever mention another woman? I understand lawyer-client privilege, but you can answer yes or no."

"Answering yes or no would render the privilege meaningless," Barton said, "but I'll tell you he never mentioned another woman to me."

"Thank you."

Mattie picked up the pen and signed the first document.

The cottonwoods along the Fall River were leafed out more than the ones at the ranch because the sandstone cliffs radiated heat. Mattie leaned into the railing by the road and watched the river. There was no dam above Hot Springs to slow the water, and stones tumbled and groaned along the bottom. Dead limbs bounced in the current. They would end up in the Angostura Reservoir seven miles downstream.

She was free now. She owned what she owned, including half of four thousand acres. She had power to decide what to do with her possessions. But what *would* she do? What did she want? She'd never asked herself that question before.

The last time she was so uncertain she was sixteen, the year she'd worked at Rosa Saenz's bakery. The job paid her rent and food, but more important, it gave her a place to be. Tomás Cruz was the baker. He had a wife and four children in Mexico and was as lonely as she was, but he laughed and whistled and made eyes at her in a joking way and sang and laughed again. He spoke little English, but he showed her how to mix dough, knead it, how long to bake cinnamon rolls and muffins. She learned to laugh and whistle and sing, though she wasn't so good at it as Tomás Cruz.

Every morning Rosa Saenz opened the bakery and kissed her. Such a little thing, a kiss good morning from an old woman, but the pleasure of it! Mattie looked forward to that kiss every morning and long afterward, all through college, when Rosa wasn't there.

"Mrs. Remmel?"

She turned at the sound of her name and saw the man from the museum standing at the railing. "I wanted to apologize for yesterday," the man said. "I know Jane can be pushy."

"I can push back," Mattie said.

"Do you have any questions about the maps?"

"Yes, one. Why did you give them to me when you already know my opinion?"

"People can change their minds," the man said.

"That's a generous view."

"Didn't you think they were beautiful, though?"

"Beauty doesn't have much to do with digging up bones."

"Have you ever been to the museum?" he asked. "I could give you a tour, if you have time."

"Do you think persistence changes minds, too?"

"Sometimes it does."

"The maps are in my truck," Mattie said, "which is at the Amoco station."

"Is that a yes? See, you're already caving in."

"I don't want to owe you any favors," Mattie said.

Lee Coulter's truck was not the fancy one he'd come to the ranch in. It was a worn-out blue Nissan 4x4 with rust on the body and a pock-marked windshield. The bed was filled with cardboard boxes, tire chains, and plastic five-gallon buckets of junk—rock specimens, fossils, tools—pretty much like hers. He didn't drive slowly, either. On the by-pass he bore into the arroyo so hard she felt G-force on the uphill.

"You're not from here?" he asked.

"No, but I've been here fifteen years."

"And before that?"

"Maine and Arizona."

"You went to college?"

"I started at Arizona State, but I transferred back east."

"Back east is a big place."

"Cornell."

"The Red Raiders of Ithaca," he said. "What'd you study?"

"I liked science, birds in particular, but I wanted a job, so I majored in communications. Why are you asking me these questions?"

"And did you get a job?"

"I worked for Channel Two in Boston before I met my husband."

"Where'd you meet?"

"At a party."

"How old are you?"

"I don't have to answer that."

"You don't have to answer anything."

"I'm forty-four."

"I'm forty," he said.

He turned into the Mammoth Site parking lot. The museum was modern and looked like a high school gymnasium with the center spine of a whale. Lee coasted into an official parking spot near an unmarked door.

"Let me ask you a question," Mattie said. "Is Haney's brother in on the conspiracy?"

"Your husband said you were opposed to the dig, but we assumed you knew everything."

"That's not an answer."

"Earl Remmel signed, yes. But if we don't have your cooperation, we won't explore the site."

"You won't proceed without my agreement?"

"I'm the director," Lee said. "I decide what our projects will be."

They got out and walked toward the unmarked door.

"Or would you rather pay admission?" Lee asked. "I don't want you to feel obligated."

Inside, huge skylights illuminated the space. Full-scale replicas of a Columbian mammoth and a saber-toothed tiger sparred in one corner, and there were cases of bones along the walls, but most of the mammoths were still in the ground. A walkway ascended gently and overlooked the worksite, where bones lay tilted oddly in the sediment, half buried, and lying across other bones.

"A guy on a bulldozer was scraping this hill for a housing development," Lee said, "and he unearthed a jawbone. Fortunately he asked somebody what it was, and—surprise—the developer had a conscience. This was in 1974. A few years later he sold the site to the museum trust."

"So this hill was a sinkhole?"

"What probably happened was a cave collapsed and filled with warm water. In the Pleistocene and Tertiary, the climate was cold, and animals were attracted to the plant life that grew around the hot water. Mammoths stumbled into the sinkhole and drowned or couldn't get out and starved. Over thousands of years the collapsed cave filled with sediment, and then, over more thousands of years, the shale on the outside eroded away, leaving this hill."

"This is what you think occurred on the ranch?"

"Maybe." Lee pointed to a spot near the bones of several mammoths jumbled together like the pieces of a jigsaw puzzle. "Those are three compacted mammoth footprints."

"And you believe this work is worth doing?" Mattie asked.

"I think it's worth knowing one's history. I grew up in Scottsbluff and moved to Oregon when I was ten. My grandfather had a sheep ranch. My great-grandfather came from Scotland and met my great-grandmother on a Ferris wheel in Toronto. Aren't you interested in where you came from and who your family was?"

"It doesn't have to be public knowledge," Mattie said. "There should be privacy, even for mammoths."

Lee climbed farther up along the catwalk. Below, two women were excavating a three-foot-long mammoth tusk in a pit strewn with bones.

"We've found fifty-four mammoths here," he said. "Over ninety percent are males. Do you know why that should be?"

"I have no idea."

"They refused to ask directions." Lee smiled. "Now, tell me truthfully, isn't this wonderful to see?"

Chapter 15

Mattie didn't want to think about the past—not the Pleistocene or the Tertiary, not seven years ago, or last week, or yesterday. She wanted to stay in the present, in the very moment the sun was slanting from the clouds. Lee had continued to ask her questions as he drove her to get her truck—about Shelley and Haney and even about Loren's death—and she was so upset when he pulled into the Amoco station that she jumped out and forgot to give him his maps.

She didn't want to think of the future, either. The future was blank. She'd thought in passing of getting a job, maybe in Rapid City, or volunteering in a hospice, even of going back to Tucson, but equally possible was enlisting in the Peace Corps or looking for birds in Costa Rica. She had no intent, no desire, no plan, except to get the hay cut and baled and moved to the hay pens.

The pickup hummed along the section lines, and she averted her eyes from the cemetery and turned east. At Hector Lopez's driveway she slowed and turned in. Hector lived next to the Pollards on the north on forty treeless acres above the river. Only ten of it was irrigated, and on the rest he pastured two Hereford bulls, Jorge and George—Jorge, with the white spot the shape of Texas on his shoulder, and George, the follower.

To the neighbors, a Hispanic in Indian country was suspicious, and everyone thought Hector had had a scrape with the law. People predicted bad things would happen. But they hadn't yet. Hector worked harder than anyone else Mattie knew. He planted corn on shares, ran cows on whatever land neighbors leased him, and still held a full-time job troubleshooting for the phone company. He had a tiny house, kept neatly, and a mutt named Rafe.

Rafe yapped a couple of times when Mattie drove into the yard, but he stopped when he recognized her. Hector was lying on a workcloth, with his legs sticking out from under a New Idea corn picker.

"When are you going to plant some trees around here?" Mattie asked.

Still holding a crescent wrench, Hector rolled out from under the corn picker in greasy overalls. His black hair was haloed under a Buffalo Gap Feeds cap, and he smiled. A tattoo, the bottom of something Mattie couldn't see, was hidden by the sleeve of his T-shirt. "Maybe someday," Hector said. "Did you come to lecture me about my landscaping?"

"I was on my way home," Mattie said. "I wanted to ask you about that pasture up north."

"I'd rather have my cows and calves closer than the Westcotts'," Hector said. "You got it fenced yet?"

"Just about. I thought maybe you'd want to look at it."

"All right."

"What about the corn?"

"The ground's drying out. I should be able to get it in pretty soon now."

"And I was thinking about buying calves."

"To pasture or to feed?"

"I have that permit on the government."

"Shame on you, taking advantage of the taxpayers."

"Am I supposed to not use my permit?"

"You could buy pairs," Hector said, "but it's kind of late for that, too."

"I have that fallow section out east, too."

"People sell what they don't want," Hector said. "You have to be real careful."

"That's why I'm asking you."

"I'll keep my eyes open," Hector said. He found a larger crescent wrench in his toolbox and levered himself back under the corn picker.

"Oh, listen, Hector?"

"Yeah?"

"I found an invoice for that hauling hay you did. Did Haney ever pay you?"

"He paid me."

"What'd you haul the hay in?"

Hector wrenched and banged and wrenched again. His legs contorted with the effort. "It wasn't for hay hauling," he said. "It was for what he did to my truck."

"What'd he do to it?"

"It wasn't his fault, really. Someone hit him."

"That dent in your passenger door?"

"I didn't get it fixed," Hector said. "I bought two cows instead."

"When was this?" Mattie asked. "What was Haney doing with your truck?"

Hector grunted, and whatever it was he was working on came loose, and he slithered out from under the machine again. "His car broke down, and he had to get somewhere. It was a few months ago now."

"Like, where did he have to get?"

"I don't know."

"Well, then, where was the accident? Do you know that?"

"In Rapid somewhere."

They exchanged glances, Mattie's asking and Hector's not wanting to be asked. She understood Hector's reluctance to talk. She was a woman, and he was a man, so he was on Haney's side. But he was her friend, too.

"Okay, Hector. Keep an eye out for some calves."

"All right."

"That's all you can tell me?"

"That's about all I know," Hector said.

Mattie nodded and walked back to her truck. Rafe stayed where he was, in the shadow of the tire.

Chapter 16

"She said she was the morning star," Shelley said. "I found that a little much."

"Dawn is a little much," Mattie said, "but I see the Case is out by the Ironweed Patch. Does it run?"

"It didn't get there walking."

"Maybe she did magic."

Mattie kneaded the bread dough on her cutting board, and Shelley poured herself a beer.

"How'd the Indian boy do?"

"The piles were bigger. I guess he did okay. Did you know Dawn hung Daddy's wind chimes in that yukky shower."

"I was tired of them myself," Mattie said.

"So, anyway, then she starts quoting Percy Bysshe Shelley, something about a blithe spirit and a bird. She thought there was a divine connection between his name and mine."

"What did you say?"

"I said I was the evening star."

"So you got along?"

"I guess, sort of, maybe. She said people call Venus the evening star, but it's a planet."

"You think we should hire her? I told her I'd let her know."

"She's goofy, but I liked her. Maybe you ought to test-drive the tractor."

"I guess I will. Maybe I'll go get the grader blade across the river."

Mattie put the bread dough in a bowl and covered it with a damp kitchen towel, and then she went out and started the Case. It fired up well, and she idled it back and tested the hydraulics. They worked all right. She shifted into gear and ran along the track to the river.

Mattie crossed the bridge slowly—the planks were just wide enough for a tractor to make it—and before she got the grader blade, she turned off toward Dawn's camp.

Dawn waved to her and scrambled down the gully and up to where Mattie had idled the Case.

"I was figuring to pack up if I didn't hear from you," Dawn said. "And I was going to be sad."

"You don't have to be sad. But listen, Dawn, if I hire you, it's provisional."

"Yes, ma'am. Provisional, at ten dollars an hour."

"I pay a hired man eight."

"Ten is way cheap for a mechanic, but I'll take eight-fifty, plus board. If it's all right with you, I'll camp where I am."

"What about a bathroom?"

"I already dug a pit, and I can shower in the Morton."

"If you stay on for a month, I'll raise you to nine-fifty."

"Deal."

"And I don't want you in bars with cowboys."

"Cowboys don't know which end is up."

"Will you stick to one name?"

"Dawn is the new day."

"I don't want any trouble. That's what I'm saying."

"Neither do I."

"Okay, then, tomorrow let's go out and look at the pivot sprinkler."

"What's wrong with it?"

"It doesn't work," Mattie said. "That's what I've hired you for—to tell me why."

After supper Mattie got out Haney's sculptures to polish, and Shelley finished up the dishes. Shelley was fine with hiring Dawn; it was the Indian boy she didn't trust. "There's just something about him," she said.

"Like what?"

"He worked hard today. I'm not arguing that. You're not afraid he'll steal us blind?"

"He could have already. I think he likes us."

"*Likes* us? Why would he like us? We're white, and we took his land away."

"Maybe he's forgiven us for that."

"He smells, too," Shelley said.

"I don't care. And I don't like that talk."

"It's a fact, Mom. And I don't want him sleeping in my Lincoln."

"Since when is it yours?"

"You aren't going to drive it."

"I'm going to sell it," Mattie said. "Are you telling me you'd drive a Lincoln around?"

"In the absence of anything else."

"We'll see," Mattie said.

The moment of agitation faded. Mattie dipped the cloth and rubbed paste on the bronze woman's back. "By the way, I talked to Hector, and he wants to look at that pasture."

"The pasture or the fence?"

"I'd say the fence."

"Then we're all right. I am a fence-building genius."

"Did you get all the wires clipped on?"

"Mom, I'm not helpless."

"Good. I figure if we have Dawn and the Indian boy, we'll have enough of a work force to make it through the summer. What's Warren going to do?"

"I'll ask him." Shelley paused. "So, Mom, when you were a girl and moved out of your house, were you afraid?"

"I was petrified. It wasn't like going off to college. I was only sixteen, and I'd never been on my own."

"Neither have I."

"My father was mean, or he *got* mean, especially to my brothers. I don't know whether he couldn't deal with my mother's leaving us or what, but he started drinking. Sometimes he came home with presents—a bracelet or a scarf for me—but mostly he brought home anger for my brothers. One time he broke the neck of David's pet rabbit because David hadn't picked up a beer bottle from the yard, and another time he whipped Sean for a wrong look. My brothers absorbed his anger and played it back to me. David beat me up once when I asked him to turn down his radio, and one night I woke up and found Sean masturbating at the end of my bed. I had nowhere to go but away."

"What'd you do?"

"I took a job in a bakery." Mattie dipped her cloth again and rubbed hard at the bronze. "All I know is when I moved out of my house, I didn't know any more about the world than this boy does."

"You think he's that desperate?"

"I think he is," Mattie said. "Why else would he be here?"

That night Shelley called Warren and launched into a tirade about picking up rocks, pounding in fence posts, and stringing up barbed wire. "I'll tell you one thing, Warren," she said. "I don't like manual labor."

"On the other hand, you accomplished something," Warren said. "Good for you. I've been sitting on my butt all day studying."

"How's it going?"

"I won't know till after finals."

Shelley looked at the posters on her walls and hated them, especially the *Space Odyssey* one. And Julia Roberts—Was she still alive? "So you don't miss me?"

"Sure, I miss you."

"Are you screwing around?"

"I'm screwing around with sodium ions and valences."

Shelley flopped down on her bed and stared at the ceiling. "What about Kenya?"

"I'm not thinking about Kenya right now."

"I mean, I should tell my mother if you're coming here or not."

"Can't we talk after my chemistry test?"

"Jesus, Warren, why can't you decide? Is that asking too much?"

"I'm trying to pass my exams," Warren said. "Why are you giving me all this grief?"

"It's not *grief*," she said, and slammed down the phone.

She lay on her bed for a few minutes, shaking. Warren was a dweeb. Why couldn't he make up his fucking mind? And she was such a bitch. She got up and ripped down all her posters from the walls and stuffed them in her wastebasket.

She heard voices downstairs and put on her robe and tiptoed down the back stairs.

"He might have been going on business," Trini was saying.

"What business does he have in Seattle?"

Shelley came in. "Who?"

"Your father," Trini said.

"That plane ticket I asked you about? Your father was going to Seattle in June."

"What for?"

"That's the question," Trini said. "All we know is that he bought an electronic ticket."

"One-way," Mattie said.

"Your mother wants to imagine the worst."

"I don't," Mattie said. "I don't want to *imagine* anything. I want to know."

"Well, maybe you can't know," Trini said.

"Then let's not talk about it," Mattie said.

Shelley got a beer from the refrigerator and twisted off the cap. She and Trini looked at each other across the table. "So how are Keith and Dylan?"

"Boring," Trini said.

"They could be stealing cars," Shelley said.

"I wish the little bastards were robbing banks. Keith's leading a prolife rally next week at school. Where does a son of mine get the idea a woman doesn't control her own body? And why aren't prolifers in Guatemala or Somalia feeding children who are already alive?"

Silence. No one had an answer.

"Did you know he had Hector Lopez give him a false invoice?" Mattie asked. "He borrowed Hector's truck and had an accident, and he didn't want me to know."

"I thought you didn't want to talk about it," Trini said.

"I mean, here we are out in nowhere, and he's had some other life."

"Mom, there'll be an explanation."

"Do you think?"

"I think you're hyperimaginating."

"Then who's in Seattle? Where are the letters he got from friends? And why did he want to be buried in Maine? I think he's been covering things up all along."

Chapter 17

The layers of hills were shadowless and stark; the air was empty of birds. The river had smoothed out again, and the green coin of the pivot field shone in the sun. Dawn and Mattie drove past the Indian boy, already at work picking up rocks.

"You could sure graze some buffalo here," Dawn said.

"My husband had the pivot hauled from Chadron last year and put it together himself. But I'll bet it hasn't run in a long time. The sprinklers are rusted, and the generator doesn't start."

"I've never worked on a sprinkler system before," Dawn said. She pointed beyond the gate to the road on the other side. "Who lives over there?"

"The Pollards. You met Jimmy. That's their trash in the ravine. Hector Lopez lives past the Pollards, and over there Trini and Allen Decker have the place on the road."

"I guess your husband left you a lot of work piled up, huh? How long ago did he die?"

"About three weeks ago."

"And what about the Indian kid? Does he work here?"

"He's been here a few days," Mattie said. "He's pretty skittish. Won't tell us his name. I guess he doesn't want us to send him back to his parents. But I figure he'll tell us someday."

"Maybe he'll choose a new name for himself."

Mattie forded the river and drove up the embankment and past the enormous pile of rocks the boy had assembled. From ground level the sprinkler's myriad legs dwarfed the truck. Mattie drove to the center of the field and stopped at the generator.

"Four hundred volts," Dawn said. "A buzz from that could send you to Mars."

"If you weren't already on Mars," Mattie said.

Dawn got out and tinkered with the wires and hoses, while Mattie walked out to inspect the alfalfa. The first few blades were up, and if the seeds took, even without irrigation they'd have a good first cutting. If they could get water to it, the second and third would be better because there weren't any gophers or thistles yet.

Mattie heard a *thwack* and looked around. Dawn was up on the pivot, twenty feet off the ground, beating her shoe on a piece of metal.

"What are you doing up there?"

"Seeing what moves and what doesn't. Can you throw me a wrench from the truck?"

"What kind of wrench?"

"A big one."

Mattie walked back to the truck and rummaged in the bed and found a pipe wrench.

"That'll work," Dawn said.

Mattie carried the wrench over, but Dawn was looking at a coyote dancing in the sage and rabbitbrush at the edge of the field.

"We've got lots of coyotes," Mattie said. "Maybe he's got a rattlesnake there."

"You have rattlesnakes, too?"

The coyote jumped straight into the air and fell back, then circled and jumped again.

"Maybe he's trying to fly," Dawn said.

They watched for a minute more.

"What'd your husband do to you?" Dawn asked.

"I'm sorry?"

"You don't seem to be grieving."

"I don't think that's any of your business."

"Oh, I know that," Dawn said. "But something was going on."

"He died. That's what was going on."

"No woman is an island," Dawn said. "To misquote John Donne."

"Goddammit, Dawn. Do you think you can fix this sprinkler or not?"

"I need the wrench," Dawn said.

Mattie flung the wrench up at Dawn, who caught it easily.

The diesel roared and whined, and Mattie urged the loader forward. The water had receded enough that she could shove earth and rocks back onto the bank. The last time they'd rebuilt the bridge, Haney had wanted to pour concrete, but Mattie argued for the river. Floodwater undermined cement, too, or if it didn't, it changed channels. That's what had happened downstream, where they had a bridge, but no water under it.

She filled the loader bucket several times from the pile of rocks and dumped them at the edge of the current. She didn't know how many trips she made or how many she'd have to make. Farm work was repetitive; everything took time.

How could Dawn say she wasn't grieving? Of course she was. And what did it mean to grieve? Was it adjusting to the rent in common habits? Haney had been there every night—his footsteps, his weight in the bed, his breathing. Was she merely cognizant of the steps not there, the fading indentation on his side of the bed, the absent breathing? Anyway, she sensed his being. At the same time, Dawn was right—their lives had diverged before he died. They'd stopped making love. She'd felt his withdrawal from her, and hers from him. Maybe she'd been grieving long before he died.

The moment at Hector's resurfaced. He knew more than he was saying, more than he wanted to say. Why had Haney needed to borrow the truck? The only reason she could think of was the Lincoln had broken down. That thought struck her: the Lincoln. That was it!

She dumped the load of rocks from the bucket onto the bank and idled down the tractor. Then she ran all the way back to the house.

The Lincoln was under the cottonwood where it always was. A flock of starlings nattered above it and then flew off toward the barn.

Shelley came out onto the porch. "What's going on?" she asked cheerfully. "Are you ready to lay the planks for the bridge?"

Mattie stared at the car. A film of dust made it look plum-colored. She opened the passenger door and leaned inside. The Indian boy's sleeping bag was rumpled in the back seat, the dirty pillow crammed against the door. His smell was in the upholstery, but she didn't care about that. She opened the compartment between the seats, sorted through the litter of road maps and spare change. Nothing. She tried the glove box, but it wouldn't open.

Shelley opened the driver's door. "What are you doing, Mom?"

"The keys are in the house," Mattie said, and leaned back out of the car.

"You want me to get them?"

"I'll get them."

Mattie went in through the vestibule, got the keys from the hook, and came back outside.

"Will you please tell me what's going on?" Shelley said.

"We're about to find out why your father was buried in Maine," Mattie said.

She opened the glove box—a flashlight, car registration, receipts for the last time the Lincoln was serviced, and a $582 repair bill dated from last fall at the Texaco in Hermosa.

"What about the trunk?" Shelley asked.

"I'm getting to it."

Mattie stepped around, and her shadow and Shelley's fell across the dusty trunk. She put in the wrong key, then the right one, and the trunk popped open.

"I want to do this alone," Mattie asked.

"He was my father."

"He was my husband."

They looked at each other.

"Please," Mattie said. "You'll know soon enough."

Shelley backed away.

The first thing Mattie saw was a case of wine, four empties, the rest unopened: Joseph Phelps cabernet. Mattie had never seen the wine before. She lifted the case out and set it on the ground.

"You need help?" Shelley asked.

"Not yet."

Mattie lifted a blue and silver space blanket folded over a cardboard file box. The box was fastened with a string wound around a rivet. She unwound the string, took off the lid, and dropped it on the grass. She heard blackbirds squawking in the marsh, and a bobolink sang somewhere, but the songs of birds receded to silence; she didn't hear the breeze tattering the leaves of the cottonwood above her or feel the ground she was standing on. The box contained bundles of letters held together with rubber bands. The return address on the top envelope was Dennis Burke, Plaza de Luz 17, Barcelona. The red stamp was a picture of Juan Carlos. The letter was addressed to Haney Remmel, 3213 West Main, Box 63, Rapid City, SD 57701.

She scrabbled through the other bundles, all addressed to Haney in

Rapid City. She didn't recognize the names of most of the writers. At the bottom of the box were receipts from restaurants and motels, mostly in Rapid City, together with several magazines—*Gay Life* and *men and men*.

"What is it, Mom?" Shelley asked.

Mattie looked up into the cottonwood tree where light scattered among the leaves. She felt nothing, then surges of anger and hurt, then nothing again for a long time. She walked away from the car to the picnic table and knelt there on the grass. She didn't know how long it was before Shelley knelt and put her arm over her shoulder.

Part II

The eternal silence of these infinite spaces terrifies me.

—Blaise Pascal

Chapter 1

For three weeks there was no rain, and the alfalfa was high in the fields. It was mid-May, still two weeks to first cutting, and irrigating was well under way. Mornings and evenings Mattie and Shelley and the Indian boy put water on the Upper East and north of the river and on the Long Narrow and the West Main, moving the water down the ditches several notches at a time, and then starting over. Hector had planted the corn, and Mattie and Shelley laid out Nu-Flex plastic pipe to irrigate it, and they supplemented water from the district with the overflow from Haney's pond. There was plenty of water from the early rains.

Dawn worked into her own schedule. She welded the grader blade, tuned up the International, and read up on sprinkler systems. She drove to Chadron once and talked to the man who'd sold Haney the pivot. Mattie couldn't have been more pleased with her work. But Dawn stayed apart. At lunchtime she fixed herself a sandwich and ate it reading and sunning herself in the glare of the Morton. Most evenings she came in late, when they were done with dinner, and got herself a snack to take back to her camp.

Even Shelley worked hard. She irrigated and helped plant the garden and fixed lunches and often dinner, too, and she helped Mattie lay the bridge planks. They chained one end of a plank under the loader bucket so that when the bucket was raised, the plank was cantilevered across the river. Each one was eighteen feet long and four inches thick, and as Mattie lowered it, Shelley, on the far bank, guided it into place beside the one next to it. The bridge saved fifteen minutes each round trip over using the river ford.

Mattie worked herself to exhaustion. She rechanneled the river so it ran again under the east bridge, cultivated the alfalfa north of the river with a Vibra Shank cultivator borrowed from Sigurd Olafsson, rototilled and planted and weeded. Avery Bishop's hired man turned the West

Tip, but Mattie seeded it with Sudex from a seed spreader mounted on the four-wheeler. She helped Hector move his cows to the north pasture, and they agreed on a month to month lease, the price exchanged for Hector's slightly smaller share of the corn.

Hector said he hadn't found any calves, or pairs, either, but Mattie had plenty to do without a cow-calf operation to manage, too.

No one talked about Haney.

There wasn't a single call about the Lincoln.

Mattie paid the Indian boy in cash every other day, thinking he might use the money to pay his way home, but he didn't. He picked up all the rocks from the pivot field and irrigated and mended fences. He didn't complain about the greenflies or the horseflies or the heat. For overtime, if he wanted it, Mattie put him to work on the three scourges of the ranch or, as Haney had called them, the Three Stooges.

Moe was gophers. They tunneled under the alfalfa, and irrigation water ran from a ditch fifty feet into a field and disappeared into catacombs. The gophers didn't drown, but the alfalfa beyond the holes went dry. And when the alfalfa was high, the gopher mounds were impossible to see. When the cutting bar of the windrower hit one, the whole machine lurched sideways and skipped over the alfalfa, and skipping alfalfa cost money. So did sharpening the cutting bar. Gophers couldn't be shot or trapped, so the only thing to do was to put poison into their holes. Poison cost money, too.

Curly was thistles, pretty lilac-colored flowers when they bloomed, but terrible for cattle and alfalfa. They started along the ditches and creeks and spread their seeds in the wind, like dandelions. Every spring Haney had hoisted a tank of Round-Up on the back of the pickup and sprayed the ditches from a nozzle hanging out the window. Round-Up worked, and it didn't work. It killed the thistles, but wind dispersed the spray, and Haney missed more than he hit or could ever reach.

Larry was starlings. Though she loved birds, Mattie detested starlings. A hundred years ago a misguided soul set loose a half dozen in Central Park in New York City, and the birds spread across the continent like a plague. They usurped other birds' nesting places and raised three, sometimes four broods of young. They ate everything—seeds, insects, corn. In late summer and fall they collected in dense flocks in the cotton-woods, littered the ground with guano, and made a terrible racket.

Mattie offered the Indian boy ten dollars an hour to get rid of go-phers and to spray thistles, and she gave him a quarter for every starling he shot with the .22 rifle.

But there was a new scourge on the ranch now that no one could fight and no amount of money could eliminate. Driving to the Upper East, or planting peas, or running the Vibra Shank, Mattie thought of it. It was in her mind constantly, turned her stomach, made her crazy. The new scourge was named Haney.

Mail Boxes Etc. was a private post office. Since Haney's death, the let-ters had accumulated there, but Mattie didn't have the combination to his box, and the clerk refused to give her the mail. "Not without his sig-nature," the clerk said. "When the box expires, the letters go back to the sender."

But even without the recent letters, she knew Haney's intentions. She'd read the letters in the file box. A few were innocent correspondences from friends, addressed to the ranch: John Kipp Wessel telling about lob-stering and his new girlfriend; Ames's account of his tribulations with a publisher; Arnulf's description of what he'd done to his boat.

The rest of the letters from his Maine friends were sent to Mail Boxes and were different in tone and intimacy. For example, Jen Smith wrote:

> Arlo drinks a bottle of wine, and he's pleasant for an hour, but from one moment to the next, he starts raving, and some-times he takes off into the streets. Once I found him directing traffic on AOA. I might be amused if he were someone else's husband, but after a while his aberrant behavior wears thin. Is this the fate of a miniaturist?
>
> The question is, what should I do? I'm a loyalist like you, but how long can I endure this? You mentioned the cross-roads—well, that's where I am, too.

The other letters were from lovers. Franz liked opera. He'd gone to Dartmouth, was married, and worked for a radio station in Spearfish.

Apparently they'd met in a gay bar. His first note said, "So nice to see you at The Stage. I'd love to get together for dinner." Jeff Hopkins lived outside Chadron and lamented how difficult it was for gay farmers. "Are we supposed to be celibate?" he wrote. Toby was Toby Cushing, a soccer coach, almost illiterate, to judge from his handwriting, but handsome in the photograph Haney saved: blond, maybe thirty-five, good legs, not very tall. No other history.

A lot of the letters were from Dennis Burke. Though he wasn't a regular at Ames's beach, Mattie had met him there. He was tall and sleek, and occasionally he'd shown up with different men. She'd liked him. She'd even visited his studio once, and she'd admired his paintings. The circles and triangles juxtaposed, the blues and yellows, suggested sea and sun, but as well-explored variables of composition. She hadn't noticed anything different in Haney's behavior then. Apparently their affair started later, when Haney went back east to close his studio and ship his sculptures to the ranch. Who besides Jen Smith knew about it? How many of the Maine crowd had kept it from her or felt sorry?

The worst of it was Haney's deceit. Once he'd flown to New York to see friends before she joined him on their way to Europe, and he met Denny. Later, the time he'd hurt his knee, they'd spent three days in Vail together, and after Haney and Earl looked at property in New Mexico, he met Denny in Santa Fe. And all the time Haney had been tortured by what to do in the present.

January 25
Blue Hill

Dear Haney,

Got home yesterday. Hope your knee is better. What a nightmare after such joy. Ah, the life of crime. I felt sorry for you—you looked childlike, as if you possessed something once that you didn't anymore. I was so lucky to know early on who I was. I know it must be puzzling to feel in your body what you can't admit in your mind.

(undated)

Dear Haney,

. . . What's the point of confession you might later regret? Yes, you'd live anonymously in San Francisco or Seattle, but is that really what you want? You love your family, and what would they do without you? Why not settle into ambiguity? Isn't that best? . . .

March 15

Dear Haney,

So glad you met someone nearby. Franz sounds like a perfect person for you. And married, too! Your coming here again so soon isn't a good idea. As I've said before, I have a life-in-progress. . . .

I'll be in Spain six months, traveling with Joel the first part, and then on my own for two weeks. Kevin's meeting me in Barcelona. Of course I'll miss you. . . .

It had never occurred to her to cross-examine him about where he was or how he spent his free time. At the ranch there wasn't much leisure. When he came home from a meeting or from errands in Rapid City, he was tired. She was tired. Tomorrow was another workday. He never said much, but now she understood his silence was lying.

Yes, she'd seen him look away from her or stare out a window when he spoke. She heard his wistful tone of voice, watched him go to the fields early and come back late. Perhaps being alone so many hours on the tractor, or in the Morton, or at his desk atrophied his ability to speak. Perhaps it was his predisposition. Or had it been the discovery of his true sexual nature that had made him silent?

Once he'd been close to telling her. She was sure of it—the time after the pig roast at Trini's. Haney had been in a good mood, teasing Becca Haffner about the weight she'd lost and playing horseshoes with the men. He could be charming when he wanted to. He'd talked up Rose Parsons about her daughter's upcoming wedding to Ken Wickham. "Tell her to say ouch," he said, and they all laughed. When they left the party around ten, he put his arm around her on the way to the truck.

"You're riding with me?" she asked.

"I'll get the Lincoln tomorrow," he said.

He'd opened the passenger door for her. "Can you drive?" she asked.

"I'm as sober as you are."

She got in and reached across and opened the door for him. He climbed up and started the engine and pulled out of the driveway. The moon was close to half, not bright, but pretty against the clouds. For minutes she committed herself to the quiet, and she felt the ease of being with him. In that ease she wanted to ask only what was natural, what puzzled her—why didn't he want to make love with her anymore? But she didn't want to risk hurting him or making him answer. She thought: *Each of us is afraid of what the other is thinking.* Then she felt the ease change to unease, as if passing the first mile and descending the hill had worn the fabric of their quiet. The change made her brave, and she asked, "Why don't you hold me anymore?"

"I held you tonight," he said.

"When other people were around."

She felt him tense up. "Maybe I'm at that age," he said. "I feel old."

Then he looked at her, and she thought he wanted to say something more. The moonlight caught his face, and she saw tenderness there, or imagined she did, and sadness, too. He didn't feel old, but he wanted to absolve her from blame. *It's not your fault,* was what he meant.

But the moment passed. He didn't say anything more. They reached the mailbox and turned in, crossed the cattle guard, and drove between the moonlit pastures. Her opportunity was gone, and the lie went on. That he hadn't told her had been his failure, but not reaching him was hers.

Chapter 2

One morning early Mattie started fires in the dry weeds by the weir at the head of the West Main ditch. The weeds should have been burned off months earlier, but Haney hadn't done it, and then it had been too wet. Now new weeds had grown up under the husks of old ones. The Indian boy lit a fire at the middle of the ditch and another at the culvert where the ditch ran under the road, and the fires burned toward each other. Smoke, brown and gray and angry on the breeze, rose into the air.

In the distance a car horn sounded, and Mattie waved to Shelley, going out the driveway. She was taking the Lincoln to Boulder for the weekend to see Warren, and Mattie was glad she was getting away. Since they'd found out about Haney, they hadn't volunteered much to each other. Mattie hoped Warren could get her to talk. At least the turmoil about Haney had made her cancel the date with Mr. Adler.

Not that Mattie hadn't encouraged her to open up. One night after supper Mattie had poured brandies with the idea of conversation. "I don't want any brandy," Shelley said.

"I thought we'd discuss your father."

"Mom, he was gay. You had a gay husband. I had a gay father. What is there to say?"

"We could say what we feel."

"I don't feel anything."

"Well, you should. Don't you want to read his letters?"

"No, I do not want to read his fucking letters." Shelley drank her brandy, threw the glass into the wastebasket, and stormed from the room.

End of dialogue.

The Lincoln disappeared behind the birch trees by the mailbox, and Mattie called to the Indian boy to set another fire. "At the far end," she said. She motioned him farther along. "I'm going to make lunch."

The Indian boy gave a thumbs-up.

He was a blessing, no doubt about it. A Doogsend. She didn't have to get on him to do his chores. He mowed the yard, chainsawed a dead cottonwood tree into firewood, towed the old Nu-Flex to the dump, cleaned the incinerator. His work harbored no grudge or anger, and he didn't plot to avoid her. He worked well alone, and when she needed him to, he worked well with her.

She learned not to ask him questions—*Where did you go to school? Where are your parents? Do you have brothers and sisters?*—because he wouldn't have answered them. Still, it was the nature of awareness that silence be filled. She watched him set the fire at the far end of the ditch, the way he bent down with the match; he was dressed in one of the white T-shirts she'd bought him. But that was only what she saw. Her imagination filled the other spaces around him. He had come from somewhere else. He knew animals. He had someone left behind. She saw the pale smoke rise from the ditch and the boy's body tilt over the rake as he drew weeds into the fire.

There was a message on the answering machine from Trini: "Do you want to play tennis? Rose can't play, and we need a fourth. Call me as soon as you can."

Mattie dialed and, while she waited for Trini to answer, got out the makings for sandwiches from the refrigerator.

"Hello," Trini said.

"Are you kidding me?" Mattie asked. "I don't have time for tennis."

"I thought it would do you good. You used to play, didn't you?"

"I have lunch to make, a fire in the ditch, and irrigating to do. If I played once upon a time, I don't remember it."

"It's like riding a bicycle," Trini said. "You don't forget how. It's country tennis at the city park with Becca and Gretchen Wright. You can borrow Allen's racquet."

"Gretchen's eighty years old."

"If you have errands in town, you can deduct the gas."

"Dawn did say she needs some parts for the sprinkler."

"There, see how easy that was? Why don't you drive up here after lunch?"

Dawn tinkered with the three-wheeler that morning, and during lunch she rode into the yard on it. The Indian boy got up from the picnic table, and Dawn spun a turn around him, tipped a wheel, and caught herself on one leg.

"Can I ride it?" the boy asked.

"It hasn't got brakes yet," Dawn said. "That's a disadvantage."

"Three-wheelers aren't safe anyway," Mattie said. "You stick to the four-wheeler."

"I used to ride one," the boy said.

"Oh, where?" Dawn asked.

"Before."

Dawn took a half a sandwich and some carrot sticks and sat on the bench beside him. "There's a sick calf across the river," she said. "I saw it from my camp up in one of the arroyos."

"It must be one of Hector's," Mattie said.

"I'll go," the Indian boy said.

"No, I'll go," Mattie said. "You watch the fires."

The boy gave her a disheartened look.

"You can have some ice cream," Mattie said.

Dawn grabbed four Oreos from the bowl on the table, and she and Mattie got into the truck.

The calf was at the edge of the thick brush, halfway up the arroyo. Mattie climbed up the sandy bottom, and Dawn skirted the rim and angled down toward the calf from above. It didn't get up when either of them approached.

"It's breathing funny," Dawn said. "What do you think's wrong with it?"

"Pneumonia. Maybe a lung defect."

"Buffaloes don't get sick," Dawn said. "Where's the mother? That's what I want to know."

"A cow won't stay with a sick calf. And of course buffalo get sick. I think we'd better take this guy down and feed him, or being sick won't matter."

Dawn lifted the forelegs and Mattie carried from behind, and they maneuvered the calf down the arroyo to the truck. He weighed maybe seventy pounds and was too weak to struggle.

"Put him on the front seat," Mattie said.

Dawn opened the door with one hand, and they slid the calf up onto the seat.

"What'll Hector do with him?" Dawn asked.

"I don't know. He might let him die. Vets are expensive."

"There's always hope," Dawn said. She pulled a stone from her pocket and laid it in the cab beside the calf.

Chapter 3

"Gretchen gets testy if we're late," Trini said. She pulled the Suburban up close to Hector's mailbox. "Just leave the note there. He won't get it any faster on his door."

"But I'd feel better."

"If he isn't here, what difference does it make?"

"What difference does it make to you?" Mattie asked.

But Trini didn't back up, so Mattie put the note in the mailbox. Then Trini drove on, raising dust behind them.

"What'd Hector do?" Mattie asked.

"He didn't do anything," Trini said.

"You're the one who says confession's good for the soul."

"It depends on whose soul it is. Isn't it irritating to have all those wires littering the sky? Why doesn't anyone complain?"

"Because in three million years the earth will be a frozen snowball hurtling through space."

"That's my point," Trini said. "Now is all the more important."

They drove past the alfalfa and corn and alongside telephone and electric lines.

"If people were to choose between beauty and telephones, they'd take telephones," Mattie said. "That's the way it is."

The windbreak pines at the cemetery appeared in the midst of the fields and open sky, and Mattie fell to silence. The arch was decorated with ornate metal flowers painted white, but they were rusted and weathered. Far away, cars moved along an invisible highway in front of the foothills.

"Are you glad now Haney wasn't buried here?" Trini asked.

"It might have been better for Shelley."

"It wasn't as though he did evil," Trini said.

"What would you call it?"

"He didn't mean to, do you think?"

"What's intention got to do with it?"

"Remember that night last winter when our pipes froze? Haney spent two hours under our house with a welding torch."

"I didn't say he didn't do good things," Mattie said. "But I can't forgive him for lying."

"If he'd told you, would you have stayed with him?"

"I might have. I think he loved me. I know he anguished over what he was doing."

"Of course he loved you."

"But really, I don't know what I'd have done."

Hitting a yellow ball back and forth over a net was not Mattie's idea of how she should be spending her time, but she had fun despite herself. Becca Haffner was pretty good. She knew where to stand and how to hit a backhand and a real serve, not a tap and float like Trini's. Trini's game was the tease and ridicule of lobs and sidespins. Gretchen was a marvel. She covered lobs to the backcourt, and she was a tiger at the net. Every time Trini tried to pass, Gretchen either let the ball sail wide of the alley or put away a winner.

What Mattie liked was that it wasn't the end of the world if she double-faulted or missed an easy forehand. They laughed a lot, and no one cared who won. Between sets, they ate oatmeal cookies Gretchen had made and drank lemonade, and they talked about what so-and-so's lungs must look like after smoking twenty years and Jennifer Parsons's wedding and the old days of Hot Springs, when Gretchen was a masseuse at the Evans Hotel. They never would have talked about men if Trini hadn't brought up the subject.

"Mattie's looking," Trini said. "I want everyone to keep an ear to the ground. She wants a rich, younger man who is smart."

"Don't be greedy, dear," Gretchen said. "Men are not smart."

"No one ever accused Ben of intelligence," Becca said, "but he has compensations."

"It isn't the size, but the fit," Trini said.

"Do we have to talk about this?" Mattie asked. "I am *not* looking for a man."

They played another set—Gretchen and Mattie against Rose and Trini—and on set point, Mattie hit a backhand past Trini down the alley.

"You'll never be invited to play again," Trini said.

"That's about when I'll have time."

They stopped at Pamida on the way home, and Trini bought a rake, a garden hose, and four pints of two-cycle oil for the rototiller. Mattie got parts Dawn said she needed for the three-wheeler and more ammunition for the .22.

"So you're not going to tell me what happened with Hector?" Mattie said.

"I told you, nothing happened."

"That's it?"

"That's all I'm saying."

They passed the sprawling feedlot and its terrible stench. A harrier, tilting its wings on the wind, glided low over the fields.

At the ranch, when Mattie stopped at her mailbox to get bills and catalogs she never looked at, she heard three small pops from the direction of the house and, at regular intervals after that, four louder reports. She drove on to the yard, checked on the calf, and then heard more gunshots. They were coming from down at the river. "That second gun isn't a .22," she told the calf. "What do you think they're doing?"

She got back into the truck to go find out.

Dawn's Mercury was parked in the cottonwoods, the front passenger door open, and she was standing with two hands resting on the door, aiming a pistol at a suit of men's clothes impaled with sticks on the mudbank. She fired two shots and lowered the pistol.

"What is going on?" Mattie asked. "Where's the boy?"

"Right there."

Holding the .22, the boy stepped out from behind a tree. "We're practicing," he said.

"I thought you were watching the fire at the ditch."

"It burned out," he said. "You didn't say what to do next."

Mattie turned to Dawn. "Is that my pistol?"

"I found it in a drawer in the kitchen. It hasn't been cleaned in a long time." Dawn raised the pistol and squeezed off another shot, and the suit of clothes on the mudbank jerked. "You want to try?"

"I want you to stop," Mattie said. "I don't want you practicing to kill."

"We're not practicing to kill," Dawn said. "We're practicing to defend ourselves."

"We don't need guns," Mattie said.

"We do with the Pollards around," the boy said.

Dawn held the gun out toward Mattie, but she refused to take it.

Chapter 4

Squash and the melons hadn't shown themselves yet, but the peas were up, and the beans an inch high. Five rows of beans were a lot. Mattie admitted that, and she hoed out one whole row. Then she picked the first lettuce and washed it at the spigot. The air was a perfect temperature, with a slight breeze, and she was glad there were no wind chimes at the Morton.

The phone rang, and she answered it; she'd brought it with her to the garden in case Shelley called. But it wasn't Shelley.

"Mrs. Remmel?"

"Oh, it's you." She recognized the voice of the man from the museum. "I was expecting my daughter to call."

"I was wondering about those maps," Lee Coulter said.

"Yes. I'm sorry I haven't got them back to you."

"I'm over at a dig site in the Badlands. If it wouldn't inconvenience you, I could drop by later and get them."

"You might as well inconvenience me," Mattie said. "Are you any good with directions?"

"I'm not a mammoth," he said. "Tell me where to go."

"I will if I have to," she said.

When she hung up and was carrying the vegetables in, she felt bad for being rude. His coming for the maps saved her a trip to town, and it was one fewer thing to think about. It was almost a favor, though not one she'd have to repay.

She fed Hector's calf—no word from Hector yet—and then, in case Hector would stay for dinner, she decided to cook the pork roast Shelley had got. She peeled six russet potatoes, then two more for Dawn as an afterthought. She quartered them and scattered them in the pan alongside the roast, added carrots and flaked garlic, and put the roast in the oven. For a salad, she had fresh lettuce, red pepper, and avocado. Out the window she saw the Indian boy on the four-wheeler zooming up the county gravel to the Upper East and wondered too late if he liked garlic.

A car buzzed the cattle guard behind the Morton, and at first she thought it was Hector coming home from work, but it was Lee Coulter's blue truck that circled the garden. Mattie put on her visor cap and walked outside just as Lee pulled in.

"You got here faster than I thought," Mattie said. "The maps are in the pickup."

"I saw a lot of smoke coming down the mesa."

"We were burning ditches today."

Lee pointed toward the cottonwoods at a dark plume of smoke curling into the air. "It looks as if it's jumped the ditch. Get in. I have buckets and a shovel in back." He leaned across the seat and pushed open the passenger door.

Mattie climbed in—she didn't have much choice—and Lee drove west into the creek bottom and up the hill toward the smoke. Across the horse pasture the sky was divided by smoke, blue on one side of the roily black funnel of smoke and blue on the other. Off to their right Tom Mix and Dale Evans galloped across the pasture.

"The horses got wind of the smoke," Lee said. "Is there water in the ditch now?"

"We dried it out to burn it."

"Then let's fill the buckets here."

Lee stopped at the weir. He dumped out the tools and rock samples, and Mattie took the first empty bucket and filled it.

"We need to get water in the ditch, too," Lee said. "It'll be slower getting there than we will."

Lee scooped water into the other two buckets, and Mattie stacked boards into one of the cement gates so water would flow into the burned ditch. Then they loaded the full buckets and rode on.

The fire had burned over the embankment, and the wind had caught it, and now a narrow red-orange band curled through the high grass under the cottonwoods. Lee poured water on the flames, and Mattie took the empty buckets back to fill. Then Lee worked with the shovel, digging at the lead edge of the fire and a little ahead of it.

The water in the ditch had barely reached the truck and wasn't deep enough yet to fill the buckets, so Mattie fetched a tarp from across the road and was carrying it back when she saw the Pollards' red Dodge bumping down the lane.

It was Jimmy. She made out his square shoulders and big head, hatless. He pulled up and got out wearing a clean white shirt.

"I was going to town and wanted to see if Dawn would go," he said. "Looks like you got yourself all kinds of problems."

"I think we're all right," Mattie said.

"Kinda late to be burning ditches."

Mattie set the tarp in the ditch, and Jimmy stripped off his shirt and spaded earth to hold the corners of the tarp.

"Whose truck?" he asked.

"A man from the museum. He happened to come by."

Mattie used one bucket to fill the other and her cap to fill the first.

"I'll carry those," Jimmy said.

"Then I'll go get more buckets from the house."

Lee had left the key in his truck, and she got in and did a three-point turn in the lane.

She fetched more buckets and a shovel from the Morton, and when she got back, the dam was full. She didn't care about the pain in her wrist. She filled two buckets and carried them to the top of the embankment, where Jimmy, coming back, took them from her. The weight of the buckets made the veins bulge in his neck and arms.

The fire had burned farther toward the trees, the flames brighter, or so they appeared in the diminishing light. Dawn had shown up, too, apparently having waded the river, and she was shoveling hard alongside Lee to dig a firebreak.

A grassfire was capricious. It held its breath for hours, barely smoldering, and then flared up even when there wasn't much breeze. Mattie filled the buckets, and Jimmy carried them. When Jimmy tired, Lee switched with him, and they worked through dusk toward dark, the smoke merging finally with the night sky.

Then, at last, the fire was out. Jimmy went back for two more buckets, and Lee and Mattie walked the perimeter, kicking the leaves and grass to make sure there was nothing but ashes.

"I guess I owe you one," Mattie said.

"Maybe two," Lee said.

"Where'd Dawn go?"

"She was on the embankment," Lee said. "Maybe she went back with Jimmy."

"You got introduced to them?"

"More or less."

"I don't trust Jimmy," Mattie said. "I'm going back. Do you mind?"

"Go ahead. I'll walk around one more time."

Mattie climbed the embankment and heard Jimmy's and Dawn's voices below her at the ditch.

"Dawn?"

"Hello. We're down here."

Mattie sideslipped down the slope. Jimmy had his shirt on again, white visible in the air. He and Dawn were standing beside Jimmy's truck.

"Then another time," Jimmy was saying, "but I bet you'd like to see them."

"Maybe I would."

"I didn't mean women couldn't fix machines."

"Oh, I know," Dawn said. "The contention was so blatantly untrue."

"Well, come over, then," Jimmy said. "Anytime is okay."

"To see what?" Mattie asked.

"Just some birds I have," Jimmy said. He turned to Dawn. "You sure you don't want to ride into town?"

"No, thanks. I have work tomorrow."

"So do I."

"Not tonight," Dawn said.

"I appreciated your help, Jimmy," Mattie said.

"No problemo."

"I'd be glad to pay you."

"Naw," Jimmy said. "I don't want money." He looked at Dawn again. "Listen, I'll see you."

Jimmy got in his truck and started it and pulled on the headlights. Then he backed into a gate apron and turned around.

"Thanks again," Mattie said.

Lee came down the embankment in the dark and joined them.

"I have a burned pork roast in the oven," Mattie said. "Is anybody hungry?"

Chapter 5

Shelley had a half hour's delay for the bridge construction at Edgemont, but she didn't see Dwain, working or loafing, either one. Past Edgemont, she took the Red Bird cutoff to Lusk, Wyoming. She wasn't particularly thrilled to go to Boulder, but maybe it was a good idea to see Warren. She'd talked to him on the phone a lot, but she hadn't seen him since the funeral, and that barely counted as seeing him. She still hadn't told him her father was gay. What was she supposed to say? *Listen, Warren, my father liked men. He kept it hidden so my mother and I wouldn't suffer, but we understand it now, and we're fine. Absolutely fine.* He'd think she was a sideshow freak, which was how she felt.

Nothing good came of bitterness. Trini said that all the time, but Shelley couldn't help her feelings. The father she thought was honest and hardworking and loving instead was a cheat, and she was part of him. She had his eye color, hair, the stocky body. Her blood was half his. If he was a cheat, she was at least half a cheat.

And it was worse for her mother. To find out—God, not that your husband was having an affair with another woman—but that he was screwing men! That was disgrace. That was humiliation. And of course they had to lie. They hadn't done anything wrong, but they had to make up excuses, to say good things about her father to save face. They were forced to do exactly what he'd done—cover up his life and pretend everything was normal.

Normal. What was that?

Warren had the male gene for squalor. He washed dishes only when he ran out of clean ones, never swept the floor, never made the bed. His apartment was a petri dish. She'd assumed he'd grow out of it, or he'd make an effort when she was around, but he hadn't. Not that she needed him to be perfect. In idle moments she thought they'd get married— Marriage with a capital M. That's what all her friends hoped for. College was their chance to meet someone with an education, someone who'd make money. Ha! She wasn't that eager to tie the knot—what a strange expression. It made marriage sound confining. Why shouldn't partners be freer for being together? They could relax, explore, and experiment without having to worry about finding sex.

Warren wasn't exactly a sex fiend. He was new to it; so was she. Inexperience was okay. But he didn't want to learn. He touched her as if he were patting a dog, and when they made love, he never even took off his pajama bottoms. He rolled onto her, and it was over before she got started.

She stopped for gas in Lusk, bought a Pepsi, and dialed Warren's number from the pay phone. His answering machine picked up. "Warren, it's me. I'm in Lusk. That's with a k. I'm on my way to see you." She paused, then clicked the receiver.

It was forty-one miles from Lusk to I-25, and the whole way she played Barbie Lou Scott.

> We've all got places to go and things to do
> But I don't ever want to do 'em with you,
> No more, no more.

The song conjured up Dawn in Shelley's mind. Now there was one ugly woman. How could her mother think Dawn was pretty? Big lips, crooked nose. Good figure, though. And did she have the junk! *I'm the morning star*. Shelley laughed. Dawn might be a druggie, but she was likable, and Shelley preferred being around a crazy woman to a smelly runaway Indian boy.

The Lincoln rode smoothly at eighty. Mindless asphalt. Blank land. Sun, wind, sky, hills separated from her by safety glass and speed. Vistas moved past without sinking in. Driving the interstate was like watching television. She thought of Bryce's teaching poetry to the television generation. How relevant was poetry to sit-coms, cars, and sports?

She supposed she was glad she canceled her date with him, though she'd done it more for her mother than for herself, more because she'd have felt weird about going, having just found out about her father. Later. Maybe another time.

Shelley passed a car and a truck, and the driver of the semi honked at her. She gave him the finger. Cheyenne loomed ahead: plastic, glass, and cement stuck out there on the plains. Air Force jets torpedoed the sky. At every intersection through Cheyenne there was fast food and gas.

Boulder was windy and warm, the sun low over the Flatirons. She took Baseline to Chautauqua Park, where picnickers were sitting on blankets and dogs chased Frisbees. She made a right on 11th and coasted downhill past the parked cars. Every house had a student apartment, so there was never parking. She cruised past Warren's brick house, parked too close to a fire hydrant in the next block, and walked back. The sun shot down through a pine tree across the street, or rather, she moved so the sun came from a different angle. That's the way things felt to her—the world stayed the same, but she kept moving. Evolution was too goddamn slow. She wanted something to happen *now*.

His basement apartment was in back, past two street-level windows, and she could see he wasn't there because no one was at the computer. She went down four steps and let herself in with her key.

The kitchen was clean—no dishes in the sink, the stove immaculate. No food was left out on the counter. The bathroom was clean, too—no slime in the basin, no dirty clothes in the bathtub. If Warren's toothbrush hadn't been in the holder, she'd have thought he'd moved.

The bed was made, and his clothes hung up in the open closet. Hers were to the far left—blouses, skirts, a few dresses. She took out the blue dress she'd worn to a classmate's wedding and held it up in front of her. It was knee-length, cut high up on the neck. She took off her jeans and shirt, slid the dress over her head, and zipped it partway up the back. The material snugged over her breasts and curved in at her waist. She looked at herself in the mirror. From ranch hand to model. *Not bad.* Her breasts weren't huge, but they weren't tiny, either. She imagined Warren behind her, their eyes meeting, his hands on them. But he wasn't behind her, and if he had been, he wouldn't have thought of touching her.

She lay down on the bed and closed her eyes. In her body was the lingering vibration of the Lincoln at eighty.

The microwave door closed, and the machine whirred. Warren was home. A gray dusklight shone into the bedroom from the windows at the top of the room. Shelley rolled onto her side and pulled the hem of the dress above her knees. Warren's footsteps went into the living room. She heard the clicking of the computer keys, but apparently there wasn't any e-mail because he got up and went to the bathroom. Then he came into the bedroom.

He peeled off his T-shirt and threw it on a chair and put on another. Then the timer dinged on the microwave, and he went back out to the kitchen. *Unbelievable!* He clattered a plate from the cupboard and got silverware from the drawer. She smelled pizza with anchovies, sausage, and mushrooms.

She rolled off the bed and walked to the kitchen in her bare feet. He was cutting the pizza with his back toward her. She noticed he'd had a haircut because his hair was short above his ears.

"Hello, Warren."

He jumped and whirled around with the knife. "Jesus," he said, "you scared me."

"That's what you always say."

"Where did you come from?"

"From the bed. I was lying there in plain sight. Are you going to stab me with that?"

"I didn't expect to see anybody," he said. "I was thinking about the Goths sweeping across Europe. You want some pizza?"

He got another plate from the cupboard.

"You don't seem very glad to see me."

"I am, though. How's the ranch? Is your mother driving you crazy?"

"Aren't you even going to kiss me?"

"Oh, sure." He hugged her with one arm and kissed her cheek without putting down the knife. "How many slices do you want? There's Pepsi in the fridge. Get me one, too, will you?"

She opened the refrigerator door and wrenched two Pepsis from the plastic rings of the six-pack. "Your place is pretty clean," she said.

"You weren't here, so I hired a housekeeper."

"A housekeeper?"

"A sophomore from the KKG house."

"Let me get this right," she said. "You thought I was your maid?"

Warren forked the pizza onto the plates. "I didn't say that. You bitched all the time about the mess, so I did something about it."

"Well, fuck you, Warren."

"Look, do you mind if we argue about this after we eat?"

He brought the plates to the table, Shelley's with one slice, and his with four, and sat down.

Shelley opened her can of Pepsi and flung it across the room.

Warren stared at her, as Pepsi ran down the wall.

"Get your fucking maid to clean it up," she said. "And I hate anchovies."

Chapter 6

Mattie carved the roast while Dawn cut red pepper and avocado. The Indian boy set the table and put the silverware in the middle of the plates. "Don't forget napkins," Mattie said. "They're in the drawer by the sink."

"Where are the glasses?" Lee asked.

"In the cupboard where Dawn is. Butter's in the refrigerator."

The Indian boy got out the butter. Lee got glasses and poured water for everyone.

"I thought Hector was going to come get his calf," Dawn said.

"He's probably on an emergency assignment for the phone company."

"Should we move him into the barn?"

"He's been out in that arroyo," Mattie said. "He'll be all right in the lee of the house."

Mattie served the pork roast, and everyone sat down. The Indian boy bowed his head.

"We don't have to say grace," Mattie said.

"It won't do any good," Dawn said. "Grace. There, it's been said." She looked at the Indian boy and smiled.

The Indian boy cut his potato with his knife. "I didn't help because of the spirit," the boy said. "It was out when I went to shoot the twenty-two."

"If there was a spirit," Dawn said, "it was Styver's."

"Who's Styver?"

"You don't want to know," Dawn said. "He was a boyfriend once."

"It was a grass fire," Lee said. "Nothing terrible happened."

"I should have checked it," Mattie said. "The wind came up and started a few embers." She passed the plate of roast pork. "What's wrong, Dawn? Don't you eat pork?"

"No, thanks. I'm a vegan."

"I thought you wanted to raise buffalo."

"What's a vegan?" the boy asked.

"No meat, no fish, no eggs, no animal fat," Lee said. "How long have you been a vegan?"

"Since yesterday."

"What kind of birds does Jimmy Pollard want you to see?" Mattie asked.

"Eagles."

"Where would he get eagles?"

"He just said he had some."

"Jimmy Pollard's as bad as a cowboy," Mattie said. "Worse, even. You saw the Pollards' trash in the gully by the river, and every dry year they steal water from us. I don't want trouble with them."

"I haven't caused any trouble yet."

"Don't be about to."

For a few minutes they ate in silence.

"Where do you come from, Dawn?" Lee asked. "I thought I heard a southern accent."

"I came from Utah last," Dawn said.

"What about you?" Lee asked the boy.

"I didn't come from anywhere."

"Hey," Dawn said, "why don't you make up a name for yourself?"

"What for?"

"So we can call you something. Indians name themselves, don't they? Like Red Cloud or Crazy Horse. You ought to know that from your tribe."

"I don't have a tribe."

"My original name was Katharine," Dawn said. "I didn't like it when people called me Krazy Kat, so I named myself something else."

The boy took more meat and potatoes.

"I tried Sage for the smell and Yvonne because it was sexy. Dawn has implications for the future."

The boy smiled faintly.

"How about Earth Fire?" Dawn said.

"Or Flamous Amos," Lee said.

"My name's Elton," the boy said. "That's my real name."

"Elton," Dawn said. "That doesn't say much about the future."

———

After dinner, Elton gave Dawn a ride back to her camp on the four-wheeler.

"Thanks for dinner," Dawn called.

"Thanks for helping put out the fire," Mattie said.

The four-wheeler sputtered and caught, and Elton revved it. "Hold on," he shouted.

He gave gas, and Dawn shrieked and grabbed Elton's waist. She waved to Lee and Mattie, and they disappeared around the house.

Then Mattie and Lee were alone.

"I need to give you your maps," she said. "Finally."

"But coffee first."

"I guess I owe you that."

"I didn't get dessert, either," Lee said.

They went inside, and Mattie got out coffee and a filter.

"I'd help," Lee said, "but I make instant, or say, 'Coffee, please.'"

"You've done enough," Mattie said. She spooned coffee into the filter and turned the coffeemaker on.

"I'm sorry Elton felt bad about the fire, but maybe that's why he told us his name."

"Why do you say that?"

"Guilt leads to atonement."

"In my experience, it leads to silence," Mattie said. "But I admit I've never heard the boy talk so much as he did to Dawn tonight."

The coffee started to drip, and Mattie got out some Oreos. Lee wandered into the living room.

He made her nervous. He wasn't an enemy exactly, but wanting her permission, he was a threat. And she didn't like him in her living room.

She heard a few chords on the piano and then nothing. She went to the doorway and found him looking at Haney's sculpture of *Man and Woman Separated by Air*.

"Do you agree with the premise?" he asked.

"What premise? Do you play the piano?"

"I used to, but not since I came to Hot Springs. You took down a picture over there. Was it of Haney?"

"I thought it would be easier not to be reminded of certain things. The coffee's probably ready. Shall we sit outside?"

It was cool outside, but not cold. Mattie sat on the steps, and Lee took a wooden chair. Close in to the house, the arc light illuminated their trucks and the white fence and a wedge of the lawn. They sipped their coffee and listened to the screech owl in the swamp.

"Did Elton come back?" Lee asked.

"Not yet. I forgot Shelley took the Lincoln to Boulder. That's where the boy sleeps."

"Maybe he'll stay over there with Dawn."

"He's fourteen," Mattie said.

"If I were fourteen, I'd want to stay with Dawn."

"You think she's pretty?"

"I think she's good with a shovel."

"She can fix machines like nobody's business, but I'm worried she wants to hide out here for a while."

"Hide out from what? Or is it whom?"

"My guess is it's a man."

"Men are shits," Lee said. "There's no doubt about it."

"They're different from women."

"At least we agree on that. I was thinking we should check on the fire one more time."

"I can do it," Mattie said.

"I know you can, but let's take my truck in case we need the buckets."

Away from the house, the sky was clear and wild with stars. Lee steered the truck into the creek bottom and uphill onto the dusty track where a kangaroo rat scurried through the headlights, jumped twice, and disappeared into its hole at the edge of the road. Mattie rolled down her window. "I like the sounds," she said.

Lee turned off the engine, and the truck drifted to a stop in the moonlight. "Let's walk, then," Lee said. But neither of them got out. The cab windows were open, and they listened.

No breeze.

Not an owl.

No moving water, even in a ditch.

No cars.

No airplanes.

Not an insect chirring.

No voices.

A quarter moon. Stars. The pale road extended ahead of the truck and disappeared into darkness.

A coyote broke the quiet with a long, eerie yapping.

"Will you do me a favor?" Lee asked.

"I just gave you dinner. And coffee."

"You owe me one more. Will you show me the sinkhole site? Jane did the preliminary studies, but I've never seen the place."

"Will you take no for an answer?"

"Of course I will, if you say it. What about Saturday? That's my day off."

"All right, but I run a ranch. There are no days off."

He got out and went around and opened her door, and for some reason Mattie allowed this. She couldn't explain why. She stepped down without help—he didn't offer any—and moved away on solid ground. Lee reached into the cab and got a flashlight, then pulled a shovel out from among the buckets in the bed.

They walked without the flashlight on, and neither of them spoke. She was conscious of him beside her and felt he was conscious of her, but Mattie sensed no silence. They turned at the weir and walked along the ditch. Water was running in the dark, and the horses moved beside them along the fence. The stars danced over them all.

Then suddenly Lee took her arm and held her back.

"What is it?" she asked.

But as soon as she heard it, she knew what it was. The sound was a buzzing, almost like running water, but not quite. Lee turned the flashlight on and zigzagged the beam across the ground until it came upon the rattlesnake, a big one coiled with its tail in the air.

"Hold the light," Lee said.

Mattie took the flashlight and aimed it at the snake. Its rattle was a tan blur, and its head swayed, and its tongue lapped the air. Lee stepped out of the light to the left, holding the shovel in front of him. "It's all right," he said to the snake. "I'm not going to hurt you."

The snake struck, and its body made the blade of the shovel ring. It fell back and coiled again, and struck, and the second time, Lee caught it with the shovel blade and flung the snake over the ditch.

They continued walking, now with the light on.

"I'm glad you didn't kill it." Mattie said.

"It was only doing its job," Lee said. "Why would I kill it?"

"Because men are shits."

"Only some men, sometimes."

They reached the burn, and Mattie jumped the ditch and shone the light back for Lee, and they climbed the embankment together. At the top Mattie played the light across the blackened ground.

"No smoke," she said. She turned the light off. "No fire."

"Look there," Lee said. He touched her shoulder and turned her toward the river.

A small flame, far away, shimmered from the dark.

"That's Dawn's camp," Mattie said.

"It looks like two shapes at the fire."

"If you had a boy, would you let him stay over there?"

"I do have a boy, and sure, I'd let him."

"Really?"

"My son is six," Lee said.

"I don't trust anyone who makes up her own name."

"You barely know her."

"That's another reason."

"So you don't trust me, either?" He took the flashlight. "Wait here. I'm going to walk the fire again."

Lee followed the flashlight beam down the embankment and circled into the trees. At the other side of the burn, he stopped and turned off the light. "I trust *you*," he called back.

Chapter 7

Shelley spent the night with friends in a sorority, and the next day, when Warren was at the lab, she went back to the apartment to get her things. The kitchen still smelled of Pepsi and anchovies.

Warren had left a note on the table:

> Shel—
> I have to monitor my project today. BUT PLEASE STAY.
> I'll be back early this afternoon. Your mother called, wants
> you to call her.
>
> W.

She boxed up her textbooks and portable phone, folded her dresses and shirts and coats into green garbage bags, and crammed her book bag full of toiletries and underwear. The TV set was too heavy, but two students passing by helped her load it into the Lincoln. Before she left, she showered and put on clean panties and jeans and a T-shirt with no bra. No one was going to see her, at least no one she knew.

On the interstate, she jetted to ninety, careless of speeding or getting caught at it. The highway raced under her. For a change she felt almost honest with herself. She'd made grievous mistakes, and there would be regrets, but the biggest one was having stayed with Warren as long as she had. How could she have known how wrong it was? She'd wasted two years with Warren, but of course she could be only as wise or as strong as the moment allowed. To imagine freedom was one thing, and to have it another. One thing was certain: The unknown was strong and bright and coming fast.

She ate lunch at a truck stop south of Cheyenne. Her mother had two helpers now, so she wasn't in any hurry to get home. But where else could she go? She folded out a map of Wyoming, and it showed lots of blank space. Interstate 25 divided the state north and south, and Interstate 80 lopped off the bottom. She'd never been to Rock Springs or Thermopolis or Jackson. Maybe she'd drive to Yellowstone and spend the night alone, sleeping on the ground the way Dawn did. What would it be like to do that? What would she feel to be out by herself under the stars?

Once when she was seven or eight, her father had picked her up from a birthday party in Hot Springs. It was winter. Cold, dark outside, snow on the ground. Ice and stones kicked up under the car. He asked about her party, and then they lapsed into their respective reveries. She was sleepy, riding in the warm car. Then strange wisps of colors danced above the horizon: vertical clouds of reds, whites, lilacs, forming and disappearing. She thought the rainbow veils of moving colors were ghosts shimmering in the sky. She wasn't afraid, exactly, though she felt something akin to fear, and she burst out crying.

"Those are the northern lights," her father said. "There's nothing to cry about."

The name gave her something to hold on to, and over a few minutes the wisps and colors grew fainter, and then it was dark again. She thought now, looking back, that what she felt so like fear was not knowing. Absence. Unknowing. Why hadn't her father explained in the beginning what the lights were?

She drove north through Cheyenne and Wheatland. The road shimmered wet with mirage; cathedral clouds burgeoned above her and shadowed the plains. In the absence of clear desire, she took the exit for Lusk.

That was her problem, she decided. She had nothing she wanted, no goal, no reason to do one thing rather than another. There had been no defining moment in her life that pointed her on the right path. She considered her past. She had dyed her hair pink. She'd shoplifted once; that was something. Loren's death had affected her. What about what Jimmy Pollard did to her? That scared her plenty. Or perhaps there was no such thing as a defining moment. Everything mattered, and nothing mattered.

One summer she'd worked at the Blue Bell Lodge near Custer, making beds and cleaning rooms with Thella, and Thella had got her into running. Every afternoon when they were through cleaning rooms, they ran trails or went to Custer High and did laps. Thella taught her to set goals for herself—a waterfall, twenty laps, a trail junction. When school started that next fall, she tried out for the cross-country team. Thella was the star—it was hard to believe now—but Shelley made the team, and her parents were so proud of her they let her buy a used Datsun so she didn't have to ride the school bus. Over the season she improved from barely on the team to third- and fourth-place finishes in the small meets, and top tens in the bigger ones. The team qualified for state, and her parents, even her father, drove to Pierre to watch her run. She finished eighteenth.

Maybe getting the car was the defining moment in her life. It gave her freedom to go to other school activities—club meetings, basketball games, dances. Because she was happier, her grades, which had been Bs and Cs, improved to all As. Mrs. Edmonds entered her non-Euclidean geometry project in the math fair, and Mr. Adler gave her A+'s on her essays and stories. (He'd particularly liked a story titled "Cherry Bombs.") Her turnaround led to her thinking of college.

But if she had to choose a defining moment, it would have been her father's death. She'd been taking it easy, stagnating, in a rut, and suddenly everything was changed. Changed unalterably—but how? What did it mean?

By three-thirty she was in Hot Springs, descending the familiar hill past the high school to the river. The closer she got to the ranch, the more she resisted, and if she were going home, at least she could take her time. What day was it, Friday? She knew where Bryce lived, or used to, because she'd had to take him written arguments when he'd appeared for her in front of the school board. On impulse, she turned left at the 7-Eleven and came out on Sixth Street. His VW was in the carport, and she parked across the street. Her excuse was to apologize for canceling their date. Or she'd recalled the poem he'd read to the class about a red tent in France—how did it go? Or she could just say hello. What was wrong with that?

Once she was out of the car, it was easy, except she was aware she had no bra on. She crossed the street and walked straight up the steps. Then she remembered he rode his bike to school, and it wasn't there. She knocked anyway and was surprised to hear footsteps.

A woman opened the door. "Yes?"

"Mr. Adler isn't home?"

"He's up at the school," the woman said. "Can I help you?" The woman was thirty-something and had on a loose gray dress. Her curly brown hair was pulled back in a barrette.

Shelley hesitated. "I'm selling tickets to the choir concert at Chadron State."

"Oh, that's so nice of you," the woman said. "Why don't you leave your name, and if he wants to go, he can call you?"

"Okay. Sure."

The woman disappeared into the house to get a pencil and paper, and Shelley ran.

Humiliated was how she felt. He had a girlfriend, so what? Why had she lied to the girlfriend about choir tickets? God, that was dumb! It was obvious she didn't have any tickets. She didn't look as though she sang in any choir. And then to run away!

She drove to Maverick Junction yammering at herself, then sat at the stop sign until a car behind her honked. "Fuck you," she said, and did a U-turn and headed back to Hot Springs.

It was early, before happy hour, and Yogi's was slow. Only two or three geezers sat at the bar, and one pool table was in play. She paused at the door, but didn't see anyone she knew. That was fine. She went in and ordered a Budweiser.

"You got an ID?" the bartender asked.

Shelley slapped her wallet open, but the bartender didn't look at it. He opened a bottle. "You want a glass?"

"No." She laid down a five-dollar bill. "Give me two dollars' worth of quarters, too."

She took her beer to the vacant pool table and fitted three quarters into the slots. The balls dropped, and she racked them for eight ball—one-ball in front, then two stripes. She swigged the beer and found a cue without much bend in it.

Two cowboys were playing on the next table, and they eyed her.

"We can do a three-way," the one with the fat gut said.

"He means at pool," said the other one. "One to five, six to ten, eleven to fifteen."

"I'd rather practice," Shelley said.

She broke, and the balls scattered over the green felt.

At CU she'd played with Warren once in a while at the rec center, but she wasn't very good. He'd taught her about weight and mass and inertia and calculating the angles, but she knew from running that a lot of it was experience.

She missed her first two shots, then made a cut on the three in the side.

"Nifty," Fat Gut said. "You look pretty good."

Shelley ignored him. She played the rack out and got another beer.

People filtered in: carpenters, shopkeepers, ranchers. She'd played half of a second rack when a man in an NRA cap came up and put quarters on the rail of her table. He had sawdust on his jeans and wore a T-shirt with César Chávez's picture in a circle with a red line through it. She didn't like him even before he slotted the quarters.

"Play for a beer?" he asked. "I'm Bill Carson. People call me Kit."

"I'm Gloria Steinem," Shelley said.

Shelley broke and, by luck, sank a stripe. She made the ten in the corner, then missed on the twelve.

"Too bad, Gloria," the man said.

He sank three solids, *bang bang bang*.

Then Shelley glanced up and saw Hank Tobuk, hatless, leaning against the door jamb.

Shelley got one more turn before Kit Carson ran the table.

"That wasn't fun," she said.

"Let's play another one," Kit Carson said. "I can drink all night for free."

Hank Tobuk stepped to the table and put down some quarters. "Let's play partners," he said, "if it's all right with Gloria."

"Sure," Kit said. "My buddy over here can drink for free, too."

Shelley got two beers from the bar, and when she came back, Kit Carson and Fat Gut were slapping hands. Hank racked the balls. "Why don't we play for real money?" Hank asked. "Say, twenty dollars a game?"

"Make it fifty if you want," Kit Carson said.

"Fifty, then," Hank said. He looked at Shelley. "I'll pay if we lose."

Hank lifted the triangle, and Fat Gut exploded the rack. A stripe and a solid went down, and he grinned. "There's balls for you," he said.

Fat Gut was a blaster. He rammed in two solids, then hit the cue ball so hard it jumped off the table.

For fifty dollars, Shelley expected Hank to shoot first, but he didn't move. "It's your table," he said. "These guys only think they're good."

Shelley made the ten and a cut on the twelve, but she left herself a bad angle on the nine. She hit the cue ball softly, but the nine kissed off the rail, and the cue ball nestled in behind it.

"Good leave," Hank said.

Kit Carson missed the bank shot and left the cue ball open.

"There's our fifty dollars," Hank said. "Excuse me a minute."

Hank went to the bar and came back with two shots of tequila, a bottle of Heineken, and a pool cue case. Hank did one of the shots and gave the other to Shelley. "We don't take checks," he said. He chalked his cue, sprinkled talc on his left hand, and leaned down and bridged. He stroked the nine gently into the side.

Shelley drank down her tequila.

The nine was the only ball Hank made. Then things happened fast. Fat Gut grabbed Hank from behind and jerked him upright, and Kit Carson stepped forward to take a punch, but Hank was quicker and kicked Kit Carson in the balls. Shelley swung her pool cue and nailed Fat Gut in the side of the head. He reeled sideways and let Hank go, and Hank jammed a fist in his stomach.

Fat Gut dropped to his knees and moaned. Hank jabbed Kit Carson in the forehead with the butt of his cue, and the fight was over. He pulled Fat Gut's wallet from his pocket.

"Plus overtime," he said, and took the wad of bills.

Then he picked up his cue and the case. "Let's get out of here," he said.

Shelley grabbed the Heineken.

A minute later she found herself on the sidewalk, running after Hank. She'd had three beers and a shot of tequila, not that much, but everything was in slow motion. "What's the rush?" she asked.

Hank steered her across the street toward the tourist information center.

His truck was parked beside a camper, and he opened the driver's side and threw in the pool cue and the case. Then he kissed her against the side of the truck.

She didn't mean to kiss him back, but she was carried into the moment, still clinging to the bottle of beer. Hank ran his hand under her shirt and twisted his palm against her breast.

She broke away. "I thought we were in a hurry."

"We are," he said.

"What about Thella?"

"She's at her sister's in Spearfish."

He pushed her up into the truck, and she slid across the seat. Keys jangled; the engine revved; tires squealed into the street.

Shelley drank from the Heineken and passed it to Hank.

"There's more behind the seat," he said.

"My car's at Yogi's."

Hank pretended he didn't hear. Shelley got a Coors from behind the seat. At the video store he turned onto the main highway. Then he pulled her over and slid his hand inside her shirt. She closed her eyes, but still felt the headlights of cars pass against them. God, that felt good.

The truck slowed. Hank took his hand away, and she opened her eyes. Trailers, each with its own pole light, stairstepped up the hill on flat spots dug out of the gravel. Hank's, near the top, was a single wide with a piece of corrugated green plastic over the door. The deck had a grill on it, two white plastic chairs, and a refrigerator.

Hank carried the beer up the steps and put it in the fridge and unlocked the door. The inside smelled of cigarettes and grease. A brown sofa, a TV. Shelley went through the living room and down the narrow hall to the bathroom. The bathroom was a mess—Thella's hairbrush, Tampax, the mirror spotted with toothpaste. She sat on the john and tried to think how she got there and how she was going to get out.

In the living room Hank was standing up smoking a cigarette and changing TV channels with the remote.

"I should probably go," Shelley said.

"You just got here. Have a beer."

He stared at the TV. She felt as if she could tiptoe past him, get outside, and run. But she wasn't a prisoner. She walked across to the door.

"Get me one, too," he said.

She opened the door, saw the trailer lights below her, and took a beer from the fridge.

When she closed the refrigerator, Hank was there. "You don't want one?"

"I've had enough," she said.

He took the can, set it on the grill. "You want to get your car?" he asked.

"I guess I should."

"We'll do it," he said.

He kissed her again, hard—she tasted the cigarette on his lips—and she kissed him back without really meaning to. His hands circled her rear end from behind and drew her closer, and she felt his cock against her leg. She put her arms around his neck.

Then he unbuttoned her jeans and pulled down the zipper, and his fingers worked their way inside her panties. She was wet, and she felt the shock of his finger inside her. She sighed through the kiss.

After a minute, he pushed her jeans and panties down over her hips, knelt, and worked off one shoe and the jeans and panties off one leg. He stood and unbuckled his belt and pressed her against the refrigerator. She held his cock and guided it into her.

Then she thought about a condom. Did he have one in his wallet? He eased almost all the way out of her and paused, but she couldn't say anything, couldn't move. She held him so he couldn't pull away any farther. *No, don't go away.* She felt the cool metal of the refrigerator.

He pushed into her again. *Yes. Don't stop.* He didn't stop. He lifted her against the refrigerator and went faster. Then faster still. He stopped abruptly, pulled her close, and spasmed inside her.

After a moment he lowered her to her feet, and his cock slipped out.

Then, lights everywhere—headlights, flashing blue lights whirled through the trees—as two police cars roared up the hill.

Chapter 8

After Lee Coulter left, Mattie practiced her ritual for sleep. She lay on her back for a few minutes, turned onto her left side till she drowsed, then onto her right side where usually she fell asleep. That night she repeated the ritual three times and was still wide awake.

Shelley hadn't called from Boulder; that was one worry. Mattie had called to make sure she got there, and Warren had told her about the argument they'd had, that Shelley had stormed off. A return call would have been considerate. But Shelley was the age of consent, if not of reason, and Mattie couldn't dictate to her. She turned onto her left side, then turned over and lay on her back and stared at the ceiling.

Who she really blamed for not sleeping was Lee Coulter. He'd made certain the fire was out and had driven her back to the house. That part was fine. She'd given him his maps, and they'd said good night, and then, instead of heading south, which was the shortest way to Hot Springs, he'd driven north. The only reason to do that was to stop at Dawn's camp.

Lee could do what he wanted, of course. He was how old, forty? And he was divorced. But she had to think of Dawn. Somebody had to, because Dawn didn't think much for herself. In a few days she'd drawn Jimmy Pollard to her and bewitched a fourteen-year-old boy, but Lee Coulter should know better. She turned over again onto her right side.

All those years sleeping with Haney—was he thinking of men? Had he been wishing to be with Dennis Burke or Franz or Toby Cushing, the soccer coach? And what had he felt for her? Disgust? Indifference? Love? What sort of love was it when it was so tainted by deceit?

She hoped the ditch fire was out. Had Lee checked it carefully enough? She remembered a fire Haney had set once to burn brush from the border of the Upper East. He'd let it burn too hot, and the flames consumed five birch trees. She begged him to call someone for help, but he watched the flames spread. Then the wind shifted, and the fire roared down the mesa toward the house. Mattie watched from the kitchen and realized the fire was coming for her. But she chose not to run. As she waited, a hawk, disoriented by the smoke, crashed through the window and fell on the table, its wing extended across her aunt's clean china plate. The cottonwood tree in the yard burst into flame.

Mattie woke in the dark and sat up in bed and listened to her racing heart and the silence.

The next morning she rose and showered and went outside into the yard. It was clear and cool, and she watched the rising sunlight travel across the mesas. She didn't see Elton. The four-wheeler wasn't at the barn or by the Morton. She thought maybe Elton had slept in the truck, but she checked, and he hadn't.

The calf had survived the night, and she fed it again.

Then she made coffee and took her cup and her binoculars to the creek. She liked May for migration—more birds every day. Sparrows scattered like brown leaves across the yard, and kingbirds had returned, their white breasts like isolated blossoms high in the cottonwoods. A common yellowthroat sang *wichety-wichety*, and a kingfisher rattled down the creek toward the river.

She scanned to the west: no smoke from the grass fire. A bright blue bird—either a grosbeak or a bunting—flew from the tangle of brush through the circle of her vision, and she crossed the creek and followed the bird along the fence line. It perched on a barbed wire, then flew farther along to the springy stalk of a sunflower: a blue grosbeak, blue with brown wing bars, stubby beak, black face. Behind the bird, against the pale green mesa, was Dawn's red dome tent with her dolphins fluttering beside it in the breeze. The dead campfire was in a ring of stones. There was no sign of Lee Coulter's truck, but the four-wheeler was there beside Dawn's Mercury.

Mattie raised her binoculars to look closer, and at that moment Dawn emerged from the tent, sleepy-eyed, her hair a loose tangle over one shoulder. She had on a gray sweatshirt and white panties barely visible under it. She stretched her arms into the air and turned a full circle, as if thrilled to be alive.

Mattie was livid. How could Dawn feel thrilled to be alive? If she had no conscience, maybe. What about Elton? Dawn slid her feet into her sneakers and walked to the edge of the butte to an animal trail that led to the river. She descended it on a long traverse. Mattie had to admit she was graceful. Her long legs gave with the terrain, and she skipped down the last ten feet to a dry sandbar. She peed in the bushes, then gathered driftwood and stacked it at the foot of the trail. Mattie watched her as she walked to the river, apparently searching for stones.

Dawn found one she liked, took off her sneakers and put the stone in one of them, and then waded into the water. Mattie knew the river there. She'd built a fence across it, but the flood had washed it out. Now the water was slow and shallow. The low angle of the sun from the east made the water look golden, and Dawn knelt and touched the river as if it were fragile. She dipped her hands and lifted the water to her forehead. Then she stood and lifted her sweatshirt over her head and shook out her tangled hair. Her breasts were small and round, her hips barely flared from her slender waist. Her body and the pale white vee of her panties reflected in the water.

Then she waded deeper into the river and peeled down her panties and stepped out of them and faced the sun. She held her hair away from her neck and splashed water on her face, using her panties as a washcloth. Her breasts, her face, her blond hair were outlined in the gold light.

What would Elton think if he'd seen Dawn then? He would marvel at her, probably, but not as Mattie did. He'd be tantalized. She shifted the binoculars to the camp, but didn't see him.

Then she looked back at Dawn. She was part of the sky, the horizon, the cottonwoods, the blue and yellow sunlit water. The grosbeak close by sang its sweet notes, and the sound made Mattie's eyes tear up. Even that birdsong, such a small event, conjured up in her the admonishments of youth. It wasn't Dawn who was heedless of the world, but she.

Dawn tossed her panties to the sand and sank forward into the current. She rose and arched her back and swam, then turned over and lay back with her head in the current and floated, her face and breasts visible, her feet kicking gently. Sunlight flowed around her face, a face as composed as Mattie wished her own to be, merged with the light from the river.

The sun was warm and dew steamed from the grass when Mattie walked back to the house. She felt mysteriously calm. The songs of warblers in the thicket and blackbirds in the marsh, the scent of wet grass, the breeze along the creek were perfectly ordinary, but her sense of them was heightened. She heard the familiar sound of the screen door's slamming.

When she reached the yard, no one was there. Just the house, stark in sunlight, and its shadow, and the leaves of the cottonwood shaking in the breeze.

As she approached, the front door opened, and Elton came out holding a basketball and eating a piece of bread. He tore the bread with his teeth and continued down the steps, tossing the ball in the air, twirling it on his fingertip. He bounced it on the ground.

"There you are," Mattie said. "Where'd you get the basketball?"

"Dawn gave it to me."

"Where's the four-wheeler?"

"Over at Dawn's camp. It wouldn't turn over last night when I was about to come back."

"So where did you sleep?"

"In her car."

"Did you see Lee over there?"

"No." Elton tossed the ball from one hand to the other. "I saw a car go by."

"Elton, you know you can sleep in the house."

"The car was okay."

"I mean, we choose each other. If you want to be here, and I want you here, we have an agreement."

"Yeah."

"Do you understand me?"

"I think so." He dribbled the ball a few times.

"There are spark plugs in the Morton," she said. "Go find the one you need."

Chapter 9

"I thought we'd go to Rapid City," Mattie said. "We don't have to work all the time."

"I don't want to," Elton said. He was eating a chicken sandwich and had a bite of it in his mouth.

"Dawn can go, too, and I'll pay your wages. Maybe we can play miniature golf."

"I don't want to play miniature golf."

"If you're nice, I'll get you a basketball hoop. And Dawn needs parts for the three-wheeler."

"And the sprinkler," Dawn said.

"I think we'll give up on the sprinkler," Mattie said. "It's already been too much work. And I don't think we can get the water there." She looked at Elton. "Elton, you change your clothes. You're going with us. I'll feed the calf."

"I'm taking a shower first," Dawn said.

Mattie gave the calf a bottle—it had an appetite, at least—and then she tried Shelley again at Warren's.

Warren answered. "I left her a note to call you," Warren said. "She was here and got her things, but I have no idea where she went."

"Did she talk to you about her father?"

"We didn't talk about anything," Warren said. "I think she's having a breakdown."

Out the window Mattie saw Lute Pollard drive into the yard. "Listen, Warren, I'm sorry about Shelley. She can be a little out of control sometimes."

"You're telling me."

"I've got to run," Mattie said. "I'll talk to you."

She hung up and went out onto the porch.

Lute had pulled his truck right to the steps, and he leaned across the seat. "We got a problem up at the house," Lute said. "Can I borrow some gas from you?"

"I was about to go to Rapid. How much do you need?"

"I got a ten-gallon canister here. I'll pay you for it."

"All right."

Lute smiled. "Jimmy says you got a woman working for you now, a mechanic. Kinda pretty."

"Is that what you came down here for?"

"No, I need the gas for my four-wheeler. Oh, and Jimmy wanted me to give her these." Lute handed Mattie two long dark brown feathers.

Just then Dawn came across from the Morton. She'd had a shower and her hair was wet, and she had on a T-shirt and shorts. She had a walk she didn't need to try for, and Lute watched her all the way to the house.

"Go get your gas, Lute. I'll give Dawn the feathers."

"Right," Lute said. "If she wants extra work, I got a backhoe needs a look at."

The Black Hills lay to the west of the highway, and the plains spread out to the east, farther than they could see. Elton rode between Mattie and Dawn and spun the basketball on his finger.

"Elton, you're going to have to stop that," Mattie said, "or we'll have a wreck."

Elton juggled the ball from hand to hand.

"Why are you so nervous?"

"Who said I was nervous?"

"You're acting nervous," Dawn said. She took the ball and wedged it behind the seat. "What are you nervous about?"

Elton stared straight ahead.

"Did you ever hunt buffalo?" Dawn asked.

"Are you talking to me?"

"You're the Indian, aren't you?"

"There aren't any buffalo."

"There used to be. And there could be still."

"We're not getting buffalo," Mattie said.

"Is there a Moroccan restaurant in Rapid City?" Dawn asked. "I like lamb and couscous." She looked at Elton. "Do you know what couscous is?"

"It has something to do with girls," Elton said.

"I thought you were a vegetarian," Mattie said.

"I'll bet you don't know where Morocco is, do you, Elton? Or the Sahara? Have you ever heard of Africa?"

"Duh," Elton said.

"Do you know what geography is?"

"No."

"Geography is where things are," Mattie said, "like oceans and landmasses. It's where the house is and the Upper East and Sheep Table and where rivers start and end."

"Rivers start in the mountains and end in the ocean," Elton said.

"That's geography," Mattie said.

"Can you read?" Dawn asked. "Did you ever go to school?"

"Sure, I can read."

"You can't go to the moon until you dream the dreams to take you," Dawn said.

"I don't want to go to the moon."

"Maybe you'll want to someday."

"If you stay with me," Mattie said, "you'll have to go to school."

"But not till fall," Elton said.

"I want to know the geography of stars," Dawn said. "Did you know all the stars we see at night are not really where they appear to be?"

"Where are they?" Elton asked.

"They've moved since the time they emitted the light we see."

"What are you talking about?" Elton said.

"The starlight we see started from very far away. Way far. So far it takes thousands of years for its light to reach us. In that time, the star that emitted the light has moved or maybe even died."

"I don't get it," Elton said.

"All things are moving. We know the earth moves around the sun, but the sun is also moving through space. We think space is finite—that's how we conceive of what's around us—but it isn't. And we think we're the center of the universe even though we know we're not. The universe is in chaos."

They crested a hill, and Rapid City appeared before them.

"Now *that* is chaos," Mattie said.

"What I love to think about is deep space," Dawn said.

"You're already in deep space," Elton said.

"Do you think so?" Dawn asked. "I hope it's true."

Chapter 10

D awn had never considered herself in deep space in the way Elton meant it. All her life people had accused her of being scatter-brained, flaky, eccentric, unbalanced, whimsical, and strange. She didn't *feel* eccentric or scatterbrained. Impulsive, maybe, but not crazy. She hated that word, "crazy."

Her high school counselor had called her a nitwit, and her fellow students called her Krazy Kat. The girls in Dublin, Georgia, were fuck-ups and sluts, and the boys fuck-ups and brutes. They stayed away from her because she was unpredictable. In science class a boy called her Krazy Kunt, and she beat his desk to splinters with an aluminum base-ball bat while he was sitting in it. Another time a rumor started she had breast implants, and she'd locked the rumormonger in the janitor's closet with three lab rats and a king snake. When the counselor asked why, she said she didn't want the snake to go hungry.

Also, she was smart, though no one knew it. She spoke too fast and left out parts of sentences, and her mind skipped details, so what came out of her mouth were often disjointed phrases and unintelligible ideas. She couldn't help it. Her grades were only so-so, but she read Russian literature and got upper 700s on her SATs.

She'd been born in Dublin in Laurens County in the state of Geor-gia in the United States of America, but borders never made sense to her. Did a deer or a wild boar know state lines? Did a bird understand national boundaries or a fish international waters? Every animal had its habitat and territory according to its needs. *Homo sapiens* was the only species that knew what country it belonged to, and that knowledge was catastrophic for millions of people.

Her parents were odd. It was her father who conceived of Doog. Doog was the force of interrelated matter, the connection between a frit-illary's wing and the ice pack in the Arctic Ocean, rain in Ecuador and the decay of a dead raccoon in longleaf pinewoods in Alabama, the song of a warbler and the redistribution of sand in the Negev Desert. It was not cause and effect, but the principle of constant recomposition, not a religion, but a way of seeing and being. The best thing about Doog, according to her father, was you didn't have to go to any doogdamn church to ask for forgiveness.

Her mother was German and read mystery novels in her native language. She crocheted "Home Sucks" on dishtowels that sold well as far away as Atlanta and Tallahassee. On occasion, she ran off to visit Disneyland or Six Flags—she liked the rides—or Cincinnati, where she knew no one in particular, or that's what she said. Why not believe her?

The spring of Dawn's senior year, her mother and father were killed in a car crash on a bridge—two drunk drivers hitting each other head-on. Her mother was one driver, and her father the other. They'd been to different parties, and both were under the impression they were to meet at the other party. Fate. From then on, Katharine considered fate the governing principle of the universe.

After she graduated from high school (with "Krazy Kat" under her yearbook photograph), she joined the army. The army was imbued with God and patriotism and the conviction of being right, and if she could endure the army, she could endure the world. Besides, in the army, living was free.

Basic was at Fort Benning. She climbed ropes, scaled walls, slithered, slogged, sprinted. She accustomed herself to communal living, relied on others when she needed help. By fate, she was stationed at Fort Carson, Colorado. In the blink of a plane ride, she inhabited an arid land with a wide sky. Instead of humidity, green, and no horizon, she confronted a land as bleak as the moon. Colorado was vulnerable to the sun. Her skin parched and burned; her lips cracked; her eyes ached with dryness. There were no trees to hide her, no azaleas to draw attention away. She was tall and blond and talked southern.

Men weren't afraid of her, so she befriended them, not because she liked them, but because they listened to her garbled ideas. The problem was finding one bright enough to understand what she said. She sorted through dozens of men willing to try, and she made mistakes, but in time she found three who were smart and kind: an officer, an enlisted man, and a cabdriver from Cañon City. The first, Drew, was from Beaumont, Texas, and was in the JAG. He had a tendency to break bones—

his foot, his nose, his wrist. Hudson worked with computers and was likable for his bumbling, though twice he rolled condoms on the wrong way. Gordon was the cabdriver.

Love was not an issue. For what she wanted, these men were fine, but she had to juggle them like grapefruits. She didn't lead them on. Each knew about the others, but still called her. From them, she gained confidence, and that was how her trouble started. Confidence got her a promotion, and instead of being an anonymous cog in the motor pool, she became the front-wheel axle, in charge of work orders for three dozen soldiers.

She didn't want to be a leader. Leaders believed in God and the supremacy of the United States. Leaders made decisions even when they didn't believe. She couldn't believe something false, so she lied. The more she lied, the more she was successful, and the more successful she was, the more she wanted out of the army.

As always, she relied on fate. She got appendicitis, which she parlayed into a medical discharge.

That summer she worked in Colorado Springs at an RV repair shop desperate for help during tourist season. She took the name Sage. Liberated from barracks life, she went to wine bars, where she met an assortment of egomaniacs and droners. Why did men think shooting an elk, a stock market coup, or mountain biking up Pikes Peak would interest her? She wanted someone who read books, held her in bed, and listened to what she said. After a time, because men were such idiots, she decided to have nothing to do with them.

Her winter of celibacy coincided with dreams of dolphins leaping from the water. She swam with them and danced with them in the tides. She remembered dolphins she'd seen in childhood on a trip with her parents to Cumberland Island. Images came to her in daydreams, too—conversations with dolphins, making love with them, being in a family. In essence, the dreams freed her by making her comfortable being alone.

This freedom was the impetus to create herself in a place she'd never been, preferably somewhere not overrun with right-wing pseudo-Christians. She went to the library to do research on where to live. Fate: Behind the main desk in the library was a picture of the National Bison Range in Polson, Montana.

She walked out of the library and across the street to the Phantom Canyon Brew Company to celebrate finding a place to go. It was four o'clock on a warm spring afternoon. She read outside under a red and white umbrella, now and then aware of the couple arguing at the next table. The man was lank and dark-haired, blue eyes, and he wore an absurd red and green Hawaiian shirt. Finally the woman got up, stepped around her, and said, "Excuse me."

Sage glanced up and saw not the woman disappearing, but the man left behind. His smile was a skyrocket. "*Novel with Cocaine,*" he said. "Ageyev. I like the Russians. Do you know Chekhov?"

"Not personally."

"May I?"

He took the book from her and read several pages. She liked the audacity of his shirt and the bright green concoction he was not ashamed to be seen drinking. He knew Chekhov was not something one did to a list.

The woman he was with appeared again on the sidewalk. "Styver, we're late," she said.

"Can I borrow this when you're through?" he asked. "I promise I'll return it." He slipped a business card into the book, handed it back to her, and smiled the same powerful smile.

The card said "Lester Styver, Real Estate Appraisal" and gave an address, telephone, e-mail, and fax in Salt Lake City. When she finished the book, she mailed it to him with her return address and signed her new name, Yvonne.

Weeks went by. She quit her job at the RV repair, bought a pickup truck, and drove to Montana. Instead of Polson, she settled south of Missoula in Lolo, because she liked the name. She had no trouble as a pretty blond veteran finding work on a construction crew. She camped for two weeks in the national forest, then sublet a cabin from a woman who was going to Alaska for the salmon season.

Life as Yvonne smoothed out. She liked pounding nails, and the Bitterroot Valley was not overrun with vapid Christians. Evenings she was sweaty, tired, and deserving of wine, a shower, and a book.

One particular Friday she threw her leather tool belt into the truck, pried a Moosehead from a six-pack in her cooler, and drove to the post office. In the mail was a letter from her aunt, a final phone bill from Colorado Springs, and her official discharge from the U.S. Army. She came out of the post office whistling, and there was Lester Styver leaning against her truck. "I told you I'd return the book," he said.

She was naive enough to think his finding her was a compliment.

He'd cajoled her name from her landlord in Colorado Springs and charmed her forwarding address from the postmaster. Then he'd flown to Missoula in his Cessna and had waited three days at the post office. "I've done appraisals for Holiday Inn," he said, "so I have some comp time."

They talked a few minutes about the book—whether Vadim Maslennikov was a coward or a hero and whether his mother was the cause of Vadim's addiction. Did human beings have free will or were they victims?

"So is it Sage or Yvonne?" he asked finally.

"I'm Yvonne for now," she said. "I've been cutting floor joists all day, and I'm a mess."

"Well, thanks," he said. "Thanks for the book."

He shook her hand, got into his rental car, and drove away.

Later, in her cabin, she pondered this. He'd flown a thousand miles and waited for three days at the post office to return a book. Had he been so appalled she worked construction and drove a truck? Did she look so much worse than he remembered? At least he could have invited her for a drink.

She showered and, in the midst of washing her hair, thought how he had so delicately let drop where he was staying. She put on clean shorts and a blouse instead of a T-shirt, drank a glass of chablis, and found she couldn't concentrate on the Ivan Doig she was reading. Instead of dinner, she drove to Missoula to the Holiday Inn.

He wasn't in the lounge or the dining room, and she asked the woman at the desk if there were a Mr. and Mrs. Styver staying there. "I want to surprise them," she said.

The clerk understood the nature of surprises and, against policy, gave her the room number.

At Styver's door, she listened. No voices. No TV. She knocked twice. Styver opened the door holding hand weights.

"Will you take me up in your plane tomorrow to see buffalo?" she asked. "I want to fly over the bison range."

He smiled his skyrocket smile.

The Mission Mountains were blue snow, gray rock, black trees sweeping upward. Styver followed a river course past the church at St. Ignatius and over the yellow hills. From the air it was apparent how water flowed. At the bison range the animals browsed the yellow grass, their massive heads fixing them to the earth. Like the river courses, animal paths were worn along the easiest contours to the streams or along the perimeter fences.

"They don't have much to hide from, do they?" Styver said.

"Indians, wolves, maybe a bear. Later, of course, settlers and soldiers."

"Shall we fly to Yellowstone?" Styver asked. "We can look for wolves, too."

He banked the plane, and they flew the Bitterroot River south to Hamilton. They talked about Russian writers—Kuprin, Mayakovsky, Shokholov. Apparently he did his homework.

"You don't read women?" he asked.

"Colette," she said. "Sometimes Alice Munro or Leslie Silko."

"I like Grisham, Clancy, Stephen King, and Robert James Waller."

"You do not. You couldn't."

"They make money," he said. "I'm curious how they do it. I want to have a million dollars before I'm thirty."

"How old are you now?"

"Twenty-eight. And I want to break seventy."

"Seventy what?"

"Strokes," he said. He thumbed toward his golf clubs in the back of the plane.

"What happens when you make a million dollars and break seventy?"

"I don't know," he said. "I'll think of something. Don't you have ambitions?"

"None that I know of."

"You don't want to get married and have children?"

"No, why would I?"

"Women want to get married and have children," he said.

"That tells you something about me," she said.

Yellowstone was lakes and rivers and deep canyons, turquoise pools with steam rising, trees, grasslands, acres burned black in the fire of 1988. The bison looked lazy. Styver circled Old Faithful, then flew south over Jackson Lake and in front of the Tetons, and came in low over the golf course west of town.

"Why don't you play?" she asked.

"You want me to? We'd have to spend the night."

"I'll be able to see how close you are to quitting."

They landed at the airport and rented a car. Styver explained par was usually four, and par for eighteen holes was seventy-two. He had to shoot under par three times in a round to break seventy.

"So what's the problem?" she asked.

Styver teed off with a hook, and after three holes she understood the difficulty—chips from near the green and two-foot putts counted the same as the long drives. Styver couldn't hit the ball straight. For nine holes he shot forty-one.

"What about the million dollars?" she asked. "Are you any closer to that?"

That night he booked two rooms at the Snow King resort. She was flattered he hadn't assumed she'd sleep with him, but mildly insulted he didn't want to. They had a drink, dinner, and said good night in the lobby.

She lay in bed in black panties, thinking he'd knock on her door to visit. She watched *ER* on TV, then a rerun of *L.A. Law*. Her experience with other men was irrelevant to the particular case, but if he spent the money on aviation fuel and flew her to see buffalo, why wouldn't he sleep with her?

She wrote the reasons on hotel stationery:

> (1) he's married
> (2) it's too soon
> (3) he's deformed
> (4) he's gay
> (5) he's too tired
> (6) he's a Mormon or a moron (omit the second m)
> (7) he doesn't think I'm attractive
> (8) he's bullshitting me

Number eight sounded the most logical—he was taunting her. One thing was certain: She hated wondering. She put on a T-shirt and stomped down the hall and rapped on his door.

He opened it right away. He still had on his green checkered slacks from playing golf.

"Are you fucking with me?" she asked.

He knew what to say: nothing. He held his hands out and drew her inside.

His laptop was on. Lists of whatever were on a blue screen.

"At least you're not playing video golf," she said.

"You don't accumulate a million dollars by taking vacations," he said. He took off his glasses and laid them beside the laptop.

She felt awkward then. He still held her hand. Then he turned her toward the mirror.

"See how beautiful you are?" he said. "But I'll make you more beautiful."

She saw herself in her T-shirt as a pale white bird. What she imagined he saw was what his money could make her into—a woman in new clothes, jewelry, a different hairstyle. He rested his hands on her shoulders, and she blushed in reflection. Her body softened. He lifted her shirt and exposed her breasts. To be revealed in the light, to be watched, was different from being touched under the covers in the dark. She watched his hands skim down her bare shoulders.

He was right: With his hands on her skin, she was even more beautiful.

Chapter 11

Each time she was more beautiful. He knew how to kiss her, *when* to kiss her, when to touch her lips with his fingers, the precise pressure she liked on her nipples. He knew when to pause. Each touch, every small gesture, escalated her yearning.

Once, lazing on top of him, with his penis still inside her, she asked what he felt.

"I feel how wet you are."

"But what emotion do you feel?"

"Joy."

"That's all?"

"What do you want me to feel?"

"Close."

"Is that an emotion?" he asked.

There was nothing wrong with joy—she felt it, too—but she was open, naked and willing, *vulnerable*. She wanted him to be equally scared.

Every other weekend he flew to Missoula. She drove once to Park City, where he played golf, and they stayed at the Blue Church Inn. Doing nothing in a strange place made her edgy. Why did he want her there if he was playing golf?

"For sex," he said. "What did you think?" He was lying on the bed in knickers and a pink polo shirt. "Come over here."

"No more sex," she said. "I want attention, not sex."

"I'm attentive." He rolled onto his side and smiled.

"Your cock is attentive. The rest of you is playing golf."

He took her wrist and pulled her toward the bed. His other hand moved up her thigh and under her shirt. She shivered when he pressed the swale of her back. Then he let go of her wrist, and she didn't move away. She hated herself for allowing him that, for letting him unfasten her skirt, for letting him trace the line of her panties. She hated herself for moving her legs apart. She hated herself for sighing when he eased her panties aside and his fingers found her wet. Her whole body shook with hatred.

After that night she hated Styver. She hated him when she moved with him to Salt Lake City so he could be near his mother, when he drove his Lexus to play golf, when he made her body burn while he felt nothing but joy.

Styver's mother was seventy-four and lived in Springville. She still had her stuffed animals from childhood, her prom corsage, her first Bible. Her 1968 Mercury was preserved under a tarp in the garage. Styver was solicitous toward her. He brought flowers, carried out her trash, took her car for exercise. But his mother barely paid him any mind. In the odd moment Yvonne was alone with her, his mother unraveled to her Styver's upbringing. "I swear he screamed so much until he was three I couldn't bear the thought of another child. That's still the way he is—completely selfish."

"He acts as if he's generous."

"He lives on credit cards and borrows money from me."

"He owns an airplane."

"Lester doesn't own anything except you."

"I don't think he owns me."

"But he thinks he does. You're pretty."

"Thank you."

"It wasn't a compliment. That's why he wants you."

Yvonne suddenly felt her skin swarm and her eyes water. She itched. A cat pranced across the room and jumped up onto her lap.

"That's Hercules," Styver's mother said. "Isn't he precious?"

Styver's house was in the foothills east of the city, three thousand square feet, with a view of the Great Salt Lake. Mornings he stretched, lifted weights, showered, and ate breakfast naked. He speed-read a novel for thirty minutes, read the financial page of the *Tribune*, then dressed and went to his office. It was true Styver paid for dinners and groceries with credit cards. He bought gas on credit. He got cash from ATMs. If he owed money, it never showed on his face.

Once, midafternoon, she dropped by his office, hoping to meet his secretary, to visualize where he sat and what was on the walls. The building was a modest one-story. No lights on. Locked. Nearly empty.

At home, she searched his office and found business cards:

> Lester Styver, Fine Gifts and Antiques
> Lester Styver, Travel Consultant
> Lester Styver, Mobile Home Sales
> Lester Styver, Gourmet Foods
> Lester Styver, Office Maintenance

At dinner, serving the veal, she dropped the cards beside his plate. "I was looking for a stapler," she said. "I didn't know you sold mobile homes."

"Those are businesses I used to have."

"What do you know about gourmet foods or antiques?"

"I know people are irrationally enamored of them."

"And now you appraise real estate?"

"For almost two years."

"Your office building was empty."

"I start single proprietorships," Styver said. "I get them to show a profit, and then I sell them."

"You're a con man."

"Yvonne, there's no law against selling people what they want to buy."

In May, after they'd lived together four months, Styver's mother died choking on mashed potatoes. She was cremated, and her ashes kept in an urn on the mantel. Styver grieved strangely. He wanted to move his mother's house to his own backyard, but zoning laws prevented it, so instead as compensation, he replaced his oak dining room table with her Formica one, his leather sofa with her flowerprint settee. He sold his Lexus and drove her Mercury, and worst of all, he adopted his mother's cat.

As if to placate Yvonne, Styver became more expansive than ever. They flew to Dallas for a golf weekend; they flew to Hilton Head, South Carolina, where he shot eighty-nine at Harbortown; he made a pilgrimage to Ohio to play the Nicklaus course. Her allergy worsened, and Styver's solution was to bury Hercules with his mother in the family plot in Bakersfield. On the way to California, he'd play the Furnace Creek course in Death Valley, the only golf course in the world below sea level.

On the way, they spent a night at Caesars Palace, and while Styver was shooting seventy-five at the South Course, Dawn got her nails done for the first time in her life. That evening they drove to Death Valley in 115-degree heat.

People starved in Bangladesh and Somalia, but Death Valley had an eighteen-hole golf course. Crops died in Mexico and Bhutan for lack of water, but there were sprinklers on the fairways at Furnace Creek. While Styver played golf, Yvonne waited in the air-conditioned clubhouse drinking wine. She read, and she'd had three glasses of chardonnay when two college boys came in clicking their golf spikes.

The bartender had stepped out, and the blond boy walked around the bar and mixed rum and Cokes. "So who's winning?" he asked, looking up at the TV, where a football game was on.

"I hate football," she said, "but I think someone is ahead."

"What's your name?" the blond boy asked. "Can we buy you a drink?"

"Leave her alone, Ray," the other one said. "Her husband's playing golf."

"Maybe she wants a drink," Ray said. "She's a golf widow."

"A drink in return for sex, is that what you mean?"

"Now we're getting somewhere," Ray said.

"I'll have a double Stoli on the rocks."

Ray brought a full bottle and a glass of ice to her table and poured. "Say when."

"Now's always the best time," Yvonne said. "Meet me in the ladies' room in five minutes."

Ray stopped pouring.

Yvonne drank a swallow, stood up, and put the rest of the bottle in her backpack. She carried her drink with her to the ladies' room.

It was empty, and she locked the door and looked at herself in the mirror. Her clothes were modest—just shorts and a blouse—and she had on no make-up. She'd been reading quietly, drinking wine. What gave that boy the idea she could be spoken to, much less that she'd have sex?

She ran a brush through her hair, drank another swallow of vodka, then unlocked the door, and walked out past the pro shop and into the parking lot. Styver was standing beside the car doing curls with his hand weights. The keys were in the trunk lock.

"Did you break seventy?" she asked.

"Seventy-one," he said, and gave her his smile.

She took the keys from the trunk and got into the driver's seat. Hercules jumped over the back seat and into the passenger side. "You wouldn't have known or cared," she said, and she started the Mercury.

"Yvonne, goddammit, what are you doing? Cared about what? Hey, I'm going to drive."

She put the car in reverse and gave gas. The Mercury squealed around Styver, and she shifted to first and gunned it. The tires spun on the gravel. Right behind her head was an explosion; the window shattered and glass splintered everywhere. Then the car leaped forward, and Styver appeared in the rearview mirror shaking one hand weight in the air.

The blond boy, Ray, came out of the clubhouse and down the steps. "Hey, wait up!" he shouted.

She swerved past him and fled between the rows of date palms on either side of the drive.

Chapter 12

Rapid City was a disorganized patchwork of buildings and roads on the northeastern edge of the Black Hills. It had grown piecemeal out of supply and demand, supply being the stepchild. No one had thought to plan anything until it was already too late. Power lines and telephone wires were tangled webs in the air. As traffic increased, stoplights were put up. Modern apartment buildings rose alongside old houses; run-down warehouses and commercial buildings were cheaper to abandon than to tear down and rebuild. As the economy expanded—tourism in the Black Hills, light industry, and the air force base—confusion multiplied. The effect was of scattered obsolescence, random development, and clutter.

They stopped at a red light, and Elton woke with a start. "Where are we?" he asked. He slouched down in his seat.

"Why are you hiding?" Dawn asked. "Who do you think's going to see you?"

"I'm not hiding."

"Is this where you used to live?"

"No."

"Then sit up," Mattie said. "You have to face things."

"Oh, that's something to say," Dawn said. "Face things! You mean, the way you do?"

"What's that supposed to mean?" Mattie asked.

"Why are you giving up on the pivot field?"

"Yeah," Elton said, "I picked up rocks out there for two weeks."

"I broke loose all those rusted sprinkler heads," Dawn said.

"And I paid you," Mattie said.

"Come on, Mattie," Dawn said. "Money isn't the issue. The field's already planted. Without water, it'll be a wasteland."

"It'll be the way it was," Mattie said.

"We all put in hours," Dawn said. "You did, too. So what's the real reason?"

"I don't want to."

"I brought my parts list," Dawn said. "We could at least try to get the sprinkler working."

Mattie didn't answer.

"What he did was that bad?" Dawn asked.

"No," Mattie said. "We have too many other things to do."

Mattie got on I-90, juked among cars and trucks for a few miles, and exited at Deadwood for the Honda distributor. Elton stayed in the truck while Mattie and Dawn went in and bought a new starter housing and brake pads for the three-wheeler.

"You don't want to get the parts for the sprinkler?" Dawn asked. "The farm supply is right across the interstate."

"We'll get Elton's basketball goal and then go to a movie."

"You sure?"

"Yes."

They went to Eagle Hardware. Mattie made Elton come in with her to pick out a basketball goal. Naturally, he got the most expensive one.

"This is what you want?"

"Yes."

"You're happy?"

"Sort of."

"What else do you want?"

"A net."

"It comes with a net."

Elton looked at her. "The parts for the sprinkler."

Mattie looked at Dawn, then back at Elton. "If we do it, it'll mean longer hours."

"If we don't do it," Dawn said, "we'll be bored."

"All right," Mattie said. "We'll try."

She drove back to the farm supply warehouse, and Mattie and Dawn bought new sprinkler heads, three-inch gears, a grease gun, coolant, Teflon tape, fuses, wires, and assorted parts for $672.14. Elton refused to go in.

The movie was about an ugly fat man named Bub Barker, who worked in a meat-packing plant. His ex-wife hated him, his girlfriend shunned him, and women ignored him. He quit his job to think about his life, and thinking triggered weird events. Mosquitoes swarmed him. Leeches clamped on to his legs when he swam in the lake. Dogs attacked him. When he took his two children to the zoo, a giraffe bit his arm. He puzzled over why he was suddenly so good to eat. His girlfriend wanted him back; his wife loved him again; women found him irresistible. Meanwhile, Iris, the woman he really loved, only talked to him on the telephone.

At the end, things turned out with Iris, and even Elton laughed.

"Beware of what you wish for," Dawn said when they came out of the theater. "So now what? Where's the Moroccan restaurant?"

It was still light out. The traffic in the mall parking lot was scary.

"I'm not hungry," Elton said.

"What about ice cream?" Mattie asked.

"Not for me," Elton said.

"You don't like ice cream?"

"Not here," Elton said.

It was dark when they drove into Buffalo Gap. The streetlights were pale in the trees. They passed houses and trailers and barking dogs and Stockman's Bar, and Mattie turned east onto the plains. They'd had dinner in Hermosa, halfway back from Rapid. That was the first place Elton said he was hungry.

Out of Buffalo Gap, the moon flew among the clouds and over the silver wheatfields. Their headlights skimmed the gravel.

"Do you think Hector came and got his calf?" Dawn asked.

"He better have. And I hope Shelley's home."

"You never talked to her?"

"I never knew where she was."

"What is it, do you suppose, that we call home?" Dawn asked.

No one said anything.

A coyote crossed the road in the headlights, and they went on. The road, barely visible, ran straight ahead up a hill and disappeared.

Mattie turned to Elton. "You want to learn to drive?"

"I already know how."

"I'll drive, if you're tired," Dawn said.

"No, I want to see if Elton can. He'd be more help on the place if he can drive the truck."

"I said I know how."

"Good. Then you can drive us home." Mattie pulled to the side of the road and got out.

Dawn nudged Elton over behind the wheel. "Can you reach the clutch?"

"You be quiet," Elton said.

Mattie got in on Dawn's side. Elton pulled himself forward on the steering wheel to the edge of the seat, then gave gas and popped the clutch. The truck jerked forward.

"Now second," Mattie said.

"I know."

The truck lurched again, and Elton gave more gas.

"I want to sue," Dawn said. "Call the lawyer."

"You have to downshift to get up this next hill," Mattie said.

"Will you let me drive?"

Gravity slowed them on the uphill, and when Elton shifted, metal gnashed.

"I'd like a pound of lean," Dawn said.

"He's doing fine," Mattie said.

They chugged up the hill, and then the ride smoothed out. The moon followed them past a windmill tank and drifted through silver wheat. After a mile the road narrowed. Elton downshifted and turned ninety degrees along a section line.

"The gate's up ahead on the right," Mattie said.

Elton slowed, shifted to second, and slowed some more. He let the clutch out, and the truck coughed. He gave gas, but too much, and they roared across the cattle guard and just missed the gatepost.

"A near miss is really a near hit," Dawn said.

The truck careened over the grassy track toward the edge of the mesa.

"Maybe try stopping now," Mattie said.

Elton braked, but forgot the clutch, and the truck bucked and surged, and the engine died. Elton snapped open the door and jumped out and ran up the track.

"You go after him," Mattie said. "Be gentle."

Dawn got out and ran after Elton and caught up to him halfway up the hill.

"You have to lighten up, Elton," Dawn said. "Get a sense of humor."

"Then stop teasing me."

"All right, I've stopped."

The moment settled, and the moon drew them together.

"Maybe your idea of things is the fewer people you know, the less you can be hurt, but the truth is, the more people you know, the more they can help."

"That's what you say."

"Mattie's not going to let anybody hurt you. And neither will I."

"Would you shut up?" Elton said.

"Okay," Dawn said, "I'll shut up." She turned and walked back toward the truck, then stopped. "Don't get bitten by a snake."

Dawn walked on.

Mattie got into the driver's seat and picked up Dawn, and Dawn opened the passenger door when they came up to Elton.

"Come on, Elton," Mattie said. "Get in."

Elton ignored the open door and climbed into the truck bed.

They descended the old road along the moonlit gullies toward the river. The arc light at the Morton shone through the cottonwood trees. In the yard the Lincoln was parked where it always was, and the calf was gone.

Chapter 13

Shelley was stunned by the blue whirling lights roaring up the hill. Hank fell away and jerked up his jeans and ducked around the refrigerator into the trailer. She pulled up her panties and got her jeans on, just as two police cars passed behind the lower trailer. She crouched down, and her heart thumped in her ears. Two officers emerged from their cruisers holding pistols.

So much for afterglow. She lay down and dropped off the deck to the ground and slithered under the trailer.

"He's in there," one of the cops said. "I saw him go in."

Blue lights thrummed against the trailer, and she heard static on the police radio. "We're at Sunnyside," the other cop said. "The suspect's in sixteen. No sign of the woman. She's probably inside, too." A pause. "Yeah, right. Okay." He apparently hung up the radio. "Stay down, George. Backup's on the way."

"I don't want backup," George said.

One of the cops turned a spotlight on the trailer door, and the light flew back and forth across the side of the trailer. Then someone fired a shot. Shelley couldn't tell which cop it was, but she didn't hear it hit anything.

"You heard that, Larry," George said. "He fired on us. Am I right? You heard the shot."

Then one of the cops fired several more rounds, and the windows above her shattered. Then it was quiet again. Far off she heard a siren. She edged out and behind Hank's truck, then around the cab, where she was in plain sight of the police. One of the cops turned and leveled his pistol at her.

She put up her hands, and the spotlight glared on her. "Hank didn't do anything," she said.

"Who's that?" the radio cop said.

"It ain't Tobuk," George said.

Three more police cars turned into the trailer park, sirens wailing, and their blue lights cutting through the dark trees.

Shelley and Hank were taken in separately, and Sheriff Nolan came in to talk to Shelley personally. "You're that Remmel kid," he said.

"So?"

"I remember you from when you broke your arm in that squabble with Jimmy Pollard."

"It wasn't a squabble," Shelley said, "and I remember you, too. You didn't do a damn thing."

"Well, now you're in some real trouble," the sheriff said.

"We were playing pool. Those assholes owed us money."

"According to them, there was an assault and robbery."

"They thought Hank was hustling them."

"Was he?"

"All I know is they grabbed Hank and were going to pound on him."

"It's against the law to play pool for money," the sheriff said. "What were you doing at Hank's trailer?"

"We were talking."

"Were you buying or selling?"

"Buying or selling? You mean drugs?"

"We've got a warrant to search the trailer."

"I don't do drugs," Shelley said. "And besides, I have more on Officer George than you'll ever have on Hank and me."

"Hitting a man with a pool cue is assault with a deadly weapon."

"George fired into Hank's trailer without provocation," Shelley said. "I was there."

Sheriff Nolan was quiet for a moment.

"I heard what George said to Larry," Shelley said. "They wanted to kill Hank."

"George said he was fired on first."

"I know what I know," Shelley said, "and I'm not going to be quiet."

The sheriff scowled at her, and Shelley held his gaze.

"If I let you walk—"

"Hank, too."

"I haven't talked to Hank yet."

"I told you, the other guys started it. There were twenty people in Yogi's. There have to be witnesses. If I didn't do anything, he didn't, either. We did everything the same."

The sheriff turned away. "You get out of here before I change my mind," the sheriff said. "And I'd better not find your fingerprints on any drugs at Hank's."

Shelley got her purse and was on the street in ten minutes. She walked back to Yogi's and got her car, then stopped at the 7-Eleven and called Thella at her sister's. "I think you'd better get back here," she said.

"Did Hank get in trouble without me?"

"I bet he'll tell you about it."

Thella sighed. "He always does."

It was nine-thirty when Shelley got back to the ranch, and no one was there. She went straight to her room, took a shower, and lay on her bed in the dark and pondered what she'd done. A shot of tequila and a few beers weren't an excuse. Neither was love; fucking Hank Tobuk against a refrigerator wasn't exactly love. And what about fucking a girlfriend's boyfriend?

She was home, though. The sheriff had let her go. She remembered when she'd shoplifted. That was another time she wanted to forget. The junior class had taken a field trip to the museums in Rapid City, and when they were walking from the Heritage Museum to the geological museum, she and Thella and some other girls sneaked into a drugstore. Thella wanted to buy condoms to drop beside Mr. Armitage when he lectured on rocks, and while Thella was deciding which brand to buy, Shelley put a tube of coral lipstick in her pocket. A security guard saw her on the surveillance camera.

Shit flew. While the class went on to the museum, the store called her parents, and Shelley had to wait for them. She hadn't cared about punishment from the school. She'd be suspended for a few days and get zeros in her classes. At home, her mother would lecture her, and she'd be grounded. But what would her father do? Her father had always embraced her. That was how she took his silence. He accepted her excuses for where she'd been, and he never said anything when she came home late or got a bad grade or talked too long on the telephone. He loved her.

But now he'd see who she really was, a thief. His silence that had accepted her before would now be disapproval.

All that time waiting she dreaded that, and when the door opened to the security area, it wasn't her father who'd come, or both of them together, but her mother alone. Her mother paid for the lipstick and signed some forms, and when they got out of the store—right there on the sidewalk, as if she weren't ashamed—her mother hugged her.

Shelley remembered the ride home, too, how the wind pushed the truck and whined through the side window. Her mother never questioned her about what happened and hadn't yelled at her. Now and then she'd looked over and smiled carefully and bravely. It was the first time Shelley understood her mother was in pain, too. Whatever had made Shelley steal the lipstick was in her mother, too—that terrible, terrible need to be loved.

Neither of them ever said a word about it

And that was what she felt now, lying in bed in the dark.

It was a half hour before she heard the Toyota truck come into the yard, the doors open and slam closed. Downstairs the front door opened, and she heard Elton's voice, then her mother's muted through the floorboards. She got under the covers in case she had to feign sleep.

Chapter 14

I t was Saturday morning, and two dozen cliff swallows sat on the telephone wire out the kitchen window. Mattie should have been out with Dawn working on the sprinkler or up at Hector's checking on the calf, and she *would* have been farther into the day if Shelley hadn't unnerved her so. Her breaking up with Warren was almost expected, but her getting into a fight at Yogi's Bar worried her. That wasn't like Shelley. Not like the recent Shelley anyway. And she was afraid Shelley hadn't told her everything.

With all that, and the work she had to do, the last person Mattie wanted to see that morning was Lee Coulter. He was sitting in his truck by the gate, not getting out, not even looking at the house. He was reading. After ten minutes she finally went out and rapped on the hood of his truck.

Then he jumped.

"Did you come all the way out here to annoy me?" she asked.

"I was studying the site information," he said. "Have you changed your mind about showing me the place?"

"If I promised, I promised."

Lee closed his notebook. "Look, Mattie . . ."

"Who said you could call me Mattie?" She glared at him. "Let's get this over with."

"If you're going to be distressed, we don't have to go up there."

"Up where?" Shelley asked. She was on the porch. "What are you doing, Mom? You said we were laying pipe today."

"I told Mr. Coulter here I'd show him your father's dig site."

"Are you Shelley? Your father told me about you."

"I'd like to see it, too. Can you wait till I get my boots on?"

"We're not in any hurry," Lee said.

Shelley went back into the house.

"Look, Mr. Coulter, all I want is to be left alone. I see what you're doing."

"What am I doing?"

"I'm telling you in advance it won't work."

"What won't work?"

Shelley came out with her boots in her hand and sat on the porch step and put them on.

The most direct route to the mudmounds was on a steep four-wheeler track that ran up above the swampy ground east of the Ironweed Patch. Lee scraped bottom on rocks, braked down into a swale, and then churned full-tilt-boogie uphill to the lip of the ravine. The truck pitched at such an angle on the hill Mattie had to hold to the grip above the window, and Shelley in the bed was almost standing on the side rail.

"The sinkhole's up on the grassy knoll there," Mattie said. "You can see the tops of the trees. There's a spring a little to the east."

"Not an irrigation seep?"

"I don't think so. There are alders and wetland flowers like buttercups and shooting stars."

"Our investigation of the site would do far less damage than irrigating that tabletop."

"Are you saying I should stop growing alfalfa up there?"

"I'm not saying you should or shouldn't do anything," Lee said. "The human race should stop wasting its resources on cattle and sheep."

"What would we eat?"

"We shouldn't graze forests and nonreplenishable prairie or grow cattle feed on marginal land like that mesa. Arable river bottoms revitalize themselves. If we took care of the land, it would take care of us."

"The enlightened despot," Mattie said. "What else would you like to do?"

"I'd like to take you to dinner."

The truck cracked on rocks in the swale, and Lee revved it up the next hill.

"I meant politically," Mattie said.

"All the dams broken on all the rivers."

"So we'd have floods?"

"We have floods now. The dams silt up. I'd close wildlife refuges to hunting, outlaw clear-cutting, eliminate grazing on public lands."

"You have a serious agenda."

"I'm in favor of guaranteed national health care, a one hundred percent inheritance tax, and the death penalty. Three strikes and you're out. Why should society bear the cost of keeping around miscreants who don't know the minimum standards of decency?"

"You could run on the liberal-fascist ticket," Mattie said.

"There's no question capitalism undermines democracy. We're losing our bird and mammal species to deforestation, global warming, and habitat destruction. Do we, as a people, choose this, or does business choose it for us?"

"Are you asking me?"

"Did you know Americans consume ten times more energy than Chileans and a hundred times more than poor Africans?"

"And what do you see as a solution?"

"Ecoterror."

"I don't see how terrorism solves anything," Mattie said.

"Do you really want to be left alone?" Lee asked.

"What's wrong with wanting peace?"

"You didn't say you wanted peace. That's different."

"Doesn't everyone want peace?"

"My ex-wife wanted turmoil. If our life was calm too many days in a row, she threw something at me or wanted to move."

"What did she throw at you?"

"A plate of food once, my guitar, a typewriter. She threw my manual Triumph typewriter at me from across the room."

Mattie laughed. "So you argued?"

"We argued about who was going to change a lightbulb or whether to put dressing on the salad before it was served."

"Haney and I didn't argue," Mattie said.

"We could discuss this further at dinner," Lee said.

"I don't want to go to dinner."

"That sounds like a no."

Mattie smiled, though she didn't want to.

Lee was quiet a moment, driving across the rolling hills. "When we got divorced, she took the children," Lee said. "That wasn't fair."

The green spot was a mound of earth in the midst of a hillside of sparse grass. Lee stopped, and Mattie and Shelley stepped down, shaking out muscles and testing for broken bones. "It doesn't look like a sinkhole," Shelley said.

"Our maps suggest a compacted density," Lee said. "If it's a sinkhole, it would look like this, filled with dirt and debris."

"And maybe animals?"

"We don't start digging and leave a mess. That's what I was trying to tell your mother. We'd drill a core sample first. It might be a sinkhole that had cold water and no vegetation around it. You have to remember the climate was wetter and chillier a few hundred thousand years ago."

"But Daddy found that tooth."

"A fragment," Lee said. "It could have come from any mammoth passing by."

"So what if you found something in the core sample?" Shelley asked.

"It depends on what we found and what we were allowed to do. We might drill several core samples. Or we could do an exploratory dig of a few square meters. We wouldn't bring in a backhoe. You don't have to decide anything for a while."

Mattie was aware Lee was trying to persuade her through Shelley. He was respectful of Shelley's questions and cautious not to build up any expectations. But Mattie didn't want to hear what he said. She drifted away from their conversation and walked to the edge of the gully to the east. Alders and brush filled the ravine, and she heard water trickling. A wren sang in the thicket, but she couldn't see it for several minutes until the bird stopped singing and revealed itself by fluttering deeper into the thicket.

She heard Lee's voice on the moving air and felt the sensation of memory—the night when they'd walked out in the dark to check the fire and had occupied the same world. Perhaps it was easier to believe such a feeling when sounds came from no particular place, and the sky beckoned with swarming stars. In daylight the sky held her where she was, and voices were divisions in silence. Lee was talking with Shelley, and she was at the edge of the arroyo, impatient, waiting for the wren to sing again above the sound of the water.

Part III

O dear white children casual as birds,
Playing among the ruined languages,
So small beside their large confusing words,
So gay against the greater silences
of dreadful things you did. . . .

—W. H. Auden

Chapter 1

During first cutting the weather was sunny and breezy, and the hay dried fast. Evenings were cool, so there was enough dew to make bales stick together. The teeth on the cutting bar of the windrower weren't so often dulled by gopher mounds or broken on rocks, and the dry hay didn't clog the conveyor. With four of them sharing the work, everything went smoothly. Mattie and Elton did most of the windrowing, but Dawn took a turn, too. Mattie liked windrowing, even though the machine was decrepit. Haney had bought it thirty years' used at a farm sale, a Deere with no cab, no sunshade. The engine purred, and the meshing of the cutting bar and the canvas conveyor had a rhythm to it. It chopped the alfalfa low, threw it onto the wide canvas belt, which carried it to the center and dropped it beneath the machine into windrows. She marveled at the sheer inventiveness and convenience.

There was more work after that. Mattie had to bale at night or in the early morning, when there was enough dew, and the bales had to be stacked. Meanwhile Shelley irrigated the corn and Sudex and cooked and now and then took a turn moving bales.

Dawn was the grease. When the windrower didn't start one time, Dawn hot-wired it and fixed the starter that evening, and when the tying mechanism on the baler failed, Dawn had it working again in a couple of hours. The Case ran without any trouble pulling the baler; so did the International moving bales to the hay pens.

One evening Mattie and Dawn were lubing the windrower, and Hector stopped by to say hello. He leaned from the window of his pickup. "I was checking for worms in the corn," he said. "Things aren't looking too bad. But it's looking a little peaked from midfield on down. Who's irrigating?"

"Shelley mostly."

"I walked down into the field, and the ground looks dry. Is she running twelve hours?"

"I think so."

"And how many gates?"

"I don't know. I'll ask her. She should be opening ten gates. I sure hope the Pollards aren't taking water."

"They don't need to yet," Hector said.

"How's the calf," Dawn asked. "You still have him?"

"Right here," Hector said.

Dawn came up to the passenger side and patted the calf through the open window. "He's gained some weight," she said. "What've you named him?"

"I haven't. He's gained only about half of normal, but I admire his persistence, so I take him with me to work. There's no point in naming him, though, if he's going to die."

"Maybe he won't die if you give him a name," Dawn said.

"I guess that's a way to look at it. Mattie, part of the reason I came around is to tell you if you get tired, I can bale some for you."

"Thanks, Hector. We're all right for now."

"We all have plenty to do," Hector said, "but it's a standing offer."

"It's strange to be out there at night," Mattie said. "I want to see if I can do it."

The pivot field was the easiest to cut. There weren't gophers or rocks, no cheatgrass or thistles or weevils. But it took them three days in shifts of four hours each to finish it, and when the hay dried, Mattie baled it in two consecutive nights. It was grueling work, running the tractor so many hours, the headlights following the windrows, the noise, and looking back at the baler to see how the bale was rolling, up and back, up and back, spitting jellyrolls out behind. She thought of calling Hector a hundred times, but she didn't because she wanted to know what Haney must have thought all those hours he'd done it. Had he stayed focused on the work? Or had he longed for a man?

Shelley moved the bales with the International—two bales on the carrier in back and one on the prongs in front—and stacked them near the rock pile. That was the extent of her operating machinery, though she couldn't put the bales on the top tier of the stacks because she was afraid a bale would fall on her. Mattie did that, or Elton.

One Thursday evening, when Mattie was about to leave for a meeting at the irrigation district, Jimmy Pollard showed up. Shelley immediately disappeared upstairs. Jimmy had his dog with him, a mangy-looking, bull-headed mutt. He barked when Mattie came out onto the porch.

"Shut up, you," Jimmy said. He hit the dog in the head, and it shut up.

"You aren't going to the meeting?" Mattie asked. "We're voting on rates."

"Nah, they do what they want anyway."

"Maybe that's because you don't vote."

"Is Dawn here?" Jimmy asked. "Did you give her those feathers I sent over with my dad?"

"I gave them to her," Mattie said. "She's working now. I don't want you bothering her."

"It's kind of after hours. What's she doing?"

"We don't have hours," Mattie said. "She's welding a tooth on the cutting bar."

Jimmy got out of his truck and folded his hands across his chest and under his biceps. "I just wanted to say hello."

"I'll tell her—"

"You're going to your meeting," Jimmy said.

Elton came out onto the porch and picked up the basketball from a chair.

"If it isn't the Indian brat," Jimmy said.

"He works for me," Mattie said. "He isn't a brat."

"Let me see the ball," Jimmy said.

Elton hesitated, then passed Jimmy the ball.

Jimmy rolled the basketball down his arm. "You any good?"

"Okay."

"If I had time, I'd whip your ass in horse," Jimmy said.

"No, you wouldn't."

"Goddamn, if I wouldn't."

"We haven't put up the basket yet," Elton said.

Jimmy rifled the ball two-handed back to Elton. "I got to say hello to

Dawn," he said. He looked at Mattie and smiled. "Have fun at the meeting."

Jimmy turned and walked off toward the Morton.

"You go ahead," Elton said. "I'll take care of Dawn."

He dribbled the basketball down the steps and followed after Jimmy.

With the pivot, they put up more hay than ever before, but everyone else had a good crop, too, because of the rain in April and early May. The price at the feedlot dropped from $65 a ton to $35, and Mattie decided to wait to sell.

One crop with rain was possible, but two would have been a miracle, and when the fields were cleared, they worked in earnest to get water to the sprinkler. They loaded eight-inch pipe from the Ironweed Patch onto a trailer and unloaded it where Mattie marked the river crossing. Another load had to go up Sheep Table, but the farm road was too steep for the trailer. The choice was to hand carry each piece uphill from the river or to drive the trailer around the back way through the Pollards'. Mattie hated to ask Lute and Jimmy any favors, but it made sense to save the time. Neither Shelley nor Dawn wanted to ride with her, but Elton did, to protect her, he said. That was what he'd done for Dawn the night Jimmy came over. For a half hour he'd dribbled the basketball or thrown it against the wall of the incinerator right next to the open bay of the Morton until Jimmy left.

As it turned out, the Pollards weren't there when Mattie and Elton drove through, and that was lucky because, out of curiosity, Mattie wanted to see their hay crop. It wasn't bad, but it wasn't good, either, especially considering the rain. It looked as if they had let the hay lie in the field too long. But Lute had never done the little things—cultivating out cheatgrass, spraying for weevils, or reseeding weak patches. It was always someone else's fault his yield was small. Mattie knew they borrowed every year to keep their equipment and their cows. They prayed for a boom in cattle prices or maybe to win the lottery. That's what Sigurd Olafsson told her.

Haney had set in four lengths of pipe from the weir, but they still had to lay pipe down the cliff, over the river, and uphill on the other side to the sprinkler intake. They slid pipes downhill with ropes, fitted new gaskets, and horsed the pipes together, pushing and wiggling and shaking them until they locked into place. Then they canted steel fence posts against the pipes so the pipes wouldn't roll when they were filled with water.

It took three days of mucking back and forth to get the pipeline over the river. They braced twelve-foot cedar posts with horizontal two-by-sixes and looped cables around them, then waded the pipes across and fitted them together. According to Haney, the weight of water in the pipe would stabilize the structure.

After that, the task was easier. The land rose slightly from the river to the field, but the field was flat. In a morning they got the pipeline to the sprinkler. By then Dawn had assembled the gears, put on the new sprinkler heads, and greased and lubed the fittings. She'd cleaned a bird's nest and debris from the end, checked the timer, and replaced the wires and coolants in the generator. The sprinkler sections were driven by the torque of the one in front, but she couldn't test her work until there was water in the pipe.

On the afternoon of June 21 they all gathered on Sheep Table. Shelley opened a bottle of red wine, Mattie offered a benediction, and Elton fitted the boards into the weir. Water ran into the pipe, and they followed its rush to the edge of the cliff. It trickled first, then gurgled, then roared. Leaks sprang up from the pipe joints, but nothing serious, and the pipe didn't roll. They passed the wine—Elton took the biggest swig—and they all crossed their fingers.

Dawn rubbed stones together. "It'll work," Dawn said, "because it's the summer solstice."

Shelley and Dawn took the truck to the sprinkler, while Mattie and Elton climbed down the pipeline to the river. The pipe over the river filled slowly because the water had to go uphill on the other side. The Xs sagged, and in one of the sections a gate was open and water spurted out. Elton walked out on the slippery pipe and closed it. Finally the water collected and had nowhere to go but uphill to the sprinkler.

They all met up at the center of the pivot, Dawn switched on the generator, and they waited, passing the wine back and forth. Then water coughed in the sprinkler intake. The sprinkler heads sputtered and jerked, and finally water sprayed out. The huge insect inched forward.

Mattie ran out into the alfalfa and stood under a sprinkler, and Elton joined her in a rain dance.

"Weird," Shelley said. "That is weird, even for my mother."

Chapter 2

Then there was a lull. Mornings and evenings they irrigated the corn and the Sudex and the alfalfa. Mattie cultivated north of the river; she and Elton built a fence around the hay pen at the pivot; Dawn sharpened the cutting bars and tuned up the Case and put up the basketball goal at the west end of the Morton. She had apparently discouraged Jimmy Pollard because he hadn't been back to see her. Elton sprayed thistles and punched gophers and in one week killed fifty starlings, one for every state in the Union. Every day the sun stared from a blue sky.

During these days Shelley slept, read mysteries, and did laundry. For the hay cutting she'd operated on nervous energy, but now she collapsed into self-examination. What was she doing with her life? The only thing that got her going was arguing with her mother about the dig site.

"I want to keep the land as it is," Mattie said.

"But irrigated land isn't as it was. That's not preserving land. Why can't we ever do what I want?"

"Because you never follow through."

"Because you never follow through," Shelley said in a singsong voice. "Are you worried about the sinkhole or Lee Coulter?"

"I was against this before I met Lee Coulter."

"I don't see the harm in getting preliminary studies," Shelley said.

"Preliminary studies lead to further studies," Mattie said. "Why allow the first step?"

"Because I want to see what's there. You're the one who's always saying it's better to know than not to know."

"Will you deal with the museum people?"

"Yes."

"All right. Preliminary studies. But that's all I'm agreeing to."

"Okay," Shelley said. "It's a deal."

On a slow Thursday, Trini asked Mattie to go with her for an overnight in Rapid City to stay at the Hotel Alex Johnson and eat in a fancy restaurant. "An old women's night out," Trini said.

"I can't imagine anything worse," said Mattie.

"You need a break. And you liked the country tennis."

"That was different."

"You never want to enjoy yourself?"

"If there's one thing I can't stand, it's having a good time," Mattie said.

But Trini was persuasive, and Shelley and Dawn urged her to go, too. Mattie made Shelley and Dawn agree to rebuild the shower in the Morton; if she had to suffer, so did they. The next day Trini picked Mattie up in her Suburban, and they drove to Rapid City.

The Hotel Alex Johnson was built in the 1920s as a tribute to the Great Sioux Nation, though it was constructed of red brick and had German *Fachwerk* at the top. The lobby was opulent Indian: blankets, sculptures, paintings of chiefs, together with an immense red-patterned oriental carpet and a table exhibiting miniature flags of the world.

Mattie and Trini checked into a suite on the tenth floor. Their two rooms were of turquoise-and-western decor. They had carved pine furniture, dried flowers in a vase, and zigzag Indian quilts on the beds. A bellhop brought up their bags and opened the curtains, revealing the gray buildings of Rapid City sprawling toward the Black Hills.

When they'd traveled in Europe, Haney liked pensiones. He wanted to be in the essence of a place, in the music and the smells and the shouting in the streets. In Paris they stayed in Montparnasse, and in Rome on the Via Margutta near the Piazza del Popolo. He absorbed the neighborhoods. The last hotel she'd stayed in, though, was the Copley Plaza in Boston when Haney needed to entertain gallery owners. Mattie remembered that time as bliss—breakfast from room service, swimming in a heated pool, sleeping in a king-sized bed. But the memory was altered; bliss long ago was tainted now.

Trini made two gin and tonics at the bar, and Mattie took hers into the bathroom. Trini had the idea of going dancing later, but that was the last thing Mattie wanted to do. She showered long and hot and, as she dried herself, heard Trini talking on the phone.

"Who was that?" Mattie asked when she came from the bathroom.

"I ordered something from room service," Trini said. "Why don't you lie down and relax?"

"I'd relax if you'll promise to forget about going dancing."

There was a knock on the door, and Trini opened it, and a young woman in a loose white cotton smock stood there.

"Come in," Trini said. Then she turned back to Mattie. "I'll be back in an hour."

The woman in the smock wheeled in a portable table, and Trini closed the door and was gone. "I'm Nadine," the woman said. "You're the one who's getting the massage?"

Mattie and Nadine stared at each other. Nadine was in her twenties, Mattie guessed, and nondescript—a sunless face, limp brown hair, eyes of indeterminate color. The smock hid her plumpish body.

"It's paid for," Nadine said.

Mattie didn't want a massage, paid for or not, and she'd have said so if she hadn't felt sorry for Nadine.

"Do you want music?" Nadine asked.

"No, thank you. No music."

Nadine wheeled the table to the window and unfolded it. "Incense?" Nadine smoothed a sheet over the table.

"No music, no incense," Mattie said.

"You're already undressed," Nadine said. "Climb up and lie down. Let's untie that robe."

Nadine untied the belt on the robe, and Mattie climbed up and lay on her stomach and put her face into the doughnut headrest. She felt foolish. And: *Goddamn Trini!*

"Usually I ask if there's any pain or soreness," Nadine said. "But we'll just be quiet. Do you agree?"

Mattie didn't answer.

Nadine slid Mattie's robe off her shoulders, and Mattie felt a sheet flutter over her body. It had been years since she'd been undressed in front of anyone else besides Haney. It wasn't that she was so much self-conscious as that she'd acquired the habit of privacy. And who could relax in such a position? Her arms and shoulders were skewed; her stomach and legs felt as if they were sodden weights.

Nadine's hands moved over her back, together and then separate, down her spine, up her sides and over her shoulders. The room was quiet. That was good, and out the window city lights were coming out of the dusk. Nadine's hands were soft hands, inquisitive, intrusive, flaring over her shoulders and then along her shoulder blades, forcing their way inward, blaming. Mattie supposed she was to give in to Nadine's hands, but instead she coiled and uncoiled her fists. She took deep breaths, but there wasn't enough oxygen in the room.

Nadine stood directly in front of her in thick-soled shoes. The hands kneaded her shoulders, pressed her neck, and Mattie closed her eyes, feeling guilty for resistance. Her muscles were hard, like petrified rock. Nadine's fingers arced, punctured, bore in. A few minutes seemed forever. The heels of Nadine's hands dug into the back of Mattie's right thigh, her calf, legs hard as obsidian from shoveling and lifting earth, walking and carrying pipes. The long muscles of her upper thighs were blunt stone. Nadine rubbed the heel, the sole, the ball of her foot, the toes one by one.

Erosion. Nadine's hands glided over her skin, and Mattie felt herself weaken.

Her body wore away.

Breaking.

Chipping.

Loosening.

Smoothing out.

Nadine's hands were wind and water, like light. The light broke the stone into colors.

Yellow.

Orange.

Red.

Lilac.

Azure.

Smooth strokes up her legs, up her back to her shoulders again, down her arms. The pounding, lifting, driving, carrying, picking, cooking—all the work in her arms and legs melted into light.

A key fitted into the lock, and the door opened. "Mattie?"

Mattie woke and sat up.

"Are you okay?" Trini asked.

"I think so." Mattie pulled the sheet over her breasts. Her body took its shape again, muscles and bone reconstructed from nothing. Blood flowed back into her capillaries, her arteries, her heart.

"Nadine said she'd get her table later. Are you ready for dinner?"

"I'm ready to sleep for two months," Mattie said.

"So it wasn't a waste of time?"

"No, it was wonderful," Mattie said. "Let's go dancing."

Chapter 3

The shower Haney had put in the Morton was mildewed. The iron pipes leaked, and the wooden walls were rotted out. While Dawn broke apart the cement shower pad with a sledgehammer, Shelley dismantled the walls with a crowbar. "This is a man's work," Shelley said. "Why can't my mother hire a man?"

"It's the work of the person who does it," Dawn said. "There isn't much to know about plumbing except shit runs downhill and payday's on Friday. Whatever happened to that guy who was with you in the bar fight?"

"I don't know. Living out here, you never know what's going on unless someone tells you."

Dawn shoveled chunks of cement into a wheelbarrow. "Were you scared?"

"Hell, yes. I've seen fights in movies, but it's different when you're in one. I hit a fat guy with a pool cue, and the guy I was with, sort of with, pretty much laid both guys out cold."

"Who was he?"

"Just someone I know. I was drunk, I guess. I've thought about that, whether I'd have done what I did if I hadn't been drunk."

"People will do just about anything," Dawn said. "Being drunk gives them an excuse."

"Have you ever used a Skil saw?" Dawn asked.

"You're kidding me, right?"

"You're going to saw studs and floor joists," Dawn said. "Press the trigger to start it. Brace the wood, and keep the guide straight." She sawed a board and then handed the saw to Shelley. "What do you know about Jimmy Pollard?"

"He's a creep."

"Is he a liar?"

"Jimmy doesn't know what the truth is, so maybe he's not a liar. Why, what's he told you?"

"He invited me to a movie."

"Probably *Lethal Weapon Sixteen*," Shelley said.

Dawn slid two-by-fours across the floor. "Here, these are measured. Saw them."

Shelley sawed the studs where Dawn had marked them, and when she'd done the first several, Dawn gave her more. Shelley liked sawing. She liked the smell of sawdust and the noise of the saw, and she could see her accomplishment.

But she was still caught up on Jimmy Pollard, and she turned off the saw. "So did you accept?"

"What do you think?"

"I think maybe you did."

"Give me some credit."

"I was trying to, but I thought better of it. I mean, if you say you're the morning star, and you've got dolphins flying around at your camp . . . Then there are the magic stones."

"So you think I'm ignorant?"

"And look at your body."

"You don't think a woman can have a good body and a good mind? That's garbage. That's what men want us to think."

"Is that right?"

"The body is only the residence of the spirit."

"Please," Shelley said. "Anyway, why aren't you with a man?"

"I haven't found one good enough."

"Have you been in love?"

"Once. That's how I know how bad things can be."

"My friends are all sure they'll live happily ever after."

"That's not love. That's romance. If you believe that, you're dead in the water. What do you think about love?"

"It's like a dream," Shelley said, "something not real. My mother loved my father, but when he died, she woke up and there was nothing there."

"But dreams are real," Dawn said. "Haven't you ever come in a dream?"

"What are you talking about?"

"Orgasm," Dawn said. "You know . . ."

Shelley turned on the saw and cut three more floor joists. Then she turned off the saw again. "No," she said. "Not in a dream or any other time."

Dawn smiled. "It's worth trying for," she said. "But an orgasm isn't love, either."

The phone rang, and Shelley answered it at the workbench.

"I'm trying to reach Mattie Remmel," the man said.

"She's not here," Shelley said. "May I take a message?"

"Is this Shelley?"

"Who's this?"

"This is Dennis Burke. I'm calling—"

Shelley hung up.

"Who was that?" Dawn asked.

"Nobody."

The phone rang again.

"You want me to answer it?" Dawn asked.

"It's for my mother."

The phone kept ringing, and finally Shelley picked up the receiver.

"Don't hang up," Dennis Burke said. "I'm a friend of your parents."

"I know who you are," Shelley said. "We have your letters."

There was a pause on the other end of the line. "I just heard the terrible news about your father. If I could explain—"

"You can't explain. There's nothing we don't know."

Shelley clicked off again and looked at Dawn. Then she ran out of the Morton.

The phone rang again, but Shelley kept running until she reached the barn. She heaved open the door, grabbed one of her father's sculptures, and carried it outside and pitched it into the ravine.

Then she went back and got another and another and another.

Chapter 4

That evening after dinner Elton wanted to play basketball, and Dawn played him one-on-one to ten. Elton won both games. "What about horse?" he asked. "You any better at that?"

"I'm tired," Dawn said. "I've been working all day."

"So have I."

"But you're younger."

"You're chicken."

"If there's anything you should know about me, Elton, it's that I'm not chicken. No more basketball today."

Elton dribbled and shot more baskets, and Dawn went inside. Shelley had done the dishes and cleaned the stove and was sitting at the table looking at a clothes catalog.

"How much energy do you have left?" Dawn asked.

"Not enough to do more plumbing."

"Will you go somewhere with me?"

"I promised myself to stay out of town for a while."

"It isn't in town."

"Where is it then? What's 'it'?"

"If I tell you, you might not go."

"Why should I go if you won't tell me?"

"Because you're curious."

"No, I'm not."

"Okay, then, don't go."

They took the four-wheeler. Dawn drove because she knew where she was going, and Shelley rode behind, carrying a small backpack. The sky was broken with scattered moonlit clouds. Shelley thought they were going to do a ritual sacrifice in the pivot field, or maybe on Sheep Table, or maybe they were looking for dolphins. Clouds were islands, and dolphins might cascade through the stars.

They headed west and up the hill to Sheep Table, where Dawn cut the engine. "Now we walk," she said.

Shelley unsaddled, and Dawn took the pack. "What's in there?" Shelley asked.

"Leftover chicken from dinner. Gloves, pliers, and a crowbar."

"Any beer? I could use a beer about now."

Dawn shouldered the pack, crossed the pipe from the weir, and stopped at the Pollards' gate.

"We're going to the Pollards'?" Shelley asked.

Dawn climbed over the gate and strode away, and Shelley followed. She ran to catch up.

"Jimmy wanted me to see his eagles," Dawn said. "He told me anytime."

"But he didn't mean this way."

"Probably not. But we're not making a social call."

"So I gathered."

The track dropped off into a small glen where cows grazed the meadow. They climbed to the next ridge, where they looked down into the Pollards' yard. The house was a stucco shack with a low A-shaped tin roof, and the changing blue-gray light of a TV moved at one of the windows. A pole light illuminated the other buildings—a run-down metal silo, a shed beside a corral, an open barn where a tractor was parked. The hay pen was only half full of bales.

"Not much of a ranch," Dawn said. "Have you ever been in the house?"

"No."

"Are they drinkers?"

"They're Pollards," Shelley said. "I expect they drink."

"Do you think there are any eagles?"

"How would I know?"

"Jimmy gave me feathers," Dawn said. "And he said I should come and look at them."

"Maybe he wanted to get you over here."

"And he did," Dawn said.

The back door opened abruptly, and light spilled out of the doorway. The Pollards' dog wandered out to the shadow of a tree and lifted his leg, and a man came out after and peed into the weeds.

"Is that Lute?" Dawn asked.

"He's mean," Shelley whispered. "So's the dog."

"So was Styver," Dawn said.

Lute went back inside, and the dog sniffed Lute's mark and peed on it.

"If there are any eagles," Shelley said, "they'd be behind the silo or the shed, somewhere you couldn't see them driving in."

The dog looked across the road and started to bark.

"Well, shit," Shelley said, "We can't go down there with that dog out. Let's go home."

Dawn picked up a stone and flung it toward the house. It cracked on other stones, and the dog barked louder, and kept barking when Dawn threw another stone.

"I hope those aren't lucky stones," Shelley said.

After a minute Jimmy came to the door. "Gizzard, get in here," he yelled.

The dog turned back to the house, and Jimmy let him in. Dawn and Shelley waited another minute, watching the house.

"Two of us will make twice as much noise," Dawn said. "You're staying here."

"I was going to," Shelley said.

Each measured the other. Dawn put out her hand, and Shelley squeezed it.

Dawn stayed as far from the light as she could, though with moonlight she could see pretty clearly where she was going. She picked her way downhill slowly, quietly, watching for snakes. A couple of times she looked back at Shelley, and Shelley waved.

Halfway down, a rock kicked loose and rolled to the bottom of the hill, and Dawn stopped for a minute. The TV still flickered in the house. Gizzard didn't bark. No one came outside. Shelley gave a thumbs-up.

At the edge of the yard Dawn paused to listen. Cattle stirred. She heard faint voices from the TV. Then she ran across open ground to the silo, into light and back into darkness, where an acrid smell rose around her. It wasn't manure or mildewed hay, but something rotting—the reeking carcass of a deer splayed over a tractor tire. A little farther on, she saw the eagles' cage.

She inched closer. The cage was a pipe frame, five feet square, set on two sawhorses. Woven wire spaced with barbed wire braids kept the birds in. The eagles—dark bodies with tapered heads—were at the back. They were beautiful birds.

Dawn opened the eye hook latch, swung the door open, and jostled the cage to encourage the birds out. They flapped their wings, stubby wings clipped at the shoulder. She hadn't thought of what to do if the birds couldn't fly. She'd brought gloves to hold the birds if she had to, pliers to cut wire, and a crowbar to pry nails, but what now?

She put on the gloves and took out scraps of chicken from her pack. "Here, baby," she said. She jiggled the cage and held out the scraps. "Here, sweetheart. You know what I want. I know you know. Come and get it."

One of the eagles raised its clipped wings and hopped down from its perch. It stretched its head toward the meat, and as the bird did that, Dawn caught it against the side of the cage, maneuvered its neck against the pipe frame, and held it there. The bird clawed and flapped, and then it shuddered and went limp.

She turned to the other bird, whose eye glittered in the moonlight. "Here, baby," she said. "I know you know."

The other bird wouldn't come to her, and she reached with her crowbar through the door and flailed at it. The bird backed into the corner of the cage, and Dawn trapped it there with her hand. The bird tore her forearm with its beak, but she stunned it with the crowbar and then snapped its neck.

Blood flowed into her glove and pooled in the fingers, and she picked up her pack and backed away slowly. Then she turned and saw the Pollards, Lute with a shotgun across his chest.

"They dead?" Jimmy asked.

Dawn didn't move.

"See about them feathers," Lute said.

Jimmy pushed Dawn away from the cage and turned on his flashlight. "One's clean," Jimmy said, "but the other's beat up pretty bad."

"This the woman who works over to the Remmels?" Lute said. "I think she come here to get our attention."

Lute jabbed Dawn with the barrel of the shotgun.

"I think she did," Jimmy said. "I asked her to come over."

"We better wash down the feathers 'fore the blood soaks in. They'd be worthless to the damn tribe."

"Now?" Jimmy said. "We got important things to take care of here."

"Now," Lute said.

Lute grabbed Dawn's arm and dragged her across to the water trough at the side of the yard, and Jimmy carried the dead eagles. He laid them in the dirt, then clamped a hose on the spigot, and turned the water on. He sprayed down the bird with the blood on it.

"She's got blood on her, too," Lute said. "Better hose her off while you're at it."

Jimmy turned the water on Dawn, soaking her thin shirt and her jeans.

"I like that wet look," Lute said.

"Take off the gloves," Jimmy said. "Wash your hands before supper."

Dawn peeled off her bloody glove and threw it at Jimmy.

"That's enough," Lute said. "We don't want her too clean."

Jimmy turned the water off and propped the wet eagle on the trough to dry. Lute poked Dawn again with the shotgun.

"Move over onto the grass."

Dawn recoiled and knocked into Jimmy, and then she ran. There was nowhere to go except across the yard.

Lute fired a blast over her head, and buckshot skittered against the silo.

Dawn ran full speed, but there were footsteps after her. She was near the backhoe when Jimmy caught her and pulled her down.

"Okay," Dawn said, breathing hard. "Okay."

"I'm not letting you up."

"Just not in the house," Dawn said.

Lute came up to them still lying on the ground, and he swung the barrel of the gun into Dawn's knee. "There. She won't run anymore."

Dawn twisted on the ground, and Lute raised the barrel to hit her again.

"Wait," Jimmy said. "We want her awake. It's more fun if she makes noise."

"Get her jeans off then," Lute said. "Maybe after, we'll give Gizzard a turn."

"Let herself get her jeans off," Jimmy said. "That's consent. She does that for us, maybe we won't call the sheriff about the trespassing and stealing."

"Or maybe we won't do worse," Lute said.

"All right," Dawn said. She got up slowly to one knee and unbuttoned her shirt, pulling each button loose deliberately. When she was done, she held the corners of the shirt out like wings.

Lute handed Jimmy the shotgun, unfastened his belt, and pulled his pants down to his knees. "I guess we should take what's offered."

Then headlights flew up beyond the hill, and a motor roared. A truck came fast around the curve and straight ahead into the yard. Jimmy whirled and fired the shotgun, and a headlight went out on the truck. The truck careened forward and stopped twenty feet away, the one headlight splayed out into the yard over Dawn and Jimmy and Lute with his pants down and his cock dangling from his underwear.

Hector Lopez opened the driver's door and stood in the doorframe with a 30.06. Dawn limped toward him.

Chapter 5

Two long-billed curlews squawked from side-by-side fence posts when Mattie and Trini turned in at the north gate. The sun shimmered across the neighbor's wheatfield, and on her side of the fence, Hector's cows were bunched at the corner of the pasture. "The herd mentality," Mattie said. She got out and opened the gate.

They crossed the bridge and curved up from the river bottom through the cottonwoods. Shelley and Dawn were sitting at the picnic table drinking Coronas when Trini pulled in. Dawn had a bandage on her arm.

Mattie and Trini got out and stretched, and Shelley came over.

"What happened to Dawn?" Mattie asked.

"She had sort of an altercation."

"With whom?"

"The Pollards."

"What kind of altercation?"

"You'd better drink a beer first, Mom."

"I don't want a war with the Pollards."

"It was a skirmish," Shelley said, "not a war."

Trini opened the back of the Suburban and handed out two sacks of groceries. "I think I'll put my frozen stuff in your freezer and sit a minute. Is that all right?"

"Of course it is," Mattie said. "You bought the Redhook."

Shelley took the two sacks, one in each arm. "The bottom line is Hector saved Dawn's ass."

They all carried groceries to the kitchen, and Trini put her frozen juice and ice cream into the freezer in the vestibule.

"You all had a good time?" Shelley asked.

"It was all right," Mattie said.

"She had a great time," Trini said. "She wants to go to San Francisco next."

"In my dreams," Mattie said. "Did anyone call?"

"Uncle Earl wanted to know about first cutting. And Lee Coulter. The museum is doing a plant inventory this week. And who else? I can't remember."

"Did you finish the shower in the Morton?"

"Of course. What did you think?"

"Is Elton irrigating?"

Trini levered open two Red Hooks and handed one to Mattie. "Calm down now, Mattie. Work doesn't start until tomorrow. Let's you and me go out and sit."

"I want to know how Hector saved Dawn's ass," Mattie said.

"Ask Dawn," Shelley said. "I'll bring out a cooler and some beer."

Mattie and Trini went outside to the picnic table where Dawn was sitting. The table had four empty Corona bottles on it and a plate of limes.

"Tell me what happened," Mattie said. "I told you I didn't want any trouble with the Pollards."

"It wasn't that bad," Dawn said.

"They hurt you?"

"One of the eagles hurt me."

"You went over there to see the eagles?"

"At ten o'clock at night," Shelley said. "She wanted to let them go." She set the cooler on the ground beside the picnic table.

"I didn't expect the Pollards to find out I was there," Dawn said.

"But they caught you?"

"Shelley was on the ridge and ran and got Hector."

Mattie looked at Shelley. "You were there, too?"

"Dawn wanted me to go. It was a good thing I did."

"Well, Jesus," Mattie said.

"It was a near hit, but nothing happened," Dawn said. "Tell us about Rapid City."

"Mattie was spectacular," Trini said. "We went to AJ's Ballroom at the hotel, and we danced with a group of Japanese businessmen."

"You danced, Mom?"

"I used to know how," Mattie said. "But who would I dance with out here?"

"Not Dad."

"The Japanese men weren't much for conversation," Mattie said. "But they were good dancers."

"And she had a massage," Trini said.

"Not willingly," Mattie said.

"Yes, willingly," Trini said.

Dawn got up. "I'll go make some nachos."

They gabbed and finished one beer and had another. Dawn came back with a tray of hot nachos, and Trini took a gooey one with a jalapeño on it. "Do you know what they say about nachos?" She sniffed the one in her hand.

"We don't want to," Mattie said.

Trini took a slow, oozy bite. "They taste like Mexican food."

Shelley groaned, and Dawn smiled. Mattie didn't get it.

"Here's another one," Trini said. "A girl asks her mother about the birds and bees, and the mother explains when the man puts his penis in the woman, his sperm swims up and fertilizes the egg, and that's where a baby comes from. The child nods seriously and asks, 'What happens when the man puts his penis in the woman's mouth?' 'Well, sweetheart,' the mother says, 'that's where jewelry comes from.'"

Shelley and Dawn laughed, but Mattie stood up.

"Oh, come on, Mom. It wasn't that bad."

"I'm going to get more limes."

"And more beer," Trini said.

Mattie walked across the lawn and felt the skew of the world. One beer was her limit, and she'd already had three, and not much for lunch, and she was going to have more. She was going to have a half dozen if she wanted to.

She heard thumps on the other side of the house, Elton dribbling and shooting baskets, and she went to the corner and watched him for a minute. He was good. He arced in a shot from long range, and he could dribble like a madman. He was maybe imagining himself an NBA star— that's what Loren had done about baseball—but how could an Indian be a star basketball player? The ball shuddered on the rim and fell away. Maybe Elton had played on a team somewhere, the name of a team might help them find out where he'd come from.

She got the limes, and more beer, and Haney's bottle of Jack Daniel's and four jelly glasses, and went back outside to the picnic table. Trini and Dawn were discussing haircuts.

"That's what Mattie needs," Trini said. "A new hairstyle."

"I like Mom's hair," Shelley said. "She needs a different personality."

"Why, thank you," Mattie said. She skewered Redhook ales into the ice in the cooler. "Who wants Jack Daniel's?"

Everyone raised her hand, and Mattie put ice in the four glasses and poured them full.

"I could cut your hair," Dawn said. "I learned to cut hair in the army."

"When were you in the army?"

"I lied about going to vo-tech school in Montana, but I can fix machines, and I can cut hair. Let's take a vote."

"A vote about what?" Shelley asked.

"Why do you always think there's a vote?" Mattie asked.

"Get the scissors," Trini said. "Dawn can cut my hair. I don't care what Allen thinks. He has a beard, and he's screwing that paraplegic woman."

"What's a beard have to do with anything?" Shelley asked.

"He's not screwing a paraplegic," Mattie said.

"Just get the scissors."

Shelley took four Redhooks from the cooler and passed them around. "I'll be right back."

"Bring a chair, too," Dawn said, and she stripped the top of her beer with her thumb.

Shelley came back with scissors, a comb, and a brush, and a stool from the kitchen.

"I'll go first," Mattie said, and she sat down on the stool.

"Oh, oh, Mom's drunk," Shelley said.

Dawn brushed Mattie's hair out. "How many years since you've cut your hair?"

"A long time. At least twenty years."

"Do you really want it cut?"

"Cut it all off," Mattie said.

"Do you remember when Shelley shaved her head?" Trini asked. "She looked like a baby bird."

"Not that short," Mattie said. "Medium."

"But it's so beautiful," Dawn said.

"I need a different personality," Mattie said.

Dawn snipped and shaped, and Mattie's hair fell, beautiful reddish curls on the green grass.

They went on drinking and talking while Dawn worked. They yakked about dresses and whether cowboy boots made the man and about health foods, and Mattie told about dancing with one Japanese man who called her darling. They drank Jack Daniel's and opened more beers. Mattie warned everyone to slow down, but she didn't slow down, and neither did they.

When Dawn was done cutting, Shelley walked all the way around, inspecting the job.

"Pretty good," Shelley said. "You look younger, Mom."

"How much younger?"

"She looks stylish," Dawn said. "Look in any magazine."

"So what I want to know is whether we need rottweilers," Mattie said.

"Rottweilers? What for?"

"The Pollards."

"We need guns," Shelley said.

"Let's take a vote," Dawn said.

Mattie poured the last of the Jack Daniel's, and Trini raised her glass. "Here's to sex," she said.

"Here's to PMS," Dawn said. "Problems men start."

"Everything is their fault," Trini said. "They think with their dicks."

"'Dick' is such a terrible word," Mattie said.

"So is 'penis,'" Shelley said.

"'Cock' is bad, too," Trini said. "What about 'pecker'?"

Mattie giggled.

"'Lever'? 'Schlong'? 'Woody'?"

"'Woody'?" Mattie laughed out loud.

"Why do we think of hard objects?" Dawn said. "Why not 'dishrag'?"

"How about 'Johnson,'" Shelley said, "or 'one-eyed snake'?"

"Peter, prick, pole, prod, poker," Trini said.

"You've given this some thought," Mattie said.

"Let's take a vote," Dawn said.

They laughed and drank some more.

"Let's vote on Lee Coulter," Shelley said.

"Who's Lee Coulter?" Trini asked.

"Lee Coulter is my mother's suitor," Shelley said.

"He is *not*," Mattie said.

"He asked you out."

"You had a date and didn't tell me?" Trini said.

"There was no *date*."

"Is he a decent man?"

"That's an oxymoron," Dawn said.

"He was heartbroken when she said no," Shelley said. "All in favor say aye."

"Why are you in conspiracy?" Mattie asked. "If I don't want to, I don't want to."

"Mattie's right," Trini said. "There are other choices besides men."

"Aye," Dawn said.

"Aye," said Shelley.

"Aye," Trini said. "Three ayes and one abstention."

"This is not a democracy," Mattie said.

"Next case, Shelley," Dawn said.

"No prospects," Shelley said.

"What about the English teacher?" Mattie asked.

"He's got a girlfriend."

"Serious girlfriend or frivolous girlfriend?" Trini asked.

"At least he isn't gay," Mattie said.

Dawn leaned forward. "Why don't you inquire about the girlfriend?"

Three hands went up.

"What about you, Trini?" Mattie said. "All you do is complain about Allen."

"Well, he's deficient."

"What about Hector Lopez?"

"Hector *Lopez?*" Shelley said, making her voice tease.

"Hector's a decent man," Trini said.

"Why didn't you want to stop at his house the other day?" Mattie asked.

"Because I hit on him, and he turned me down."

"You hit on Hector?" Mattie asked. "Is that what happened?"

"That's what happened. I wanted to make Allen jealous. Is that pathetic or what?"

They were all silent a moment. A meadowlark sang from the Iron-weed Patch.

"Dawn's the last case," Shelley said.

"Dawn's been dealt a winning hand," Mattie said. "She doesn't need any help from us."

"I have to pee," Trini said.

She got up from the bench, pushed her jeans down, and squatted by the hedge.

"Me too," Shelley said. She reeled over to where Trini was.

Mattie and Dawn came over and pushed down their pants, too. They all squatted by the hedge.

Mattie burbled out a fart, and Trini keeled face first into the grass, laughing, with her rear end in the air. Dawn pushed Trini sideways, and Trini rolled over, still laughing. Then Shelley pushed Dawn and Mattie. In a minute they were all writhing on the grass.

Chapter 6

The sinkhole site was measured and photographed from the ground and from the air. Tests were done of the surface soil. A casual list was made of mammals, reptiles, and birds, though, as Shelley said, the main concern of the preliminary studies was plants:

> Little bluestem (*Andropogon scoparius*)
> Blue grama (*Bouteloua gracilis*)
> Buffalo grass (*Buckloë dactyloides*)
> Prickly pear (*Opuntia* spp.)
> Yucca (*Yucca glauca*)
> Western wheatgrass (*Agropyron smithii*)
> Prairie June grass (*Koeleria pyramidata*)
> Blue larkspur (*Delphinium nuttalianum*)
> Yarrow (*Achillea millefolium*)
> Indian paintbrush (*Castilleja sessiliflora*)

Shelley spent her spare time at the site, and even some of her work time. She liked being there with Lee and the crew—two or three people, usually, depending upon the task. They couldn't very well refuse the volunteer help of the owner's family.

In the evenings Shelley read geological history or researched questions Lee had posed: How had the water table changed since the last immersion by an inland sea? If they were to dig, what invertebrate fossils could they expect to uncover? What forces besides climate would be evident in the substrata?

She studied the fossils in the boxes in the barn. Her father had a few books, and Lee lent her more. She spent the evening hours at the rolltop immersed in ancient history. There were four geological eras: the Pre-Cambrian, Paleozoic, Mesozoic, and Cenozoic. In the first phase of the

Paleozoic, the Cambrian period, five hundred to six hundred million years ago, the climate was tropical, and water covered most of the earth. Multifarious life forms teemed in the sea and left a rich fossil record, mostly of trilobites. In the Paleozoic, life evolved from shell-bearing creatures to bony fish to miraculous microscopic land-dwelling herby plants. During this profound change the earth re-formed itself several times. Mountains rose, and inland seas subsided. Plants grew from seeds instead of spores, struck roots into the soil instead of taking nutrients from seawater. As forests and the supply of oxygen increased, air breathers emerged: spiders, scorpions, and slightly remodeled fish. Ray-finned fish—precursors of catfish, salmon, and sailfish—were still the most prolific forms of life.

Fish with lungs were new. Crossopterygians were fish with lobed fins useful for moving from a dried-out pool to one with water. The land became hospitable to amphibians. Seas were shallower; the climate was milder. Forests spread, and trees died and toppled into bogs. Insects were born: dragonflies and cockroaches, more than eight hundred species. The land dried further, and the eggs of amphibians evolved to tolerate the drier world. The creatures that emerged from eggs on land were reptiles, no longer tied in any way to the sea.

Reptiles led the way into the Mesozoic era. They ate plants and flesh; they ate one another. Some were mammal-like, with jaws, teeth and palate, and warm blood. Many of these died out, perhaps because as the climate warmed, they couldn't regulate their body heat. They cooked inside their skins. Reptiles with thinner skin and longer legs—thecodonts—took over the earth.

The megareptiles like dinosaurs were most powerful during the Cretaceous period of the Mesozoic, but other lines of evolution were equally significant. Huge sea dwellers, flowering plants, and flying reptiles emerged. At the end of the Mesozoic, dinosaurs disappeared. Explanations for their demise—sudden climatic change, vast clouds of dust from a meteor impact, or an explosion of a supernova that bathed the earth in gamma rays—interested Shelley less than what happened after, the rapid evolution of mammals.

Mammals appeared along with the dinosaurs in the beginning of the Mesozoic, but not much of their record was found. In the 1960s researchers discovered fossil remnants of a seven-inch-long shrewlike mammal in southern Africa that dated to sixty to seventy million years ago. There were an astonishing variety of small mammals—catlike, hyenalike forms, ungulates and grazers—in a variety of habitats.

"Why didn't they grow bigger," Shelley asked, "especially after the dinosaurs were gone?"

"Are you talking to me?" Mattie came into the living room from the kitchen.

"I was pondering the evolution of mammals. Why was one adaptation, like a hoof or a paw, successful instead of another? Why did the climate change and the sea dry up? Did you know a one-inch rise in the sea inundated *thousands* of square miles?"

"A one-cent increase in the price of milk puts millions of dollars into the pockets of dairy farmers. Or middlemen."

"How did herds develop? The suckling of young? Or birdsongs?"

"I'd like to know about birdsongs," Mattie said.

The phone rang.

"I'll bet that's Lee," Shelley said. "He said he'd call about the core drill."

"I'm not here," Mattie said, and she went back into the kitchen.

Shelley answered and carried the phone to the kitchen doorway. "Hi, Lee, we were just talking about you. Yeah, my mother was just saying she wants very much to go to dinner with you after all."

"I did *not* say that," Mattie said.

Shelley listened a moment, then held her hand over the receiver. "He wants to know if you want to be present for the core drill."

"No."

"I guess not," Shelley said. "Schedule it to suit the crew. When are they done at the Wild Horse Sanctuary? I've been meaning to get over there." She listened again. "I'm studying about the Mesozoic. Why didn't those little mammal guys take over the world?"

Shelley talked another twenty minutes, and then she hung up and stood in the doorway. Mattie was counting out money to pay Elton. "He says anytime you want to go to dinner, just say so."

"I will," Mattie said.

Midweek, at lunchtime, July 2, a U-Haul drove into the yard. Mattie, Shelley, and Elton were eating in the kitchen with a fan in one of the open windows. "This wouldn't be some of Lee's people, would it?" Mattie asked.

"Not that I know of. Maybe somebody's lost."

Shelley went to the screen door to look.

"Maybe they're basketball scouts," Elton said.

"Not with a U-Haul," Shelley said.

The driver got out and looked around the yard. He wasn't a farmer. Shelley saw that much. He wore slacks and loafers and a blue polo shirt with a collar. His hair was cut so short it was impossible to tell the color, though he had a neatly trimmed blond mustache and two earrings in his left ear. Dawn appeared from around the house, went up to the man and said a few words, then shook hands.

Shelley took her sandwich out onto the porch, and Dawn and the man walked to the steps.

"This is Shelley," Dawn said.

"I can see the resemblance," the man said. He climbed two steps and stopped. "Dawn said I should just arrive. I took the liberty of renting the truck, just in case."

"A truck for what?"

The man looked at Dawn.

"I didn't tell them you were coming," Dawn said.

"Oh, well, then." The man turned back to Shelley. "I'm Dennis Burke. I assumed Dawn—that is, I talked to Dawn about it. . . . I was hoping I might—that you and your mother would consider letting me take some of your father's sculptures back to New York. Ames McGill said they were sitting in a barn."

"They're over there in that ravine," Shelley said.

"I don't understand," Dennis said.

"I threw them away."

"But that's your father's life's work."

Shelley looked at Dawn. "How could you do this to us?"

"I had to do something," Dawn said.

"I recognized him right away," Mattie said into the phone. She looked through the curtain. "He's down there right now with Shelley and Dawn."

"Every moment is an opportunity," Trini said. "You and Dennis Burke have something in common."

"Don't remind me."

"Come on, Mattie, we talk about the weather and the price of alfalfa, but at the same time, Tom Parsons bashes the Lakotas, the Pollards harass women, and your friend Sigurd Olafsson denigrates gays and blacks. Why do we not speak up?"

"By talking to Dennis Burke I will be speaking up?"

"For yourself, yes."

"I don't see—"

"I'm not saying Haney was right, but what's the point in hiding from it?"

"Okay, okay," Mattie said. She leaned closer to the window and heard Shelley shouting at Dennis Burke.

"I'll call you later to find out what happens," Trini said.

Mattie admitted she'd savaged Dennis Burke. The day they'd all sailed to the Isle au Haut, he was the catalyst for merriment, shinning up the mast, and cracking wise in a Maine accent about Tricky Dick Nixon. At night in the cabin he kept starting "The Whiffenpoof Song" *"We are poor little sheep . . . Oh, no, it's lambs!"* He started again in a strong tenor, and they'd all joined in.

At his studio he'd paid her the compliment of not explaining his work, but rather how he prepared the canvas and composed the spaces. He hadn't condescended to her, and she'd admired him for it, even liked him. She'd barely thought about his homosexuality.

But after she'd discovered his letters, she'd made him a monster.

Now she thought: *Trini's right. There's nothing anyone can do about it now.* And what else would help Shelley more than demonstrating her tolerance? So she went downstairs and talked to her husband's lover.

As much as anything else, Dennis wanted a sense of the place where Haney died, and Mattie drove him up to Sheep Table on the same road in the same truck. But in sunshine now, in summer, on a dry road.

"Ames told me you're in halves with Earl."

"Not halves, exactly. I work the place."

"Earl's an arrogant bastard," Dennis said.

"I forget you've known Haney's family longer than I have."

"The parents were supportive in direct proportion to how well Earl and Haney agreed with them, so naturally Earl got the encouragement and praise, and Haney the approbation. Over the years Haney's friends in Maine became his family."

"Why do you think he abandoned you, then, and came out west?"

"I don't think he abandoned us. He was uncertain about himself. Of course he wanted to please you. He wasn't conscious of his feelings then. He knew something wasn't quite *correct*, if I might use that word, but he didn't know what."

"He came here to escape, is that what you mean?"

"He couldn't have said so, but that may have been his intent."

"What I've never understood is why he gave up his work," Mattie said. "I know Earl disapproved of it, but Haney had sculpted for years without caring about Earl's opinion. He loved what he was doing in Maine, and even with ranch work, he could have made the time."

"We talked about that a few times," Dennis said. "I think art drew him toward the person he was afraid of being, and he resisted it by working the ranch."

"But he didn't resist it," Mattie said.

"He tried. He never wanted to hurt you."

"I read his letters," Mattie said. "I know he tried. But he hurt me anyway by saying nothing."

"Either way he would have," Dennis said. "I'm sorry for that."

Shelley wanted two sculptures for her room, and Mattie kept *Man and Woman Separated by Air*. The rest were rescued from the ravine and loaded into the U-Haul. Mattie and Shelley signed an agency agreement for these, giving Dennis the right to deal with galleries and museums on their behalf. "All art can hope for is a chance to be remembered," Dennis said. "I'm glad to do this for your father."

"And what if it isn't remembered?" Mattie asked.

"Haney wasn't guaranteed success. He didn't expect it. He only made the stuff."

"I wish he'd made more of it."

"So do I," Dennis said. "I'll be in touch."

Relief was an understatement for what Mattie felt when Dennis drove away. She was grateful for his devotion to Haney's memory, but this didn't free her from the darkness of her body and soul. Every moment was tinged with questions, and in her meeting with Dennis the reality of the past was forced even more strongly upon her: what fear Haney must have felt all his hours—when he'd sprained his knee at Vail, or when the Lincoln broke down and he had to call Hector, or when the telephone rang. And yet he'd betrayed himself, too, in keeping his life secret. Instead of being with artists who might have understood him, he'd isolated himself in a place where there was no hope of understanding. Instead of being openly gay, he'd had to live with her. With her, who didn't know and was pained by watching him. With her. With her.

Chapter 7

The days of early July elapsed. Electricity surged through the transformers at the east edge of the ranch. Thistle seeds exploded into the wind, and gophers dug new tunnels in the alfalfa. Fledged brown starlings, a third brood, crisscrossed the sky.

Elton moved into Loren's room. Mattie had never kept the room as a mausoleum, but as a place to store winter clothes and blankets, a love seat she meant to recane, a broken chair Haney was going to glue, boxes of magazines. The boxes and broken furniture she and Dawn carried to the barn, but to move the winter things, Mattie had to empty Haney's closets and drawers. She threw away the knickknacks she had no use for: a wine bottle lamp, a Haverford mug in which he'd saved pennies and nickels, a basket of filthy, worn-out gloves. She packed his clothes and shoes to the Goodwill, remembering Haney in the boots he'd bought in Rome or the suit he'd worn to Jennifer Parsons's wedding, in the T-shirt she'd given him with warblers on it. Had he worn that shirt out of convenience or love or guilt?

It stayed hot. Alfalfa grew again in the fields; the corn heaved up; the Sudex rattled. Blue grosbeaks fledged young near the mailbox, and a burrowing owl took up residence in an abandoned prairie dog hole near the rock pile. Elton found a dead redtail chick fallen from its nest in the cottonwoods downstream from the east bridge.

With the dry weather, water was more precious. Elton usually irrigated north of the river and the Upper East, and Shelley the West Main, the Long Narrow, and the corn—mornings and evenings, twelve-hour sets. Mattie took an occasional turn, too, to keep an eye on how the alfalfa was coming along and to check the levels in the ditches. Every time she measured, the district was delivering the water she paid for. The corn Hector had worried over came back—Shelley had been doing the right sets—but now the West Main alfalfa petered out at the bottom of the field, and Mattie was suspicious the Pollards were stealing water at night. But the damage wasn't much yet.

Since Dawn's skirmish with the Pollards and her secret invitation to Dennis Burke, Mattie trusted Dawn less than ever. What would she do next? The problem was, Mattie couldn't fire her now. There was no question she'd proved herself as a mechanic, and she was willing to do whatever other tasks there were, too. So Mattie's strategy was avoidance. She stayed clear of Dawn and let her set her own schedule and looked at the evidence. Over two weeks Dawn painted the workbench and reorganized the tools. She upgraded the welding equipment, did maintenance on the water control valve at the edge of the swamp, and greased and adjusted the timing on the pivot sprinkler.

Once, on a slow day, she asked Mattie whether she could resurrect the '72 GMC three-quarter-ton flatbed sitting in the Ironweed Patch.

"You think you can get it to run?" Mattie asked.

"I hope that's not a serious question. If you decide it's not worth keeping, you can sell it for more than we'll put into it."

"Wages included?"

"What would you rather have me do?" Dawn asked.

"You could build the road out to the north gate."

"I looked at your husband's plan," Dawn said. "With those elevations, a new road would wash worse than the one we've got. Why don't I fix the GMC, and I'll haul in gravel and grade the old road?"

"You do what you want," Mattie said. "You always do."

"I'll have to build a crane to take the motor out of the three-quarter-ton, but we'll need a crane anyway in the fall when I overhaul the International."

"It's July," Mattie said. "Fall is a long way off."

"What are you saying?"

"I'm saying fall is a long way off."

Thursday morning could have been any morning of the summer. Mattie drove the Toyota past the dry runoff pond up to Sheep Table to watch the weather over the Black Hills and to make sure the pivot sprinkler was running. Towhees rustled in the thickets, and a lark sparrow sang from the twisted fence wire zigzagging down the mesa.

Dividing what from what do you think? Haney had never answered.

The sprinkler turned its slow circle through the alfalfa, a green circle in a yellow background. She wished the days now to be as they were, each moment as *this moment,* defining itself and random, the sky containing all possibilities, memory and inarticulateness composing the past. She felt in her body how the sun made the land move, made the song of the lark sparrow, the known and the unknown. She was knowing and unknowing. Memory rolled the past into the present, a past that couldn't be changed. So many words in muddled sequence had been spoken and not spoken. Peace. She couldn't imagine that now.

At least Lee Coulter had let her be. No one from the museum came to the house, not even to use the telephone or to ask for water or ice. What she knew about the dig site was from Shelley—a recent delay in the core drilling—but the odd thing was, the less Lee was present, the more she was aware of him. She imagined what he did evenings, what restaurants he went to, what his children were like. She wondered whether he'd ask her to dinner again, and if he did, what she'd say, or rather, how she'd refuse. She wondered if he'd like her hair short.

She scanned with her binoculars—far off Elton was shoveling earth at the ditch in the Upper East, though she couldn't tell whether he was filling a void or creating one. She thought of Loren's doing that work; he'd have been old enough. Or would he have been traveling the country, or Europe, or working in Hot Springs, or Chicago?

She saw cattle coming down the abandoned road west of her, maybe twenty head on the run. No one was moving them, no four-wheeler or horseman. Mattie recognized the two bulls at the front—Jorge and George, Jorge with the white spot on his shoulder. The herd skirted the trees along the Pollards' fence line and descended toward the river. From the river there was nothing between the cattle and the pivot field. Cattle weren't that stupid. They knew what food was.

Mattie turned the truck around, crossed the ditch, and stopped at the Pollards' gate. They'd tightened it since she'd been through it the last time with Elton, and she couldn't open it either by shouldering it or with a stick lever. She cut the wires with a Vise-Grip and collapsed the gate still fastened to the post. She raised dust along the ditch road, climbed the ridge of the Pollards' overgrazed swale, and hairpinned down into their yard. Gizzard barked and snapped at her tires, and his barking brought Lute out of the house in overalls and no shirt. He stood in the road and shielded his eyes from the sun.

She had no choice but to stop. "I cut your gate open," Mattie said. "I'll have it fixed by noon."

"Well, shit," Lute said, "that's why I got it tight, so nobody gets in."

"I'm in a hurry," Mattie said. "If you'd keep your fences instead of your gates, Hector's cows wouldn't be about to run into my alfalfa."

"I run my place."

"Then what are you doing in the house at this hour?" Mattie asked.

She drove on, mad as sin, and turned right at the county road. She skidded into Hector's driveway, but Hector's truck wasn't there. Rafe yelped from his tether.

"Sorry, Rafe, I can't visit now."

She did a U-turn in the yard. Hector was probably on his way to work, so Mattie drove to the Deckers' and barged into their kitchen, where Allen was fixing eggs. "Hector's cows are in my alfalfa," she said. "Can I borrow Keith and Dylan and a couple of four-wheelers?"

"They're going to their jobs in town," Allen said. "They ride in with me."

"I'll bring them in later," Mattie said.

Trini appeared in her robe, her hair just washed and in tangles. "You boys get your boots on," she said. "You heard Mattie. She needs some help."

"I'm afraid of cows," Dylan said.

"*Move,* I said." Trini turned to Mattie. "What can I do?"

"You can get Elton from the Upper East and meet us at the pivot."

"What about Hector?" Allen said. "They're his cows."

"He's gone to work," Mattie said. "And it's my field. I'll pick up Shelley on the way."

Mattie did fifty on the straightaway, coasted the hill, and at the culvert to the West Main met Shelley coming the other way on the four-wheeler.

"I was coming to look for you," Shelley said. "I heard shots over there."

"Where over there?"

"West. Not that far."

"Hector's cows are loose," Mattie said. "Let's look from the mesa."

The Decker boys zoomed past, and Mattie led Shelley up Sheep Table to get a view. It was the same panorama as half an hour earlier, though the hills were in starker light.

"I don't see any cows," Shelley said. She was standing on the seat of the four-wheeler.

"They've got to be somewhere." Mattie scanned with her binoculars. "There. Look up the hill. They're at the corner."

The cows were all huddled at the intersection of two fences.

"I don't see the bulls with them, though."

"Look by the river, Mom. Something's moving over there."

Mattie traced back to the river. "Well, fuck Jesus," she said.

"What is it?"

George was lying in the shallows kicking and spitting blood, and Jorge was on his knees on an island between two smooth-flowing pools. He was struggling to get up, but couldn't, as if there were a weight on him. Blood poured out from his nose.

"What do you see?" Shelley asked.

"Go find Dawn," Mattie said. "Tell her to bring the pistol."

Chapter 8

Mattie sent Keith and Dylan to head off Trini, and Shelley fetched Dawn, who brought the pistol. George was already dead in the shallows. Dawn shot Jorge in the head, and he died on his knees. Then Mattie went back to the house and telephoned Hector's supervisor to tell Hector there was an emergency at her place. After that she called Sheriff Nolan.

Dawn drove the Case out to the pivot, and she and Mattie chained the bulls' legs and winched them to their side of the river. That's what they were doing when Hector arrived. He stared at his bulls like a man whose house had just burned to the ground.

"I don't know how they got out," Mattie said. "But I know who shot them."

"It's my fault," Hector said. "I knew the cows were in heat. I didn't build the corral strong enough."

"Even if they were loose, nobody had to shoot them."

"Nobody had to," Hector said. "We should skin them out and let the meat cool."

"We can hang them in the barn," Mattie said.

"The funny thing is that I was going to move them to Haffners' this afternoon," Hector said. "Three in two days. The calf died yesterday."

"I called the sheriff," Mattie said. "Shelley's meeting him at the house. Dawn went back for the loader."

She watched an eagle drift along the mesa until the rocks gave way to the broken fence line, and then, without a wingbeat, it scaled higher and northeastward over the cottonwoods and merged with the distance.

The loader coming along the river road disturbed the quiet, and behind Dawn the sheriff's tan Blazer came into view.

"I'll put the cows in the north pasture," Hector said. "They're tagged, so I can pull them later. Do you mind if I have too many on that ground for a few days?"

"That's fine, Hector. Whatever you want to do."

The Blazer passed the loader and disappeared into the river bottom, then reappeared at Elton's rock pile. The sheriff steered the circumference and jerked over cactus and prairie dog mounds.

When it stopped, Shelley got out and slammed the door hard and stalked over to Mattie and Hector. "What a fucking asshole," she said. "Fuck him."

"Calm down," Mattie said. "What's wrong?"

"He was giving me shit about—Never mind what."

The sheriff was a no-special-hurry kind of man, and Mattie supposed he was in less of a hurry than usual, having to deal with her and Shelley. They knew Nolan's background from elections and his performance on the job. And he knew them, too. Haney had called him a half dozen times about the Pollards' stealing water.

He opened the door of the Blazer, but instead of getting out, he fiddled with his radio and then with his clipboard. For a good three minutes he was writing something as the loader chugged around the pivot.

Dawn's hair swirled under her cap, and she drove past the Blazer and down to the river where the bulls were lying. Then Elton showed up, too, on the four-wheeler by the rock pile on the far side of the pivot. He came toward them across the diameter under the sprinkler arm.

The sheriff finished writing whatever it was and took forever to put his hat on. Then finally he got out of the Blazer. "Morning, Mrs. Remmel," he said. "Looks to me you have a problem here."

"You know Hector Lopez?" Mattie asked.

The sheriff ignored Hector and walked over to the edge of the shelf. "Those the bulls you called about?"

"You think they're raccoons?" Shelley asked.

"We dragged them over to this side," Mattie said, "but you can see where they were shot."

"That Luther Pollard's over there?"

"Yes. That fence was barely standing," Mattie said.

"Who's 'we'?" the sheriff asked. "'We' dragged the bulls . . ."

"My hired man, Dawn, there on the loader."

Dawn was beside Jorge then, and she idled down the engine. Elton came up on the four-wheeler, but stayed a little apart, sitting there and watching.

"What I'm hearing is that nobody saw them get shot," the sheriff said.

"Who else but those scumbags would have shot them?" Shelley asked.

The sheriff waved vaguely in Shelley's direction. "You, tell Don to come on over here."

"Are you talking to me?" Shelley asked.

"You, yes, you. Get him over here."

Shelley glared at the sheriff, then whistled at Dawn, but the loader drowned out even the whistle so Shelley walked halfway down the slope and whistled again and waved until Dawn saw her. Then she went back to the others.

"So the bulls were on the Pollards' property, and you dragged them over here?"

"There was no reason to shoot them," Mattie said. "And they left them to die."

"They look dead now, don't they?" the sheriff said. He looked at Hector for the first time. "They're your bulls?"

"Yes, sir."

"So what'd you do to the Pollards?"

"He didn't do anything to the Pollards," Shelley said.

"I'm asking the questions here," the sheriff said. He paused and watched Dawn come up the hill toward them.

"Look," Hector said, "let's forget about this."

The sheriff looked back at Hector. "You think the Pollards shot your bulls, don't you?"

"We don't know who shot them," Hector said.

"I'm not understanding this," the sheriff said. "You want to forget about it?"

"Yes."

"The Pollards must have had a reason."

"He's Mexican," Dawn said. "That's the reason."

The sheriff smiled at Dawn, then turned back to Hector. "You think that's it, Hector? You're Mexican?"

"I don't know."

"I mean it's not like you're an Indian or anything. You're not an Indian, right?"

Dawn stepped forward and slapped the sheriff hard in the face. The force of the blow staggered him sideways, and his hat flew off. He put his hand on his pistol.

Hector stepped in front of Dawn.

"Saying things like that gets us riled up around here," Mattie said. "You're supposed to be on the side of the law."

"I am the law."

"Then act like it," Mattie said. She picked up the sheriff's hat and handed it to him.

"Good for the Pollards," the sheriff said.

The sheriff retreated a step and brushed off his hat.

"What'd you say?" Mattie asked.

"I said, 'Good for the Pollards.'"

Mattie lunged and caught Nolan off guard, and he fell backward. She jumped on him with fists flying. "You shithead," she said. "You goddamn bastard."

Nolan held his arms across his face. "Get her the fuck off," he shouted. "Get *off*."

Shelley and Hector dragged Mattie away, still kicking and screaming.

Chapter 9

It was funny right afterward. They all laughed about it, even Hector. "Did you see his face when Dawn slapped him?" Shelley said. "God, that was sweet."

"I should have slapped him, not Dawn," Mattie said. "I'm sorry I didn't."

"You got him, though, Mom."

"I was mad and made things worse," Mattie said. "I'm sorry Elton had to hear that."

"I've heard it before," Elton said.

"How does someone like that get to be sheriff?" Shelley asked.

"By saying those things to most of the voters," Hector said.

"Well, politics sucks," Dawn said.

"We need to skin those bulls," Hector said. "No sense wasting the meat."

"Let's do it," Dawn said. "That's what they say in Utah."

Dawn and Mattie pulleyed Jorge by his hind legs from the loader bucket to a rafter in the barn, and Hector slit open the stomach and pulled the entrails into a garbage bag. They saved the liver and kidneys and heart and tongue. Hector sawed off Jorge's head, while Mattie and Elton started skinning. Dawn went back to the river for George.

Wherever Elton was from, he'd hunted before, because he knew how to skin an animal. He didn't care about blood on his hands, on his clothes, in his hair. He slid the knife along tissue smoothly and cleanly without cutting muscle.

Shelley had no stomach for skinning, so she made egg salad sandwiches and popcorn and cut up carrot sticks, and at noon they ate under the cottonwood tree. It was hot, and birds were quiet. They drank water and lemonade, and they were hungry. But the mood was restrained.

They'd joined together against Sheriff Nolan, but there was a sense of more to come. They weren't done yet with the Pollards.

"Maybe they think they're even," Dawn said.

"Let's hope so," Mattie said. "Let's not do anything crazy in retaliation."

"I got rid of a lot of bullshit," Hector said. "Let's look at it that way. I can still pay a stud fee."

"Maybe you should get a buffalo," Dawn said. "You could raise beefalo."

"Don't start on buffalo," Mattie said.

Elton finished the last sandwiches and the carrots and drank the dregs of the lemonade from the pitcher and fingered the spilled egg salad from his plate.

"We should make you pay board," Shelley said.

"I can't help it if I'm starving."

"And remember, Mom, those great days when he didn't talk?"

Mattie collected the plates, and Shelley carried in the pitchers and as many glasses as she could hold.

"Is there dessert?" Elton asked.

Dawn and Hector fell to quiet, eyeing each other.

"My mother had a buffalo robe," Elton said. "She sold it before I was born."

"Where's she now?" Dawn asked.

"Dead," Elton said.

"Then she's in heaven," Hector said.

"There's no heaven," Dawn said. "That's a crock of shit. Excuse my Spanish, Elton. But don't get any wrong ideas."

"What wrong ideas?" Hector said.

"Oh, jeez," Dawn said. "I bet you're Catholic."

"I was raised Catholic," Hector said. "Is there something wrong with that?"

"Yes, there is. You're essentially telling me you can't help what you believe."

"I can't believe what I want to?"

"We should finish skinning George," Elton said, and he got up from the table.

"Sit down," Dawn said. "Mattie's getting dessert. I want you to listen."

Elton sat down.

Dawn turned back to Hector. "You can believe what you want to if it's the truth."

"And you know the truth?"

"No, but I don't get my opinions from a guy in Rome. I have the sense to do my own research. You believe God created the world and there's an afterlife? What evidence do you have?"

Mattie came out with a bowl of cut-up fruit, and Shelley a plate of cookies. "Are you tormenting Hector?" Mattie asked.

"Hector's trying to convert Elton to a Christian."

"I believe in God," Hector said. "Is that a crime?"

"Let's be kind to each other," Mattie said. She sat down and passed dessert.

"God created the Pollards," Shelley said. "Do you believe that?"

"No," Hector said.

"That's progress," Dawn said.

Elton took four cookies, and they all ate their fruit. Then Mattie said, "Besides, I want to tell you all something."

"You're pregnant," Shelley said.

"I don't see how I could be." She paused. "Awhile back I was talking to Hector— Do you remember that day you were under the corn picker? I wanted to know about the invoice you gave Haney for hauling hay."

"I remember," Hector said.

Mattie looked around at each of them. "I don't want anyone to pretend ignorance," Mattie said. "That day I didn't know what Hector knew, and *if* he knew, about my husband, Shelley's father—"

"Mom, don't do this."

"I'd like you to hear me acknowledge— I want to be clear with everyone, partly for my sake, but partly for Shelley's, too."

"What?" Elton asked.

"My father was gay," Shelley said. "Do you know what that means?"

"I guess. Sort of."

"It means everyone hates you," Shelley said.

"It means he had sex with men. There, I said it."

"Not with me," Hector said finally.

"Of course not with you," Dawn said. "You're Catholic."

Chapter 10

A few days after the bulls were killed, Lee Coulter invited Shelley to the museum to learn techniques of excavation. If they found bones in the core drill, and if her mother let them dig, and if the find were significant, she could participate if she wanted to, so long as she knew how to dig. She was supposed to meet Lee at one, but raccoons had torn apart a section of Nu-Flex pipe, and she had to splice it, and then she was mud-caked and had to shower and change her clothes and eat lunch.

"Don't forget you have to stop at the Texaco, too," her mother said. "Our tanks are dry."

"What tanks?"

"The only ones we have. I think Lute Pollard had more than a ten-gallon can. Your father didn't pay the last bill, so they won't deliver until we settle up."

"He's supposed to pay it from the grave?"

"I never saw the bill," Mattie said. "*I forgot*. There, does that satisfy you?"

"No."

"Well, too bad."

"The Lincoln's almost empty, too," Shelley said. "It may not get to Hot Springs."

"Take the truck then. If you have time after your meeting, you can bring back some parts for the flatbed. And Elton wants more twenty-two shells."

"Why do I have to do everyone's errands?"

"We can't run a ranch without gasoline," Mattie said. "And complaining doesn't help, either."

On the road, gone, away from her mother, Shelley felt better. She looked forward to seeing the museum again, and she hadn't been to town in a while. Not that she was planning to do anything. She certainly wasn't going into Yogi's.

She dropped her mother's check at the Texaco supplier and left Dawn's list of parts at Big A, and when she got to the museum, Lee was already talking to the student interns.

He introduced her as the missing link and went on with his lecture. "Excavation is almost as slow as fossilization," he said. "We uncover a few inches every summer, but over the years we've accomplished a lot. We've mostly found mammoths—forty-nine woolly mammoths and four Columbians—and one dire wolf and one saber-toothed cat. If you want to see a site in its initial stages, you can view the one we're starting at the Wild Horse Sanctuary west of town."

At the end of the lecture he set them up with tools, and each of them worked under the guidance of a staff person. To Shelley, excavation was more like dentistry than gardening. Instead of shovels and pitchforks, they used tiny picks and brushes. And there was no real excitement of discovery. She worked on bones that had been known about for thirty years. But even in the tedium she felt a leap of her imagination. From the bones, from her brushstrokes, she extrapolated to other worlds of earlier life, and the hours flew past. When they quit at five, she was still dreaming.

She went by the Big A and picked up Dawn's parts, then got Elton's ammunition at Pamida, and after that, because she didn't want to go home, she bought a bottle of cheap wine and drove out to the Wild Horse Sanctuary.

It was hilly country, ponderosas interspersed with native grass. She had no map or directions, no idea where the site was. She thought it would be obvious—a drill, a sign, some marker—but it wasn't, so she parked on a side road and opened the wine. Her options were to swim at the Evans Plunge, but she had no bathing suit, or there was the Super 8 Lounge and the bar at Maverick Junction. None of those appealed to her. So far she liked drinking and watching the clouds lower and darken over the hills.

A dozen wild horses skirted the meadow: sleek-hoofed mammals derived from Pleistocene Ungulata. Evolution astonished her. The world of flux. Lee would have said she was evolving, though he'd have meant it with reference to time. But what she wished for was to be made whole again—a wrongdoer made a do-gooder, a scattered intelligence focused, the lazy soul made diligent. In college she'd floundered, and at the ranch how did her work matter? Was she victim or determiner? Could she choose? What would Mr. Adler say? *Bryce.* She had drunk just enough to find out.

She started the truck and drove to Bryce's house, but it looked different from the last time she was there. Choir tickets! She wasn't even sure it was the right place. A trampoline occupied most of the front lawn. Under the carport was a motorboat on a trailer, and along the front of the porch someone had planted nasturtiums and geraniums. It was the same house, but Bryce didn't live there.

A girl of about ten, in a T-shirt and shorts and ballet shoes, let the screen door slam behind her and climbed onto the trampoline. She bounced into the air and did front flips, back flips, and spins, landing perfectly on her feet. Shelley crossed the street and watched from the sidewalk.

After a few minutes the girl stopped jumping. "You're pretty to watch," Shelley said.

"I have a trainer and a coach," the girl said. "I need a manager."

"Is this your house?"

"My mom and dad's. My dad's a gym teacher back home."

"Where is that?"

"Iowa," the girl said. "Iowa's that way."

A man opened the screen and came outside. "Stephanie, you have another hour to practice."

"I was resting," the girl said.

She started jumping again, as effortlessly as before. She did a triple flip and then another.

"I'm looking for Bryce Adler," Shelley said.

"He rents from us during the school year," the man said. "Summers he works at Wind Cave."

"What about his girlfriend?"

"I didn't know he had a girlfriend," the man said, "but it's all right with me."

The little girl on the trampoline sprang high into the air, did a full twist, and landed on her feet.

Chapter 11

Shelley drank and propped the bottle between her legs as she drove toward the curtains of rain in the Black Hills. She'd been to Wind Cave only once, with Mr. Leskovitz's ninth-grade science class, and she'd screamed in the elevator going down. The guard took her back up immediately, and instead of seeing the cave, she'd had to write a report, so she knew the cave was famous for boxwork, a honeycomb-shaped calcite. And she remembered wind studies had shown only about 5 percent of the cave had been explored. It had been discovered by two hunters who'd heard a weird sound and tracked the noise to an opening in the limestone. How could these men be credited with discovering anything, she wrote in her report, when for centuries the cave had been home to spirits of the Lakota?

The visitors' center was Black Hills granite and had a bookstore, exhibitions about how caves were formed, and dioramas of birds and mammals. And bathrooms. She needed the bathroom first.

A cheerful Elder Hostel volunteer at the information desk tracked down Bryce's work schedule: He was on the Fairgrounds Tour. "All the tours start and end in the elevator building," she said. "Just follow the yellow brick road out the front door."

The path wasn't yellow brick, but a conglomerate of cement and gravel, and it led downhill to a low-slung building, where one after another, the elevators released their hostages. It was near day's end, so no one was waiting for the next tour.

Bryce failed to appear, and finally Shelley decided if she were to find him she'd have to go down into the earth. Darkness. Enclosure. No exit. Her fear wasn't rational, but even with a half bottle of wine in her, real, nevertheless.

She didn't scream in the elevator, a good sign. When the elevator door opened, Bryce was standing there talking to a couple dressed in bushwhacker khaki from Banana Republic. "You know Philadelphia?" the man asked. "We live in Wynnewood."

"I know the Eagles are a sorry group of impostors," Bryce said.

The couple joined the other tourists crowding past her into the elevator, and she and Bryce were left alone on the platform.

"I'm selling concert tickets," she said. "Is your friend still living with you?"

"My sister was visiting from Sioux Falls."

"Why didn't you call me back?"

"You invented the story, so obviously you wanted to be invisible."

"Maybe I didn't."

"But I'm not a mind reader."

"I get nervous underground," Shelley said. "Is there a way out of here?"

Up above they agreed to go to a movie in Custer, but Bryce wanted to change out of his uniform. Shelley got the wine from her truck, and they took his VW.

"How was New Orleans?" she asked.

"The symposium imposed, but the city was fabulous."

"I thought you were taking the summer off to write."

"I'm on probation at school," he said. "If I quit, I wanted to have some money saved."

"Probation for what?"

"I teach seditious material. Isn't Keith Decker your neighbor? He complained that *Portrait of the Artist as a Young Man* was obscene because Stephen Daedalus considers going to a prostitute."

"I'll beat the shit out of the little bastard."

"Maybe you should beat some shit into him."

The VW heaved and yawed in the wind, and Bryce turned at an intersection onto gravel. Within seconds, lightning cracked down into rocks a hundred yards off the road. Thunder snapped in the air a split second after.

"Close only counts in horseshoes," Bryce said.

Rain swept over them, and Bryce leaned close to the windshield. The car slithered on mud. Then it started to hail. White pebbles jumped like popcorn from the grass and on the road, and the noise on the car roof was deafening.

After a minute or two Bryce pulled to the side of the road. "The wipers don't do much," he said. "We can walk."

"Walk? Are you kidding me?"

"It's not that far." He pushed the door open against the wind and rain and hail and got out. The door slammed in the wind, and Bryce started running.

"I don't believe this," Shelley said to no one.

But what else could she do but go after him? She found two copies of *American Poetry Review* in the back seat and held them over her head and got out of the car.

She ran slowly, not trusting her knee. A minute. Two minutes. The world was nothing but gray. She jogged into a long swale and up a hill, following Bryce's tracks. Mud splattered up the backs of her legs. The magazines over her head became saturated.

Around a bend she came into some ponderosas, and the tracks in the mud led to a chinked log cabin. At the top of the hewn-board steps, Bryce was waiting for her with a towel.

"Poetry wasn't much help against the rain," she said. She traded him the soggy magazines for the towel.

Water dripped from her elbows, from her chin, from her clothes. Bryce was wet, too. His shirt was soaked, and his green uniform trousers were black. She went in, drying her hair with the towel.

"I started a fire," he said. "Go stand by the stove."

"Why did you do that?"

"Start a fire?"

"You know what I mean."

"Because in the car I wanted to kiss you."

"And now you don't?"

"Now you're not trapped in a car."

She dried her face and her hair and rubbed her arms, and he put a piece of pine into the stove box. She stepped closer. A kiss. Tentative, barely touching lips. A chill ran up her back.

Then the teakettle whistled from the stove, and Bryce broke away. He poured hot water, and the scent of mint tea rose around them.

"I should get out of these wet clothes," she said.

"That was my plan."

Another kiss, barely touching. His lips were soft. He touched his tongue to hers. Drops of water ran from his cheek onto hers. She curled a hand around his neck and leaned in.

He knelt and untied her shoes and pulled them off, and her wet socks. He pushed her back into a chair and kneaded her toes, her instep, her heel. She was aware of the stove's heat on one side of her and the cold room on the other.

He kneaded her other foot, then raised up on his knees and kissed her again. His fingers found the top button of her shirt, and he looked at her with a question in his eyes. Her answer was yes. At each button, the answer was yes.

She slid her arms from the sleeves of her shirt and shrugged off her bra. His gaze stayed with hers. She didn't dare look away.

He unfastened the button of her shorts and tugged the zipper down, and she lifted her body from the chair. The room, the heat of the stove, the evening light coming through the window slid from her awareness. She felt his mouth on her nipple, the electric sensation run between her legs. She moaned, not intending to. He kissed across her bare stomach, and she shivered, but she lifted her body toward his mouth.

Chapter 12

Lee Coulter's truck came down the mesa, bumping over rocks and splashing in the seeps. Mattie tried not to think of the noise it made, the rocks dislodged, the man inside the cab. She was tying up tomato vines. She looped twine around the stems and stakes and tied bows.

She wouldn't ascribe the profusion in her garden to the one empty row, but the fact remained it was one of her best years. The weather had been hot, and she'd mulched and weeded, and watered it every day, sometimes twice. The beans were prolific; the carrots were up. Squash and melons were blossoming. Every night for dinner they ate lettuce, and the peas were coming in on the chicken wire.

The truck came closer. She admitted the museum crew had been inconspicuous. Except for the drill rig, the crew had made no noise. There was no traffic. Now and then Shelley reported a census of birds or plants, a measurement, or a sampling, but Mattie had no other awareness they were there. Now she hoped Lee wasn't coming to tell her a bulldozer was scheduled first thing Monday morning.

The truck stopped; the door opened and closed. Mattie didn't look up. She tied up the last tomato plant, without glancing over at Lee.

"I like your hair," Lee said.

"What?"

"I have the preliminary results from the core drill," he said. "Do you want to see them?"

"Just tell me."

"Why not see for yourself?" he asked. "It'll take five minutes."

She stood and stretched her back, then picked at the fingers of her gloves and pulled them off. "You are so persistent," she said. "Don't you get tired?"

Lee laid his clipboard on the picnic table, and Mattie went over.

"First, Shelley's been an extremely conscientious and willing helper."

"I'm glad." Mattie looked at the top page, but the numbers were gibberish.

"A sinkhole is essentially sediment," Lee said. "Leaves, tree trunks, fill dirt, effluvium—whatever blows or washes in."

"I know what a sinkhole is."

"Over thousands of years, when the water dries out, whatever is there hardens like cement. It's called settling. We drilled two test cores, and it appears to be a sinkhole. We went down a hundred feet." Lee folded over the next page on the clipboard, which showed a murky picture. "We analyze everything—soil, leaves, fossil shells."

"Will you get to the point? Which parts are the bones?"

"There aren't any bones."

"I thought you said it was a sinkhole."

"It's a sinkhole. There are a few fossils, a bone fragment or two, but nothing to get excited about."

"And you want to drill more holes?"

"No, that's it. We're done here." He handed Mattie a folder from beneath the clipboard. "I made copies of our inventories, the geological data, and the aerial maps."

"So all this was for nothing?"

"It wasn't for nothing. We all learned something."

Mattie stood away from the table. Lee picked up his clipboard. They looked at each other.

"I'm sorry for being so contentious," she said.

"You were right to express your concerns."

"I was about to pick lettuce and peas. Do you like vegetables?"

"I love zucchini."

"I didn't offer you zucchini."

"What kind of lettuce?"

"What kind do you like?"

"Romaine."

"I have butter lettuce and green leaf."

"Okay, I can live with peas."

"Don't do me any favors," Mattie said.

"Is that your motto in life, Mrs. Remmel? That's pretty sad."

Mattie turned and went into the garden. Lee stayed outside at the fence.

"Okay, butter lettuce," he said. "I have green leaf in my own garden."

"You have a garden?"

"Did you know many men are farmers?"

"I didn't picture you with a garden."

"Did you picture me without one?"

She picked two heads of butter lettuce and threw them at him. He caught one in each hand.

She put leaf lettuce in her basket, then moved the basket to the peas. He was leaning against the gatepost, holding the lettuce on his arm.

"You want me to help?"

"No, thank you." She picked peas, wishing she'd never offered vegetables of any kind.

Then she heard the gate close, and she glanced up. He was walking away toward his truck.

"Mr. Coulter? You don't want these peas?"

He kept walking.

"What about dinner?" she said.

He stopped and turned around.

"Well, I thought I could cook something here. I'm grateful for your being nice to Shelley."

"I was going to put the lettuce in my truck," he said. He looked at his watch. "It's four o'clock. Why don't we meet at the Dakota Rose at seven? We'll celebrate the discovery of nothing in the sinkhole."

"All right," Mattie said. "Seven o'clock."

"I do like your hair," he said.

"Well, thank you."

Mattie took a shower, washed her hair and dried it, and then stood in front of her closet. It had been years since she'd needed to decide what to wear to go out. She was sure Lee didn't care what she wore, and she wasn't about to make herself different from who she was, but should she put on jeans and the yellow blouse or the print dress? And shoes? She'd once skydived from an airplane, but she couldn't choose which pair of shoes to wear.

She was hoping for inspiration when Shelley called. "Did it rain there?" Shelley asked.

"No, why?"

"It poured here. I left the check at the Texaco. The guy will deliver tomorrow. Do you need the truck?"

"As it happens, yes, I do. Where are you?"

"In the Black Hills near Wind Cave. Where are you going?"

"I have a meeting in town."

"Can't you drive the Lincoln this once?"

"You said it doesn't have any gas. What are you doing at Wind Cave?"

"Spending the night with Bryce."

There was an awkward pause. Mattie stared into the closet at blouses, shirts, dresses.

"Mom, I can't believe you didn't tell me what it was like."

"Tell you what *what* was like?"

"I thought mothers and daughters were supposed to talk."

"You never wanted to talk."

"Can't you borrow a car from Trini? I'll bring the truck back early in the morning."

"Maybe I can," Mattie said.

"Thanks, Mom. Have fun at your meeting. I'll see you tomorrow."

They hung up, and Mattie said, "Now what's she doing?"

After a minute she found she was still holding the phone, and she dialed Trini's number, but she didn't even let it ring before she clicked off again. Borrowing Trini's car meant Trini would know she was going out with Lee.

The only choice, then, was not to go. She'd have to call him.

Then someone came in downstairs and rattled ice from the refrigerator.

"Dawn, is that you?"

"Who wants to know?" Dawn asked.

"Come up here a minute, will you, please?"

Mattie took a beige dress from a hanger and pulled it over her head. She'd worn the dress to the irrigation district banquet, and she'd looked all right in it. Dawn appeared holding a glass of cranberry juice. "I'm covered with grease," she said.

"Grease won't change your advice. What kind of shoes should I wear with this?"

"Where are you going?"

"To dinner."

"With Lee?"

"It's not a date."

"Are you going to sleep with him? That will make a difference in what shoes you wear."

"I'm not dignifying that question with an answer." She pulled a pair of black shoes from the bottom of the closet.

"Not those," Dawn said. "Why not cowboy boots? Or sneakers. Sneakers would make you look younger."

"I'm not trying to look younger."

"Does Shelley have shoes you could borrow?"

Mattie thought for a moment. "She has some gold sandals. I might try those."

Mattie went to Shelley's room and found the sandals—gold leather ones with straps.

"What about makeup? Do you want me to help you with that?"

"Did you learn that in the army, too?"

"Of course."

"There is one thing you could do," Mattie said.

"Anything," Dawn said.

"You could lend me your car."

Chapter 13

The flatbed was a '72, and Dawn guessed it had been sitting idle ten or twelve years. The motor turned with a lug wrench, so it wasn't frozen up. Half the problem was natural erosion—gas evaporated from the carburetor and the gas tank, the gaskets and seals dry-rotted, the spark plugs rusted. A couple of days earlier she'd left the carburetor in an acid bath, and now she rinsed it and tinkered and put it back into the engine. The truck was still sitting on its four flat tires in the Ironweed Patch.

She siphoned out the acid she'd put in the gas tank, then siphoned in gasoline from the four-wheeler. She poured Marvel Mystery Oil down the spark plug holes so the pistons wouldn't turn over in dry cylinders. Then she cleaned the points and hooked up a spare battery. The engine turned over, but didn't catch. She hadn't thought it would. The fuel line needed to be replaced, and the fuel pump, too. Shelley was getting those. Some of the gaskets, when they got lubrication, would probably close up by themselves. After the engine ran a few days, she'd see what leaked and what didn't.

She spent the rest of daylight puttering with the truck, and at dusk she took the three-wheeler to irrigate. She'd promised Mattie she'd set water in the West Main and check the pressure in the sprinkler.

From the West Main, she saw Hector's truck on the mesa. Since they'd butchered Jorge and George, she hadn't seen much of him. Mattie spoke to him once in a while in the yard, but mostly he passed through like a ghost. He was shy anyway, and it hadn't helped saying those things to him about being Catholic. She waved to him, but he didn't see her. He was checking the fence.

She braked the three-wheeler—a shiny stone had caught her eye— and she pried it out of the road with the heel of her boot. It was dull brown, but had a bluish crystalline cast to it, and she rubbed the dirt off. Then she looked up the hill again, and Hector waved to her.

The sprinkler looked all right. There was good pressure, and it moved steadily, and the water sprayed out, but she had a feeling of unease about it. The hay didn't look as high as she remembered it from first cutting. And it was about time to cut it again. There was nothing to do, though, so she turned toward the house.

She passed Elton heading through the yard to irrigate the Upper East, and she coasted the three-wheeler into the open bay of the Morton. She preferred bathing in the river—she liked the deer and the sunlight in the eddies and the reflections of the hills—but the water was low now, and last time she'd met a snapping turtle. Besides, there was a new shower in the Morton.

She pulled off her boots, unzipped her greasy coveralls and threw them into the hamper, and turned on the shower. Then she stripped off her shorts, shirt, and underwear and stepped under the hot. She scrubbed her hands with Lava, but she could never get her hands clean, so she put on rubber gloves to wash her hair. The shampoo foamed and rinsed away. She put on conditioner and leaned back against the wall. She turned the spray to cool, and her nipples hardened.

She hadn't been with a man since Styver and hadn't wanted to be. No one in particular came to mind; she felt unconnected desire. She slid her hand down her stomach to the shadow between her legs. She braced her feet apart and arched her back, moved her fingers faster, until she groaned and her body felt as if it were flying through the air.

The sound of a motor brought her back. For an instant she thought of Elton. Had he come back for something? She turned the water off and grabbed a towel and slitted open the shower door. She saw Hector's truck driving past the house and receding up the driveway.

Elton set the table and put glasses on, and when he sat down, Dawn slid a grayish yellow coagulum from the skillet onto his plate.

"What's that?" Elton asked.

"An omelet," Dawn said.

Elton turned the glob with a fork. "Doesn't an omelet have eggs in it?"

"Eat it," Dawn said. "How's the hay look on the Upper East?"

Elton put a bite in his mouth. "Not too bad."

"The omelet or the hay?"

"The hay."

"You want milk?"

"I'd rather have a beer."

Dawn poured milk. "After supper I'm going out to check the sprinkler again."

"Is that why you're dressed up?"

"I'm not dressed up. I'm clean."

"I thought after supper we'd play horse," Elton said. "A dollar a game."

"Maybe later."

"Is there more omelet?"

"I'm not your slave, Elton."

"Then who is?" Elton got up and scraped the rest of the omelet from the pan onto his plate.

"What did you eat on the reservation?" Dawn asked.

Elton sat down again and forked a bite into his mouth.

"You must be from some tribe," Dawn said. "You know, even when you don't talk, you're telling me something."

"Yeah, like what?"

"You and I are alike, Elton."

"I don't think so."

"We're homeless. Right now we have good food and a place to sleep, and we're saving money, but it's not going to last. What are we going to do in the fall?"

"You think Mattie will kick us out?"

"It's economics. She won't have work for us."

"I'll go to school, and you can fix machines. Shelley will be at college, so you can have her room."

"Maybe Mattie will be lonely," Dawn said. "She'll keep us around to talk to."

"Maybe she will," Elton said.

"Can we hope for that?" Dawn asked.

A glimmer of heavy blue shone above the horizon, and the stars were out. Dawn drove the three-wheeler past the West Main and down the hill to the river bridge. The three-wheeler had a lighter chassis and was more susceptible to tipping, but Dawn liked it because she'd resurrected it from oblivion. She drove across the bridge and up the hill and under the sprinkler, which against the stars was not moving. The giant silver insect was stopped in the field.

She checked the generator with her flashlight, inspected the switches and wiring. Everything looked okay. She turned off the three-wheeler and listened.

Silence. There was no water in the pipe.

It was too late to troubleshoot—too little light. But she knew what had happened. There was no leak in the pipe. The bridge supports hadn't gone out. No, the Pollards were stealing water.

She drove west through the shallows where the bulls were killed and followed the abandoned road along the river for a quarter mile until she came out at the bottom of the steep slope below Hector's house. She left the three-wheeler there and climbed on foot.

Halfway up she paused to catch her breath. The reflection of the sky in the river brightened the hillside, and she heard a nighthawk buzz in the air high overhead. The house above her was tiny—not more than two or three rooms. Two windows were lighted. She fingered the new stone in her pocket, and then she heard music below her. Wordless notes stirred the air, mixed with wind. Sweet, like a flute. But all she saw was the silky blue in the water opposed to the dark hills.

She owed Hector. She owed her being to him. Dying had never scared her, but she hoped at death her thoughts would be unhurried and of her own volition—dolphins leaping from sea spray or buffalo surging over yellow hills or stones shimmering in a stream. Except for Hector, she might have died smelling the Pollards' beer breath and manure and ditch mud.

Rafe barked above her, whether at the music or at her she didn't know, and then Hector appeared at the corner of the house with his rifle raised to his shoulder.

"It's Dawn," she said.

Hector lowered the rifle, and he said something to Rafe, and Rafe stopped barking. "I thought you might be a Pollard."

Dawn climbed to the empty corral and then angled up to the house. Hector was barefoot and had on jeans and a T-shirt. He sat down on the step of the deck, and Rafe slumped down beside him.

"I heard music a minute ago," she said. "Did you? A flute, maybe."

"There are birds around."

"It wasn't a bird."

"I heard you coming along the river."

"I was at the pivot," Dawn said. "I knew from the other day this road must come to your place."

"I haven't been playing any music," Hector said. "What are you doing here?"

"I wanted to thank you."

"You don't need to thank me."

"I was a little shaken the other night, but I've been thinking about it. I thought I could work off my debt."

"What debt?"

"I want to pay for the bulls. It's my fault they were killed."

"Those bulls were worth more than you could work off."

"I can check on your cows. I could fix your machines."

"You have a job already."

"I have a laptop. I could put your whole operation on spreadsheets."

"I might think about doing that," Hector said. "Modernize and save."

"Why didn't you want the sheriff to file charges?"

"The bulls were dead. I have to live next to the Pollards. It wasn't worth the hassle."

"Was there something you didn't want the sheriff to know?"

"I've lived here six years," Hector said. "People have seen who I am."

"They know what you let them know," Dawn said. "You're Catholic, Hector. You know your sins."

"Maybe I do," Hector said.

Dawn tilted her ear. "There. Do you hear that?"

"No."

Rafe got up, and Dawn followed him to the edge of the deck.

"Rafe hears it."

The flutelike sound faded away, and Dawn looked up into sled-runner clouds. "Maybe it was water over stones," she said. "Maybe it was a dream."

"I didn't hear anything," Hector said.

Dawn looked out over the river. "Is this where you want to die?"

"I guess so. Nothing lasts forever."

"But why here?"

"Why not here?"

"Because you're from Mexico. Oh, I forgot. You can go to heaven from anywhere."

"That's my plan. Do you have a better one?"

"My plan is to raise buffalo."

"Now there's eternal life."

"I want to raise calves, sell the yearling bulls, breed the cows, and buy more. I want to make enough to get my own place. Why isn't that eternal life?"

"I thought it was, too," Hector said, "but I learned I couldn't control the variables."

"Like which ones?"

"Weather, market price, land. It takes time for land to open up and for people to trust you with it. If you don't have money, you need permission."

"I'll get permission," Dawn said.

"Do you know anything about buffalo?"

"I know they tolerate cold better than cattle, and they're worth more in the niche market."

"You need a lot of ground," Hector said. "And patience. You have to have patience to leave them alone."

"You don't think I have patience?"

"Not so far."

A coyote moaned in the river bottom, and Rafe perked up his ears. They were quiet a moment.

"That's not what you heard?"

"A coyote is not a flute," Dawn said. "Were you at the Morton this evening?"

"I needed a cable clamp to fix Rafe's line."

"Did you get it?"

"No, I haven't got the cable yet, so it didn't matter."

"I saw you drive away."

Hector looked down. Dawn patted Rafe.

"You listened to me."

"I didn't listen."

"You heard then."

Hector sat forward. "I couldn't not."

"It's all right," Dawn said. "I don't need a man."

"Good, because I don't need a woman."

"At least we agree on that," she said. "We'll talk some more about the spreadsheets for your business. I want to give you some compensation for the bulls."

"What's done is done."

"That's what I think, too. It's what comes after that you have to figure out." She moved from the rail. "I have to get back to Elton. I promised him I'd beat him at horse before he went to bed."

Chapter 14

Dawn's car was an adventure for Mattie to drive. The seat was too far back and sunken behind the wheel, the shocks were bad, and the steering was loosey-goosey. Dawn said it would get her there and back, though saying so wasn't a guarantee. It got her there anyway.

Lee was sitting at the bar in the Dakota Rose with two margaritas in front of him, and he stood up when she came in. "I took the liberty of ordering one for you," he said. "I was going to drink both if you didn't show up."

"I invited you," Mattie said. "I like margaritas."

"On the other hand, I didn't mean to usurp your authority."

"My authority isn't that easily usurped."

"You look very nice. Your shoes are spiffy."

"They're my daughter's. Is 'spiffy' a word still being used?"

"It was a compliment. I didn't know you owned a dress."

"Most women own a dress."

Mattie picked up her margarita and sipped it through the salt on the rim of the glass.

"Our table's ready anytime you are," Lee said.

Mattie nodded. "Maybe we'll get along better at a table."

"Are we not getting along?"

They carried the margaritas to a booth by the window, and a waitress came with menus. Outside were the parking lot and the moving headlights of cars and trucks on the highway.

They talked about ordinary things—greenflies and mosquitoes, Shelley, Elton's love of basketball. "Is there a verdict on Dawn?" Lee asked.

"She's a good mechanic," Mattie said. "Elton likes her."

"But you still have doubts."

"She has no tact," Mattie said, "and with her looks she thinks she can get away with anything."

"Maybe she can. Give me an example."

"Do you mind? I want to forget the ranch for a while, and talking about Dawn gets me upset. Tell me about your children instead."

"They live in Oregon. A boy and a girl, six and eight. I call them, write them letters and postcards, and send them birds' feathers, butterfly wings I find, pressed flowers. I visit when I can, but even so, they move away from me. In a few weeks I'm driving out to take them camping on the beach."

The waitress came back, and Mattie ordered salmon and a second margarita. Lee chose lamb brochettes and switched to red wine.

While they waited for dinner, Lee told stories about a dig he'd been on in Manitoba where the mosquitoes were so bad they had to eat with gloves on and one in Lebanon where bombs exploded every day.

"I guess bombs would test your love for your work," Mattie said.

"I already loved my work," Lee said. "What about your life with Haney? Were you happy?"

"I think we were. We lived in Boston for a while, and then Maine . . ."

Mattie talked, and she listened to herself as voice and audience, conscious of her lies. Lee nodded and apparently believed what she said. "There was camaraderie among his friends," Mattie said. "I wish for that still."

"We'd all like to go back."

"When we came to the ranch, it turned into mostly work, though I don't mind, except . . ."

"What?"

She smiled. "Nothing."

Their dinners were served. The salmon was fresh frozen, but without bones, and as Lee said, it was hard to get bad lamb. When they'd finished, the waitress cleared the plates and offered dessert.

"They have good chocolate mousse," Lee said.

"I don't need dessert."

"But do you want some?"

Mattie shook her head.

"What about coffee?" the waitress asked.

Mattie shook her head.

"One chocolate mousse," Lee said.

The waitress nodded and left them alone again.

"Shelley said a friend of Haney's took his sculptures to New York."

"Yes, I was glad of that. I didn't know what to do with them."

"Because they were beautiful, or because they reminded you he was gay?"

"Who told you that?"

"Shelley. But I talked with your husband a good deal when we negotiated the permission to dig. He didn't tell me in so many words, but I knew. I gathered from Shelley that you didn't."

Mattie folded her napkin and set it on the table and stood up.

The waitress brought the chocolate mousse. "The ladies' room's in back," she said.

Mattie hurried through the tables, down a hallway, and pushed through the cowgirls' door to the bright light. She went into a toilet stall.

A moment later she heard the outer door open. "Are you all right?" Lee asked.

"Fine."

"Then I'll wait for you outside."

She sat on the toilet, then came out and composed herself in the mirror. At home she'd been pleased with how she looked—her hair done up, understated makeup, the dress and the gold sandals—but now she looked garish. She wasn't herself in a dress. And what was she thinking wearing makeup? So Haney was gay. What was she supposed to do about it?

She took a deep breath. Be silent. Be silent like Rosa Saenz. Rosa's silence was sweet. Rosa's silence kissed.

Mattie tucked a strand of loose hair behind her ear and dabbed on fresh lipstick. She was all right. Fine! Goddammit, she was *fine*.

Lee was sitting on the fender of his truck watching the cars pass on the highway.

"Thank you for dinner," she said.

"I didn't mean to upset you."

"I know."

"I saved you some chocolate mousse," he said, and handed her a paper bag.

"Thank you."

"Maybe we can do this another time."

"Maybe we can," she said.

"I know you want peace," he said. "But if you'd like to, call me. I'll leave it up to you."

Chapter 15

Dawn had a radio, but Mattie didn't turn it on. She liked the quiet, the moonlight sliding in, the surrounding darkness. Lee followed her south to the country road, and when she turned, he beeped his horn. She watched him do a U-turn and his truck recede in her rearview mirror.

She drove a half mile and beeped her horn, too.

Lee had been solicitous and respectful, but he made her nervous anyway. At least he hadn't tried to hold her hand or kiss her good night, though he might have. But that was nonsense. She couldn't expect him to keep his distance and embrace her at the same time.

Well, the evening hadn't been as terrible as she'd imagined. She hadn't lost anything, and Lee had asked her out again. Or she thought he had. *Maybe we can do this another time.* That wasn't exactly asking her out, but it was close, and she'd been as noncommittal as he was uncertain. If she wanted to go out again, she should call him. Of course she wouldn't do that. But she might have said, "How about tomorrow?" Or, "Have you ever tried the Elk Horn Diner?" But she couldn't telephone him. On the other hand, she might call and thank him. That was politeness.

She smiled and turned at a section line. A fox scooted across the road and dived into the weeds, and ahead the cemetery came up in her headlights. On impulse, she slowed and turned in under the archway. Always there was that sadness. The moon shone down over the graves, and the pine windbreak cast a line of moon shadows. She got out and sat on Loren's grave and ate the chocolate mousse with a plastic spoon.

Having a child die was beyond pain. The pain she'd felt that night driving to the hospital, the numbness, the silence she and Haney maintained, for what was there to say? There were no words. *Hurry! What if he dies? Do something.* They had done everything they knew to do, everything that could have been done, and still he died, still he left her and went into darkness while she had to stay in the light.

She sat awhile and then got back into the car. She was almost home. She passed Hector's mailbox, the Pollards' driveway, the Deckers' house right on the road. A mile farther, at the edge of the mesa, the light at the Morton appeared in the air.

The Mercury whined in second going down the hill. Then, in the rearview mirror, moving headlights caught her eye. She hadn't noticed any cars on the road, though sometimes teenagers parked at the gravel quarry. The headlights came up fast behind her.

Was it Lee? There were three houses on the county road beyond the ranch—the Haffners, the Bishops, and the Appletons—but as the headlights came closer, she saw it wasn't a pickup. It was bigger than a pickup. At the bottom of the hill she clanked over the cattle guard and expected the car behind her to turn east, but it followed right on her tail and turned on its brights.

The high beams scared her, and she thought of the Pollards. They'd seen Dawn's car head into town and waited for her to come back. But it wasn't the Pollards' truck, either. It was one of those suburban assault vehicles, a Jeep Cherokee or a Pathfinder. She lowered the rearview mirror and sped up, but the lights moved up fast on her bumper.

Then the Pathfinder rammed her. The Mercury jumped forward and up onto the ridge at the side of the road. Mattie tightened her grip on the wheel, and the Pathfinder hit her again. She swerved, held the wheel, and then veered left, away from the house toward the West Main.

The Pathfinder stayed with her. She fishtailed to raise dust, and when the other car dropped back a few yards, she saw the hay pen loom up in front of her. Weeds and sunflowers had grown head high around it, and she careened into the weeds, hoping to gain enough ground to loop back to the main driveway. She gave gas and cut back toward the house.

Past the hay pen the track was grassy, but she had to slow over the bumps to keep the front bumper from digging into the ground. The Pathfinder caught up and butted her again and then swung out wide and cut in front of her. She had no choice but to stop, but she didn't do it willingly. She gunned the motor and hit the other car in the left rear fender and scraped alongside almost to the driver's door. The impact spun the Mercury sideways and to a stop. Mattie's immediate impulse was to get out and run, but she couldn't. She laid her head on the steering wheel, and the horn blared.

A moment passed. Then she heard a man screaming. "You fucking bitch. You fucking, goddamn bitch. I'll kill you." He yanked open the car door. "Did you think I wouldn't find you?"

He pulled Mattie up by her hair and the back of her dress.

The horn stopped, and the man dragged her out of the car. "Do you know what you've done? Do you have any fucking idea?" He pushed her against the side of the car and shone a light into her face. "Fuck," he said. "Where's Yvonne?"

"I don't know Yvonne," Mattie said.

"You have my fucking car. You have the fucking *keys*." He ripped the keys out of the ignition. "*My* fucking keys."

He pulled her around to the trunk, but her legs hardly moved. He held her with one hand and opened the trunk with the other and shone the light inside. "Where's the computer?" he asked. "Where's the fucking *computer*? Where's my mother? Where's *Yvonne*?"

"I don't—"

The man pushed her away and tripped her, and Mattie sprawled into the grass.

"I'll find her," the man said. "She's here, and I'll fucking find her."

Mattie took a breath. She smelled grass and manure and rose to her knees. She looked into the flashlight, and the man kicked her in the head.

Chapter 16

Shelley woke to the alarm at 4:00 A.M. to get the truck back for the workday. Bryce had to get up, too, to drive her to Wind Cave. That was the deal they'd made. They got dressed and had coffee and walked out under the cool stars.

In the night the storm had moved east, and in its wake was clarity and reason. "Monday's my day off," Bryce said. "Can you find your way back here?"

"I turn where the lightning hit the rock."

"You won't change your mind?"

"I might. I have before."

"Then this will be a test."

He put his arm around her, and she put hers around him. She meant to be there Monday. That was what she felt as they drove to her truck and how she felt in the truck all the way to Hot Springs.

The streets in town were empty. Yogi's was closed. So was the 7-Eleven. Streetlamps illuminated the scattered parked cars. Then she was out of town, and the lights from Maverick Junction made a pale halo in the distance.

She was amazed more than anything else. She'd never felt anything like what he'd done to her in the chair. Science classes had taught her about nerve impulse firings, increased heartbeat, blood flow to certain parts of the body. She'd read *Our Bodies, Ourselves*. She'd seen X-rated movies in which women screamed in feigned ecstasy. But books and movies didn't explain what she felt. How could she know what it felt like until it happened to her?

After he'd made her come the first time, she'd taken a shower, and Bryce had cooked rice and chicken. They'd talked about Faulkner. She cleared the table. He put on Chopin's *Nocturnes*. Every moment was anticipation.

Then they were naked in bed. She'd never cared to know a man's body before, but now she smoothed the curve of his thigh as far as she could reach, then up again, her hand in touching speaking the unspoken words.

And he touched her, too—and how quickly she was wet!

At Maverick Junction she turned south, drove the eight miles to the county road, and turned east. As always, at that intersection, she thought of Jimmy Pollard, and now the memory came to her vividly. It had been just before Dwain Skutch had graduated—she was a sophomore—and she'd agreed to park with him again if he hit a home run for her in a baseball game. He'd hit two, and the next afternoon she missed the bus on purpose and waited for him in the Laundromat across from the school. He hadn't shown up, though, and she'd got madder by the minute. Then Jimmy Pollard drove up and leaned across the seat of his truck. "You want a ride home?" he asked. "I'm going out there. They got Dwain in detention."

"What for?"

"I don't know what for. If you want a ride, get in."

She never had liked Jimmy from riding the school bus. His teasing was mean, and he was gross, and she was glad when he got to drive and wasn't on the bus anymore. But Dwain hadn't shown up and she'd missed her bus, so she got in Jimmy's truck, and they coasted down the hill to the river. She stared straight out the windshield.

Outside of town the truck started to shake. "Needs alignment," Jimmy said, "but I don't have the money."

"Tires cost money, too," she said.

They turned right at Maverick Junction, and the truck shimmied as they built up speed.

"So how was fucking Dwain?" Jimmy asked.

She felt her face heat up, and Jimmy laughed. "Everybody knows you sucked him off."

She turned toward the passenger door. The country was a blur. She was angry and hurt and afraid, too, hearing Jimmy say that.

"I have a big one needs a vacuum," Jimmy said. "You want the job?"

"I want to get out," she said. "Stop right now."

The truck drifted. She heard Jimmy's zipper being pulled down. Then suddenly he grabbed the back of her neck and twisted her head around. "Suck it," he said.

His cock was half hard, swaying in front of her face. He pressed her head down. Then she felt the truck slow for the left turn at the county road, and she knew once they were off the main highway, something bad was going to happen. The truck slowed more—he was holding the wheel with one hand and a knee—and she hit his knee, and he had to grab the wheel with both hands. She sat up quickly. Luckily a car was coming from the other direction, and Jimmy had to brake almost to a stop before he could turn, and when he did, she opened the passenger door and jumped. She put out her arms to cushion the fall, but her right arm buckled. Her shoulder hit the pavement hard, and she rolled over with her broken arm under her.

The sheriff had investigated the accident, but she hadn't said what really happened, partly because she was ashamed and didn't want her parents to know, but mostly because she was afraid of what Jimmy might do to her. But that intersection still made her think of it.

What would Dawn have done? She would have punched Jimmy out. She'd have bitten off Jimmy's Johnson. God, Dawn wouldn't have kept quiet, that was for sure. She was either brave or crazy. Maybe both. And reckless. Not being afraid of the Pollards was reckless.

She should have warned Dawn that night at the Pollards'. *They'll do anything.* Running to Hector's, she'd been filled with such hatred it scared her. If only someday she were able to run with as much love.

She passed the feedlot and followed the moon east. She was tired of having to drive sixteen miles from the ranch. How many times had she done that? Sixteen miles for groceries or a beer or a movie. She wanted other vistas. She wanted the feeling Bryce gave her to last much longer; she was so surprised what gentleness could do.

> . . . more than the hand that touches,
> it is the touching that lasts.

She'd read that in the poetry book by Bryce's bed.

No rain here, as her mother said. The gravel road was dry. She descended the hill and aimed for the arc light. It was almost five-thirty, but there were still stars as daylight seeped up in the east.

She coasted in beside the three-wheeler, but the Lincoln wasn't there. Surely her mother wouldn't have driven it to town. If she had, where was she? Or had Dawn taken it? Shelley sat for a moment with the truck window down, wishing for Monday, now that she knew what to long for.

A mist rose from the creek, and the yard was shadowed by the light from the Morton. The birds had not yet waked. Even insects were silent. She was tempted to sleep there in the truck so as not to wake anyone in the house, but she wanted to sleep late and wake dreaming.

Finally she got out of the truck. The front door of the house was open—her mother always locked the door—and she pushed through the screen quietly. There was an odd smell in the kitchen. Sweat, maybe damp—she couldn't identify it. She flicked the light switch beside the door, but there was no light.

She tiptoed across to the vestibule and turned on the light there.

What she saw: a man lying facedown on the linoleum with blood pooled beneath his head, and Dawn slumped in the living room doorway, sitting up, blood soaked through the back of her shirt.

For a long moment Shelley couldn't move.

Then at last she stepped over the man—she'd never seen him before—and leaned down to Dawn. Blood dribbled from Dawn's mouth and matted her hair and ran down her neck.

Then she stood up in panic. "Mom?"

She ran into the living room. "Mom?"

Shelley took the stairs by twos, ran down the hallway, and threw open the door to her mother's room. The light blazed. The room was empty, the bed made and not slept in. She picked up the telephone and dialed. Trini Decker's number was the only one she could think of.

Part IV

'Tis visible silence, still as the hour-glass.

—Dante Gabriel Rossetti

Chapter 1

A week before second cutting, Shelley started looking for another hired man. Elton had been gone two weeks, and Dawn was still unable to work a full day. Her mother was incapable of doing much of anything. She was lethargic, uninterested, and sad. The doctor had wired her broken jaw, but he couldn't give an explanation for her malaise. "She's had trauma," he said. "People respond to it in different ways. There's nothing to do but wait."

"We're waiting," Shelley said. "The hay doesn't."

Hector offered to bale, but he didn't have time to windrow, too. Trini, who came to visit Mattie every day, suggested one morning that Shelley call Gretchen Wright.

"Gretchen's a little old to run a windrower."

"I mean, people offer to help her, so she knows who's available."

"I'll call her."

"Your mother any better today?"

"No, go see if you can cheer her up."

Shelley called Gretchen.

"Homer Twardzik needs work," Gretchen said. "He's out of the VA hospital, and he used to be a pretty fair poker player."

"We're not looking to lose money at cards," Shelley said.

"I just meant if you're looking for a man's body, his has a mind attached to it."

"Isn't Homer as old as you are?"

"Well, then, there's Latrell Wiggins."

"My father put him on here once," Shelley said. "He smokes more than he works."

In the end, Shelley called Homer Twardzik, and Homer agreed to work three days a week, starting Monday.

For the first several days after Styver was killed, Sheriff Nolan came personally to find out if Shelley had heard from the Indian boy. His office had put out an APB on the Lincoln, but nothing had turned up. After Sheriff Nolan got no information, he sent Deputy Kroupa because, as Kroupa put it to Shelley, "It's snakes and coyotes when you and the sheriff talk." Then nobody came for a while, until her mother got home from the hospital.

One morning Mattie and Shelley were sitting on the porch, watching the swallows flutter back and forth to their nests under the eaves. On the doctor's recommendation, Mattie was knitting to keep herself occupied, but she hated it. She miscounted rows and dropped stitches, and seeing the sheriff's Blazer come through the heat and into the yard didn't help her mood.

When he parked and fiddled and finally ambled over, her mother threw her ball of yarn at the lilac bush by the steps.

"We haven't heard from him," Shelley said.

"How's your mother feeling?" the sheriff asked.

"She's right there. You see her."

The sheriff picked up the knitting and set in on the porch steps. "How are you feeling, Mrs. Remmel?"

"It's none of your business," Mattie said. "But sometimes I get dizzy and fire my pistol randomly."

"Would you tell me if you'd heard from the boy?"

"You must think we would, or you wouldn't be here," Shelley said.

"I'm here because I'm not sure."

They all knew Elton had killed Lester Styver. The theory was through the window Elton saw Styver beating up Dawn, and he shot him once from the porch, where a .22 shell was recovered. The bullet had struck Styver in the left side of the head and passed through the top of his earlobe. Then Elton went into the kitchen and shot Styver again twice from close range. He left the rifle on the kitchen table.

After that, what happened was pure speculation. Elton probably hadn't understood what he'd done was justifiable, and whether out of fear or panic, he'd taken the Lincoln and disappeared.

"You'd think it wouldn't be hard to find a 1994 Lincoln in South Dakota," Shelley said.

"He could be in Wyoming or Montana."

"He could be in Florida," Mattie said.

"But probably he went home," the sheriff said. "That's what most people do."

"We told you, we don't know where that is," Shelley said. "My mother reported him as missing when he first came here."

"Some parents don't like their kids," the sheriff said. "We talked to the tribal police in Rosebud and Pine Ridge, and even the Northern Cheyenne, but we didn't get much cooperation."

"What've you found out about the man who was killed?" Shelley asked.

"He had five arrests in Utah for fraud—creating bogus companies and then selling them—but no convictions. Apparently Styver showed up in Hot Springs posing as a detective asking about someone named Yvonne."

"That's Dawn," Mattie said. "What'd you learn about her?"

"Nothing at all. We couldn't trace her. But as far as we can tell, she wasn't involved in Styver's crimes." The sheriff paused. "Listen, Mattie, I'm not saying the boy's going to be charged with anything. But a man was killed, and we want to talk to the person who killed him."

"Then you better find the Lincoln," Mattie said.

Dawn hadn't been hurt all that badly, though she'd looked bad when Shelley found her. She'd bled a lot from a scalp wound, and she had bruises on her throat and cheek and arms, and she was in shock, but she stayed only for observation overnight at the clinic in Hot Springs.

In the clinic she'd dreamed of Styver, inky dreams of flying at night in his plane. Lights whirled through air, the motor died, and the earth flew up at her. When she woke, Styver was still there. She could feel him nearby.

When she was released, Shelley invited her to sleep in Elton's room, and she accepted because she was afraid Styver would come back for her. But she couldn't sleep in Elton's room. She was used to the wind and coyotes' songs, to meadowlarks and sparrows. Unlike the Pollards' near rape, Styver's beating was real, with a real aftermath, and it unnerved her in a deeper way. That was the consequence of evil. Anything could happen at any time. It had finally happened to her.

Her only consolation was when Mattie came home from the hospital. Dawn kept vigil over her, sitting with her at night. She rubbed her back, put cool washcloths on her forehead, kept the covers on her. She was mindful not of the companionship offered, but of Mattie's need. She needed to love herself. What solace could Dawn offer? What could she give Mattie to make her feel worthy again?

Once Mattie woke in absolute calm, as if no troubled dream had wakened her. "You've been here the whole time, haven't you?" she asked.

"Part of the time," Dawn said.

"Is it late?"

"It's the middle of the night."

Mattie looked toward the dark window. "How long's Elton been gone?"

"Two weeks. I think a few days more."

"He could call. He knows we're worried about him."

"Maybe he's some place he can't."

"Is Shelley here?"

"She's at Bryce's."

"Does she love him?"

"She can't love him until they stop fucking."

Mattie looked away. "Do you have to use that word?"

"Love?"

"You know which word. Women don't say that."

"Women say it all the time."

Mattie pushed against the headboard to sitting, and Dawn propped the pillow behind her. "We have to consider where Elton might be," Mattie said. "I think he's here on the ranch."

"Why do you think that?"

"When he first came, he was here for weeks before he came out into the open."

"Then we'll look for him," Dawn said. "Tomorrow, when you're better."

Mattie lay down again. "Tomorrow, then," she said. And she drifted back to sleep.

Shelley, too, was affected by what Styver had done. She'd driven home that night with Bryce's scent still on her and had opened the door of her house to carnage. She'd called Trini and then Lee. Lee said he'd been to dinner with her mother, that he'd followed her to the county road, so they knew she'd made it that far. That had been a little before ten. Lee had called the sheriff's dispatcher and the state patrol and then had driven to the ranch, looking for Dawn's car on the way.

But even then they hadn't found her, and Shelley was sure she was dead.

Trini and Allen Decker showed up, and the ambulance took Dawn. When the sheriff and Wade Griffith, the state patrolman, got there, there was a flurry of questions. Allen went up to Hector's to look for Mattie, and Shelley checked Dawn's camp. They thought maybe she'd gone with Elton, but they wouldn't have taken both the Lincoln and the Mercury. Had someone else been there besides the dead man?

Finally Lee had found Mattie collapsed at the creek a quarter mile from the house.

God, what a nightmare! At the same moment Shelley had felt so tenderly toward Bryce, a stranger had kicked her mother into unconsciousness, and Dawn had been beaten by a man now dead. Shelley wasn't harmed, but as a panicked witness she was a victim, too.

Mattie got worse instead of better. Physically she improved, but her behavior became more erratic. She woke early, but didn't eat breakfast or do any chores. Instead she saddled Roy Rogers or Dale Evans and took long rides, looking for Elton.

"Mom, if he's around here, where's the Lincoln?"

"I never liked that car."

"I know you never liked that car, but, Mom—"

"He might be here," Mattie said. "I have to make sure."

She wore jeans and boots and a wide-brimmed straw hat and carried in a saddlebag a snakebite kit, crackers, and water. She searched the gullies and thickets along the river, the ravines below the mesas, the dense cottonwoods to the east. Four thousand acres was a lot of territory to cover. She discovered a prairie falcon's nest not far from the fence she and Shelley had built. Dickcissels were in the pasture in the far northeast corner of the ranch. She found the bones of a coyote, a badger's den, a broken spearpoint.

She returned from these excursions midafternoon and slept, and when she woke again, she sat on the porch and watched the sun go down.

Shelley sat with her sometimes, thinking she should. She hoped the details of the ranch would draw her mother out of her depression. They'd stopped irrigating to let the ground dry for second cutting. The hay looked okay on the Upper East, but not so good on the West Main and Long Narrow. The pivot wasn't going to produce as it had first cutting, either. Dawn had remembered the sprinkler wasn't running the night she'd gone to Hector's. Mattie was uninterested.

"Homer Twardzik will help us," Shelley said, "but I don't know whether he'll do any good."

"When does all this start?"

"Monday. The day after tomorrow."

"Good," Mattie said. "Look at those colors in the clouds."

Homer Twardzik was sixty-two and totally deaf in his left ear from looking around for so many years at the disk breaking up ground behind him. He was some help to start, but by afternoon on his second day, dust and pollen and alfalfa particles had left him so short of breath he wasn't able to speak. Thursday Dawn did a couple of hours' cutting, and on Friday Shelley put Homer to irrigating the corn and Sudex. What should have taken him an hour took four.

On the next Monday, Homer came at eleven instead of at six, and Shelley fired him.

"I had to see the doctor," Homer said.

"I don't care if you saw a priest," Shelley said. "I need someone I can count on."

"Who'll cut the hay?"

"We will," Shelley said.

"We" meant Dawn and her. There wasn't anyone else.

That same Monday afternoon Dawn taught Shelley to run the windrower in the Upper East. Her mother thought the machine was tame, but to Shelley its noise was daunting. The engine roared; the teeth gnashed; the conveyor belt snapped and popped. Even with earmuffs, the noise was bad. Dawn explained the gears and hand levers and how to turn at the end of a row. She made two perimeter cuts with Shelley riding beside. "The perimeter cuts give the machine space to turn around. Then it's back and forth and up and down. It's not exactly rocket science."

Dawn did two rows and rode another four while Shelley drove. Then Shelley was on her own.

Shelley did six more rows. Her windrows weren't exactly even, more like lightning bolts trailing behind her, but she was cutting alfalfa for the first time in her life. At the end of the seventh row, she forgot to raise the reel and cranked the wrong hand lever, and instead of turning ninety degrees, the windrower went straight ahead into the ditch.

It took them the rest of the day to tow the windrower out and for Dawn to fix the cutting bar.

In the next several days Shelley got the hang of it. She finished the Upper East and started the West Main. Her windrows straightened out. The hardest thing was to concentrate, to fit the right edge of the cutting bar at the edge of the mowed field. The second hardest thing was being bitten by horseflies, greenflies, and blackflies. And she breathed dust, pollen, small bugs, engine fumes.

Once, to drown the noise of the machine, she put a Walkman inside her earmuffs and listened to "Watertower" by the band Maytag.

> I've got skies and antenna skylines
> Take a breath if you want to be fine
> I'm with a friend and he's lacking devotion
> I want the breeze and estrangement of motion
> Way out of this, let it begin.

The tape stopped abruptly, clogged with dust, and when she took off the earmuffs, she heard a wild screeching. The conveyor was working, the cutting bar clacked away, but something wasn't right. She shut the machine down and drove the four-wheeler back to the house.

"Sounds like a bearing went out," Dawn said. "It's not major unless you ran it a long time."

"Can you fix it?"

"In the army I worked on tanks and jeeps," Dawn said. "The principles are the same for most machines. I guess that's what I'm paid for. We have a supply of extra bearings."

But taking apart an old machine was tricky. Wear and tear weakened metal. Someone else had welded on some brackets because a bolt hole was broken. Twice she had to drive back to the Morton—once because she needed pince-nosed pliers and another time because both the hack-saw blades she had with her broke.

The disaster was, when the windrower was down, haying stopped.

"You think it'll be all day?" Shelley asked. "If it will, I think I'll drive up and see Bryce."

"I'm going as fast as I can."

"Yes or no?" Shelley asked.

"Yes," Dawn said, "but I thought you were adjusting your social life to the haying season."

"I am," Shelley said. "I concentrate better when I've had sex."

Each time seeing Bryce was a revelation. He keened as much to her plea-sure as to his own, and her pleasure made her willing to give. God, it was so simple! If each person cared about the other's pleasure, power disap-peared. Why were men so dense as to care only about their own?

Still, she wanted more. She wanted not only the sex, but more time with Bryce. She wanted the immediate pleasure and the prospect of the future. What would happen in a month, in a year, in five years?

Neither of her parents had ever encouraged her to find a man. A ca-reer was first. To do what she wanted and not to limit herself: That was paramount. Trini was more vocal, even, than her mother. "Too many women's lives are wasted on men," she said. "That was the fate of your mother's and my generation, but it doesn't have to be that way."

"You're the one who said you always slept with a man on the first date."

"Because there might not have been a second one."

"That's not exactly a great strategy."

"That's exactly what I'm saying. Now you can do it for the plea-sure."

"Of course, there's AIDS and STDs."

"Don't forget pregnancy," Trini said.

Shelley hadn't been like her mother or like Trini. She wanted to de-fine herself separately from other women, to identify a central point in her life and work from there. But what central point? She'd been taught to do great deeds, but what? Sell real estate? Work in a bank? Get a de-gree in journalism and work at a newspaper? Those weren't great deeds. To do something great was impossible. Life wasn't a movie. Even if she hadn't wrecked her knee, she'd never have been great at running. She might have done weights, sprints, and trained a hundred miles a week, but wanting it badly wasn't enough. Her genetics were insufficient. Her body was too slow.

Could she have a life of her own and closeness with a man? Was that possible? Certainly it hadn't been feasible with Warren. He was both selfish and reliant, two bad traits. But Bryce was different. His work left her free, and he wasn't possessive. And the way he made her feel! A future appeared in vague form, a blurry vision of being with someone for a long time. The idea scared the shit out of her.

That was how she felt when Bryce greeted her at the cabin door in his underwear. His body was soft, his shoulders thin, his skin pale from being underground, but she didn't think about his body because he was aware of *her*. He leaned into her and smelled her neck, her hair, her forehead.

"I've been running the windrower," she said. "I have to take a shower."

"Do it after." He smelled along her shoulder and the inside of her elbow.

"Bryce . . ."

"I smell hay, wind, and sunlight."

"You smell alfalfa dust, sweat, and diesel smoke."

He unbuttoned her blouse and smelled her breasts. He smelled under her arms. He unfastened her jeans and kneeled and smelled her stomach, her hip, her thigh. He peeled her panties down and smelled the soft hair between her legs. He moved her legs apart and smelled and tasted, and she was willing to do anything with him.

She suffered this torture as long as she dared and then pushed him backward onto the floor. She pulled his underwear down and guided him. Oh, yes. He pressed into her gently and held her hips tightly. She leaned over and kissed him, the smell of her still on his mouth.

Chapter 2

The next morning Dawn tested the windrower. Shelley was supposed to have been back from Bryce's, but she hadn't shown up yet, and the work had to be done. The machine ran *clackety-clackety, swish-swish, clackety-clack*. Dawn felt all right, though she'd been up most of the night and was achy-sleepy. She attuned herself to the rhythm of the cutting bar and the movement of time. She felt the changing light, minutes less in the mornings and evenings. All things were intertwined, but not causally. Establishing causality was the appeal of astrology—that celestial occurrences had repercussions in human enterprise—but she believed in fate and the magic of stones.

She dwelled on events not reconcilable with science or common sense—the woman from New Jersey who, under hypnosis, spoke an Austrian peasants' dialect from the eighteenth century, the mysterious circles of mown hay in fields in England, the overnight disappearance of the golden toad from the cloud forests of Costa Rica. Some of these could be malevolent, she supposed. Styver was present every moment.

Early clouds built over the mesa. Gray rain clouds. She considered the omen.

Suddenly a cock pheasant lifted its head black and green with a splash of red on its cheek, from the uncut alfalfa. The bird burst from cover and sailed down into yellow weeds at the edge of the field. The windrower vibrated in her body; the slapping of the canvas conveyor entered her hands. Right after the pheasant flew, a fawn stood up on its spindly legs. The first slat of the windrower reel struck it; tumbled it forward, and threw it upside down. Dawn shut off the cutting bar and the reel, and the fawn fell to the ground. She expected it to be ripped to pieces, but the fawn righted itself and stepped deliberately through the slats, and traipsed away along the edge of the uncut alfalfa.

Then it rained for the first time in six weeks. The rain fell as a hush and lasted only a few minutes, not enough to wet the ground, but plenty to clog the conveyor belt and the cutting bar. Dawn had to shut down and wait.

Lee called several times and came twice to visit before he went to Oregon to see his children, but both times he appeared, Mattie claimed she felt sick and went to her room. Shelley couldn't explain it to him. "The doctor says time will heal her," she said, "but so far it doesn't look good."

"She needs to find Elton," Lee said.

"Believe me, she's looking for him. She's covered every inch of the ranch."

"Has she looked on the reservation?"

"She says she has to be done here first."

"And what about Dawn? How's she doing?"

"Steady improvement. She's taking care of my mother at night."

"You know, I was thinking after I was here the last time, does your mother even know what happened?"

"What do you mean?"

"I found her passed out by the stream. How did she get there? Does she know what happened to Dawn? Maybe she doesn't have the whole picture."

"She knows Elton shot Styver."

"See if Dawn would go look for Elton with her. Maybe they'd talk."

"Mom wants to go alone."

"Oh, I know she wants to. But there are ways, and there are other ways."

"I'll see what I can do," Shelley said. "Anything is worth a try."

The next morning, clear and bright, Mattie climbed to the green gully near the sinkhole. She had been there before looking for Elton and hadn't found him, but perhaps he had eluded her the way deer did, by coming around back to the same place. Surely Elton must be in that tangle of brush and flowers, in such a place as birds sang and water danced from the ground.

She made her way down the dry slope through rabbitbrush and

yucca to the green tangle, where she heard the water and felt the cooler air rising. At the edge of the thicket she was comforted again. Tiger swallowtails and fritillaries fluttered among the buttercups and shooting stars and blue lupine, but she realized that while raccoons, foxes, and coyotes might find their way in and out, there was no path big enough for a deer, much less for someone upright.

"Mattie?"

A voice muffled by water: Mattie looked up and saw Dawn on the ridge.

"What are you doing down there?" Dawn asked.

"I thought Elton might be here."

"And is he?"

"Have you followed me?"

"No, but I came to find you. I need to know what you know."

"About what?"

Dawn perched herself on an outcropping of rocks, and Mattie climbed up the hillside at an angle toward her. Dawn offered her a hand up the last pitch.

"I need help remembering," Dawn said.

"What do you want to remember for?"

"I want to get past that night," Dawn said. "I have to remember before I can forget."

"And you think I know something?"

"Yes."

"I know my husband died, my son died, and now Elton is gone."

"That night, do you remember, I found you by the creek?"

"Lee found me. That's what Shelley said."

"He found you the second time, but I found you first. I was coming back from Hector's on the three-wheeler."

Mattie shook her head.

"Do you remember what you were wearing?"

"No."

"That beige dress . . ."

"And Shelley's gold sandals. I'd had dinner with Lee. I remember that."

"Do you remember driving the Mercury?"

"Yes."

"They found the Mercury over by the hay pen in the West Main."

"At first I thought it was the Pollards."

"What do you mean, at first? What happened?"

"I was cold. I woke up on the ground."

Dawn waited.

"My head hurt, my chin, and my shoulder, too. I had on those gold sandals."

"Before that. Do you remember what happened?"

"I remember the bright headlights. I wanted to lead him away from the house."

"You knew it wasn't the Pollards?"

"Yes. He rammed the back of the car. Several times. Then he cut me off, and I hit him."

Dawn waited again.

"He pulled me out of the car. . . . He wanted his mother's ashes and a computer. He said he was going to kill me."

"Kill you?"

"Kill Yvonne."

"And he almost did," Dawn said. "Except for Elton." She paused. "When I found you, you were in the pasture. Lee said you were at the creek."

Mattie thought for a moment. "He kicked me," she said. "When I woke up, I wanted to get home to Haney and Loren and Shelley. I was so cold on the ground."

"That was years ago."

"I walked toward the light. I was dizzy. At the creek I knelt down and dipped my hands, but the water ran through my fingers. . . . The water spilled out."

"I left you to get help," Dawn said. "When I got to the house, it was dark. I assumed Elton was in bed. I ran up the porch steps, and Styver stepped out of the shadow and grabbed me. Mattie, when I left him, I thought he'd never find me. Not here. I never meant for you and Shelley and Elton to be in danger."

"Why did he come after you?"

"I had his mother's ashes in an urn," Dawn said. "They were in the Mercury. So was his computer. When he grabbed me, he started raving about his golf clubs, too. I told him I didn't have his fucking golf clubs. I went into the house to call, and he followed me in. He smashed the light with his pistol. It was eerie, Mattie, this man waving his gun around in the dark, yelling about his golf clubs and his mother's cat. I never thought he wanted his mother's ashes."

"What cat?"

"I threw everything in the river. The golf clubs, his mother's ashes, the cat, too. His mother wanted to be buried with her cat. When I told him all this, he punched me. 'Maybe I won't kill you,' he said. 'I'll scar your face and kill that bitch out there by my car, so for the rest of your life you can think about what you've done.' I went crazy then. I had a stone in my pocket, and I threw it at him and hit him with it, too, and then he cracked my head against the doorjamb. All I remember after that is his hands around my neck, and his thumbs under my jaw. I couldn't breathe. That must have been when Elton shot him."

Mattie sat still.

"I guess he would have killed me," Dawn said. "Maybe you, too."

"But he didn't," Mattie said. "We're still here."

"We lived through it," Dawn said.

"We're alive. We're survivors."

"We are survivors," Dawn said. She held Mattie's arm. "That's how we should remember this."

Chapter 3

The next day Mattie was different. She was up early reading the history of the Pine Ridge Reservation; then she irrigated the corn and walked the ditch all the way to the West Main. After that she rode out to the pivot with Dawn. "The generator checks out," Dawn said. "The timer's on, but we're not always getting the water to turn the sprinkler."

"The Pollards are diverting it at night?"

"That's how it looks."

"Well, it's stealing, but the sheriff's not going to help us. Haney tried that approach and didn't get anywhere."

"So what are you going to do?"

"I guess I'll have to talk to Lute."

"I don't know, Mattie. Maybe Allen Decker . . ."

"Allen Decker isn't going to do squat," Mattie said.

She weeded the garden for an hour, tied up the tomato plants that had been neglected, then fertilized the squash and zucchini. She harvested the last of the peas and lettuce, then packed a lunch and drove the truck across the river to where Shelley was irrigating the Sudex.

"Are you ready?" Mattie asked.

"Almost."

Mattie got out of the truck, and they walked up the ditch together, Shelley in the mud in rubber boots, and Mattie on the road in sneakers. Shelley shoveled a channel from the edge of the ditch.

"I never thought I'd see you work this place," Mattie said.

"Somebody has had to. I think I'd like cutting hay if we had a newer machine. But I don't want to be out here in the winter."

"I guess you've been thinking about alternatives."

"I think I might go back to CU and do geology."

"There's still gold in the earth," Mattie said.

"I like fossils," Shelley said. "That's what I'd go back to study."

Shelley shoveled another cut in the ditch and waded back across to the road.

"I brought you some other shoes," Mattie said. "Let's get going."

East of the ranch were wheatfields and pastures, but when they crossed back over the river, the terrain changed to arid country—rocky hills, mudmounds, alkali flats, and desolate arroyos.

"A landscape inhabited by ghosts," Mattie said.

"Not exactly a place of milk and honey," Shelley said. "No wonder the Lakota feel cheated."

From the top of the crest above the river, a serrated wasteland stretched as far as they could see: Mako Sica, the bad land.

"A million acres, give or take a few," Mattie said. "And not many roads. Elton could be anywhere."

Shelley dodged as many ruts and holes as she could and ran over washboard. Scraggly antelope watched them pass. A vulture tilted close by over a mudmound. Where the gravel intersected pavement, they turned north toward Red Shirt.

Tumbleweeds and white plastic grocery bags were caught in the fences along the road. Now and then they passed a dryland field burned out for lack of rain.

"So I guess the Indians fought and lost," Shelley said. "I learned about it in school, but I never remember exactly what happened."

"After all the battles with Custer and the others, the Oglala Lakota were given all of western South Dakota, including the Black Hills, and some of North Dakota and eastern Wyoming as unceded Indian Territory. This was by treaty at Fort Laramie in 1868. The terms couldn't be changed, or lands ceded back, without three-fourths of all male Indians signing off on it. Everyone admits the Indians never consented to giving up the Black Hills."

"Do you think they'll get the land back?"

"Do you?" Mattie asked.

"Daddy used to say it was not a nation of laws, but one of convenience of the rich. But I never thought Daddy was very political."

"His politics didn't play out here," Mattie said. "This was Reagan/Bush territory, so he kept his opinions to himself."

"Neither do Bryce's. He's always in trouble with the school board. Keith Decker is a little shit."

A water tank a hundred feet in the air announced the village of Red Shirt, a knot of government-issue houses and double-wide trailers. Rattletrap trucks and new compact cars littered the yards.

"It should be easy to spot a Lincoln," Shelley said.

"Let's stop at the school," Mattie said.

The school was three trailers beside each other. A pickup and a dented Camaro were parked in the lot.

"You think there's summer school?" Shelley asked.

"We might as well see whether anyone knows Elton."

Mattie walked up the wooden access ramp, and suddenly music came through the open window—clarinets, a trumpet, a trombone. In the entryway were lines of coat hooks and pictures of Crazy Horse and Theodore Roosevelt side by side on the wall. In one of the classrooms were a half dozen children with their instruments. "Listen to the notes," the teacher said. He tapped his baton. "Do you hear what you're playing?"

Mattie stepped into the doorway, Shelley right behind her. The children giggled.

"Can I help you?" the teacher asked.

"We're looking for a boy named Elton," Mattie said. "About fourteen. He's pretty good at basketball. He might have been on a team."

"Not in Red Shirt," the teacher said. "Maybe in Pine Ridge."

"He's driving a maroon Lincoln," Shelley said.

The children giggled again. The man shook his head.

"Thanks," Mattie said.

Shelley smiled at the children. "We liked your music."

The schools in Pine Ridge were closed, but they talked to the tribal police and with the principal of Red Cloud School and showed them Elton's photograph. No one knew Elton or had seen a maroon Lincoln. They talked to the basketball coach at the junior high, and he'd heard of a pretty good kid in Wanblee.

On the way to Wanblee they drove through Kyle, but the school was closed, and they didn't see a Lincoln. In Wanblee the good basketball player turned out to be a girl. They searched Oglala and then headed back south.

"What made you do it, Mom?" Shelley asked. "Why were you faithful to Dad?"

"I loved him."

"You were never tempted by the pilot who took you skydiving, or Ames McGill, or whoever else?"

"No, I was never interested."

"So you were moral?"

"I never decided anything. I don't know if you could call it moral. I never imagined sex without love."

"I never imagined it *with* love," Shelley said. "Until Bryce it was as if I'd been in a dark room crashing into furniture, and then a light was turned on."

"Having an orgasm doesn't mean you're in love."

"Well, I know that."

"Does he love you?"

"He acts as if he does. We haven't talked about it."

"I guess how he acts is all you can go on."

Ahead of them, among the dry, rolling hills and long vistas of sky, were a few scattered houses. Shelley slowed at the outskirts of the town, where brush and trees grew along a creek. A white church appeared on a hill.

"This is Wounded Knee," Mattie said. "Have you heard of it?"

"I'm not that lame, Mom."

They stopped at the sign at a turnout, and Shelley and Mattie read about the confusion of events that led to the deaths of two hundred Indians and twenty-nine soldiers, December 29, 1890.

Chapter 4

That evening Trini came down wanting to know what they'd found out in Pine Ridge. Dawn had made a casserole, and they ate at the kitchen table with the door open for the gusty breeze. It was still light, and clouds came in from the northwest.

"You'd think if he were from Pine Ridge, someone would know him," Mattie said.

"He wasn't from there," Shelley said, dabbing at her casserole. "I keep thinking of the movies—how the woman gets terrorized by a crazy man, and the hero gets beaten up, and five minutes later the man and the woman act as if nothing ever happened to them. They're kissing each other and smiling, right back to normal."

"We may never be back to normal," Mattie said.

"There's no hero to kiss," Dawn said. "But there will be. I have that feeling."

"Did you think Styver would show up, too?" Shelley asked.

"Don't talk about that," Trini said.

A few raindrops thudded in the yard, and a gust of wind came through the screen door.

"Yes," Dawn said. "He's coming back again. It's as if he's the rain."

Dawn turned toward the window. Rain moved across the horse pasture, gray against the gray dusk. A few more drops sounded on the tin roof.

"I'll be right back," Dawn said.

She went out and let the screen door bang closed.

The room fell to hesitation. The rain swept in.

"It's eerie," Trini said.

"Dawn's eerie," Shelley said.

Mattie got up from the table and cleared the plates. "Where was he lying, exactly?" she asked.

"By the stove," Shelley said. She pointed at the floor. "Dawn was by the door to the living room so Elton must have dragged Styver over there. His head was this way. We couldn't get all the blood up, so we covered the spot with a throw rug."

"Let's think of something else," Trini said.

Mattie rinsed the dishes, and the rain sizzled on the roof.

Then Dawn came back, her shirt wet, her fist around the neck of a bottle of Stolichnaya.

"I don't drink hard liquor," Trini said, "unless of course it's offered."

"You've been holding out on us," Shelley said.

Dawn set the vodka on the table. "I've been saving this," she said. "I didn't know for what until now."

"We're not doing that again," Mattie said.

"I got this in Death Valley," Dawn said. "I know about these things."

"From the army, probably," Shelley said.

"No, not from the army, but I know."

She gazed at each of them for a moment, then picked up the bottle and walked around the table. "Styver came here to get me," she said. "All of this happened because of me."

"No one's blaming you," Shelley said.

"But maybe you should."

"It was random occurrence," Mattie said. "Maybe you picked up some bad stones."

"Listen," Dawn said.

Rain roared on the roof. There was nothing else to hear.

After a moment Dawn rolled her eyes back so the whites showed. *"Doog,"* she said. *"Golf. Mobile homes. Mother. A million dollars."*

"Jesus Christ," Shelley said. "Lighten up, Dawn. This is too much."

But Dawn didn't stop. She swooped through the room. *"Death Valley. Titleist. My country 'tis of thee . . ."*

Mattie came over from the sink and sat down by Trini and Shelley. Dawn pulled away the throw rug from beside the stove and splashed vodka over the bloodstains. Then she flicked a match.

"Stop," Mattie said.

But the floor burst into flames.

Mattie jumped up, and her chair clattered backward. Shelley grabbed her mother's arm. Blue flames licked across the wood.

"*Styver, Styver, Styver.*"

Dawn whirled through the room, sloshing vodka everywhere.

Mattie stamped at the flames, but the vodka seeped into the cracks of the floorboards and kept burning. The curtains ignited, and fire flew upward along both sides of the window.

Dawn danced around the table. "*. . . doog. Cessna. Styver! Styver!*"

The smoke thickened. Trini filled a pan at the sink and threw water at the curtains. The water hissed and steamed, and the flames diminished, but burst back alive. Mattie pulled the door to the living room closed and leaned against it. Trini filled the pan again.

Shelley grabbed her mother's hand. "Come on, Mom, let's get out."

They pushed through the screen door to the porch.

"Get the hose," Mattie said.

In the kitchen Dawn went on jabbering and chanting and shouting.

Shelley vaulted the railing and turned on the spigot and grabbed the hose. She yanked it free from a stone and handed the nozzle up to Mattie, who pulled it toward the door.

Thick smoke was pouring out now, and Mattie sprayed water into the kitchen. Shelley ran back up the steps.

"Give me that, Mom."

"Where's Trini?" Mattie shouted. "Trini?"

Shelley took the hose and opened the door. She couldn't see into the room, but she held her breath and stepped inside and sprayed the hose blindly.

"Trini? Trini? Get out! Dawn?" Mattie kept shouting the names.

Shelley retreated and took a breath. "I can't see anything in there."

Then Trini appeared at the corner of the house. "I'm here. I came out through the vestibule."

"Where's Dawn?" Mattie asked.

"Dawn's still in there," Shelley said. "The smoke—"

"Dawn!" Mattie peered inside.

Seconds went by.

Then Dawn appeared from the billows of smoke and knelt on the porch.

"The fire's out," she said. "Styver's gone."

Chapter 5

Mattie picked beans and thought of the new kitchen she wanted to build. Whoever had lived in the house before hadn't cooked—a man probably—and she'd tried to get Haney to remodel or tear out the old kitchen and start over. But it was another project he'd never got to.

In the days after the fire, Dawn pulled down burned wallboard and studs and took up the charred floor. Using the balky flatbed, she carried quarter-inch plywood from the barn and laid a makeshift floor between the porch and the living room. She levered the refrigerator onto cinder blocks and rewired the stove, leaving them with an open-air kitchen covered by a blue tarp, where the roof had burned through.

Dawn hadn't intended the fire. She'd thought the vodka would burn out the way it did in strawberries flambé. "There was more evil in Styver than I realized," she said. "And once everyone else was out of the kitchen, I sensed how close he was. I kept chanting, and he got smaller and smaller, and from one moment to the next, he disappeared."

"And that's when the fire went out?" Mattie asked.

"Yes. I knew he was gone."

There had been that one rain, but then the weather was clear, not a cloud in the sky. The cut hay in the Upper East was still too wet to bale, and the alfalfa on the pivot field hadn't dried out enough to windrow, either. They were already way behind schedule, but Mattie was back among the living and able to work again.

While they waited for the hay to dry, she worked in the garden. That's what she was doing now, picking beans and imagining her new kitchen, when Dawn came up unheard.

"A lot of beans," Dawn said.

"Yes, but I wouldn't say we've had good luck since I took out that row."

"You have in your garden."

"If you're looking for something to do, Dawn, you could drive to Rapid City and pick up the new stove and refrigerator."

"I'm replacing some of the gaskets on the flatbed. Have you talked to Lute Pollard yet?"

"We haven't even cut the pivot field," Mattie said. "We have to cut and bale and move bales, and then we'll need water. Anyway, I was thinking of letting the field go back to desert."

"It wasn't desert before."

"Haney never thought about the added labor to keep that field producing. He only thought of the possibility of getting it started."

"You aren't going to talk to Lute Pollard, are you?"

"Shelley's probably going back to school, and I can't manage that field alone."

A corner of the blue tarp on the kitchen flapped in the breeze. Dawn entered the garden, picked a bean, and chewed it raw. "Is it Elton?"

"I'm still hopeful about Elton."

"We'll see Elton again. Yes, we will."

Mattie straightened up. The blue tarp flapped again.

"Don't you believe me?"

"Dawn, I believe anything you'd tell me."

"Not true," Dawn said. "You haven't believed anyone since your husband died."

"Is that so?"

"You don't trust anyone enough to believe."

Mattie and Dawn looked at each other. Dawn chewed the bean.

"You have no right to say that to me." Mattie turned away toward the sound of the tarp.

"See?" Dawn said. "You turn away. Why do you always turn away?"

"Shut up, Dawn."

"Then you say, 'Shut up, Dawn.'"

"I don't judge you," Mattie said.

"Of course you do."

"All right, I judge you." Mattie threw the beans she was holding, and they struck Dawn in the face.

"Is that all you can do?"

Mattie picked up some beans she'd dropped and threw them, too.

"What else do you want from me?"

"More than that. I want you to admit you're scared."

"I am scared."

"You want to be strong, but you can't be. You can't do it."

Mattie turned away toward the Ironweed Patch—the rusted machines, the empty space where the flatbed had stood for as long as she'd been there, the stack of pipes by the swamp.

"You're always faking it," Dawn said.

Mattie turned back and slapped Dawn across the cheek.

"That's a start," Dawn said. She stepped closer.

"Get away from me."

Mattie edged through a row of beans, but Dawn sidestepped in front of her.

"Move."

"Aren't you going to fire me? Or are you afraid to do that, too?"

Mattie pushed Dawn away.

"Fire me. Go ahead."

"You're fired."

"Good," Dawn said, "now I don't have to do what you say."

Mattie lowered her shoulder and tried to step past, but Dawn nudged her into the wire fence, and Mattie sprawled facedown in the strawberries. Dawn straddled her back and whacked Mattie's butt. "Ha, ha! Whoopee!"

"Stop."

Dawn slapped Mattie's butt again.

Then Mattie raised up on her knees, and Dawn rolled off. She grabbed Mattie's arm and pulled her down again, and they struggled— Mattie to get loose, Dawn to stay close. Dawn was stronger, and Mattie weakened, and suddenly Mattie was in Dawn's arms, crying and crying, and Dawn was holding her and letting her cry.

Chapter 6

Three nights later Dawn woke at 2:00 A.M. for no reason she could name. She'd taken a turn on the windrower that afternoon; the hay had dried enough to cut, and Hector was going to start baling the Upper East. She felt a tremor, a vibration. She listened, but heard nothing. That was what woke her, she decided, nothing, though far off, north of the river, she saw the headlights of the tractor cutting through the cottonwood leaves.

In the morning there was a note scrawled on the seat of the four-wheeler: "BALER BELT BROKE, NORTH OF RIVER."

The baler was a priority, and Dawn spent the morning figuring out how to thread a new belt. She lined it up alongside a good one, and crawled into the baler, and looped it around the rollers—how many goddamn rollers were there? Ten, twelve? Twice she had to start over. A baler worked on compaction, the belt tightening around a small roll of hay, then stretching the springs as the jellyroll expanded. She got it the way she thought it should be, put in the linchpin, and bent the ends. She tested it, and the belt slipped off again.

Mattie came out midmorning to check on her progress. "We can call someone," Mattie said. "I didn't think when you started out that you'd know how to do everything."

"If I figure out how to do it once, the next time it won't take me but a minute."

"There's no rush," Mattie said. "Hector's not coming till after work."

"Maybe I'll grease it then, too. What's Shelley doing?"

"Windrowing the pivot. I'm going to move bales off the Upper East. Is the flatbed running?"

"Yes, but there are still some leaky gaskets," Dawn said.

"What kind of tires are on it?"

"Recaps."

"Can you build some crib sides to carry topsoil?"

"Sure."

"When you finish here, do that next. I'm going to dig up a few birch trees and plant them up at Hector's. He's already taken a sick day, and he's helping us at night when he doesn't have to. I thought it would be nice."

"What if he doesn't want them?" Dawn asked. "Maybe Hector likes open ground. In Togo the villagers sweep the bare earth around their houses to see the snakes coming."

"This isn't Togo."

"Still, it wouldn't hurt to ask."

"He'd also say this wasn't Togo," Mattie said. "And if we asked him, it wouldn't be a surprise. Besides, I don't want him to say no."

"Would he?"

"Why are we talking about this? When you finish the crib sides, scrape some manure from the corral and get a loader bucket of topsoil from the creek bank."

"Yes, ma'am."

"And don't 'yes, ma'am' me."

"Yes, ma'am."

After lunch Dawn hammered crib sides for the flatbed, and Mattie picked out seven ten-foot birch trees, dug them up with the loader, and tied the roots in seed sacks. Dawn drove the flatbed over. "We might as well do this now," Mattie said.

They wrestled the trees onto the back of the flatbed beside the manure and topsoil and drove the moany-groany flatbed out the drive.

The ground at Hector's was soft from the rain, and they spent an hour digging six holes. They planted trees on either side of the front door, and two more on the south where they would provide shade for the bedroom window. They planted another two on the north so visitors, if Hector ever had any, might see some balance to the arrangement.

"Let's put the last one by the fence for Rafe," Mattie said. "He ought to have a tree of his own so he can lie in real shade instead of next to a machine."

"A machine gives real shade," Dawn said.

"*Living* shade, then," Mattie said. "Animals like living shade."

Dawn dug the hole, and they hosed water, set in manure and soil, and planted the last tree.

That evening Dawn took down the tarp over the kitchen, and the late sunlight glanced in through the open roof and made patterns and shadows on the walls. Mattie steamed the beans and grilled salmon, and the three of them ate outside, fending off mosquitoes at the picnic table. After supper Shelley showered, washed her hair, and put on a clean blouse and shorts. She was off to Bryce's.

Dawn did the dishes, and Mattie, instead of drying and putting away as she usually did, mixed herself a gin and tonic in a Mason jar, and went outside. Dawn heard the four-wheeler start and move away from the house. "Doog" was "good" spelled backward. Dawn thought she'd done as much as she dared, and she had to let Mattie be.

Mattie drove west and left the four-wheeler at Haney's dry pond below Sheep Table. From there she walked partway up the road and cut cross-country to the broken fence below the rim of the mesa. For several minutes she drank her gin and tonic and considered the reflection of the pink and gray clouds in the river. A few yards beneath her, three does stepped soundlessly across the scree. Mattie touched the grip of Haney's pistol in her windbeaker pocket.

The gin soothed her, but didn't erase her fear. She watched the deer pick their way down toward the river, where on the surface, pink turned to lavender. The gin worked into her as the darkness consumed the land. An owl hooted in the cottonwood bottoms below.

To possess her revised history was her general task. Was it possible to draw a curtain across the past and remember nothing? Or could she select moments she wanted to hold in her mind, isolated among the ruins? The waiting and the darkness grew in her, and when she heard what she was listening for—the low whine of an engine—she climbed higher along the fence line to the flat. Had it been light, she could have seen the ditch weir from there.

In a minute a truck without headlights separated itself by movement from the dark.

The truck stopped at the gate, and Lute and Jimmy Pollard got out. A flashlight beam jerked across the ground and settled on the wire looped around the gatepost. Jimmy pressed his shoulder against the post, and the gate fell open.

"Come on, Gizzard," Lute said.

The dog jumped down from the truck bed.

The flashlight was what Mattie went by. It lit up the road, the grass beside it, a clump of yellow clover. It created the silhouettes of things—men's bodies, a shovel, the truck receding behind them. Gizzard slouched beside Lute as they walked behind the circle of light moving on the ground.

The Pollards didn't speak, already knowing what they were doing. When they got to the weir, Lute took the light, and Jimmy got down on his knees and fitted the cut boards lying there into the cement box. The flow to the pivot field was cut off. The ditch behind the weir filled with water.

"Hand me that last one," Jimmy said.

Lute kicked the last board across the grass and leaned on the shovel. Then Gizzard barked.

"Shut up, ratface," Lute said.

The dog lowered on his haunches and barked again.

"I can't see shit," Lute said, "but something's there."

He waved the flashlight in Mattie's direction, and Mattie raised up into the light.

"Is this your special sense about water, Lute?" Mattie said. "You can take those boards out again, Jimmy. I've seen what I came to see."

"We got to have water," Lute said.

"That's what the district is for. You can buy it."

Jimmy stood up beside the weir. "We got rights, too."

"Then what are you doing out here in the dark?"

Mattie stepped forward from the fence post, and Gizzard barked again. Lute shone his light into Mattie's face.

"Pull the boards and leave them on the grass," Mattie said, "and put that light out of my face."

Lute didn't move the light. "Leave the boards, Jimmy. If she pulls 'em, we'll come back later. She ain't staying out here all night."

"I hope I won't have to," Mattie said. "We're going to have a talk."

Mattie took out the pistol and her own flashlight.

Lute lowered his light. "What are you going to do, shoot us?"

"You shot those bulls that were on your property. Now you're on mine. Jimmy, you've got to three to pull the boards."

"Leave 'em, Jimmy," Lute said.

"That's one already," Mattie said. She held the pistol at arm's length.

"She ain't going to shoot nobody," Jimmy said.

Mattie stepped to the pipe, ten feet from Lute. Lute leaned his weight off the shovel, moved his other hand to it, and raised the shovel slowly. Gizzard growled.

"Gizzard don't seem to like you," Lute said.

"I don't like him, either. And that's two."

Mattie positioned herself as the point of a triangle between Lute and Jimmy. "You think I don't know what you did to Shelley, Jimmy? I know. And I know what the two of you were about to do to Dawn. Stealing water is the least of things here."

She took another step closer.

Then Gizzard lunged at her. Mattie turned and fired once, and the dog collapsed on the ground.

"That's three," Mattie said.

Jimmy yanked the top board out of the weir, and the next, and threw them on the grass. Water rushed back into the pipe.

"Now I think you both ought to kneel down," Mattie said.

Jimmy knelt by the weir.

"You, too, Lute."

Lute dropped the shovel and knelt beside the dead dog.

"Your prayers better be promises," Mattie said. "I want to hear them out loud. And they better include never coming around any of us women over here."

Lute mouthed words, and Jimmy, too, louder than Lute.

"You understand me now? You stay away from everybody I care about. And leave my water alone." Mattie fired another shot into the air. "Say it."

Lute and Jimmy spoke up louder.

Chapter 7

Dawn found Mattie the next morning on the porch. It was a little beyond sunup, and the hills were an array of different yellows. "What's that hammering?" Dawn asked. She had on a long shirt, but her legs and feet were bare.

The hammering came from behind the barn.

"Maybe you ought to go look," Mattie said.

The hammering stopped for a moment, and a towhee sang in the creek bottom.

"Is Shelley back?"

"She said she'd be here at eight."

The hammering started again.

"Who is it?" Dawn asked.

"It's Hector. He baled all last night."

"Why's he still here?"

"I don't know everything, Dawn. Go ask him."

"I don't want to ask him."

"Well, you're the reason he's hammering over there. If I were you, I'd get dressed and go see."

Dawn went inside and put on a rain poncho and came out again. The hammering had stopped.

"Did he leave?"

"His truck didn't leave," Mattie said. "I think he must still be here."

Hector's truck was by the barn, backed up to the corral, which hadn't been used much except as a holding pen when Hector vaccinated his calves. Dawn went down the steps and crossed the yard. The hammering resumed and got louder as Dawn walked through the sunflowers not yet bloomed. Then it stopped again.

Dawn turned the corner of the barn and saw Hector climbing over the corral fence. He jumped down into the lee of the barn and came toward her.

"I was just coming to get you," he said.

"Here I am. I thought you worked for the phone company."

"I'm going in late," he said. "Thanks for planting the trees."

"It was Mattie's idea."

"And I'm sorry I haven't been around."

"You've been around. You've baled every night this week."

"You know what I mean. I didn't know that much about what happened. I'm not in touch with many people, and when I found out, I thought it was better to stay away."

"You might have seen to Mattie."

"I talked to her about it already," Hector said. "She didn't need help from me except in the fields."

"She needs help in more ways than you think." Dawn looked past him toward the corral. "The baler run all right with that new belt?"

"Fine."

"I guess you saw I burned up the kitchen."

"Yeah, I did."

"What are you beating on over here?"

"Loose rails. These corrals fall apart even when you're not using them. You want to see the new calves?"

A frantic bellowing came from behind the barn, and Hector climbed back over the fence. Dawn stepped up onto the lowest rail. A brindle-colored calf had caught its head between the fence rails and was bawling. Three others were bunched at the far gate.

Hector ran across to the calf and got its head loose, and the calf skittered over to the others.

"They look kind of funny," Dawn said. "What kind of calves are they?"

"They're your kind. You said you wanted buffaloes."

Dawn looked at Hector, and Hector grinned. "A guy I ran wires for up in Hermosa raises them. They've had their colostrum, and I brought some lamb milk replacer for extra protein. You've got to feed them every four hours."

"I thought you didn't know anything about buffalo."

"You can't leave them too long in a corral. They get stressed out with too little space."

Dawn laddered up the fence and jumped down into the corral. The calves divided and wove around her. "What are they? Girls or boys?"

"If you can't tell, you've got more to learn than I thought."

"Two of each," Dawn said. "What'd Mattie say about this?"

"She's willing to give you the east pasture. My guess is she hopes they'll be an incentive for you to stay on."

"She fired me yesterday," Dawn said, "but she hired me back."

"Did you hear what she did last night to the Pollards?" Hector asked.

"No, what'd she do?"

"She caught them stealing water. She shot their dog and ran them off."

"Mattie did?"

"I guess she scared them pretty bad," Hector said, laughing. "She scares me now, too."

Dawn caught one of the calves, but it squealed and pulled away. "Strong little bastards."

"Wait till they grow up," Hector said.

"I'd better name them," Dawn said. "Maybe for poets—Keats, Byron, Dickinson, and Elizabeth Barrett Browning."

"One, two, three, four," Hector said. "That's how I name cows."

"Or the Four Winds," Dawn said. "North, East, South, and West. I'll remember them as the directions of the world."

"I hope you don't have to eat them," Hector said. "It's hard to eat animals with names."

"Thank you, Hector."

"You're welcome."

Shelley was back before eight, and all morning she ran the windrower in the pivot field. She called the machine the green monster. It roared and whirred and spit out hay between its wheels. She was more vigilant since Dawn had told her about the fawn she'd almost run over, and though she concentrated, her mind still wandered to Bryce. When it did, the windrower wandered, too. Once she left a fifty-foot swath of uncut alfalfa across the middle of the field.

She couldn't back up that far, but she couldn't leave all that hay standing in the middle of the field, either. But there was no choice. She righted her course and went on. A row took forever. She took her shirt off and felt the warmth of the sun on her breasts.

At the end of the row she did a one-eighty and set her watch to see how long it took to cut the next row. She raised the cutting bar, did a quick left, and then another, and lowered the bar into the high alfalfa. In the middle of the row she steered right and cut the swath of hay she'd missed going the other direction. It was a short, funny-looking windrow, but at least her mistake wasn't obvious from a distance.

Then far off she saw Hector's truck on the river road, and she put her shirt back on.

Now what? It was only ten o'clock, and she hadn't been out there long enough to be spelled by anyone, and what was Hector doing there? He waved to her out the cab window to stop, and she raised the cutting bar and idled the engine down. Hector drove straight to her across the windrows, which wasn't a good sign. He pulled up a few feet away.

"I'll take over for a while," he said. "You go home."

"What happened? Did the Pollards do something?"

"No," Hector said. "The sheriff called. They found the Lincoln."

Chapter 8

The evening before, the Lincoln had been stopped heading west near Sundance, Wyoming, on Interstate 90. The state patrolman had checked the license and found the car had been stolen, and he arrested the three teenagers in it. Because the car was in the NCIS computer, the Crook County sheriff in Wyoming had called Hot Springs to verify the information, and Sheriff Nolan called Mattie. Elton wasn't in the car.

The sheriff wanted Mattie to ride with him to Sundance to see whether anything was missing from the car, but Mattie wasn't about to ride three hours anywhere with Sheriff Nolan or to drive the Lincoln back, either. They were already late with the hay, so it wasn't the best timing, but the world didn't run on their clock. Mattie elected Dawn to drive with her to Sundance because Elton liked Dawn. If they found him, she might be an asset.

They took Dawn's Mercury and drove north on 79. Dawn babbled about buffalo—how they could endure twenty more degrees of cold than cattle could, how much foreigners liked the meat, how there was an upward spiral of demand.

"You've only got four," Mattie said.

"Everything big starts small," Dawn said. "You'd be surprised how fast multiples work. Hector's friend says he'll market my calves."

"You'll be surprised how many problems there'll be."

Rapid City was its usual stop and go past oil depots, silos, train storage areas, used car lots, casinos, and cheap motels, but once they were on the interstate heading west, Mattie dozed and Dawn boogied, and when Mattie woke up, they were only a few miles from the state line.

"What is that thing there?" Dawn asked. "Off in the distance?"

"Devils Tower."

"I know that, but what is it?"

"Which part didn't you understand?"

"It has to be more. I can feel it."

The tower was a granite block that ascended straight up from rolling hills, a volcanic plug five hundred feet in the air, lit by the sun, framed by blue sky.

"It's a sacred place to the Indians. I climbed it once after Loren died. That was what Shelley calls one of my tangents. I guess my tangents are all inward now."

"It has something to do with Elton," Dawn said. "We're getting closer."

"We always are," Mattie said. "Or farther away."

Deputy Kroupa, instead of Sheriff Nolan, met them at the state patrol office in Sundance. "I'm sure you don't mind he couldn't make it," Kroupa said. "I've filled in the sergeant here about the case."

"I'm sorry for what you went through," the sergeant said.

"So are we," Mattie said. "What about these three kids?"

The sergeant had closely cropped hair and a pockmarked face. He slid a folder toward Mattie. "Three juveniles—two boys and a girl—were arraigned this morning and released to their parents. We don't see any connection to your Indian boy. That's the arresting officer's report."

"These three weren't Indians?" Dawn asked.

"No, ma'am. There aren't any Indians around here."

"Did they know Elton, someone of Elton's description? Or where they got the car?"

"The kids haven't been real cooperative," the sergeant said.

"What do you want us to do?" Mattie asked.

"The state can prosecute with or without your help, but pressing charges greases the track a little."

Mattie read from the first page of the report. "Joyriding, possession of stolen property, exhibition of speed. How can they be charged with possession of a stolen car when it wasn't stolen?"

"Where do these kids live?" Dawn asked. "Can we talk to them?"

"If they'll talk to you," the sergeant said. "One boy lives here in Sundance, and the other in Hulett. They're cousins. The girl lives out west of Hulett."

"Let's go see them," Dawn said. "Maybe we can figure a way to get them to cooperate."

Jason McCants lived in a tin-sided house on Pine Street with scraggly Dutch elms in the yard. Three cars were angled in along the curbless street. Mattie and Dawn had insisted on going without Deputy Kroupa, but they promised to report back.

They walked up to the door, knocked, and waited.

"I feel like a Jehovah's Witness," Dawn said.

"Except you're a heathen."

"Other than that," Dawn said.

A skinny woman in shorts and a thin blouse appeared behind the screen, along with a little girl of about six.

"We're looking for Jason," Mattie said. "I'm Mattie Remmel. It was my car he was in last night."

"So?" the woman said.

"Mattie might not press charges if we can ask Jason a few questions," Dawn said, "assuming he gives the right answers."

The little girl took off running. "Come through the house," the woman said. "He's in the backyard."

The kitchen smelled of hot dogs and fried food, and Mattie and Dawn followed the woman through it to the back door. Jason was shooting tennis balls with a hockey stick at a box spring. He was a rangy kid with hair buzzed around the ears and long on top. The girl was talking to him. Mattie and Dawn went outside.

"So what do you want to know?" Jason asked.

"Where you found the Lincoln," Dawn said.

"Do you know an Indian kid named Elton?" Mattie asked.

Jason flicked a tennis ball at the box spring, and Dawn grabbed the hockey stick and yanked Jason around toward her. "You're being spoken to."

"It wasn't my idea," Jason said. "I was a passenger."

"We don't care whose idea it was," Dawn said. "We also don't care if you go to jail."

"We're concerned about an Indian boy named Elton," Mattie said. She held out Elton's picture, but Jason didn't look at it.

"I don't know any Indian kids."

"Where did you get the car?" Dawn asked.

"Justin drove it down from Hulett. We were going to Gillette."

"Where's Justin now?"

"Home, I guess."

"We'll follow you," Dawn said. She whacked a tennis ball over the box spring into the neighbor's yard.

Jason's mother wasn't about to let him drive her Geo, and she had to deliver some clothes to her sister anyway, so she was the chauffeur. The little girl sat in back with her face pressed against the rear window and her hands cupped over her ears. It was clear an argument was going on in the the car.

"Styver and I used to argue," Dawn said. "He had a temper."

"Haney and I never argued."

"Yelling at each other never solved anything," Dawn said.

"Neither did our way," Mattie said.

The Geo slowed for a truck turning into the lumber mill outside Hulett—a cone incinerator and piles of sawdust, stacks of logs along the polluted Belle Fourche River. Hulett was a town both dead and alive, like an old man in a broken chair wheezing from years of smoking too much. The company houses that lined the streets were rotting. The Geo made a left at a fading lilac bush, and Dawn followed it down a driveway toward a turquoise and white trailer.

"Jail might be a step up from this," Mattie said.

A rusted-out washing machine was in the yard beside a loose stack of firewood. Jason's mother pulled in beside an identical blue Geo. The door to the trailer flew open, and two small boys raced out and down the stoop. "Aunt Janette," they shouted. "Jason! Jason!"

The boys ran to the Geo before anyone else in the car had opened a door.

A woman, lank and thin as her sister, came outside, too, and waved as if a ship were coming in. The sisters hugged each other and jabbered, and Jason's mother wrestled out the clothes in garbage bags from the back seat. The younger boys clamored around Jason. Then Jason's cousin sauntered out in baggy red shorts and a Wyoming Cowboys T-shirt. He stared at them indifferently.

The confusion of the families worked loose. The little boys tussled with each other about who was going to get Jason's Smashing Pumpkins T-shirt. "You kids shut up," the mother said. "These folks have business. Get out back, *now.*"

The kids retreated around the trailer. Justin, the whole time, hadn't budged from the stoop.

"They want to know where you got the car," Jason said.

"What car?"

"Just tell them, man," Jason said, "and get rid of them."

"Up the road toward New Haven," Justin said. He nodded west. "I noticed this car'd been sitting off in the pine trees for a couple of days, and Arlene and I stopped to see if anyone was dead in it. It was just sitting there, so I opened the window with a rock and hot-wired it."

"How far from here?" Dawn asked.

"Four or five miles."

"You want to show us where?"

"Fuck that," Justin said. "I'm not a guide service."

"I'll bet you will be, though," Dawn said, "because otherwise I'll break your knees."

The turnout was 6.3 miles up the gravel toward New Haven. Justin stopped his mother's Geo, and Dawn pulled beside in the Mercury.

"Over in those pine trees," Justin said.

"Okay, thank you."

Justin turned around and hightailed it away.

An abandoned road ran into a glade of ponderosas, and beyond the trees were rolling hills and limestone ridges. Devils Tower was far off to the southeast.

"I can see why the police didn't find it," Mattie said, "but why would Elton leave it here?"

"We don't know he did."

"We assume he did. Maybe he lived around here, or he knows someone who does. The sheriff's idea was he'd go back to the place he came from."

"We might as well ask the neighbors," Dawn said, "if we can find any."

It was a country of distance to look at and distance between. At intersections were signs with names and arrows:

WILKERSON 4 →
JOHNSON 3 →
← PINEY SHEPHERD 7
NEW HAVEN 9 →
← OSHOTO 10

The names could have been towns or families. Ranches were big, and spaces between houses several miles. Gates at the road were often locked, and Mattie and Dawn had to climb through the fences and walk to find out whether anyone lived there. Sometimes someone did, sometimes not.

The stories they heard varied. People said there were no Indians in the area. The only reservation in Wyoming was near Lander. Others said Indian families worked at the ranches from time to time. A woman with frazzled white hair told them two Indian families had moved to Moorcroft, but hadn't stayed long. "If you want to see Indians, you have to go to South Dakota," she said.

A man out irrigating said one crazy drunk Indian lived a ways off the road not too far away. The man pointed southeast. "That way."

"That's pretty general," Dawn said. "How far is not too far?"

"You don't see him very often," the man said, "unless you go to bars."

They aimed southeast and asked more questions. The drunk Indian might work in Gillette. He might live in Rapid City. He hadn't been around for six or seven months. A woman pumping water at a well said she saw the man three weeks ago on the interstate, but she couldn't remember which direction he was going.

"Hitchhiking or driving?" Mattie asked.

"I don't remember," the woman said, "but I thought it was him."

Toward dusk they backtracked to Hulett, where they found out the names of two school board members from passersby. The one they got hold of said there weren't any Indians in the school in Hulett, but ranch kids were sometimes bussed to Sundance.

From a pay phone Mattie called Shelley and left a message they'd be spending the night in Sundance. "I'll call you from the motel," she said. "You need to stay there in case Elton comes home."

As they drove back south, the last of the sun shone orange on the serrated spires of Devils Tower.

"What's your feeling now?" Mattie asked.

"Strong," Dawn said. "Still very strong."

"We'll see what we find tomorrow."

"Yes, ma'am," Dawn said. "Isn't that tower beautiful?"

Chapter 9

Shelley finished cutting the pivot field at around three-thirty that afternoon and went back to the house for a cherry Coke with ice. She drank it in the shade of the burned-out kitchen. She hadn't broken anything and, except for the glitch in the middle of the field, had done a solid job. She felt proud of herself. Next she was going to move bales in the Upper East. No one had told her to, but it had to be done.

It was weird being alone at the ranch. Hector was at work. Trini was two miles up the road. She was the only person on four thousand acres of land in the middle of nowhere. She filled a thermos of water and ice and drove the four-wheeler to the Upper East.

The prongs on the front of the International were four feet long, and they tilted front to back and moved up and down. She stabbed a bale, lifted it, carried it to a second bale, and set it down. Then she reversed and steered the tractor backward and picked up the two bales on the hay carrier in back. She forked the closest single bale with the prongs in front and carried all three to the hay pen.

The stacks were pyramids of twenty-six bales, each stack movable as a whole by a hay-hauler semi. Building the stacks was easy, except for the top three jellyrolls. Her mother and Elton had topped the stacks first cutting, but there was no reason Shelley couldn't do it. All she had to do was move the levers, raise each bale fifteen feet in the air, and set it down.

But it was easier said than done. She had to lift the bale, tilt it flat, lift it higher, tilt it again, all the while being sure to use the correct levers so the bale didn't tumble back on her. When the bale was as high as the front prongs could reach, and horizontal, then she had to drive the tractor forward and let the bale down on the top row. She had to do this three times to complete each stack.

Each time she finished a stack, she laughed and steered the International out of the hay pen, shouting out loud, "I have defied death! I am a farmer! I have defied death!"

She built two stacks and carried more bales, and the whole time she pictured a life there with Bryce. He'd write poems, and she'd do research at the Mammoth Site, and they'd have two children riding the bus to and from school every day. From his royalties and her salary they'd travel in the fall—Bali, Costa Rica, France. But if they had children, how could they travel? What was she thinking? She didn't even *want* children. She didn't want to get married, either.

The gas gauge dipped to low, and she had no choice but to drive the four-wheeler back to the yard and fill the gas canisters. She loaded them into the truck and then stopped at the house to go to the bathroom. There was a message from her mother; she and Dawn were spending the night in Sundance.

"Well, shit," Shelley said. Her first thought was of the Pollards. Her second was to call Bryce at Wind Cave, which she did. She left him a message to drive down and spend the night.

Thinking of Bryce made the last hours of the day go more quickly and yet more slowly. She was happier in the tedium of work, but anticipation made time crawl. If Bryce got the message, he might get there by seven-thirty or eight, still light. *If he got the message. If he wanted to come.*

If he didn't, she was going to spend the night at Trini's and throttle Keith.

She backed into two bales side by side, forked another, and steered toward the hay pen. She wasn't going to rush things with Bryce. Take it slow. Play it cool. Wait and see. She made five more trips to the hay pen—fifteen bales—and had one single bale left. So she wouldn't have to walk back to set water, she idled the tractor where it was and let water flow into the ditch and staked her orange tarp. She made four cutouts so the water would flow out onto the dry ground.

Then, walking back to the tractor, she saw Bryce's VW coming down the hill toward the mailbox. Her first impulse was happiness, but then she thought if no one was at the house, he'd leave. That set her running. She crossed the field, broke through the weeds, at the edge, and careened down the four-wheeler track. *If you run, you'll fall. Relax, he'll wait. How will you cook a meal in that kitchen? Why haven't you ever learned to cook a real meal?*

She slowed and walked. All she needed now was to fall and hurt herself. Bryce wouldn't care what she cooked. If he'd driven seventy miles to see her, that meant something, didn't it? *It meant he wanted to fuck her.* No, it didn't.

She ran down the hill and around the swamp and past the Ironweed Patch and came out by the Morton. Bryce was inspecting the garden, and she came up behind him out of breath. When he turned, she kissed him, and he put his arms around her.

"Did your mother find the boy?" he asked.

"Not yet. I was moving bales up on the mesa. I left the tractor running. She and Dawn aren't coming home."

"That's why you called? You wanted to—?"

"No, I . . . Do you want to see the place while it's still light?"

"Sure."

"We can take the four-wheeler."

Shelley drove, and Bryce rode behind. She steered across the bridge, accelerated up the hill, and opened the throttle on the straightaway.

Shelley turned her head and shouted. "Am I going too fast?"

"Not if oblivion is our destination."

"It is."

They bumped over rocks and ruts going up the old road, and Bryce clamped his arms around her waist.

At the top of the mesa they turned around, and Shelley killed the engine. For a moment they sat and let the noise dissipate. "I see why your mother likes it," Bryce said.

"And you see why I don't."

"It's where it is. You're where you are."

She leaned back against him. The sun skimmed the fields already cut and glowed in the tops of the cottonwoods below. Most of the river was in shadow, but a curve of flowing light arced in front of the cliff beyond. Bryce put his arms around her and kissed the back of her neck. He pressed his hands to her breasts, and his touch changed what she saw. The river, the mesas, light and shadow receded into the sensation of his moving hands. She closed her eyes and listened to the wind swirl the grass.

Then there was no cliff, no breeze, no distance, no song of bird. Only blood moving. *Don't rush.* But she was wet before he touched her. *There. There. Right there, almost there.* She slid her zipper down and raised her body slightly. *Yes, there.* She shuddered and couldn't stop.

He folded his arms around her, and the wind returned, and the windblown song of the bird.

He slid off the back of the four-wheeler, and they walked along the edge of the mesa. She pointed out the pivot field she'd windrowed, Sheep Table, where her father died, the sinkhole, where Lee Coulter had drilled the core sample, the Upper East, where she'd been moving bales and left the tractor running.

"I'd better go turn off that machine," she said.

They rode down a different way, and at the bottom of the mesa they turned west past Dawn's camp along the high bank. They stopped at a couple of washes to see what the rains had brought down—fossils of worms, fragments of clamshells, part of a baculite with the nacre intact.

Where the bluff closed to the river, they turned sharply uphill to a flat and rode a half mile to a view over the pivot field. The sun lived now in the crowns of the cottonwoods, in the edges of gullies, and was bright only on the rim of the far mesa—an orange wisp like a new moon. Why was the sun so luminous now, the hills so vibrant with sun and shadow?

Her mother used to say, "Look at that light, Shelley." She saw sunlight, but never what her mother saw. Or her mother said, "Can you believe the colors in the sky?" And she'd seen a hundred colors—oranges, reds, lilacs, deep violets—but until that moment they had been familiar. Now, with Bryce, light lengthened and shone in the clouds like neon.

Bryce pointed up a side gully, and Shelley let off on the gas. A young coyote sat on the rim, thirty feet above the dry wash where a hen grouse pecked sand. Wind came down the gully, and the noise of the four-wheeler went unheeded. The coyote stared down at the grouse; the grouse scratched at the ground.

Then the coyote leaped into the air. It was a long way to jump, and the coyote must have known in mid-flight he was off target. He flailed his legs and dropped fast and landed *whump*.

The grouse cowered, but didn't fly. The coyote was there, and the grouse took off, but the coyote caught her in midair. Feathers erupted. The coyote pinned the flapping bird to the ground. Only then did he glance at the intruders.

"I wonder how he decided he could fly," Shelley said.

"The same reason we all do," Bryce said.

The coyote picked up the dead bird and carried it up the arroyo.

Chapter 10

When Shelley and Bryce got back to the house, there was another message from her mother that they were at Dean's Pine View Motel. Shelley called, and her mother answered.

"It's me, Mom. Are you hanging in there?"

"I guess so, except I'm with Dawn."

"No word on Elton?"

"Tomorrow we're getting the Lincoln, and we'll talk to the superintendent of schools."

"Dawn's driving you crazy?"

"Dawn *is* crazy," her mother said, "but really, she's been a help. Did you finish at the pivot?"

"And I moved the bales on the Upper East and set water."

"You're becoming a real positive asset," her mother said.

"That's redundant," Shelley said. "An asset is positive. I even topped off the stacks. Then Bryce showed up—he brought steaks—and we rode up to the north bluff. We saw a coyote that thought he could fly."

There was a pause on the line. "Coyotes can do a lot of things. I hope you and Bryce have a good time."

"We will."

"I love you, sweetheart," her mother said.

Shelley hung up and went out onto the porch. Bryce was starting the grill, squeezing lighter fluid on the already burning charcoal. New flames shot up.

"We already tried to burn the place down," Shelley said.

"How's your mother?"

"She told me she loved me."

"Is something wrong with that?"

"It's unusual for her to say it."

"Maybe she needed to," Bryce said.

Shelley came down the steps. "You could pick salad stuff from the garden. I'd better go turn off the tractor before I forget."

"Okay."

She drove up on the four-wheeler, and when she got there, the field was almost pitch black. She skirted the ditch where the water was running and drove toward the tractor, a beast muttering to itself, a jellyroll bale still in its mouth.

She left the headlight of the four-wheeler on to illuminate snakes, then climbed up onto the plate, then to the tractor tire, and leaned up and shut off the engine.

Sudden quiet. Like death. She mounted the seat and looked at the emergent stars. The world went on. Her brother was dead; her father dead. Her mother was going to die, too. And *she* was going to die, and Bryce, and Dawn, and Elton. Everyone was going to die. The earth would die. The sun, too. The thought panicked her. She would not be missed. No one would be missed. She would not know what happened, what her great-grandchildren would become, perhaps not even her grandchildren or children because she would be dead, while the universe went on.

The land was still in the dark. She and Bryce had made half love, and she wanted the other half. His half. She wanted all. All was what made her alive, the prospect of *all*.

Bryce had cut up potatoes and put them on the grill with the steaks. Shelley opened a bottle of red table wine and brought it and the telephone outside onto the porch, where they sat together and watched the stars. Bryce held her hand in the space between them.

" 'The last scud of day holds back for me,/ It flings my likeness after the rest and true as any on the shadow'd wilds,/ It coaxes me to the vapour and the dusk./ I depart as air, I shake my white locks at the runaway sun,/ I effuse my flesh in eddies, and drift it in lacy jags.' "

They were quiet for a moment. The resident screech owl called from the swamp, and the familiarity of the owl's call made Shelley feel old. In the days of the future, Bryce would not recite poems, nor would she leave the tractor running in the field to go to him, nor writhe so under his touch on the seat of the four-wheeler. They would be quieted, vaguely happy and unhappy, maintaining allegiance out of habit, accepting the time's passing. Already she resisted it.

"What about one of your poems?" she said finally.

A moment went by. Bryce shifted his chair. "'The Boy in Pulan, Yugoslavia.' 'One moment more than any other—/ On that afternoon in Pulan, a town I had never dreamed of even once—/ the air was filled with centuries/ of languages other than mine—'"

He stopped.

"Why did you stop?"

"Mine aren't very good," he said, "especially in the shadow of Whitman."

"I think they are. Say the one about the red tent in France."

A pause. Bryce took a breath. "'Our tent blew down the street/ twirling end over end—/ a red decahedron filled with air./ You and I, lost without language,/ watched the children chase it,/ shouting and laughing,/ until it snagged against two trees./ That night we slept under one blanket,/ deep in that red space,/ the wind in our sleep and the children's voices in our bodies.'"

"Who were you with?" she asked. "Who's 'we'?"

"Maybe the 'I' is a woman," Bryce said. "Maybe they are two women."

"But is it?" she asked.

The phone rang, and Shelley answered in case it was her mother.

"Is this a bad time?" Lee Coulter asked.

"Lee, hi. No, yes. Bryce was just reciting a poem about an ex-girlfriend."

"I'll check the steaks," Bryce said.

"I was calling to see how your mother is," Lee said.

"I guess she's okay. The police found the Lincoln in Sundance, Wyoming, so she's up there with Dawn."

"Did she find Elton?"

"Not yet. Where are you? You sound far away."

"Coos Bay, Oregon, in a phone booth." There was a hum on the line. "So you're left with all the work?"

"We're done with the cutting. Hector still has to bale the pivot. You can't believe what all's happened here. Dawn burned down the kitchen. Then my mother caught the Pollards stealing water. Now this saga with the Lincoln. But she's better, I think. The more upheaval there is, the more she improves."

The phone beeped. "I have to put in more money," Lee said.

"Let me give you her number. She's at Dean's Pine View Motel. 307-555-7820. And when you get home, I want to talk to you about graduate schools."

"I'll be home Friday," Lee said. "Maybe I'll come out there and help." The phone beeped again. "But I don't want to do your mother any favors."

Then the line went dead.

Shelley and Bryce ate in the living room because the tarp made the porch blue from the interior light. She forgave him for avoiding her question, and instead they talked about the silly questions tourists asked at Wind Cave—"Is there a bottom to this place?" "How did the Indians read in the cave before there was electricity?" "Where did the dirt go they dug out of here?" Shelley told Bryce the joke about how women acquired jewelry.

They did the dishes, and then Shelley took Bryce's hand and led him up the back stairs to her room.

Chapter 11

Dawn snored in the next bed and turned in her sleep, and Mattie heard every breath and movement. She kept reviewing the day's events—confronting the joyriders, driving the back roads looking for Elton, hearing the conflicting stories people told. What did Dawn mean her feeling was strong? Where was Elton at that very moment she was awake?

In the middle of the night Dawn went to the bathroom and then came over and sat on Mattie's bed. "You're thinking about Elton."

"I'm worried we won't find him," Mattie said. "And I'm worried we will."

"If he's with his parents, he may not have a choice of what to do. You don't own him, Mattie. You have no right to him."

"But I care about him."

"Even if he doesn't have parents, he may not want to come back with us. You have to risk that."

"That's why I can't sleep," Mattie said.

Dawn hugged Mattie and got back into her own bed, and in a few minutes Mattie heard Dawn's sighing again. Mattie, eyes wide open, turned over onto her side.

When light seeped through the curtains, Mattie got up and left Dawn a note and walked down the street to Tammy's Café.

Mattie was finishing toast and eggs when Dawn sat down across the booth. The waitress appeared with a menu. "You want coffee, doll?"

"Please," Dawn said.

The waitress was in her sixties and already looked tired on her feet. She poured coffee. "You girls didn't sleep so good, huh?"

"My mother has boyfriend trouble," Dawn said.

"I know what you mean," the waitress said. "Men have their brains in their you know whats."

"I'll have French toast," Dawn said, "and sausage . . . no, bacon."

The waitress wrote down the order, took the menu, and cleared Mattie's plate. A grizzled rancher and his wife with a bouffant hairdo sat down at the table next to theirs.

"So what's your plan," Mattie asked, "now that Styver's not looking for you?"

"You mean, for my life?"

"If you're leaving, I'd like some advance warning."

"I don't have to hide," Dawn said, "but I don't have to run, either. I could use a raise to feed my buffalo."

"I was thinking of reducing your salary to pay for the kitchen."

"I want to buy some land, too," Dawn said. "I was hoping you'd lend me the money."

"Lend you—?"

"I'd be around for a few years to fix your machines."

"You'd be my indentured servant."

"But only until my herd gets big enough."

The waitress came with the French toast. "Waking up, are we?" she asked. She held the coffeepot poised.

"We're waking up a little," Dawn said.

"No more for me," Mattie said, holding her hand over her cup. "Around my daughter here, I don't want to be too awake."

The paperwork at the sheriff's office took twenty minutes, and afterward Dawn drove the Lincoln back to the motel from the Sinclair station that had towed it. The driver's side window was shattered, but there hadn't been anything in the car to steal.

"We can leave our stuff here until one," Mattie said. "I asked the owner. By then we ought to know what we're doing."

"About Elton, you mean. Not in general."

"About Elton," Mattie said.

Dawn fetched ice for the cooler, and when she came back, Mattie was waiting by the Mercury.

The superintendent's office was in an old house near the school. The foyer had a secretary's desk, but no secretary, and the superintendent, Matt Harpling, greeted them. He was a very tall man with a graying beard and kindly, wrinkled eyes. He knew Elton immediately from the picture Mattie showed him.

"Elton Biddle," Mr. Harpling said. He found Elton's picture in the school yearbook. "He was a good student, but he was absent a lot. It's always hard to know whose fault that is."

"Why is that?" Mattie asked.

Mr. Harpling rolled his chair to his computer and typed for a minute. "Sometimes the parents move. Sometimes the kid drops out. There's no law that says anyone has to tell us what's going on." He leaned closer to the computer screen. "Elton did pretty well on the standardized tests. In February he stopped showing up."

"Do you know why?"

"No. He was in Peggy Schumacher's class. She might know more, but she's gone for the summer. Have you checked with social services?"

"Not yet," Mattie said.

"Let me call over there." Mr. Harpling dialed a number and got someone on the line. "Dolores, do you know anything about Elton Biddle? I have two women here in my office looking for him. . . ." He handed Mattie the telephone.

"Hello," Mattie said. "This is Mattie Remmel."

"Dolores Mancos," the woman said. "Why don't you come on over? I'm in social services right off Main Street."

Dolores Mancos was small and big: five feet tall, 160 pounds, no waist, wide shoulders, thin legs. She met them in the entry wearing a beige sack dress and cowboy boots.

"I'm receptionist and caseworker," Dolores said. "You must be Mrs. Remmel."

"And this is Dawn," Mattie said.

"What do you want with Elton?" Dolores asked.

"I owe him wages," Mattie said. "He worked on my ranch down by Hot Springs most of April and all of May and June."

"And you came all the way up here to pay him?"

"No. He got into a circumstance—I wouldn't call it trouble—and I'm worried about him."

"What kind of circumstance?"

Mattie and Dawn looked at each other.

"There was an incident," Mattie said, "and he took off with my daughter's car. The car was found two days ago here in Sundance."

"I heard about that," Dolores said. "I know the families."

"We talked to the delinquents," Mattie said. "Justin found the car out west of Hulett, and we asked around, but couldn't find anyone who knew Elton until we talked to the superintendent."

"Elton's father has a shack out there," Dolores said. "He works sometimes in Gillette, but mostly in Rapid City. Elton's had a real hard time. His mother died in January last year. She was drinking in Moorcroft and tried to hitchhike home and nobody picked her up. It was real cold. Two or three days later someone found her in a field. The father's a drinker, too. We had to put Elton in the care of his aunt and uncle over in Beulah. Let me get my hat. I need to make a trip out there anyway."

"Should we call first?"

"No, no. If we called first, he definitely wouldn't be there."

Dolores had a round white straw hat with a red ribbon around the crown and drove a state-issue Chevrolet. Mattie filled Dolores in on how Elton had appeared at her place, how she'd put out food for him, and how, gradually, he came into the house. "I filed a missing person's report when he first showed up," Mattie said. "But he wouldn't tell me his name."

"And I guess no one was looking for him," Dolores said.

"Not that we ever heard."

"The uncle works for the highway department, and the aunt has three little kids at home. I don't know why he ran away. Social services gets involved only when we know something's wrong. We try to protect the kids, but we can't force people to get help."

As they drove, the countryside passed by Mattie's window—dry grass hills with scattered ponderosas. This was Elton's geography, where he had come from, what he knew, what he compared things with, and she tried to imagine how he saw her place, her mesas and river bottom and sky, her house.

Dolores exited at Beulah, Exit 205, stopped at the stop sign, and made a left under the interstate. The town clearly was kept alive by gasoline. There were three stations at the interchange and a few houses clustered nearby, lives scrutinized by truckers and tourists screaming by at seventy-five miles an hour.

They passed the general store and in a minute were out to the north on a smaller road into the rolling country. They drove through fenceless land for several miles, and then Dolores pulled over at a nameless and numberless silver mailbox. A rutted driveway descended toward a cinder-block house off the road.

"There's no reason on God's earth to build a house here," Dolores said, "but there it is."

She drove in on a crest of grass and the upside of a tire rut. As the house came closer, a skinny dog slunk out from under a car up on railroad ties. Dolores parked a respectful distance from the house, and they all got out. In the dirt yard a tricycle was tipped over, the only toy among sticks, a car tire, and rocks arranged in a circle. Dolores carried her purse over her shoulder and walked toward the house. The dog barked.

"People can't feed their kids," Dolores said, "but they always have a dog."

The dog gave way, and a woman holding a baby in her arms nudged open the screen with her shoulder. Two little girls crouched behind her skirt in the shadow.

"Hello, Betty," Dolores said. "We want to talk to Elton."

"I haven't seen Elton in months," the woman said.

"These are friends of his. Can we look inside?"

Betty was silent.

"You applied for more state assistance, so I assumed he was living here again. If we can't talk to him, I'll have to get the sheriff to come out."

"He's sick," Betty said.

"What's wrong with him?"

"He's real sick," Betty said.

"Tell him Mattie and Dawn are here," Dawn said.

Dolores squatted down to the two little girls. "You're Tensa. I remember you. And you're Ariel. What's the baby's name?"

"Leonard," Tensa said.

Dolores stood up and swung her bag off her shoulder and held her cell phone up in the air in front of the woman's face. "We need to see Elton," she said.

Betty looked out past them toward the car. Then finally she bent down and whispered to Tensa, and the girl disappeared into the house.

"Have you seen Sam?" Dolores asked.

"No."

"Did he kick Elton out, or did Elton come here on his own?"

"They had a fight," Betty said. "Henry went over and got Elton."

"When was this?"

"Two weeks ago. About then. Maybe longer."

"He's been here two weeks?" Mattie said.

Tensa reappeared, and another figure moved into the shadow behind Betty. The spring on the screen door squeaked as Tensa came outside.

It squeaked again when Elton opened the door.

It was Elton, but it didn't look like him. One side of his face was swollen and black, his eye closed and a bandage wadded into the corner. The skin was torn from his ear to his chin along the jaw, part of it scabbed over, and part oozy and raw. He held the screen open with one hand to keep himself standing. The other held a bottle of wine.

For a moment Mattie and Dawn were held away from him by invisible forces—surprise, grief, shock.

And then, together, Mattie and Dawn stepped forward slowly so as not to frighten him, slowly, to let him understand, slowly, slowly, to let themselves breathe. Slowly and together, they put their arms around him. They were awkward. Elton was on the raised step in front of the door, his hands occupied. He pushed away from them, but they refused to let go.

Chapter 12

The story Mattie pieced together from Elton's gibberish on the way to the hospital was a truth made elusive through words. Elton had been drunk against the pain from the time he got to his uncle's, maybe longer, and what he remembered may have been part dream, part memory, part darkness. He was an Indian boy who'd killed a white man.

Right after he'd shot Styver, he'd taken the Lincoln to look for Mattie in Hot Springs, and when he hadn't found her, he headed north into the Black Hills. It was the middle of the night. He drove through Custer and Deadwood and eventually came to the interstate, where he knew more or less where he was—not that far from Wyoming. There wasn't much traffic, but daylight shimmered behind him.

In daylight the Lincoln became visible. Elton was small and therefore obvious behind the wheel. At a rest area he put two boulders in the driver's seat to make himself look taller. He drove through Sundance, passed a state patrol car going the other way, and turned left at the store in Carlisle, aiming for his father's house. He knew what his father was like, though, and he couldn't show up there driving a Lincoln, so a few miles away he pulled the car off the road and slept awhile until the heat woke him. Then he walked cross-country, an hour maybe. He wasn't sure. He knew where he was by Bear Lodge, what most people called Devils Tower.

His father wasn't at the house, and Elton couldn't tell when he'd last been there. That was Mattie's understanding. The place was as Elton remembered—refrigerator almost empty, mattresses on the floors of the two bedrooms, a TV. The toilet was still broken from when his father had hit it with an ax.

He spent the night, and his father hadn't come back.

There were a hundred maybes. Maybe his father was in Rapid City—that was where Elton last knew he was—or maybe he was dead.

Elton watched the fuzzy TV, but there was no news on the Rapid City station about a murder in Hot Springs.

"Was there food?" Dawn asked. "What did you eat?"

"Trout in the freezer and canned beans. I had a little money, but not my whole stash from Mattie's. I thought about selling the Lincoln for parts."

"You could have called us," Mattie said.

His father hadn't come home the second day, either, and on the third day Elton had walked back to the car and had driven to Moorcroft. No one in the grocery store said anything to him. He unloaded the groceries at his father's house and parked the car again, a little closer, but off the road in some trees.

A couple of days passed. His spirits rose a little. Maybe the police weren't looking for him after all. Maybe his father wouldn't come back. He thought about going fishing up on the Belle Fourche.

Then after a week, in the middle of the night, a door slammed.

"Right away I knew he was drunk," Elton said. "He was swearing and mumbling, and he crashed into a chair. I hoped he wouldn't figure out I was there, but he opened the refrigerator, and I realized he had to know. He had to have seen what I'd bought. He was quiet a few minutes, and then he came into my room, and I heard him going through my clothes for money."

What happened after that was harder to follow. Elton had yelled at him, and Mattie gathered they'd fought over the money. Elton somehow got the bills and stuffed them into his underwear. Then he fended off his father with a baseball bat.

"He went into the other room, and I heard him throwing things against the walls. After a while a door closed, and I heard his truck start. A few minutes later I got up to make sure he was gone, and *wham,* he hit me with a board right in the face."

Elton remembered only snatches after that. His father took the money; that was the first thing. Then he pulled Elton out of the house feet first. Elton remembered hitting his head on the stone steps and being dragged across the yard. He woke up in his underwear in the trash gully twenty yards from the house.

Apparently he crawled from the gully to the road because a ranch couple found him. He called his aunt, and his uncle came and got him. "It was no big deal," Elton said. "My father and I had a fight. I was okay."

"So they gave you wine?"

"Wine and aspirin," Elton said. "My eye hurts pretty bad."

The hospital in Gillette was a gleaming white, blocky building visible for miles. Mattie and Dawn and Dolores followed along behind the gurney when Elton was wheeled into the ER. A woman doctor in the examining room gave the impression she'd seen much worse than Elton. "But there's some bleeding inside the eye," she said. "We need to take a better look at that."

"Take a better look at it *how*?" Mattie asked.

"Are you the boy's mother?"

"She's his friend," Dawn said. "I'm his sister."

"I think you'd both better step outside."

"I'm from social services," Dolores said. "We found the boy at his uncle's over near Beulah. He was beaten up about two weeks ago."

"We'll need a signed consent form before we can do anything," the doctor said.

"Who is 'we'?" Mattie asked.

Dawn drew Mattie out of the cubicle, but the doctor followed them. "Look, whoever you are, this boy may lose his eye. We can't treat him until we have the signature of a parent or guardian. If you're not one of these, you're a problem, not a solution."

"You mean, we need to ask permission from the person who did this to him?" Mattie asked.

"Whoever it is, you'd better hurry."

They weren't about to look for Elton's father, and the aunt and uncle weren't legal guardians, either, so Dolores thought the best course was to petition a judge to sign a thirty-day emergency guardianship in the state. They could sort out later what Elton wanted or might need permanently.

Mattie stayed at the hospital so Elton wouldn't feel abandoned, and Dawn and Dolores drove back to Crook County, with the idea that Dawn could bring back the papers.

Mattie was in the waiting room when the doctor came out again. "I gave him Demerol," she said. "He can sleep now without so much pain."

"What happens when we get the consent?" Mattie asked.

"We aren't equipped here for eye trauma," the doctor said. "We'll have to fly him to Denver. The sooner the better. It hasn't helped to wait two weeks to bring him in."

"We brought him here as soon as we found him."

"And it helps you're here." The doctor sat down beside Mattie in a molded plastic chair. "The boy's agitated, even hallucinatory."

"His father hit him with a board," Mattie said. "I'd be agitated, too."

"He thinks someone is looking for him."

"The police want to talk to him," Mattie said. "Would it help him to be reassured he isn't in trouble?"

"It might if it's true."

"It can be made true," Mattie said. "I can have the deputy sheriff here tomorrow."

Dawn got back with the judge's order by seven. "The judge was in court," Dawn said, "and then he had a meeting with attorneys. How's Elton?"

"Asleep. The doctor gave him a shot."

"How are you?"

"At least we found him."

"Now what happens?"

"Elton has to fly to Denver tomorrow. I called Kroupa, and he'll be here early in the morning. The doctor thinks Elton might benefit from knowing he isn't a fugitive."

"Are you flying down with him?" Dawn asked.

"I said I would."

"Then you'll need some sleep. Let's get some Chinese food and go back to Sundance. You have to get clothes. We'll call Shelley and let her know what's going on."

"I want to stay with Elton," Mattie said.

"He's asleep. He won't even know you're gone."

"Chinese food in Wyoming," Mattie said. "And fathers who beat their sons."

They ate egg rolls and sweet-and-sour pork driving back to Sundance, Mattie spooning a bite into Dawn's mouth as she drove and then taking one herself. When they were done, Mattie dozed with the white boxes of food on her lap and didn't wake again until Dawn bumped over the curb at Dean's Pine View Motel.

"What time is it?" Mattie asked.

"Ten-thirty. There's a note on our door."

"It can't be more bad news," Mattie said. "What else could happen?"

"What's that song?" Dawn asked. " 'I've been down so long it looks like up to me.' "

Dawn took down the note, and Mattie unlocked the door.

"It's for you," Dawn said.

"What's it say?"

"You read it."

Dawn went into the bathroom, and Mattie read the message.

> I want to know about Elton. Whatever the hour,
> knock on my door when you get back.
>
> Lee, Room 14

Mattie crumpled the note and threw it on the bed. "Did you know he was coming here?"

"How would I?"

"Well, it's too late to knock on his door."

"He says no matter what the hour," Dawn said.

Mattie took off her shoes and lay on the bed. "I'm too tired. How can he show up like this?"

"He likes you."

"Shelley put him up to this. Don't I have a say?"

"You have complete control," Dawn said.

"Good. I'm not going over there."

"Go just for a minute," Dawn said. "It's your duty."

"A duty now, is it?"

"Yes." Dawn pulled Mattie up to sitting.

"There's no duty involved."

"There is to Elton."

"To Elton," Mattie said. She stood up. "Okay, for Elton. But if I'm not back in ten minutes, you rescue me."

"If you're not back in ten minutes, maybe you'll have been rescued."

Mattie walked barefoot along the row of cars nose in to the rooms. It was quiet. How many rooms were there—twenty-five, thirty? Maybe half were filled. Bricklayers, criminals, doctors, foreigners, farmers, all thrown together in one place. Strangers. She was too tired to make conversation with Lee. The fear she'd felt walking up to the aunt's house, then seeing Elton hurt, and the worry at the hospital, and even now the worry. She hadn't noticed Lee's truck, but she saw it now; a camper shell was on the back.

She cut through the space between Lee's truck and a Saab to room 14 and knocked: two soft taps on the blue door. Lamplight shone at the edges of the plastic curtain drawn across the window. She hadn't taken a shower, or changed clothes, or combed her hair. She knocked twice more, then turned away.

Across the parking lot, a man came out of his room and got something from his car and went back inside. She assumed it was his car, his room, but maybe not. Appearances deceived. Behind her the door opened. She turned. Lee was rubbing his eyes. He was in his socks, and he wore a rumpled work shirt loose over his belt. "Hello, Mattie," he said. And he yawned.

He yawned!

But seeing him—she didn't know what happened to her—before she had a chance to tell him about Elton, she started crying. He must have thought she was crazy. He took her hand and led her inside and went to get her a glass of water. She was still crying when he came back.

Chapter 13

Mattie slept until the phone rang. She picked up the receiver and heard a woman's voice. "It's six o'clock."

She sat up. She was covered with a blanket in a strange, messy room. A suitcase was open, a man's clothes, a book on the nightstand about the worsening catastrophe of overpopulation. She was still dressed, so obviously she'd slept in her clothes. She remembered crying and not being able to stop. Lee had got a glass of water for her, and she'd lain down on the bed.

She got up and looked out through the curtains and saw Lee's truck was in front of the room.

She opened the door and went outside and stepped between Lee's truck and the Saab.

"Good morning," Lee said. "Did you sleep all right?"

"I slept all right."

The top of the camper shell was open, and Lee was making coffee with a hand filter.

"I had the desk wake you."

"Thank you."

"Dawn said you're flying to Denver with Elton. You want coffee?"

"I thought you only knew how to make instant."

"I learned how." He handed her a cup, steaming in the air.

Mattie took the coffee and looked into the camper shell. He had a foam pad and a sleeping bag, a propane stove, and several boxes of food.

"I told Dawn last night you were sleeping in my room. I didn't want her to worry."

"How thoughtful of you."

"I slept in my truck."

"Oh."

"So you're driving down to Gillette?"

"I'm meeting the deputy sheriff at the hospital." She paused. "The coffee's not bad."

"Any fool can boil water."

"Did you have a good time with your children?"

"Oh, sure. We hiked and ate butter clams and mussels. It rained a lot, and it was too short."

"It rained here, too, in the middle of haying." Mattie sipped more coffee and looked at the sky—such a clear blue. "I'm sorry," she said.

"Sorry for what?"

"Everything. Everything there is to be sorry for—your short visit with your children, my behavior, Elton's pain. How things are." She looked away, not wanting to cry again.

"Things don't have to be how they are."

"No, they could be worse." She handed the cup back to Lee. "Thank you," she said. "I have to go meet the deputy in Gillette."

When Mattie got to Elton's room, he was dazed, but awake. The alcohol was mostly out of his system, and he was coherent, though the Demerol affected him. "Can you talk?" she asked.

"I talked yesterday."

"Not very well. Do you still hurt?"

"A little. Not too much."

"The deputy is here from Hot Springs. He wants to ask you some questions. Is that all right? I'll be here the whole time. If you need a lawyer, we'll get one, but you didn't do anything wrong."

"Will I have to go to jail?"

"You protected Dawn. Everything is going to be all right."

Elton's statement to Deputy Kroupa corroborated what everyone knew, but the details were clearer. He'd been upstairs in the house, not asleep yet, when he'd seen the headlights of a car move across the ceiling. The sound of the engine wasn't familiar to him, and he'd got up and looked. It seemed odd to him that whoever it was had parked at the creek instead of driving to the house. Naturally he thought it was the Pollards, but he couldn't see much from the window except the moon shining off chrome.

He got dressed in the dark and went out through the vestibule. Someone was circling along the bushes, and his walking without a flashlight made Elton even more suspicious, so he'd hidden behind the cottonwood. The man was thinner than either of the Pollards, and it wasn't Hector Lopez, either, though Hector wouldn't have been skulking around at that hour. The man stopped and looked at the house for a minute, then mounted the steps to the porch and went inside.

Elton expected to see a light come on, but it didn't. Nothing happened. He didn't see the man for several minutes. Finally the man came out and walked straight across the yard to his car and drove it around behind the Morton. Elton ran to the Lincoln, figuring the man was going to come back.

He did, and he sat on the porch for a while, apparently waiting for someone to get home. After a while Elton dozed off.

He woke when he heard voices. The house was still dark, but the three-wheeler was by the gate, so Dawn had come back. He was surprised he hadn't heard the motor. The voices were loud, yelling, Dawn's voice and a man's. They were arguing, and then the man was swearing and threatening so Elton had run to the Morton and got the rifle.

When he came back, it was quiet—no voices—and he climbed up to the porch and looked in the window. The man had Dawn up against the doorframe and was choking her and banging her head against the side of the door. There was no time to think.

"So I shot him," Elton said.

Deputy Kroupa looked at Mattie, then back at Elton. "What'd you do after that?"

"The man was on top of her. I went in and pulled him away."

"Why'd you shoot him again?"

"I hated him."

"Did you know Dawn wasn't dead?"

"Not till after, when I saw she was breathing, but it didn't matter. I'd have killed him anyway."

"Why didn't you call someone?"

"Who would I call?"

"So you took the Lincoln?"

"I wanted to find Mattie."

"Why didn't you stop at a neighbor's?"

"I told you. I wanted to find Mattie."

"So you kept driving?"

"Yes."

Mattie stood up. "You know the rest," Mattie said. "That's enough, isn't it?"

"I guess so." Kroupa stood and closed his notepad. "There'll probably be a hearing, but I don't see how the DA can do anything with this."

"Like self-defense," Mattie said. "He saved a life."

"Maybe he'll get a medal for bravery," Kroupa said. "Lester Styver was a nasty guy."

Mattie walked out into the corridor with Kroupa. "Thanks for coming. You'd say Elton's in the clear?"

"Yes, ma'am, that's what I'd say."

"Except for remembering what happened," Mattie said. "From that you're never in the clear."

A few minutes later the doctor came in and checked the bandage on Elton's eye. "Are you ready to fly to Denver?" she asked Elton.

"Not really."

"Don't you want to see out of that eye again?"

Nothing.

"He does," Mattie said.

"You're scheduled for surgery this afternoon," the doctor said.

"And then what?" Elton asked.

"Then you recover. That's what we hope for."

After the doctor left, Mattie called Dawn at the motel. "We're about to go to the airport. I thought you'd want to talk to Elton."

"I do."

Elton took the phone. "Yeah?" he said.

"Yeah?" Dawn said. "What kind of greeting is that?"

"Hello."

"How are you feeling?"

"Nervous."

"You ever flown before? It's like riding in a boat thirty thousand feet in the air."

"I hate boats," Elton said.

"If you want to see dolphins, you have to get in a boat."

"I don't care about seeing dolphins."

"You'd better care because I want to show you one someday. Elton, you have to learn from pain and not give it to others."

Elton didn't answer.

"I love you, and Mattie loves you, too."

Elton was still silent.

"Do you hear me?"

"I heard you."

"Good. Don't be a jerk."

Elton gave the phone back to Mattie and slumped back in the bed.

"Not so good, is he?" Dawn said.

"No."

"We'll take care of things at home. You get Elton well."

"I'll try."

"No, you will."

"I will," Mattie said.

Chapter 14

L ee had a trailer hitch, so he and Dawn drove the Lincoln to Gillette and rented a tow bar. Lee towed the Lincoln, and Dawn drove the Mercury. It was afternoon when they got on the interstate, and thunderheads were building above the Black Hills.

They took it slow and easy and arrived in Hot Springs a little before four. Lee's duplex was as run-down as his truck—shingles falling off the roof and the sides peeling blue. "Paint would help," Dawn said.

"I don't own it," Lee said. "I don't spend enough time here to mind what it looks like."

"That's the hired man's creed: It's not my ranch."

"But that isn't your creed, is it?"

"No. Look, I'll take back the tow bar, and you can get some sleep."

"I told Shelley I'd come out and help with ranch chores."

"Now?"

"There's good light left. My vacation lasts till Monday. Let's get the tow bar off."

Dawn released the clamp, and they hoisted the tow bar away from the truck. Then Lee worked off the bolts under the bumper of the Lincoln.

"So we're leaving the Lincoln here?" he asked.

"I guess that's the plan," Dawn said. "Do you have carpentry tools?"

"A few."

"I'd like to rebuild Mattie's kitchen before she gets home."

Lee returned the tow bar in his truck, and Dawn drove to the ranch in the Mercury. Shelley wasn't at the house, and the truck was gone, so Dawn parked under the cottonwood beside a stack of lumber that had been delivered in their absence. The blue tarp flapped over the roof and wall of the kitchen.

There were worlds within worlds, worlds falling down and taking shape simultaneously, stars dying and being born. There was no time, just stop-time, time warp, no time at all. She gave no thought to the future, though neither did she want to be a spectator of ruins. Time was a construct people invented for themselves, and what they accomplished in the world and what they accumulated meant nothing. She believed that. Such insignificant measures mattered only in a moment that didn't last, important to those who knew nothing else. What she believed in was a way of seeing and being that needed no words, an existence without language based on sensing the world, feeling it. Words were only useful as inexact translations, clumsy tools, means to an end. They were never enough in themselves.

The house in the sun was desolate with no one else there. Dawn picked up a stone from the yard. "We'll take care of things at home," she'd promised Mattie. *Home.* This was her home, the place she lived. It was where she wished to be.

She strode across the yard to the corral, where the Four Winds were sleeping in the shade of the barn. East Wind, the bull calf with the scar on its nose, scrabbled to his feet and came over and nudged her leg. "Has Hector been feeding you candy?" she asked. "Or are you feeling lonely?"

She gave him a pellet from the bin. The other calves woke. She filled their water trough and patted each of them, except North Wind, who didn't trust her yet and stood away.

"I have work to do," she told them. "I can't be with you every minute."

At the Morton she loaded tools onto the flatbed: Skil saw, power screwdriver, nail gun, Sawzall, crowbars, a sledgehammer. The table saw would be useful, too, but she'd have wait for Lee to help her lift it. She brought along boxes of leftover plumbing materials—pipe, sealer, blowtorch—and drove the flatbed to the house.

She dragged away the blue tarp. With a crowbar, she levered the burned studs from behind the stove. When the crowbar was slow, she sawed nails with the Sawzall; when the Sawzall was slow, she shattered boards with the sledgehammer.

Lee Coulter arrived when she was pulling down the outside wall of the kitchen.

"Tell me what to do," Lee said. "Later we can have a bonfire and roast marshmallows."

"Get hold of a crowbar," Dawn said. "It's good therapy."

Lee went to work. He got into it. When he had a question, he asked, and when he didn't, he busted ass. He yanked and jerked and ripped. When debris piled up, he cleared it away to a bigger pile. They worked two hours without stopping.

They left the common wall with the living room intact, and, behind the stove, a partial row of salvageable studs. The two outside walls were air. They cobbled two-by-eights onto the weak floor joists and replaced two that were badly burned, then nailed down three-quarter-inch plywood so they had something solid to walk on.

At eight—still light—Shelley came back from moving bales north of the river. "I never want to see a hay bale again," she said. "I'm going to dream of moving bales."

"There are worse dreams," Dawn said.

"Nothing like mindless physical labor to inspire the academic," Lee said.

"Grab a hammer," Dawn said. "Remember how much you liked building the shower? That was nothing compared to this."

"I have to set water," Shelley said. "Did Elton and Mom get to Denver?"

"I didn't hear about a plane crash," Dawn said.

"Is there a blueprint?" Lee asked. "Once we finish this destruction, does anyone know what we're building?"

"It's in my head," Dawn said.

"It's going to be a tree house," Shelley said.

"Mattie didn't say what she wanted?"

"She ordered appliances," Dawn said. "We know sort of what she wants. She likes light."

"If she were here, it'd go twice as slowly," Shelley said. "And anything will be an improvement."

"I'm taking the side wall out six feet," Dawn said. "We'll reconfigure the back entry to give more interior space. And there's a solarium . . ." She looked at Shelley. "You'd better go set water so you can get back and help."

Shelley irrigated and came back. By then Lee had cut and nailed the odd-shaped pieces of three-quarter-inch plywood around the perimeter of the floor, and Dawn had framed the outside wall of the porch.

They all worked measuring, sawing, nailing until it was almost dark. They hadn't thought of food.

"We can't cook in this mess," Shelley said.

"Is there any food?"

"We have frozen stuff."

"If I can have a shower here," Lee said, "I'll treat everyone at the Maverick."

Chapter 15

Before they left the house, Shelley talked to Mattie. Elton's surgery had been delayed, but right then he was about to go in. He'd loved flying. Mattie said she'd promised to take him up in a glider when he got better. "He liked seeing the rivers from above," she said. "He thought they told stories."

They drove in Lee's truck, with the idea Shelley and Dawn could ride back in the Lincoln, and on the way they stopped to invite Hector to come with them. He wasn't home, but they left him a note to get an answering machine and to join them at the Maverick if he wanted to.

The café wasn't crowded on a Thursday, and Dawn picked a booth near the salad bar. Lee slid in beside Shelley on one side, and they ordered beers and looked at the menus. A few truckers came in from the gas station next door and passed through the restaurant to the adjacent casino and bar.

The waitress set down their beers and pulled a pencil from her matted brown hair. "Best thing's the sirloin," she said.

"I'll have the shrimp basket and fries," Shelley said.

"The sirloin," Dawn said, almost mooing. "And a baked potato without the *e*."

"You've come a ways since you were a vegetarian," Lee said.

"I try to improve myself," Dawn said. "And you're paying."

"I want chicken-fried steak," Lee said. "And another beer all around."

They settled in and talked about what Elton would do if he lost his eye. Then they debated whether Indians were better off to assimilate themselves into the economy or to resist the culture and preserve their language and identity as a separate people.

"Indians always lived at the level of subsistence," Lee said, "but now they're poor."

"We get richer in money, but poorer in spirit," Dawn said. "We're a people of Wal-Marts and Taco Bells. Every strip in every town looks the same. And where do all the mansions and second homes come from?"

"From superconsumption," Lee said.

Dawn looked over toward the cashier's counter. "Who's that?" she asked.

Shelley and Lee turned, and a heavyset woman waved at them.

"That's Thella Silverman," Shelley said.

Thella bought gum at the cash register and came over.

"We run into each other all the time," she said to Shelley. "How's it going?"

"Okay," Shelley said. "How about you?"

"Okay. I quit work in Rapid. The money wasn't good enough. Are you still helping your mom?" She unwrapped the stick of Doublemint and folded it into her mouth.

"For the time being."

Thella looked at Lee and Dawn. "Shelley and I ran cross-country together in high school." She laughed and patted her stomach. "I guess that was awhile ago, huh? Well, not *that* long ago."

There was an awkward pause.

"Oh, sorry," Shelley said. "This is Dawn and Lee. Thella." She paused. "So, how's Hank?"

"Real good. He's in there winning at the poker machine."

The waitress brought the dinners and more beers. "Shrimp basket?" she asked.

"Hey," Thella said, "I hear you're going out with Bryce."

"Who told you that?"

The waitress set the sirloin in front of Lee, and he exchanged plates with Dawn.

"Is it true?"

"I've been seeing him some."

"Good," Thella said, backing away. "Well, look, I better go. I'm Hank's lucky charm."

"See you around," Shelley said.

"Anything else I can get for you folks?" the waitress asked.

"Not a thing," Lee said. He smoothed the cream gravy over the steak. "I'm writing a book about my experiences in restaurants. It's called *Chicken-fried Steak*."

"Everyone's writing a book," Dawn said. "Mine's called *Every Married Man*. Look, there's Hector."

Hector came in and scanned the room, and Dawn raised her hand to signal him.

Hector came over. "I hope I'm not imposing," he said.

"We invited you," Dawn said. "You're not imposing."

"Do you know Lee Coulter?" Shelley asked.

Hector and Lee shook hands and nodded at each other. Dawn scooted over in the booth, and Hector slid in.

The waitress brought another menu. "Beer?" she asked.

"No, thanks," Hector said. "I'll have water."

"You're getting pretty social, Hector," Shelley said. "Coming out at night."

"I go out about once every two years," Hector said.

"Lee's buying," Dawn said. "You can order the most expensive thing."

"Do they have buffalo?" Hector asked.

"No," Dawn said, "but someday they will."

After dinner Lee faded. He'd driven all night from Coos Bay, then slept in his camper in a motel parking lot, and then had crowbar therapy at the ranch. "I'm not twenty anymore," he said. "I'm not even thirty." He stood up. "Sorry, Hector, I'd like to watch you eat, but I have to go to bed."

"I shouldn't have ordered trout," Hector said. "I guess they had to catch it first."

"What about the Lincoln?" Lee asked. "Anyone want to ride to town with me?"

"I will," Shelley said, "but I want to talk to Thella first."

"Hector can bring us," Dawn said. "If he doesn't mind."

"All right. Anyone want dessert before I pay the bill?"

"I do," Dawn said. "Is that terrible? I want strawberry ice cream."

"Fine."

"And thanks for dinner."

The waitress arrived with the trout, and Lee ordered Dawn strawberry ice cream.

"Hector?"

"I'm fine," Hector said. "Thank you, Lee."

Shelley stood up. "I'll meet you in here or outside," she said.

"Okay," Dawn said. "Outside."

Shelley walked with Lee to the cashier and gave him a quick embrace. "Thanks so much for dinner," she said. "Will we see you tomorrow?"

"I'll be there," Lee said, "bright and early."

Thella and Hank were drinking beers in front of the poker machine. Hank pressed the buttons for hold or draw, and the cards flipped up on the blue neon screen. Shelley watched surreptitiously from behind as Hank lost four hands in a row. Then he hit a flush and a full house in consecutive games, and Thella clapped her hands and squealed.

Hank grinned and looked around to see who else was watching and saw Shelley. "Well, shit," he said, "my luck's about to change."

"Hello, darlin'," Thella said. "Hank's on a tear."

"You believe in bad luck, Hank?" Shelley asked.

"Damn right I do," Hank said. "I did ten days in jail because of you."

"If it hadn't been for me, you'd have been dead."

Hank slid from the stool and pressed the cash pay button. The machine clicked down the credits and spit out a piece of paper. He took the ticket and headed to the bar.

"Don't mind Hank," Thella said. "That was an act for me. He feels bad for what he did with you."

"Which part?"

"Come on. If we don't sit right next to him, he'll buy you a beer."

They sat on stools at the corner of the bar, and Thella ordered Budweisers. Hank was sitting down the bar past two cowboys, smoking a cigarette and watching TV.

"And you're not mad?" Shelley said.

"Me? Why should I be?"

Shelley didn't answer.

"You mean about that?"

"Well, yes."

"Hank's fucked more people than you. And I've been there sometimes. You said you were sorry, didn't you?"

Their beers came, and Shelley took a long swig on hers.

"If I were you, I'd be mad," Shelley said.

"Look, there he is, right there," Thella said. "He's still with me."

Shelley drank again. "So how'd you hear about Bryce and me?"

"I don't remember. Maybe it was in Yogi's. I heard he got fired, too."

"When was that?" Shelley asked. "He was thinking about quitting."

"I'm surprised he didn't get fired a long time ago. You sort of liked him even back then, didn't you?"

"I liked his class."

"Class or ass? At least you were out of school before he fucked you."

"What are you talking about?"

"He fucked me senior year, and Julie Picard, too. She was a sophomore."

"That's bullshit."

"I was there," Thella said. "And you can ask Julie. I don't know who else he's fucked since then."

"Why didn't you tell anybody?"

"I didn't want to get him in trouble. Besides, I liked it. Probably Julie did, too."

Shelley stood up from the bar, and Thella took her hand. "Look, Bryce likes you. I could tell. What's it matter now?"

"*He* told you?"

"How is it different from what you did with Hank?"

Shelley downed the rest of her beer. "I've got to go. Those people are waiting for me."

"Don't mess yourself up," Thella said. "Bryce is a good guy."

"Thanks," Shelley said. "I'll tell him you said so."

Hector wolfed down his trout and french fries and salad in as long as Dawn took to eat her ice cream. It was warm when they went outside. Above the gas pumps, insects swarmed in the blazing Conoco sign above the parked cars.

"It's pretty dry," Hector said. "I might not be able to bale."

"It wouldn't hurt you to sleep once in a while."

"I sleep when I can," Hector said.

They crossed the parking lot to a construction site next to the bar. Whatever had been there before had been leveled, and dirt was piled at the edge of the lot. An array of pink ribbons fluttered on surveying stakes.

"It's going to be a trailer park," Hector said.

"Why here?"

"Because there isn't one."

"There isn't Buckingham Palace, either."

A semitrailer howled past on the highway, and they walked away from the light. Dawn climbed a big pile of dirt, slip-sliding backward, her shoes filling with earth. She sat on the top and looked down. "Are you going to tell me or not?" she asked.

"Tell you what?"

"I don't know. What do you have to tell me?"

"You mean, like a confession?"

"Is that what you'd call it? I'm not a priest."

"I know in general what people say about me," Hector said. "It isn't true."

"Then why did you come here?"

"My father brought me to the States when I was fifteen to work in the artichoke fields in Castroville. My mother's still in Chiapas." Hector knelt in the dirt at the bottom of the pile and looked at the stars. "Other people, you know . . . they didn't exactly cause what happened, but they let it happen."

"Who let what happen when?"

"Do you want the whole story?"

"What other kind would I want?"

"My girlfriend got pregnant, and we got married. I know what you think—I'm Catholic."

"You don't know what I think."

"When we first arrived, I had the idea I was going to be an American. I got this tattoo. . . ." Hector pulled up his sleeve to the shoulder and showed the American flag. "I was going to learn English, see, and I did. I learned from a television set. By the time I was seventeen, I was making extra money as liaison between owners and workers."

"Were you legal?" Dawn asked.

"No. We were always afraid of being sent back. It was worse than that, really. Being sent back was bad. Shameful back in Mexico. But it was worse being here. We were nothing. *Nada.* Invisible. Then my father had this accident. He caught his shirt in a conveyor belt, and it almost tore his arm off. No permit, no insurance . . ." Hector paused. "He died before they did anything."

"What about your wife and baby?"

"We had a house in Castroville next to her parents. They owned a grocery store, but they did other things, too, under the counter, like selling false papers. They thought I was too cozy with the owners and wanted me to go to L.A. to make contacts, get counterfeit documents, and so on. But I liked my job. The owners liked me, and it had possibilities for advancement. So the family sent my wife to L.A., and she gave the baby, Luisa, over to the grandparents. My wife was gone two weeks, three weeks at a time. This went on a couple of years. Then one day the welfare people came to me. The baby was in day care, and her face was bruised. Did I know anything about it? A day later one of the owners said he'd heard I was in trouble, that I'd done something bad. *I* had done something. Who'd made up this lie? It didn't matter who. The workers stopped talking to me, and if they didn't talk to me, I was of no use to anybody. The people from welfare came around again and asked more questions. Then a friend told me the police were going to arrest me. The baby was already living with the grandparents. My job was ruined. So I took off."

"You ran away."

"What was I going to do? Go to jail for something I didn't do?"

"Maybe you wouldn't have gone to jail."

"Do you believe that?"

"No."

"I worked fruit crops in Yakima and spent nights taking a course in telephone repair. I heard there were jobs in Wyoming, so I went to Casper, where I got into a fight with a cowboy who wanted to beat up a Mexican. Then I drifted east to Hot Springs. People were moving away, so I got a job right away and bought my forty acres cheap."

"So that's why you didn't want the sheriff to make a big deal out of your dead bulls?"

"I didn't see the point in his looking too far into things, especially when he doesn't like Mexicans. I doubt anyone's looking for me, but I don't know for sure. The family just wanted me gone."

"What about your daughter?"

"What about her?"

"What if she wants to see you?"

"She won't. If she does, she can't."

"And you can live that way?"

"What are the choices?" Hector asked.

"That's the whole story?"

"All I know," Hector said.

Dawn stood up and skittered down from the top of the pile of earth, and Hector caught her momentum at the bottom.

Chapter 16

Mattie and Elton flew in a thirty-seater DeHavilland Dash 8 from Gillette to Denver. Elton held on to her when the engine revved, and the plane hurtled down the runway and slid into the air, but as the ground receded, his nervousness subsided. He pressed his good eye to the window.

"What do you think?" Mattie asked. "There's some point to being a bird, isn't there?"

"Devils Tower is an anthill," Elton said.

"Look at the perfect order of water: streams, creeks, rivers. Water goes where it has to."

"There aren't many people," Elton said.

"Imagine the land when your great-grandfather was here."

An ambulance met them at DIA and took them to University Hospital. The ultrasound was scheduled at three, which gave them time to fill out papers, get into a room, and have lunch. While they waited, Mattie taught Elton a word game. They drew grids of twenty-five squares and alternated giving each other letters. The object was to make three-, four-, and five-letter words, left to right and top to bottom, scoring a point for each letter in a word. Elton won, 38 to 35.

"I let you win," Mattie said. "It was your first time."

They played again, and Elton won, 40 to 39.

"I wasn't expecting a *Q*," Mattie said. "You're vicious."

"Let's play again for money," Elton said.

The surgeon was Amos Cardenas, a gawky, hawklike man, with a mop of gray hair and a thin mustache. If anyone had hands for surgery, it was he—frail hands and long, slender fingers. "So you're from Wyoming," he said, "and you ran into a board."

"It ran into me," Elton said.

Dr. Cardenas peeled off the bandage over Elton's eye and leaned closer. "How long ago did this happen?"

"Two weeks."

"Fourteen days exactly?"

"Seventeen," Elton said.

Elton lay on a glass and metal table, and a nurse monitored the ultrasound machine. Pictures appeared on a console in front of Mattie and Dr. Cardenas. "You can see a giant tear," Dr. Cardenas said, pointing to the screen. "The force of the blow and the subsequent jarring separated the retina and caused considerable hemorrhaging. The bleeding obscures what we can see here. We'll have to do a vitrectomy to clear the blood."

After the ultrasound Dr. Cardenas showed them a plastic model of the eye. "Your retina's separated here," Dr. Cardenas said. "We'll reattach it and hold it in place with a buckle—just like a belt buckle—and then we'll lase the surrounding tissue. The laser creates a scar that will help keep the retina from moving. If the trauma is severe, we can also use a gas bubble to steady the eye."

"What does 'severe' mean?" Mattie asked.

"The success of the procedure depends on how much bad scar tissue has formed. That's our major concern, what we call bad healing."

"How long will I be out of it?" Elton asked.

"You mean under anesthesia? The procedure will take several hours. An emergency came in a few minutes ago, but I'll get to you as soon as I can after that. Is that all right with you, Elton?"

"I'm not in any hurry."

Mattie and Elton played gin rummy for a penny a point, and she let him win, and then they watched *Baywatch* on TV.

"Only this once," Mattie said. "I don't want you thinking women are like that."

"Like what?" he asked.

It was after six when an orderly wheeled Elton out of his room and took him down to surgery.

During the operation Mattie walked the corridors. *Bad healing.* She knew what that meant. She'd lived through bad healing in her life, and so had Elton. His father hit him with a board and dragged him to the dump. And her mother had left her family in shambles. But they had lived through bad healing, and they would live through good healing now. They'd help each other. She'd help Elton, if she could. She'd care for him and love him and make him well.

She thought of Lee Coulter, too, lonely and sad about his children. A man who loved his children the way he did couldn't be all bad. Not that he had ever been bad.

The surgery lasted four hours, and Dr. Cardenas spoke with Mattie right after. "It went as well as could be expected," he said. "It's a severe case that wasn't attended to right away. We'll monitor his eye every hour—keep it dilated, check for further hemorrhaging, and hope the eye stabilizes. He'll have to lie facedown for at least a week, maybe two."

"What are his chances?"

"You mean, that he'll be able to see out of the eye?"

"Yes."

"Less than fifty percent."

"He loves basketball," Mattie said. "Will he be able to play basket-ball?"

"Of course he can play," Dr. Cardenas said, "but perhaps he should learn to love something else."

Chapter 17

So what'd Thella say?" Dawn asked. She was sitting between Hector and Shelley in the cab of Hector's truck, riding to Hot Springs to get the Lincoln.

"None of your business," Shelley said.

"Something not so good."

"Not so good."

"Bryce did something bad."

"I said it's none of your business, Dawn. You can't fix everybody's problems."

"I'm not trying to fix anything," Dawn said, "but if you're angry, let's talk about it."

"I don't want to talk about it."

"Maybe it isn't so bad."

"It's bad," Shelley said.

"Like what, he has diseases?"

"Leave her alone," Hector said. "She doesn't want to talk."

They rode a few minutes in silence.

"I mean, how much should I worry about his history?" Shelley asked.

"You mean, like with other women?"

"Yes."

"Did he lie to you about it?"

"He hasn't lied to me any more than I've lied to him. Neither of us has volunteered anything."

"Will someone tell me where I'm going?" Hector said.

"Turn left at the bypass," Dawn said. "Take Nineteenth Street to Baltimore."

The town streetlights appeared, and Hector turned left at the Dakota Mart.

"Does it matter?" Shelley asked. "That's what I want to know. Should I ask him about it?"

"What do you gain?" Dawn asked. "What do you lose?"

"Is my mother better off knowing about my father?"

"Are you?" Dawn asked. "Jealousy is its own punishment."

"I don't want to be a victim," Shelley said.

"You determine that."

"I thought you believed in fate."

They turned right on Nineteenth and climbed the hill. "Left or right on Baltimore?" Hector asked.

"Yes," Dawn said.

Hector turned right, and in the next block they saw the Lincoln parked at the curb. Hector pulled in behind.

"You want us to follow you home?" Dawn asked.

"I may not go home," Shelley said.

"You're going to see Bryce?"

"I don't know."

"Don't drink too much," Dawn said. "Remember what happened the last time."

Shelley started the Lincoln and sat for a minute and watched Dawn and Hector turn the corner and disappear. Now what was she going to do? She believed Bryce liked her. He hadn't said he loved her, but he cared for her. Dwain had said he loved her because he wanted to put his cock in her, and Warren had said it because he didn't know any better, but Bryce hadn't said it. He hadn't said a word about love. But how could he do the things he'd done and *not* love her?

She hadn't said she loved him, either, of course, not because she didn't, but because she hadn't wanted to give him power over her. *What a bastard!* She could maybe understand his fucking Thella—she'd been prettier then, and she'd always been a flirt—but Julie Picard? She was a mousy waif with brown hair and freckles. Smart, though. Was it even true? She ought to call Julie and ask, but Shelley hadn't seen her since high school, and anyway, she'd deny it. Really the person she should ask was Bryce. What would he say? *Yes or no, Bryce, did you fuck Julie Picard?* She wanted to see his goddamn face as he tried to make up a believable lie.

But Thella was right. How could she ask him after what she'd done with Hank?

She put the Lincoln in gear, turned off Baltimore toward the high school, and rolled through the stop sign. Almost without considering what she was doing, she turned down the hill, crossed the bridge, and turned left toward Wind Cave.

The aim was to talk, not disparage. She wanted to understand Bryce, not accuse him. She was going to ask without rancor. *Do you know Julie Picard? What do you think of Thella Silverman?* Spoken gently. The point was to see how his eyes moved, his hands, to hear the pauses and the tone of his voice.

"Yeah, right. Be gentle," she said aloud. "You should kill the son of a bitch."

In fact, he was probably fucking somebody right now. As if that woman were his sister! Bullshit!

The notion of spying on him exhilarated her, scared her. What if there were two cars at his cabin? What if she caught him in bed with Julie Picard?

The road was little traveled that time of the night, though she had to watch out for deer or buffalo. She knew the curves now, though, where the road descended into the trees and came out into clearings. She slowed for Bryce's side road, and as she turned, the shadow of the Lincoln spilled into the moonlight.

But if she caught him in betrayal, who would suffer? She turned off the headlights and drove the last curve slowly, then parked at the berm and walked.

The cabin was splotched with shadow and moonlight. She saw candlelight in the window. Only Bryce's VW was parked in front, but he could have brought someone from work, someone from Custer. But she didn't hear any voices, no moans of love. As she got closer, she saw the candle in the window was moonlight on the glass.

Now she felt foolish. She didn't know what to do—whether to go in or leave—and as a compromise she sat outside on the steps. It was a clear night. Far away she saw the lights of a town—Buffalo Gap maybe—and the headlights of cars moving along the highway.

After a few minutes the screen door creaked and footsteps crossed the porch. "Are you staying out here?" he asked.

She didn't turn around.

He sat down two steps above her and kneaded her shoulders with his fingers. "It's a beautiful night," Bryce said.

His hands were innocent. His palms pressed inward to her neck, moved down her back. She took a breath. She might have moved away or recoiled from his touch or asked what she'd come to ask, but she didn't. It *was* a beautiful night.

He moved down a step and kissed the top of her head. She was aware he had on only a robe; his cock was getting hard. Then she stood up abruptly.

"What's wrong?" he asked.

She faced him, but it was dark. His eyes were too shadowed to see if he would be telling the truth. *Did you fuck Julie Picard?* She couldn't ask.

Instead she bent down and unfastened the robe and pulled it apart. His cock lolled from the dark hair above it, and she knelt on the step, took it in her hand, and kissed it. She swirled her tongue over the smooth tip, then leaned back and looked at him. "I've never done this before."

"You don't have to now."

"But I want to."

She knew her wanting was anger as much as desire. She kissed his cock again and then felt it rise in her mouth. She lifted her head, slipped her hand down over his cock, and followed it with her mouth. Again.

And again.

Then she paused and leaned back, holding his cock with her hand.

"Don't stop now."

"Why?"

"Because," he said.

"Because why?"

"You know why."

In the moonlight, his cock was slick with wet.

Because he was about to come?

Because he wanted the pleasure?

Because it was unfair to tease?

Because he loved her?

She bent her head again and took his cock in her mouth. She didn't care what he wanted or how it felt to him; she cared how it was to her. He pressed into her mouth. Once, twice. He was silent, and she knew what his silence meant. He spasmed hard, and she held still.

After a few moments she leaned away. "Are you sleeping with Julie Picard?" she asked. "I want to know."

"No."

"Did you ever?"

Silence.

"Is that a yes?"

"Who've you been talking to?"

"It's a simple question."

"Does it matter if I did? Would you find out what kind of person I am?"

"Why are you asking me questions instead of answering?"

"What do you want me to say?"

"I want you to say no, you never fucked Julie Picard."

"And if I say yes?" He stood up and pulled the robe around his waist and tied the belt.

"Bryce?"

She heard the screen door open again and close. Then the air was still, and the clear darkness was hollow.

She knew the area around Blue Bell Lodge from the summer she'd worked there, and she liked best the French Creek Trail because it stayed along the stream and led to the Natural Area—meadows and ponderosas and aspens. That was where she drove when she left Bryce's.

She had no tent or sleeping bag. She carried a flashlight and her father's space blanket from the trunk of the Lincoln. The moonlight was bright and patterned the trail with shadows.

> I am going out to gather broken branches
> rimed with light
> brittle as I am
> under the weight of what you say is love.

A half mile up the trail she found a cushion of grass and wrapped herself in the space blanket and lay down. She'd brought matches for a fire, but she wasn't cold yet, and she waited and watched the clouds blow among the stars. Over aeons, Dawn said, the constellations changed shapes. Leo would become a football player, Cancer a television set. The Big Dipper would become a Chevy Camaro. To Shelley they were already unconnected, not even shapes she knew from star lessons with her father.

She tilted her watch to the flashlight. Eleven-twenty. Seven hours till daylight. She thought of her mother, who'd lived alone at sixteen, and Elton in the hospital, and Dawn, the morning star, and Lee, who'd got her interested in fossils. The cold seeped into her slowly, gently, drew around her like a shroud. She hovered at the edge of sleep and waking, too cold to sleep, too tired to be awake. She imagined animals in the trees by the creek—a porcupine whose body was a tree trunk, an elk jumping from one branch to another. An owl as large as a bear flew quietly through the dark. She woke, and cried, and wished for light.

Chapter 18

Hector and Dawn drove back from Hot Springs as if everything had been said. The gravel stretched before them, bordered by weeds and fences and fields. The moonlight was true. The pastures with the shadowy hay bales, the dark hills, the river were all true. They passed neighbors they knew and did not know. Dawn clutched a stone in her hand.

Each section marker was a ninety-degree turn and a new perspective. They passed the cemetery, turned east, and climbed a knoll. The plain was a visible lightless sea.

Hector stopped at his mailbox.

"Am I to walk from here?" Dawn asked.

"It's an invitation," Hector said.

Dawn didn't say anything for a few seconds; then she got out of the truck and walked to the edge of the gravel and looked out over an alfalfa field to the moon. The field was cut and cleared of bales, and water ran from the ditch. The air was mild. Crickets and katydids called. A breeze rattled the weeds along the ditch.

Hector came up behind her. "I can't promise anything."

"Did I ask for a promise?"

"You might hope what would happen tonight would mean something tomorrow."

"I'm not hoping anything, Hector. Remember the time I heard the music you couldn't hear?"

"Yes."

"That night I thought you were dreaming of me."

"I was imagining you," he said.

"Anyone can imagine."

"You think I should dream of you? How do I do that?"

"I'll show you."

She crossed the ditch and walked out into the field and stopped where water flowed around her on the ground. Hector followed her.

"Here?" Hector asked.

"Why not here?"

They listened to the water.

"First stay still," she said.

"I am still."

"Dream your body and spirit," Dawn said. "What do you want from me?"

"You know."

"I know, but tell me without words."

Hector unbuttoned his shirt and dropped it on the ground. The flag on his arm was a mark of nothing. He hopped in the mud and tugged off his boots, unfastened his belt, peeled his jeans over his thighs. The moon glanced from his shoulder and his bare arm, from his thigh and calf so his skin was edged with silver. He slid down his underwear and stood naked in the field. "I'm dreaming now," he said.

She touched the crescent of his silver shoulder, and her hand made a shadow across his body. She kissed him and lifted her hands, not to his body, but above her head into the air.

He lifted his hands to hers.

Chapter 19

I t was two weeks after the surgery that Trini drove to Denver to pick up Mattie and Elton from the hospital. Elton could sit up for an hour at a time, depending on how he felt, but it was good to be conservative about his recovery. His eye was red, and his vision still blurred. That was to be expected, Dr. Cardenas said. The eye was mending. Elton's moving around and drinking wine may have helped him—the scar tissue was not so much a problem as Dr. Cardenas had feared—but it was too early to tell if the eye would be normal again.

"Don't be surprised if he's sad," Dr. Cardenas said. "It's not unusual for patients to get depressed about their injuries, especially children."

"I don't want him feeling sorry for himself," Mattie said. "We've had enough of that."

Elton lay in the back of the Suburban, and Mattie and Trini talked. Trini wanted to know everything that had happened, every detail.

"We found him," Mattie said. "That's all that matters. We got him to the doctor. I don't want to talk about it. How's Allen doing? And Dylan and Keith?"

"That woman in the wheelchair left town. Unfortunately, Allen will get over it. Keith got fired from Taco Bell for refusing to serve someone wearing a proabortion button, and Dylan is reading *Storm Troopers of the Lost Universe*. They're the same little shitheads they always were."

"Good."

"I guess you know Dawn's pretty much living up at Hector's now."

"I heard," Mattie said. "Dawn said Hector was still an American and still a Catholic, but he was learning. How are her buffalo calves?"

"She's jury-rigged an electric fence out east on your place, but now she wants to build a real fence for when they grow up."

"I told her she could."

"Oh, the big news . . . guess what?"

"I don't have strength to guess."

"The Pollards are selling their place. I don't know whether it's the bank making them or what."

"Maybe they were scared." Mattie turned around. "Did you hear that, Elton? We're getting rid of the Pollards."

"I'm not deaf," Elton said. "And only half blind."

Mattie looked back at Trini. "How much do they want?"

"The way they've run that place into the ground it can't be worth much. Are you interested?"

"I have the money from Haney's estate," Mattie said. "It's adjacent property. It could be made better, especially if I controlled the water."

"You couldn't run such a big place."

"I could if Hector would quit the phone company and work full-time at ranching. And Dawn will need more pasture for her buffaloes. There's Elton to think of, too."

"Thank you," Elton said.

"The Pollards would never sell to you," Trini said.

"That's why there are real estate salesmen. They might sell to Earl."

They turned east off the interstate toward Lusk and passed through rolling country of pastures and isolated limestone buttes. Even with the windows open, it was hot. A coal train loaded full inched up along the curve of a hill. Mattie dozed sitting up and dreamed herself a hawk in the air, riding thermals. She felt the current lift her, the sun warm her back. The patterned hay meadows spread out beneath her, and water flowed silver in the ditches. The landmarks resembled ones she'd known—a meandering river running through cottonwoods, a limestone cliff face, a fence dividing one pasture from another. The sun threw shadows into the gullies and the trees, but the land was too still. It wasn't the place she knew so well from the ground.

She woke with a start. "Where are we?"

The countryside was speeding past—tree-shrouded hills and a sky of blue and white.

"Almost to Lusk," Trini said.

"How's Elton?"

"Asleep. You're both real good company."

Mattie looked around at Elton on the back seat, his hair to one side of his face, his arm dangling into the footwell.

"How's Shelley getting along, do you think? She gets herself involved so fast, and when things fall apart, she keeps everything inside."

"I wonder where she gets that from," Trini said. "She's upset about Bryce, but she's young. Lee's talked to her some. He's offered her part-time at the Mammoth Site if she can figure a way to do it with the ranch work."

"Elton's not ready to work for a while, but I think she'd have time, at least till third cutting. I have to give her credit for taking over the place the way she did."

"I tell you, I'd be thrilled if she were my kid."

Elton woke, groggy and hungry. "When can we stop and eat?" he asked.

"We can get something in Lusk," Mattie said. "That almost sounded like the old Elton."

"It wasn't, though," Elton said.

In Lusk they got gas, and Mattie and Trini each got milk shakes for the road. Elton got a turkey sandwich and Fritos and a twenty-ounce Coke.

"So what else aren't you telling me?" Mattie asked.

"What else about what? About Shelley?"

"I don't know about what. That's why I asked."

"That's about all I know," Trini said. She smiled. "You'll see when you get there."

At the SunMart in Hot Springs, Mattie called the ranch and was surprised when Dawn answered. "Yep, we're still here," Dawn said.

"I thought you'd be working," Mattie said.

"Then why'd you call?"

"Do we need any food? We're at the grocery in Hot Springs."

"I don't think so. Do you want to talk to Shelley?"

"What's that racket in the background?"

The noise stopped, and Shelley came on the line.

"Hi, Mom."

"What's going on out there? Are you and Dawn drinking?"

"Not yet, but we're getting ready to. Dennis Burke called. He sold four of Daddy's sculptures."

"Four?"

"Two to a museum in Framingham and the other two to collectors. He said Ames McGill sold a story to *The New Yorker*."

There was a crash in the background.

"You better get here fast, Mom."

"Do we *need* anything?"

"I've got to go. Bye."

Shelley hung up, and Mattie stared out into the parking lot of the SunMart. "Jesus H. Christ," she said, "I'm hurrying as fast as I can."

It was after three o'clock when Mattie and Trini and Elton descended the long hill to the mailbox. As usual, the Morton caught Mattie's eye first, but then her gaze moved to the alfalfa fields cut and cleared. The jellyrolls were stacked high in the pens. This was the place of her hawk dream, but now she was on the ground, the mesas washed in sun and the shadows inching up the gullies as if the land were moving. She never tired of that closing distance between the mailbox and home. The Suburban made the familiar clank across the cattle guard and lipped the culvert over the creek. She remembered the time almost sixteen years ago, when Haney had first brought her here. The house was weathered, unpainted clapboard, but the land made it new to her. "It's beautiful," she'd said then. And it still was. Her recollection of that moment was muted now, overlaid with the hundreds of times she had driven that lane in every weather, in every mood, every sorrow. This time driving in now merged with every other. But there were still sorrows to be healed: good healing. She needed that, too, almost as much as Elton.

"You're not even looking," Trini said.

"At what?"

Elton raised himself from the back seat. "Look at the house," he said.

The house was in clear view. The blue tarp was gone, and in place of the gaping hole of the burned-out kitchen was new siding, whiter than the rest of the house. A big window on the west looked into the yard, and to the south, a solarium curved into the rebuilt vestibule. A new door opened to the porch.

Mattie looked at Trini, then at Elton. "You knew about this."

"I guess I did," Trini said.

Shelley and Dawn and Hector and Lee came out and waved. A banner across the porch said WELCOME HOME, ELTON.

The women hugged each other, and Dawn and Shelley said hello to Elton through the car window. Mattie embraced Hector, while Lee and Trini got Elton out of the car, Elton making himself as pathetic as possible, grimacing and moaning with each jerk and jostle.

"He should be upstairs in his bed," Mattie said.

"I'm not going upstairs," Elton said.

"How do you feel?" Dawn asked.

"Terrible."

"You don't either feel terrible," Dawn said. "You're home."

"Put him in the kitchen then," Mattie said. "I want to see what you've done."

The kitchen was a jumble of grocery sacks and six packs of sodas and beer, but Mattie could still appreciate their work. The sink was new; the refrigerator and stove were the matching pale green ones she'd picked out. They'd tiled the counters and had put in cabinets of hardwood and glass. The new floor was waxed and polished. In a recess by the phone was Haney's sculpture of *Man and Woman Separated by Air*.

"Barton said the house was insured," Shelley said. "We decided to go the whole nine yards. Dawn and Lee did most of the work."

"Shelley did all the ranch chores," Dawn said.

"I like it," Mattie said. "Do you like it, Elton?"

"It's okay."

"If you can't play basketball, you can learn to cook," Dawn said. "Lee can teach you."

"Cook?" Elton said. "I don't think so."

"You eat, don't you?" Lee asked. "Men should learn to cook."

Trini passed around beers.

"So how's the eye?" Hector asked.

"They put a buckle in it," Elton said, "and used a laser."

Elton told his story.

"We need you back by third cutting," Shelley said, "so you can stack the hay bales, I was scared every minute."

"I'd rather do that than cook."

"You can do both," Mattie said.

Dawn kneeled beside Elton's chair. "Let me tell you a story. When I was in the army, I saw a woman changing a tire on a jeep. The jack slipped, and the jeep rolled—a ton of metal, right? It went over her legs, but her legs didn't break. Do you know why?"

"She had fake legs," Elton said.

"Because she willed them not to break," Dawn said. "A few days later blood collected in one leg, and the doctor wanted to amputate it, but she said no, the leg was staying with her."

"Yeah, I know," Elton said. "Her leg got better."

"Not until she chose to make it better," Dawn said.

"Is that true?" Shelley asked. "Was that you?"

"The woman had picked up a magic stone." Dawn opened her hand and revealed a stone, and Elton took it.

"Did her leg get better or not?" Elton asked.

"She never even limped afterward."

The others looked away from Elton.

"So is the pivot baled?" Mattie asked. "Are the bales stacked? Is the sprinkler working again?"

"Of course it's working," Dawn said.

"Everything's done, Mom. Relax."

"How many stacks do we have?" Mattie asked. "I'll need to account to Earl."

"Thirty-two," Shelley said.

"How'd you come out, Hector?"

"All right. The price is up at the feedlot."

"Did anyone think to bring back that cultivator from across the river?" Mattie asked.

No one answered.

"I'd like to cultivate the pivot."

"Mom, we don't have to do it now. This is a party."

"I'd like to be ready for tomorrow."

"Dawn and I have had a couple of beers," Shelley said. "We shouldn't operate machinery."

"I want to show Elton my buffalo calves," Dawn said.

"I'll do it," Lee said.

Everyone looked at Lee.

"We don't need the cultivator right now," Shelley said.

"I want to."

"Do you know how to run a tractor?" Mattie asked.

"I grew up in Scottsbluff, remember? But you can refresh my memory."

"How about a forklift?"

"I'm about to learn," Lee said.

"This I have to see," Shelley said.

"Somebody take the hay carrier off the International," Mattie said. "I want to see this, too."

Dawn helped Elton outside, and Hector carried a plastic chair for him from the porch. Shelley drove the four-wheeler ahead to the Morton, and Lee and Mattie walked behind.

"I want to thank you," Mattie said.

"I haven't done it yet."

"I mean, for getting the Lincoln back, for talking to Shelley."

"I like Shelley."

"And for helping out here."

"Dawn did most of the work on the kitchen. I did what she told me to do, but I hope you still feel you owe me several favors."

Shelley disengaged the hydraulic hoses and pounded out the pin between the tractor and the hay carrier, while Dawn got Elton settled into his chair. Trini and Hector talked about spreadsheets, what all Hector needed to do since Dawn had set up the laptop for him.

Mattie and Lee walked over to the International. "You sure you want to do this?" Mattie asked. "Someone else could do it twice as fast with half the trouble."

"But I'll have four times as much fun."

"You think he can make it across the bridge?" Shelley asked.

Mattie climbed up into the seat, started the engine, then motioned Lee up. He stepped up onto the tire and squeezed into the seat beside her.

"It's pretty simple, really," Mattie said. She put her hand on the gearshift. "Low. Intermediate. High. This is the hydroglide. This is the throttle." She pulled out a knob, and the engine revved. "The clutch is a little tricky, but you'll get used to it."

"Low, intermediate, high," Lee said. "And reverse? Where's that?"

"Here. And this lever raises and lowers the forklift." Mattie pushed the lever up, and the lift groaned upward. "This is up. This is down."

"I know up from down."

"I'd stay in low or intermediate so you won't have to use the brake much. You aren't in a race. The chains to pick up the cultivator are under the seat."

"I chain the cultivator to the forklift?"

"The cultivator's in the weeds where the road divides. You edge up close to it, idle down, and put it in neutral. Now you sit where I am."

She got up, and Lee ducked under her and sat in the driver's seat. He touched the pedals and levers. "Clutch, throttle. Low, intermediate, high, and hydroglide."

"Where's the forklift?"

Lee shifted the lever for the forklift. "Up. Down."

"That's all there is to it," Mattie said. She stepped down to the tire and then to the metal plate. "Don't hurt yourself."

"I didn't know you cared."

"You're not covered on my insurance," Mattie said.

She jumped to the ground. Lee revved the engine and shouted something.

"He wants to know where you want him to bring the cultivator," Shelley said.

Mattie turned and pointed to the ground. "Right back here."

Lee gave a thumbs-up.

"Does he know what he's doing?" Shelley asked.

"I don't think so," Mattie said.

Lee went through a practice run with the forklift: up and down, then up again.

"He's like a little kid," Shelley said. She picked up a stone and gave it to Dawn.

"That's not a good one," Dawn said. "I can feel it."

Lee pressed in the clutch, and the gears groaned and engaged. The tractor lurched forward. Lee nearly ran into the corner of the Morton, but veered away across the apron.

"Steer," Shelley shouted.

He had the presence of mind to steer, but that was about all. The tractor careened toward the windrower, and Lee wheeled past it— barely—and into the Ironweed Patch. Mattie would have laughed if it hadn't been her tractor.

"Throttle down," she called. "Let off on the gas."

"He can't hear you," Shelley said.

Dawn took off after the tractor, but there was nothing she could do, either, so she stopped and watched. The tractor jumped the berm and sent several rolls of woven wire spinning like dust devils.

"Brake!" Mattie shouted.

Lee didn't brake. The tractor roared past the defunct breadloaf hay packer, past the Corvair with the hood up and the wagon with the broken axle, and straight toward the pyramid of aluminum pipes stacked in front of the barbed wire fence at the far end of the Ironweed Patch.

"Lee!" Mattie started running.

Lee hit the pipes full-on broadside with the forklift raised. The pipes burst into the air like silver toothpicks and scattered in every direction, but they didn't stop the tractor. It crashed through the fence beyond the pipes and surged ahead into the swamp.

The muck stopped it fifteen feet in. The front wheels sank, and the back wheels spun, and when the tractor was in deep enough, the engine died.

Mattie and Dawn ran up. Lee climbed slowly out of the cab.

"Are you all right?" Mattie called.

"The throttle jammed," Lee said. "The key didn't turn off the engine."

"It's hydraulic," Dawn said. "You have to idle it down."

"God, I'm sorry," he said.

Mattie surveyed the swath of damage—the aluminum pipes crunched and scattered, the broken fence, the rutted track into the swamp. Lee stepped off the half-submerged tire into the oozy water.

Shelley came up behind Mattie and Dawn. "Is he all right?"

"I told you it was the wrong stone," Dawn said.

Lee slogged through the swamp, looking shaken and haggard. One of his feet sank in the muck, and he pulled it loose without the shoe.

"You look so scared," Mattie said.

"I am scared," Lee said. "You don't have insurance."

He limped a few more steps and rose up through the reeds and out onto the grass, one shoe on, the other lost. He looked pathetic, standing knee deep in the mire.

Then Mattie laughed.

Lee stared at her.

"What's so funny, Mom?" Shelley asked.

She couldn't stop laughing.

"Jesus Christ," Shelley said. "Get a grip, Mom."

Lee dripped mud and swamp water from his clothes.

Shelley started laughing, and Dawn, too. Lee staggered up onto the grass and touched Mattie's arm.

Then Mattie stopped laughing and was still. Lee put his arm around her shoulder, and she laid her head against him. A rush of air filled her lungs, and heat came to her cheeks and forehead, and all that had made her laugh made her quiet.

That evening they ate in the new kitchen. Lee made shrimp pasta with mushrooms and garlic and grated Parmesan cheese and crushed red pepper, and Elton thought he might learn to cook after all. They talked about Elton's surgery, second cutting, the construction of the kitchen. They laughed again about Lee's running the tractor into the swamp.

"I knew the swamp would stop it," Lee said.

Elton got tired early, and Mattie and Dawn helped him up to his room.

"We're all glad you're back," Dawn said. She gave him a kiss on the forehead.

"Don't do that," he said.

"I just did," she said. "And I will if I want to."

From below the sound of the piano rose up the stairwell.

"I'll take you tomorrow to see the buffalo calves," Dawn said.

"My mother used to have a buffalo robe."

"I know, you told me." She kissed him again. "Good night."

Dawn went out. Elton turned over on his stomach, and Mattie pulled the sheet and thin blanket over his shoulders. Then she sat on the edge of the bed and listened to the music.

"Do I have to go back to my aunt and uncle's?" Elton asked.

"It's up to you and the judge," Mattie said. "I'll help you do what you want to. But if you stay here, you have to go to school."

"I will if I can drive the Lincoln," Elton said.

"Shelley's taking the Lincoln, but maybe you can drive the truck once in a while. You don't have to think of school yet. You need to think about getting better."

Mattie heard several cars start, and she got up and went to the window.

"What is it?" Elton asked.

"Trini's going home. And Hector and Dawn, too. I guess they have places to go and things to do." She turned out the light by the bed.

The notes of the piano trailed off. More headlights scattered into the cottonwood tree and across the ceiling. It had to be Shelley. Where was she going?

"Elton?"

"Um?"

"If you ever leave here again, you tell me where you're going."

Elton didn't answer.

"Good night, Elton," she said.

Mattie went out and closed the door behind her and leaned against it for a moment. She felt anxious and girlish. The house was quiet, but she wasn't alone. She crossed the hall and turned on the light in her bedroom. She hadn't slept in her bed in three weeks, but it was the same as it had been—the single pillow and the pale bedspread that showed the solitary, deeper swale where she had slept alone all the months since Haney died. She folded back the covers on her side of the bed, stood silent for a moment, then went to the closet and got another pillow. She pulled back the covers on the other side.

Then she went out of the room and down the hall.

Lee must have heard her footsteps because when she paused at the top of the stairs, he was there on the landing looking up at her.

"There you are," she said, and he came up the steps to meet her.

A PENGUIN READERS GUIDE TO

LAND THAT MOVES, LAND THAT STANDS STILL

Kent Nelson

AN INTRODUCTION TO
Land That Moves, Land That Stands Still

Mattie Remmel is no stranger to grief. At the opening of Kent Nelson's luminous novel *Land That Moves, Land That Stands Still*, her husband, Haney, dies in a farm accident. Seven years previously, their son, Loren, passed away from a sudden illness. Mattie is unable to heal these wounds, and whatever small progress she makes toward an acceptance of Haney's death is lost when she opens the trunk to his car and discovers from photographs and letters that Haney was gay and had hidden it from her for their entire marriage. Faced with this revelation, Mattie tries to sort out the illogical feelings of failure and guilt stemming from her inability to be a good wife to Haney.

Redirecting her energies into her ranch, Mattie unconsciously assembles a new family for her and her daughter, Shelley. The first arrival is Dawn, a mysterious and beautiful young woman with a troubled past and a penchant for mechanics. As Mattie's hired "man," Dawn brings with her a bizarre belief system ("doog") and a preternatural insight into Mattie's emotions, and slowly becomes an integral part of Mattie's healing process. She invites Dennis Burke, Haney's past lover, to visit the ranch and retrieve Haney's sculptures, and eventually provokes Mattie to admit her fears and denial.

The other addition to Mattie's new support system is a runaway Indian boy, Elton. Through her feelings for him and the unconditional love of her family and neighbors, Mattie begins to deal with Haney's duplicity and forge a new love and respect for those who care for her. Despite her acceptance, however, the attention she gives Elton has repercussions: He disappears after killing Dawn's dangerous ex-boyfriend, Styver, and Mattie's façade of stoicism cracks. Mattie must find Elton to recover her new family and restore herself.

Ultimately, a meditation on loss, trust, acceptance, and the changeable perception of family and home, *Land That Moves, Land That Stands Still* is a remarkable portrait of an emotional journey to acceptance and renewal.

ABOUT KENT NELSON

Kent Nelson lives in Salida, Colorado. He has worked as a tennis pro, city judge, ranch hand, and university professor, and is the recipient of two NEA grants, as well as the Edward Abbey Prize for Ecofiction for his novel *Language in the Blood*. An avid birder and mountain runner, he has searched out more than seven hundred North American bird species and has run the Pikes Peak Marathon twice, most recently in 2001.

A CONVERSATION WITH KENT NELSON

1. In many of your novels and stories, in particular Language in the Blood, *birds play a symbolic, as well as literal, role, and in* Land That Moves, Land That Stands Still, *birds and bird imagery are important. Hawks appear above the spot where Haney was killed; Shelley is likened to a baby bird; Dawn kills the Pollards' captive eagles to set them free. Mattie even mentions she once dated an ornithologist. Why do birds factor so largely in your writing? What symbolism do you assign to them?*

In my novel *Language in the Blood*, there's a line near the end which says, "They [birds] were what I first knew how to love." I was ten or so when I first became fascinated with birds, learning about them outside of school, in the neighborhood where I grew up in Colorado Springs. I've spent a lot of my travel time looking for birds, particularly rare ones—in South Texas, Alaska, Newfoundland, Southeastern Arizona, Florida. Birds are part of my life, and it feels natural to me to use them in my stories and novels. I don't consciously attach any particular symbolic significance to them. That's for readers to do, though of course I do choose which birds to put in at which particular moment. I do this not as intellectual intent, but rather because certain birds, say the hawks Mattie sees, fit better at that time in the novel. Besides, some of these moments are transposed directly from my own experience. I saw a kettle of Swainson's Hawks just like the one in the novel, though for me it was only an isolated, but moving, experience, while Mattie brings a more complete or confused psychology to the moment.

2. Dawn's belief system is highly unusual—a mixture of mysticism, New Age beliefs, and American Indian shamanism. From her magic stones to her impromptu ritualistic cleansing of the kitchen (and nearly the entire house), it seems she has taken appealing ideas from all religions to create her own version of "doog." What was your inspiration for creating this belief system for the character of Dawn? Are your own beliefs as varied as Dawn's?

As Dawn says in the novel, "doog" is good spelled backwards. There was no particular inspiration for Dawn's quirky belief system. I tried to imply it's a culmination of the sort of searching lots of people have embarked on these days to explain why we're who we are. I was worried about overdoing Dawn's character, but at the same time I wanted someone different from Mattie and Shelley to challenge them and be a catalyst for change. My own personal beliefs are very simple, but not relevant to the novel.

3. Your descriptions of the Black Hills and the surrounding areas are pitch perfect and meticulously researched. How much preparation was necessary to chart the areas surrounding the ranch that feature in the novel? What was it about the landscape of the Black Hills that inspired you to set this work there?

The short answer is the landscape was what I knew. There was no research. In 1992, I escaped Exeter, New Hampshire, and worked on this very ranch from April to late October as the hired man. I was paid seven dollars an hour for building fences, cutting and baling and stacking hay, irrigating, and in general doing the various chores on the ranch, including the laundry and cooking. I got ten dollars an hour for "hazardous duty"—spraying thistles or cleaning the incinerator or dragging plastic pipe to the dump. There were two or three of us there, depending on who was available or whether the owner was around, but I was there pretty much all the time. The work was exhausting—sometimes I'd go to sleep with my hands aching and contoured into the shape of a post pounder, and I'd wake up with them in the same position. But I liked the physical part, and I liked being outside all day.

4. The central characters in the novel are women, all highly realistic with well-defined strengths and shortcomings. What is it about the relationships between women that you wanted to examine in writing this story? When you were creating the characters of Mattie, Shelley, and Dawn, what elements in your own life helped you to further define the attitudes and appearances of these women?

I didn't have any preconceived ideas about the women characters. When I start a novel, I start with a place and assemble the characters piecemeal. I don't have anything in particular in mind to "examine." As the writing goes along, the characters become deeper and richer according to where they are and what happens in their lives. There were really no models from real life for any of these people. I made them up. At the same time, I realized that as a man I was taking a risk writing about three women. As much as possible I tried to make them separate and different people. But writing is about risk and learning from it. I've done quite a few short stories with women characters. Inventing or imagining what women would do is more absorbing and challenging to me than figuring out what men would do. Often men are too predictable, too obvious, and too superficial in their behavior; there are more nuances to women's behavior and feelings.

5. Many passages in Land That Moves, Land That Stands Still *are extraordinarily technical expositions on how a ranch would be run: how alfalfa is cut, how bales are stacked, how buffalo are raised, etc. Why did you choose to involve the mechanics of ranch life so thoroughly in the story? Do you think you could have told this story without adding that particular element to it? Did the inclusion of the characters performing manual labor add a facet to their personalities that was not there before you placed them in that setting and with those tools?*

I wanted to show what these women did and what they could do. Many early writers stereotyped women as frail and retiring, but

I don't see that women are helpless or in any way unable to do hard work. In the novel, even Shelley, who's been protected by her father from the drudgery of farm life, learns she can do manual labor if she chooses to. By the way, I think men can learn to be less determined and victimized by macho cultural dictates, too, though most men don't try.

6. *Dawn acts as a modified Greek chorus in this novel, a seer that gives pointed comments on underlying emotions and themes. When you created her character, was this a deliberate function you assigned her, or did her character evolve through your writing process?*

I never plan out ahead what's going to happen in a story or novel, so I'm as surprised as readers might be by how characters turn out. This doesn't mean the characters govern the story; they don't. And I'm not surprised in the sense of being shocked, because the characters accrete slowly, day by day. So, yes, Dawn evolved into her role. As she became more real to me, even if she might be a little exaggerated, I perceived her as a catalyst for certain events, like the rescuing of the eagles or even Styver's return, and as a mediator between what Mattie keeps to herself and what she needs to reveal. She also served this role for Shelley and Elton—Shelley can confess to Dawn what she can't to her mother, and Elton can let his emotions out because he likes her. I suppose Dawn turned out to be a little wiser than I'd hoped, but a writer can't make every character perform perfectly.

7. *Land That Moves, Land That Stands Still is an incredibly dense and thickly plotted work, full of rich characters and subplots. When you initially mapped out the novel, did you envision all of the characters existing in such an interrelated fashion? Or as you began the story of Mattie and Haney, did your other characters—Lee, Hector, Trini, etc.—increasingly appear more often than you planned, developing their own lives?*

7

I didn't know when I started that Haney was going to die in the first chapter. I didn't know they would have a son who'd died. I didn't know it would flood. I had no idea there was even going to be a Dawn or Hector Lopez. So there was no mapping out. I like this aspect of my work, the discovery of what happens as I go along, as well as the building up of the people. I suppose I try to imagine what a character might reasonably experience in her life, given the time and place and circumstances. Mattie, for instance, at her age, would have children, would have friends of fairly long-standing, would be expected to and willing to participate to a clearly defined extent in the life of the ranch. Her role changes, of course, when Haney dies. What before Haney determined, now she determines, including whether or not to finish the projects he's started. And since I lived on this ranch, I was aware of other families and their struggles. It was not a hard jump to imagine neighbors and friends because there would naturally be neighbors and friends who impinge on the lives of three women in a remote setting.

8. *During the drive home from Rapid City with Mattie and Elton, Dawn almost wistfully asks, "What is it do you suppose we call home?" At the end of the novel, the characters have built upon one another's grief and acceptance to create a new home, one that nurtures their individuality yet offers a loving support system, lending itself to the idea that home is truly where the heart is. What do you believe qualifies as your "home"?*

Since I didn't know who the characters were at the start, their yearning and understanding of "home" was a gradual unfolding that at first I wasn't aware of, but which later appears as a theme of the book. (I also like this aspect of writing: that I'm only trying to get down a story, and only later am I aware that some people may decipher from the story a theme.) Anyone can have this allegiance to place, regardless of where it is. Though I grew up in Colorado, over the years I've lived in a lot of different places and, through searching for birds, have traveled a lot, too. I hope this enables me to portray landscapes sufficiently and to instill them in my characters in the form of discovery and allegiance. I know to feel comfortable in a place I need either solace or the possibility to learn, and I think this is what Dawn comes to sense about where she is—and what Mattie has sensed, too, though over a long time. I was quite at home on an island off Charleston, South Carolina, and I liked Los Angeles, too, because the climate was different and there were new birds; I suppose I'm most at home in Colorado, where I know the seasons and the mountains and the space almost as a physical part of my character.

9. *Do you have a rough idea for your next project? Can you give us a sneak peek of what's next?*

Well, I'm always working on something. I have four new stories (two set in Colorado, one in Georgia, and one in Costa Rica) and a second draft of another novel nearly finished. I don't want to talk much about the novel, though. It's about a family that moves from Lexington, Massachusetts, to Montrose, Colorado, and I like to think it's an exploration of what's happening across the West, especially to small towns, as more and more people move here where it's supposedly unspoiled, or relatively so compared to the East or to California.

QUESTIONS FOR DISCUSSION

1. A few weeks after Haney's death, Shelley asks Mattie what her definition of a "good wife" would be. Would she be faithful, would she make her husband happy, would she obey? Throughout the brief exchange, it becomes apparent that because Haney did not reveal his secret life to her, Mattie believes that she was not a good wife to him. What is your definition of a good wife? Discuss whether or not you believe Mattie was a good wife to Haney. Conversely, was Haney a good husband?

2. Throughout the novel, Mattie is distrustful of Dawn, exclaiming, "How could someone so pretty not be trouble?" What is it about Dawn's personality as opposed to Mattie's that breeds this contempt in Mattie? Could it be that Dawn reminds Mattie of aspects of her own life as a young woman? Mattie also notes that "it wasn't Dawn who was heedless of the world, it was she." What do you think Mattie means by this observation? Does Mattie's emotional detachment make her heedless, or is it something else?

3. Hawks bear a unique symbolism in Native American culture. They are considered a messenger of totems, the bearer of a heightened awareness and a new perspective. However, the Christian interpretation of the omen of a hawk is very different, foretelling injustice, violence, and even death. In the novel, hawks appear twice specifically to Mattie, circling above the site of Haney's accident, and once as she relates the story of a hawk crashing through her kitchen window after becoming disoriented during a brushfire. What symbolic interpretation do you think the author was implying (consciously or unconsciouly) with his usage of the hawk in this way? Do you believe the hawk represents something or someone else? Discuss the appearances of all the various birds in the novel. What do they each represent?

4. Shelley reacts strangely to her father's death, hiding her grief with irrational choices, breaking up with her boyfriend, Warren, sleeping with her friend's lover, and getting into a bar fight. Do you think her choices are a direct response to Haney's death? If so, is her method of grieving healthier than Mattie's? Is it better to act out rather than keep emotions inside, despite the possibility of endangering yourself? At the end of the novel, she has made bold decisions about the direction of her life, choosing not to continue her relationship with Bryce and instead going to graduate school. How does Shelley change in her response to the various men in her life? What are the guideposts Shelley uses to determine her choices?

5. Dawn's strange belief system is a major element of the text. From her innocuous magic stones to her disconcerting actions to free the Pollards' captive eagles, and her culminating act of exorcism by fire to remove Styver's evil influence from the ranch, her actions in the name of "doog" become increasingly erratic. As she defines it, "doog" is the principle of constant recomposition and the force of interrelated matter, an idea very much akin to Dawn's other belief system, namely, fate. How do the principles of both "doog" and fate interrelate? Do these ideals sanction the behavior and actions that Dawn has expressed throughout the novel? Do you think that her behavior toward Styver and his belongings also fit into her belief system?

6. Mattie's relationship with Lee is very rocky throughout the novel. When she initially encounters Lee, she is troubled by the knowledge that Haney agreed to certain agendas for the ranch and his life without consulting her, including having Lee's museum dig the ranch's sinkhole. Yet by the end of the novel, their relationship goes much deeper than one might expect given its start. Do you think Mattie's acceptance of Lee coincides with her acceptance of herself? What is Shelley's role in their relationship? Do you believe

that after Haney's betrayal Mattie will be able to build a relationship based on trust and devotion with Lee?

7. The attitudes and actions of the Pollards are a sad reminder of the prejudice and dishonesty that still thrive in the world. What role do you believe the Pollards play in the novel? Are they the catalyst that brings the new family of Mattie, Shelley, Dawn, and Elton closer together? Analyze each individual's grievances with the Pollards—for example, Dawn's near rape or Shelley's broken arm. What is it about those confrontations that informed each character's behavior later on, both in the presence of the Pollards and in the presence of others? Did you find it realistic that Mattie would be the strength that would drive the Pollards away forever?

8. After Styver's death, Dawn approaches Mattie to discover what she remembers of the night they were attacked, explaining, "I have to remember before I can forget." This method of learning the truth in order to accept what has happened is relevant both in Dawn's atonement for leading Styver to the ranch and in Mattie's acceptance of Haney's sexuality and her own guilt and anguish. Do you believe Dawn meant her words to lead Mattie into finally confronting her own feelings of anger and regret?

9. Mattie lost her own son, Loren, seven years before this story takes place. She remembers her own and Haney's feelings of powerlessness as being "beyond pain." When Elton arrives on the farm, Mattie becomes a mother figure to him. After Styver's death, is Mattie's catatonic grief a result of Elton's disappearance and the sudden reminder of the powerlessness she felt after Loren's death, or is it the culmination of all of the loss in her life? Do you believe that Mattie is using Elton to help her grieve over her son? Consider Elton's hospital stay, during which Mattie did not leave his side. Is she caring for him as she couldn't care for her son while he was ill?

10. Dawn and Hector have a connection deeper than first appearances predicted. Despite their obvious differences in opinion, reflected in Dawn's comments to Shelley that Hector is "still an American and still a Catholic," they seem to be able to take what the other has to give with little disapproval. What is it about their personalities and experiences that makes their relationship a success? How do their accounts of loneliness and isolation help them relate to one another?

11. A defining theme of *Land That Moves, Land That Stands Still* is the ability to accept the presence of loss and grief in one's life and to overcome and accept what cannot be changed. In fact, each character in the novel is grieving for someone or something he or she lost—Mattie for her son, for Haney, for her ability to trust; Lee for his children; Hector for his home and his daughter. Trace each character's journey from loss to acceptance. How did their individual experiences inform their behavior throughout the novel? Has each character come to terms with his or her loss by the end of the novel?

For more information about or to order other Penguin Readers Guides, please e-mail the Penguin Marketing Department at reading@us.penguingroup.com or write to us at:

> Penguin Books Marketing Dept.
> Readers Guides
> 375 Hudson Street
> New York, NY 10014-3657

Please allow 4–6 weeks for delivery.
To access Penguin Readers Guides online, visit the Penguin Group (USA) Web site at www.penguin.com.